Praise for Carla Laureano

The Solid Grounds Coffee Company

"What a bright and engaging story! *The Solid Grounds Coffee Company* is full of snappy and smart dialogue, genuine characters I was rooting for, and sweet romance with just the right amount of tension. I loved getting to know Analyn and Bryan and seeing their two very different worlds dovetail into one layered, romantic, and delicious story."

LAUREN K. DENTON, *USA TODAY* BESTSELLING AUTHOR OF *THE HIDEAWAY, HURRICANE SEASON*, AND *GLORY ROAD*

"Carla Laureano is at the top of her game with *The Solid Grounds Coffee Company*. I was invested in Bryan and Ana's journey from the opening pages and had fun catching up with characters from Laureano's previous books. I enjoyed watching Bryan set out to turn his life around . . . and of course, I loved the delicious romance! (And, yes, now I'm craving a latte!) Another winner from an author who belongs on your keeper shelf."

MELISSA TAGG, CAROL AWARD–WINNING AUTHOR OF THE WALKER FAMILY SERIES AND *NOW AND THEN AND ALWAYS*

"Coffee and romance! Who could ask for a better treat?"

DIANN MILLS, AWARD-WINNING AUTHOR OF *FATAL STRIKE*

"Carla Laureano writes the kind of books I'm eager to begin . . . and that I'm just as sorry to see end. *The Solid Grounds Coffee Company* is filled to overflowing with fictional characters who readers will wish were their real-life friends, along with a how-is-this-going-to-work-out romance and a glimpse into the creation of many people's favorite addiction, coffee."

BETH K. VOGT, CHRISTY AWARD–WINNING AUTHOR OF *THINGS I NEVER TOLD YOU* AND *MOMENTS WE FORGET*

"Carla Laureano has a reputation for penning smart, sophisticated reads, and *The Solid Grounds Coffee Company* is no exception. Brimming with complex characters and a captivating storyline, it's a book readers are certain to devour and one I highly recommend."

JEN TURANO, *USA TODAY* BESTSELLING AUTHOR

"I'm an avid coffee drinker, so this book definitely intrigued me. With elements of redemption and second chances at love, *The Solid Grounds Coffee Company* was quite an enjoyable read."

T. I. LOWE, BESTSELLING AUTHOR OF *LULU'S CAFÉ*

Brunch at Bittersweet Café

"With fun food scenes and organic spiritual elements, Laureano's book will be relished by sweet-toothed inspirational readers."

PUBLISHERS WEEKLY

"The delightful characterization of baker and pastry chef Melody Johansson coupled with a realistic romance and spiritual message make *Brunch at Bittersweet Café* an exceptional pick."

MIDWEST BOOK REVIEWS

"This romantic drama portrays realistically flawed characters in messy situations."

WORLD MAGAZINE

The Saturday Night Supper Club

"A terrific read from a talented author. Made me hungry more than once. I can't wait to read what comes next."

FRANCINE RIVERS, *NEW YORK TIMES* BESTSELLING AUTHOR OF *THE MASTERPIECE*

"Bright, jovial, and peppered with romance and delectable cuisine, this is a sweet and lively love story."

PUBLISHERS WEEKLY, STARRED REVIEW

"Romance aficionados and fans of stories about overcoming obstacles and the role of faith in everyday life will eagerly await the next entry in this sweet food-centered series."

LIBRARY JOURNAL

"Writing charmingly about faith, love, friendship, and food, Laureano will leave readers hungry for the next installment in the Supper Club series."

BOOKLIST

THE SOLID GROUNDS COFFEE COMPANY

A SUPPER CLUB NOVEL

CARLA LAUREANO

Tyndale House Publishers, Inc.
Carol Stream, Illinois

Visit Tyndale online at www.tyndale.com.

Visit Carla Laureano's website at www.carlalaureano.com.

TYNDALE and Tyndale's quill logo are registered trademarks of Tyndale House Publishers, Inc.

The Solid Grounds Coffee Company

Designed by Mark Anthony Lane II

Edited by Sarah Mason Rische

Published in association with the literary agency of The Steve Laube Agency.

The Solid Grounds Coffee Company is a work of fiction. Where real people, events, establishments, organizations, or locales appear, they are used fictitiously. All other elements of the novel are drawn from the author's imagination.

For information about special discounts for bulk purchases, please contact Tyndale House Publishers at csresponse@tyndale.com, or call 1-800-323-9400.

ISBN 978-1-4964-4187-4 (HC)
ISBN 978-1-4964-2032-9 (SC)

Printed in the United States of America

26	25	24	23	22	21	20
7	6	5	4	3	2	1

For Lori, who literally prayed this book into existence.
Your friendship and your encouragement
mean more than you'll ever know.

Acknowledgments

IF AUTHORS ARE office-dwelling creatures who court their muses—or at least their coffeemakers—in yoga pants, then novels are their high-maintenance progeny who need entire teams of specialists before they can meet their public.

This book's specialists are even more special than most. I owe a great debt of thanks to: my Tyndale #dreamteam, Karen Watson, Jan Stob, Sarah Rische, Amanda Woods, Elizabeth Jackson, Andrea Garcia, Mark Lane, Danika King, and the Tyndale sales team whose enthusiasm is so crucial to the success of a book; my ever-wise and humorous agent, Steve Laube; my personal circle of awesome, who get a mention every time because they've stood by me with every twist and turn of this business, Evangeline Denmark, Brandy Vallance, Amber Lynn Perry, and Lori Twichell; my fearless assistant and de facto publicist, Audra Jennings, who didn't roll her eyes *too* hard every time I had a last-minute request; and my family, Rey, Nathan, Preston, Mom, and Dad, who would be proud of me if I never wrote another story . . . that's the kind of love that lets me write these books. Lastly, my gratitude goes to my gracious heavenly Father, who chose to give me the desires of my heart even as He uses them to mold me into the person He wants me to be.

Acknowledgments

IF AUTHORS ARE office-dwelling creatures who court their muses—or at least their coffeemakers—in yoga pants, then novels are their high-maintenance progeny who need entire teams of specialists before they can meet their public.

This book's specialists are even more special than most. I owe a great debt of thanks to: my Tyndale #dreamteam, Karen Watson, Jan Stob, Sarah Rische, Amanda Woods, Elizabeth Jackson, Andrea Garcia, Mark Lane, Danika King, and the Tyndale sales team whose enthusiasm is so crucial to the success of a book; my ever-wise and humorous agent, Steve Laube; my personal circle of awesome, who get a mention every time because they've stood by me with every twist and turn of this business, Evangeline Denmark, Brandy Vallance, Amber Lynn Perry, and Lori Twichell; my fearless assistant and de facto publicist, Audra Jennings, who didn't roll her eyes *too* hard every time I had a last-minute request; and my family, Rey, Nathan, Preston, Mom, and Dad, who would be proud of me if I never wrote another story . . . that's the kind of love that lets me write these books. Lastly, my gratitude goes to my gracious heavenly Father, who chose to give me the desires of my heart even as He uses them to mold me into the person He wants me to be.

Prologue

By all accounts, Suesca was haunted.

From everything Bryan Shaw had seen, he believed it. But for him, it wasn't the spirits of the dead that hovered over this small Colombian town. It was the memory of the living. A memory that he'd ignored, run from, and blotted out for three years without any significant success.

He zipped up his one-man tent and stood there, letting the cool, dark night surround him before he made his way toward the campfire where a cluster of other climbers gathered. Suesca was the epicenter of rock climbing in Colombia, its 8,400-foot elevation giving it the benefit of comfortable temperatures year-round, its proximity to Bogotá giving it the benefit of ease of access. The entire town was built around climbers: gear shops, hostels, campgrounds. Like most, Bryan had opted to rent a tent from the outfitter and camp here, just a stone's throw from the rock.

"Hey, mate, want a beer?" Jack, the big blond Australian Bryan had met earlier in the day, pressed a bottle into his hand as he approached and slapped him on the back. "I was just telling this mob about how you on-sighted Natalio Ruiz this morning."

Bryan made a noncommittal sound that could be taken as assent or appreciation and settled into a spare folding chair by the fire. Just because he'd never climbed that particular route didn't mean he'd never been on that pitch—he'd been climbing in Colombia on and off for most of his career. Nor did he say that for a climber of his caliber, a simple 5.9 wasn't much of a challenge. But Jack was a convivial sort who liked to tell stories, even if they weren't his own. Fine with Bryan. He didn't much feel like talking tonight.

Maybe Suesca had been a mistake after all. He could have gone on to Florián or La Mojarra without returning to the site of his old memories. Maybe he'd figured that by coming back he could reclaim them, expunge them. He'd been wrong.

Bryan took a swig of his beer and stared into the dark. He and Vivian had met here for the first time five years ago when Bryan was filming a climbing video. She'd been a production assistant, a climber herself, and even though Bryan was supposed to have his mind on the rock, half the time it had been on her. Which explained why he'd fallen on his first attempt. Embarrassing, but altogether understandable considering the nature of the distraction. Black-haired, lithe, and athletic, she was pretty much a climbing supermodel, and she naturally drew the eye of any man within a hundred yards.

A shadowed woman skirted the fire, and for a moment, he could have sworn it was her. Now he was seeing things, and he didn't even have alcohol to blame for it. He took another drink, closed his eyes, and tipped his head back to the sky.

"Hello, Bryan."

His eyes snapped open and he looked at the bottle in his hand as if it could confirm that he hadn't lost time, wasn't in the middle of some drunken vision. When his voice came out, it sounded hoarse and scratchy. "Vivian. What are you doing here?"

She dragged a folding chair over and plopped down beside him. "What anyone else is doing here, I imagine. Just got in tonight. How about you?"

"Last night, late." He looked her over as if to convince himself that she wasn't an apparition. But no, he knew her features as well as he knew his own. Hair pulled back into a severe ponytail, longer than it had been last time he'd seen her. Chiseled cheekbones. Sleek climbing pants and sport-fabric shell showing off every curve and muscle on her small frame. His stomach tightened and his heart clenched in response. "You're telling me we just happened to be in Colombia at the same time? That's some coincidence."

"It's no coincidence. I was in Peru, and when I saw your Instagram, I thought, *Why not?*" She flashed him a smile that managed to be halfway between knowing and regretful.

"In that case, I'm going to bed. Early morning tomorrow, and I want to be rested." He rose and saluted her with his mostly empty bottle.

He'd only taken a few steps when her voice trailed after him. "Since when are you so concerned with getting your beauty sleep?"

He paused for a second, then continued to his tent several hundred yards away and ripped the zipper open. He resisted the urge to shatter the bottle, setting it down carefully inside instead. Turned on the battery-operated lantern and zipped himself in, then stripped down to his athletic shorts. All the while he clenched his jaw so tightly his teeth ached.

Bryan was just reaching for the lantern's switch when the flap of his tent opened with a slow, deliberate zip. He straightened, muscles tensed, hoping it was just some drunk climber who forgot which rented tent was his own.

He couldn't be so lucky.

Vivian ducked through the opening and settled on her knees, zipping up after herself. "I don't like the way we left things."

"Just now? Or three years ago?"

"Both." She studied him carefully. "You look good."

He looked away before he could be pulled in by her pleading expression. "I'm not doing this, Viv. If you remember, you were the one who decided how we left things. I asked you to marry me, you said no, and I never saw you again. It sounded pretty definitive to me."

She crept closer. "Bryan, I'm sorry. I never meant to hurt you. I just . . ."

"You just didn't want to marry me. I'm over it." He made his face and his tone stony, as if the affectation would reach his heart.

Vivian bit her bottom lip. "Well, I guess I'm not."

Great, she was going to cry. He'd never been able to bear seeing her upset. That had been the whole problem. He would have given up everything for her, and she would give up nothing for him.

"I'm sorry. This was a mistake. I just thought—" Her voice strangled for a split second. "I thought if I could see you again, I could stop wondering if I made the right decision."

Despite the fact he hated himself for it, her imploring tone began to soften the hard shell he'd erected around the part of his heart she still owned. He reached out and smoothed a tear off her cheek with the roughened pad of his thumb. "Viv, we can't go back. What's done is—"

"Done, I know. But it doesn't stop me from missing you. It doesn't stop me from wishing I'd done things differently."

Her eyes, shining wet in the glare of the lantern, met his, and all the anger he'd held against her crumbled. For a while, he'd thought an endless string of women would help numb the pain, but they couldn't erase her memory when he'd never stopped loving her, never stopped wanting her.

Bryan didn't think when he slid a hand behind her neck and brought her closer. Acted on instinct when he lowered his lips to hers. And when her arms wrapped around him and she kissed him in return, the last three years melted away. It felt like all the wrongs in his life had been righted.

*   *   *

Bryan woke to a pale-blue glow through the tent canvas, the distant chirping of birds alerting him to the cusp of morning. He rolled to his side and touched only an empty space where Vivian should be, the chill on the nylon telling him she'd been gone for a while.

Quietly, he pulled on his clothes and shoes and unzipped his tent flap, a rush of relief coming immediately when he saw Vivian crouched in front of a small campfire. The smell of coffee drifted from the aluminum percolator set on the rocks. He crept up behind her and pressed a kiss to her neck. "Good morning, beautiful."

Instead of twisting around to kiss him as he expected, she straightened and slipped out of his embrace. "Coffee?"

"Sure." He retrieved his lightweight camp mug and held it out as she poured the thick black cowboy coffee into it. "Sleep well?"

Once more, she avoided his eyes. For the first time, a pang of fear struck him. "Viv? What's wrong?"

"Last night shouldn't have happened."

Bryan frowned and settled into the dirt beside her. "Viv, baby, I know it wasn't planned, but now that you're back . . ."

She swallowed hard and looked him straight in the eye. "I'm getting married."

He swayed in a sudden rush of dizziness. "Excuse me?"

"In May. I came here for closure. To get you out of my head once and for all. I didn't mean—"

"You're getting married?" His stomach clenched, not a single word after those three registering in his brain. She was getting married. To someone else. Not to him.

"Bryan—"

He jumped to his feet, but it didn't feel like his brain had any control over his body. "How could you? I thought—"

"Bryan, I'm sorry. You know I'm sorry." She buried her face in her hands. "If Luke finds out . . ."

"Wait, not Luke Van Bakker . . . What does he have to do with this?"

Vivian raised tear-filled eyes to his. "I thought you knew."

Bryan wiped a hand over his face, sudden understanding dawning. Luke Van Bakker, president and CEO of Pakka Mountaineering. A man he'd known for ten years, one he'd like to think was a friend. Engaged to his ex, and neither of them had told him.

Even worse, Pakka was his biggest sponsor, the one that allowed him to travel all over the world climbing instead of holding a real job.

"How could you come to me when you were engaged to him? I thought . . . I thought you were coming back to me. Wasn't that what this was all about? How much you wanted to be able to do things over?" He scrubbed his hands through his hair. "You must not think very much of me if you think I'd be okay with this."

Viv jumped to her feet. "Do you think I meant for this to happen? You can't tell him."

"Tell him?" Bryan barked out a harsh laugh. "The last thing I want is for Luke Van Bakker to know I just slept with his fiancée!"

She jerked her head around as his voice rose, and sure

enough, another climber poked a sleepy head out of a tent. He lowered his voice. "You and I are screwed. If there's anything Luke prizes, it's loyalty." It suddenly occurred to him that had Luke prized loyalty so much, he wouldn't have taken up with Bryan's ex in the first place. "How long have you been seeing him? Was that why you wouldn't marry me?"

"No! No, Bryan, you have to believe me." She reached for his hand, but he stepped out of reach. "Luke and I have only been together for a year. We reconnected at an event. Figured it had been long enough, you know? I assumed you were long over me, that you wouldn't care."

"Which is why no one told me."

"I swear to you, it wasn't like that . . ." Viv broke off, her lips pressing together stiffly, and Bryan turned to see Jack approaching them at a jog.

"Morning, you two." He beamed at them, a big blond puppy. "Wanted to know if you need a ride back to Bogotá this morning."

Right now, bugging out of Suesca didn't sound like a bad idea. "Sure," Bryan said at the same time Viv said, "No thanks. I'm climbing La Bruja today."

Bryan stared at her. "Not by yourself, you aren't."

She lifted an eyebrow and planted her hands on her hips. "And since when have you had *any* say over what I climbed?"

"As your former instructor, I do have some say. And unless you've suddenly advanced in your climbing ability, La Bruja is way over your grade."

Jack finally figured out he was stepping in the middle of something bigger than a climbing dispute and started to back away. "Okay, mates. We're leaving at eight if you change your mind."

Vivian never took her eyes from Bryan. "Go if you want. I'll find someone else to belay for me."

Bryan snorted. "You're out of your mind."

"You doubt my climbing ability?"

"No, I doubt your beta. I've watched these guys. None of them have even come close to sending that route. They wouldn't know a crimp from a hole in the ground." It was, he could admit, a little unfair; there were decent sport climbers among them, but La Bruja was the most difficult trad route in Suesca, and Bryan was betting any information they'd given her was colored by their need to impress her, not firsthand experience.

"Then come with me." Her eyes held a challenge.

"What game are you playing at?"

"No game. I came here from Peru and I'm not leaving until I climb."

"So do Azul."

"I'm not interested in Azul. You in or what?"

He knew that look. Knew that stubborn glint in her brown eyes. It was one of the things he'd loved most about her, one of the things that made her an excellent climber. She was going to do this with or without him. And however angry and hurt he might be right now, she was better off climbing with him as a partner than without.

Bryan shook his head. "Fine. You win. But I lead."

"I lead." Her eyes silently dared him to argue. "And to be clear, I got my beta from Alejandro, the guide at the shop. It's solid."

"Fine." He held up his hands. She was a good climber. As long as she placed active pro in the right spots, she'd be okay. And he'd be there on belay to catch her when she inevitably fell—as he'd always been.

They silently ate their breakfast of protein bars, trail mix, and coffee, the strain palpable. The whole time Bryan shoved down his feeling of betrayal and what felt like the awakening of his long-dormant conscience. He'd done many things in his life, but sleeping with another man's fiancée was in an entirely different class. If he felt this betrayed, how would Luke feel? And how long would it take for him to find some loophole to cancel Bryan's sponsorship contract if he found out?

He needed to finish out this day, keep Vivian safe on the crag, and get out of Colombia. The more space he put between him and Suesca, the easier it would be to pretend this whole sordid thing had never happened.

*　　*　　*

The sun was just beginning to shine down when they approached the route, loaded with their gear and a full thirty minutes ahead of the other climbers, who were just starting to poke their heads out of their tents. Bryan was used to hot climates where an early start was an advantage; here, the temperature stayed chilly well into the morning.

Vivian didn't meet his eye as she pulled on climbing shoes and set her gear. Bryan checked the length of lead rope for any frays or weaknesses before he handed it over for Viv to tie it onto her harness with a figure-eight knot, then double-checked her knot. It was a routine, not a doubt about her competence— two sets of eyes were always better than one. More skilled climbers had decked out because of a simple mistake.

"All right, so let me see your rack." He nodded toward the collection of cams, nuts, and slings hanging from her belt, ignoring the flash of amusement that crossed her face at the comment. "You'll need more active pro for this one."

She arched an eyebrow at him. "This coming from Mr. Passive Is Best?"

And here they were, retreading old arguments over whether active or passive protection was best, when in reality it was whatever best suited the rock and the route. Had he not been so irritated at her at the moment, he would have found it funny. "There're some cracks that won't take a hex or a nut, and you're not going to want to worry about conserving cams. Trust me on this one."

For once, she didn't argue and rummaged in her gear, then clipped a few more cams onto her harness. Old-timers who'd started climbing before spring-loaded camming devices existed looked at them as cheating; Bryan figured if it was a choice between a cam or a fall, he'd pick the cam every time.

"Ready?" he asked.

"Ready." She checked her rope again, chalked her hands from the pouch on her belt, and approached the rock with a look of determination.

"On belay?"

"Belay on," he replied.

"Climbing."

"Climb on." He stayed in position near the wall, feeding rope through the belay device and his hands to give her enough slack to get up to her first anchor point. He'd always loved to watch her on the rock, partly because of her gorgeous body displayed in climbing tights and a skin-tight T-shirt. The thought of that now set a sick feeling in his stomach; she wasn't his to ogle, no matter what he might have thought the night before.

Mind on her climbing, he reminded himself. Vivian made short work of the first fifteen feet, her technique steady and confident. He began to relax as soon as she took the first cam from her harness, placed it precisely in the crack where he would have, and clipped herself in. Now he had a belay point, so he took up the slack while she looked for her next hold.

She was climbing respectably, placing more pro than strictly necessary, which told him she'd taken his warning seriously. Except she hadn't yet reached for another cam after the first, choosing to place hexes and nuts where she could fit them. "Set a cam before the overhang!" he yelled, but either she was too focused on her next move to hear him or she was ignoring him outright. Stubborn woman.

She was at least seventy feet up when she realized she'd gotten herself into an untenable position. He checked the slack on the rope and waited for her to work out a solution. There— thanks to her flexibility, her handhold became a foothold and she could lever herself upward with the power of her legs. She was going to send it on her first try. Unbelievable.

Then Bryan saw the mistake, but it was too late to help her correct: her leg had crossed between the rock and the rope, the anchor below holding it taut against her thigh. Her left hand held steady near her foot, right side pushing upward to the next handhold, and then . . .

Vivian screamed as her supporting leg slipped off the rock.

Bryan automatically prepared himself for a soft catch, but there were bigger problems. The rope flipped her upside down so she was plummeting headfirst down the side of the rock. Every hair on his body lifted in dread. He jumped just as she hit the end of the slack and braced his feet against the wall, a move that should have helped soften the catch and dampen her swing back into the wall.

The nut she'd placed earlier popped out of the rock and zippered the next two out with it.

"No, no, no." Bryan barely managed to get back on his feet and yanked the rope through the brake as fast as he could, silently praying that one of the anchors would catch before she hit the deck. Then finally, the slack ran out and the rope caught on the cam and held.

Vivian careened into the side of the rock with a sickening crunch, where she hung, her limp body dangling thirty feet off the ground, unmoving. Drops of blood fell in slow motion and spattered the dirt at Bryan's feet.

"Please," he mumbled, running the rope through the brake to lower her slowly to the ground. "Please be alive. Please be alive." She never wore a helmet—Bryan rarely did either—but now he wished with every ounce of him that he'd insisted on it before she'd attempted La Bruja.

Finally, she was on the ground. He unclipped and ran to her side, carefully laying her out flat on the dirt. Blood matted her dark hair and something about her lower body looked wrong, crumpled, but her chest still rose and fell. He put his fingertips to her neck and found her pulse, surprisingly quick considering she was unconscious.

"Help!" he screamed. *"Ayuda!"*

It could have been moments or hours later, but a crowd began to form around them. Alejandro, the guide from the shop near the base camp, pushed his way through and checked her pulse and breathing as Bryan had, then pulled out his cell phone. He dialed the emergency number and then explained the situation to the dispatcher in calm, rapid Spanish. "She'll be okay," he said to Bryan, but it was an empty reassurance. No one knew whether she would be okay or not. They hadn't seen how she'd whipped into the wall, too out of control to break her own fall.

"Just hang in there," he whispered to her, wanting to do something but knowing that moving her would be the worst thing he could possibly do. He brushed her hair off her face and clasped her hand until he heard the siren from an ambulance approaching. Relief rushed through him. He hadn't been sure if Suesca had ambulance service; he'd never needed it.

Two paramedics stepped out of the ambulance and carried an unwheeled stretcher to Vivian's side.

"¿Que pasó?" the first man asked, looking automatically to Alejandro.

Bryan quickly explained what had occurred. Had it been any other situation, he would have been amused by the paramedics' surprise that the gringo spoke their language. The men examined Vivian with little more detail than Bryan and Alejandro had, then the two of them carefully transferred her to the stretcher.

"I'm going with her," Bryan said. They nodded and he climbed into the back of the ambulance with her.

They were minutes away from the camp when Vivian began to stir and cried out in pain. Her eyes opened slowly, but they didn't seem to focus.

"Viv, I'm here." He bent over her and gently squeezed her hand to try to orient her.

"Bryan?"

"Yes, love."

"Everything hurts." Tears leaked out of her eyes and slid down her face, breaking his heart more surely than her earlier tears had.

"I know. You had an accident. We'll be at the hospital soon and they'll give you something for the pain."

The rest of the afternoon was a blur. They arrived at the hospital, which was a surprisingly modern-looking white-and-blue two-story building in the small town of Suesca. Bryan said he was her husband so they would give him updates. The doctor in the emergency department examined her, pronounced her hip dislocated, several of her ribs fractured, and her skull cracked, and promptly decided to transfer her to Bogotá.

That trip took over an hour, and Bryan held her hand in the back of yet another ambulance as they traveled to a larger hospital in the capital city. She remained sedated—a mercy when he considered how many broken bones she had.

And the whole time he prayed, *Please don't let me lose her.*

He was aware of the irony. He'd already lost her three years ago, and once again this morning when she'd announced her engagement to Luke.

They finally arrived at a hospital in Bogotá, a concrete institutional structure that reminded him of a prison. The paramedics took her into the emergency department, where Bryan was immediately pushed out of the room, despite his repeated insistence that he was her husband. Instead, he paced the faded waiting room, pulled out his phone, and dialed the number he'd been dreading calling since the moment she fell.

"Luke, it's Bryan. Vivian's hurt. We're in Colombia."

*   *   *

Bryan sat in the bar of his Bogotá hotel, nursing a glass of whiskey and feeling like he'd been run over by a train. This was high rent for his usual means of travel—even if the exchange rate came out to about sixty-seven bucks a night—but he didn't have it in him to dirtbag it as he usually did. Despite his simple needs, he was still the son of a successful Denver real estate developer, and right now he wanted something that felt like home.

Vivian would be okay, or at least as okay as she could get with broken bones and a fractured skull. By now, she would be flying home on the air ambulance plane that Luke had arranged to take her to Cedars-Sinai Medical Center in Los Angeles near where they lived together. Where they had been living together, apparently, for the past year—something that Luke had been lying about or at least avoiding the last several times they'd talked. Bryan had relayed the doctor's thoughts on her prognosis in straightforward terms, not softening them or putting hope on them. Bed rest. Physical therapy. She'd walk again. Climbing would be out of the question for quite a while.

Explaining why he and Vivian were in Bogotá together was another story. Bryan tried to pass it off as a friendly climb for old times' sake, but Luke clearly didn't believe it. Maybe it was

3

something in Bryan's voice or maybe Luke just knew Vivian too well, but he'd gone silent for a long moment while he considered. Then he'd said calmly, "I appreciate you helping me get her home. But after that, I don't think we have anything more to talk about."

He'd apparently meant it literally, because the notice of termination had hit Bryan's inbox less than an hour later, almost as if it had already been drafted and was simply waiting to be sent.

Notice of termination. A fancy way of saying he'd been fired, his sponsorship ended, his means of support gone.

Of course, Luke wouldn't be so obvious as to name the real reason he was firing him; instead, he couched it in words like *exclusivity* and *conflict of interest*, despite the fact he'd been fully aware of the other, minor sponsorships when he signed Bryan. Not that it mattered when the end result was the same. Without Pakka's support, he wasn't a professional climber; he was just a deadbeat, traveling the world with his backpack and his gear rack in order to avoid having a real job. He'd become what his father had always suspected he was.

Bryan let out a sharp laugh and drained the rest of his glass, then gestured for the bartender to pour him another one. What would his father think of this whole situation? Mitchell Shaw was a good Christian man; Bryan's mother, Kathy, was practically a saint. They'd given up lecturing him about his conquests long ago, but sleeping with an almost-married woman and losing his source of income was beyond what even they could overlook. Consequences of his own actions, they'd say. And now he was going to have to deal with them. When you screwed up this badly, there was no such thing as a second chance.

"You look like a man who's had a bad day."

Bryan turned his head toward the American who had sat down beside him. Nondescript in brown dress pants and a white shirt, like a Midwestern businessman. Slightly thinning hair on top, sympathetic expression. Bryan was half tempted to give a sarcastic retort, but the man seemed sincere enough, so he just gave a single nod.

"Want to talk about it?"

"Not really." The bartender poured Bryan's drink and he took a slow sip, savoring the burn of the whiskey as it went down. Anyone who said that it was smooth was lying, or maybe he'd just turned wholly into a beer man somewhere along the line. In any case, it blurred the hard edges, and right now that was all he cared about.

The man asked for soda without ice in mangled Spanish, and Bryan quickly translated for him. He looked at Bryan in surprise. "If I had your fluency, my day would be going a lot better."

"I've spent a lot of time in Central and South America," he said. "You pick it up."

"I don't, apparently. I've made several trips to Colombia over the last couple of years, and it doesn't want to stick. Old dog, new tricks, I guess."

Bryan smiled vaguely, hoping that would be the end of the conversation.

"I don't suppose you'd be interested in a job?"

Bryan turned his head just enough to look the man in the eye, suddenly suspicious. "A job?"

"I was supposed to be headed south today, but my translator bailed on me. You know anything about coffee?"

"I know how I like to drink it."

"Do you know how to talk about it in Spanish?"

"Enough, I guess. Why?"

The man pulled a business card from his pocket and slid it across the polished bar. "This is my company, Café Libertad. We're coffee importers, but more than that, we're . . . I guess you could call us missionaries."

Bryan slid it back. "Not interested."

"Are you sure? It's an interesting story, ours. You see, for the longest time, the only option for farmers was coca, working for the cartels. But it brings violence into communities, wedges the farmers right between the government and the rebels, puts them at the mercy of the 'war on drugs.' So we come along and help them shift from growing coca to growing coffee instead. For the first time in decades, thanks to the demand for fair trade organic coffee in the States, the same acreage can produce a greater dollar yield than drugs."

"Sounds like you're doing good work," Bryan said, but he couldn't force interest where there wasn't any. He didn't have it in him today.

"It is. I'm supposed to be visiting several new farms, seeing about bringing them into the co-op. But again, without someone to translate, this was pretty much a wasted trip. You wouldn't know anything about wasted trips, would you?"

Bryan tossed back the rest of his drink and set the glass firmly on the counter. "I don't know what you want from me, but I'm the last person you should be asking to join some Christian charity." He gave the man a wan smile, then eased himself off the stool.

"Are you sure? Because from where I'm sitting, you look like a man in need of a second chance."

Bryan paused several steps away and turned. "What did you say?"

"I said maybe this is a second chance. I only need you for a week, and I pay well. What have you got to lose?"

What did he have to lose? He had nothing to go back to but the disappointed looks of friends and family. At very least, this delay to the inevitable would pad his bank account. And maybe he'd figure out a new direction by the time he boarded the flight home.

"Okay," he said finally. "I'm in. When do we start?"

Chapter One

EIGHT MONTHS LATER

In all her years as a publicist, Analyn Sanchez had never met a mess she couldn't clean up.

Until now.

She gripped her cell phone so hard her fingers began to turn white as she struggled to keep her voice level. "I don't understand how this could have happened. I have a signed contract right in front of me. June nineteenth, Bishop-Kanin wedding."

"I'm very sorry, Ms. Sanchez. I understand how upsetting this is, and I take full responsibility for it. But the situation remains, we are double-booked for the nineteenth. I've already spoken to the other party to see if they'd be willing to change. They're not, and because their contract was signed first, I have no choice but to give them the space."

Ana pressed the fingertips of her free hand into her eyelids. "What are we supposed to do, then? The invitations have already gone out."

"Again, I'm very sorry. Of course we will refund the deposit and any additional monies paid, and I'll be happy to send you a list of other venues that might have openings—"

Ana stopped listening after the second "very sorry." One job. She'd had one job and she'd blown it. Melody was handling all of the decor and working with Rachel on the menu; all Ana had had to do was negotiate and book the venue. And now, with the wedding less than three months away, her best friend had nowhere to marry the love of her life.

She almost didn't register the woman's voice still coming from the speaker; she'd ceased to exist the minute she wasn't willing to help. Ana clicked off her phone and, in nearly the same motion, dialed the other member of their little trio, Melody Johansson.

The phone rang several times before Melody picked up. "Hey, Ana. What's up? Is something wrong?"

The low hum of voices and clatter of pans in the background made Ana glance at her clock—5:20. Melody and Rachel would be shutting down the kitchen of Bittersweet Café right now, getting ready to close their doors to retail traffic at six o'clock. "Is Rachel there?"

A couple of sharp bangs, and the noise level dropped sharply. "Not anymore. I stepped outside. But you're starting to freak me out."

"The venue is double-booked and they gave it to the other party."

A long silence met the announcement. Then Melody said slowly, "That's . . . unfortunate."

"It's more than unfortunate, Melody. The wedding is only twelve weeks away and they've got nowhere to get married!" Heads turned in Ana's direction, and she quickly lowered her voice. She wasn't supposed to be handling personal matters in the office, let alone those of a friend, but it wasn't like she had a choice. "What are we going to do?"

"We're going to look for another venue, of course. This is Denver, not New York. It's not like we booked the Plaza three years ahead."

Melody had been clearly watching rom-coms again; Ana knew for a fact she'd never been to New York, let alone the Plaza Hotel. "Yes, but this is *Denver*. Meaning there's less than three months of the year we can count on good weather, so everyone gets married between June and August. Things were starting to book up nine months ago."

"That's what I don't understand. We've been talking to them the whole time. We have menus chosen. How did no one notice this?"

"I don't know. Something about a junior sales rep booking the other group and not merging her calendar."

"How about a different day?"

"We can't. Alex has family coming in from Moscow. There's no way we can ask them to reschedule."

"Well, we're going to figure this out. Hey, what about Alex's place? He has that gorgeous roof deck, and it is where their love story began in a way. It could be really meaningful."

Ana shook her head automatically. "No can do. They've invited a hundred and fifty people, and even if we could manage to stuff that many guests up there, I think the fire marshal and the building department would have something to say about it. I'm sure it's not rated for that weight or those numbers."

Several feet away, Ana's boss, Lionel, poked his head out and gestured to her from his framed glass doorway. "Ana, when you're done, can I see you in my office?"

Ana nodded and held up one finger. "Sorry, Mel, I've gotta go. Let's talk later? And don't say a word to Rachel until we have some solution to present. I don't want her worrying about this."

"Okay, I'll—"

Ana's finger was already on the End Call button before the words came from the speaker, and by then it was too late. She had hung up on her friend midsentence. She cringed, but there was no time to call back and apologize. Besides, Melody wouldn't be offended—she knew how crazy Ana's job was.

She inhaled deeply, counting to herself as she sucked oxygen into her lungs, then exhaled for twice as long. A meditation exercise meant to calm her nerves and slow her heart rate. It didn't help.

She rose from her desk, smoothed down her pencil skirt, and strode across the room to her boss's office. "You needed to see me, Lionel?"

"Yes, I did, Ana. Please close the door."

She turned around and pulled the glass door shut behind her, only then noticing that they were not alone. Morgan sat in the armchair in the corner, clutching a handful of Kleenex. "What's going on?"

"I'm going to need to you take over Christopher Mason from Morgan."

Ana blinked at her boss for a long moment, then looked at Morgan. "Why? You fought tooth and nail for that account."

Lionel cleared his throat. "It seems that Mason has been harassing Morgan and she is uncomfortable with continuing."

Ana narrowed her eyes at the first whiff of dishonesty. Morgan never had a problem with clients. As women dealing with badly behaved men, they were always fending off unwanted advances and unwarranted assumptions. Morgan was the first person to set them straight, often in painful ways if they tried anything funny. The tissue-clutching, teary-eyed victim sitting in the chair across from Ana had to be a complete fabrication.

"This is a great opportunity for you, Ana."

"I've already got a full roster of wealthy, wannabe frat boys. Why would I want to add another one?"

"Because this one's father is about to be appointed to a cabinet position, and said father happens to be a longtime friend of my family. So I would take it as a personal favor if you would get him in line and keep him out of trouble for the next month until the nomination is announced."

Ana took a deep breath and considered. It sounded like Lionel was giving her a choice, but she knew from experience that once you started turning down clients at Massey-Coleman, it was a short slide to finding yourself on the way out the door. They were hired to be can-do types, and that meant accepting even the most annoying and difficult clients. There was a reason why publicists in the crisis management division got paid so much—they earned each and every penny.

"Fine," Ana said with a sharp nod. "Morgan, I need all your files on him. I'll give him a call and figure out where we are. Lionel, are you notifying him of the change, or am I?"

"Somehow I think he would take the change better coming from you." The glint in Lionel's eye was her first indication she might have made a mistake by acquiescing so easily. "Morgan, that will be all. Please get Ana all your files before you leave today."

They both nodded curtly at their boss, and Ana preceded Morgan from the office. As soon as they were halfway across the room to her desk, Ana rounded on her. "What was that all about? And don't tell me for one minute you've suddenly lost your ability to shut a client down before he can even attempt a pass at you."

Morgan straightened, no sign of the tearful demeanor in sight. "He's called me in the middle of the night every night this week. My husband has threatened to either kill him or divorce me if I don't dump him."

"So you thought you'd make him my problem?"

Morgan grimaced. "Sorry about that. I was actually lobbying for him to go to Ryan. I figured he wouldn't be as demanding with a male publicist."

"But somehow Lionel got the idea that I was the perfect person to handle him."

"Well, they don't call you the Atomic Nun for nothing."

"No one calls me that except you." But the joking nickname loosened the knot in Ana's stomach and she managed a smile. "Fine. But you owe me big time."

"I promise. Anything you need . . . that doesn't involve Christopher Mason." Morgan sat down at her computer, clicked a few keys, and attached a file folder to an email message with Ana's address on it. "On its way."

Ana gave her a nod and strode back to her desk, concentrating on her breathing again. Morgan's email was waiting at the top of her inbox, so she wasted no time in downloading the file and beginning her perusal. From the notes, it was hard to tell that Christopher Mason was a difficult client—it was just the usual guidance for anyone related to a politician. Keep them out of the press, keep their personal activities— whatever they might be—quiet, unless it was a specifically orchestrated photo op. The media was rabid when it came to the families of politicians running on a morality ticket. The minute someone came out in favor of family values or the like, reporters combed through the dirty laundry hoping to find an illegitimate baby or a gay son they could parade around as a sign of the politician's hypocrisy. But from her reading, she didn't see much more than the propensity to drink and speak a little too freely at fund-raisers for his father's campaign. Maybe Morgan was telling the truth and she was just doing this because her husband didn't like her getting late-night calls.

Only one way to find out. Ana found his number, picked up her phone, and dialed. Mason answered on the first ring.

"Mr. Mason, my name is Analyn Sanchez. I'm Morgan Caroll's colleague at the Massey-Coleman Group."

His response was cordial, professional even. "Hi, Analyn. It's nice to meet you. What can I do for you this afternoon?"

"We've had a bit of internal restructuring here, and I'll be working on your account now. I was hoping we could get together, just to meet, get to know each other a bit."

"How about tonight?"

Ana paused and glanced at her watch. She had dinner plans with Rachel and Melody. "I'm afraid I'm not available tonight."

"That's too bad. I've got reservations at Equity Bar and Grill and my dinner date had to cancel on me. Tell me if I'm mistaken, but I seem to remember Lionel Massey assuring my father that my publicist would be at my disposal whenever necessary."

Ana let out her breath carefully. If Lionel had really conveyed that message, it went a long way to explaining why Morgan had demanded that he be assigned to someone else. Some clients seemed to think they needed to get their money's worth.

And if Mason ran back to Daddy, who then called Lionel, Ana would have plenty of free time to spend on dinner with her friends.

"Very well. I can reschedule. What time is your reservation?"

"Eight o'clock."

"Great. I'll see you then." Ana forced a smile so the feigned warmth would transfer to her voice and then hung up. She quickly sent a group text to her friends.

Sorry to bail, but I can't make dinner tonight. Last minute meeting with new (problem) client.

Moments later, Rachel replied, Come by my house when you're done. Melody brought home eclairs from the bakery. We'll save you some.

Melody's response instantly followed: Speak for yourself. Ana, if you're not there by nine, I'm eating them ALL.

Ana texted back: Fair enough. For the last eight years, she, Melody, and Rachel had been practically inseparable. Her two friends worked in the food service industry, Rachel as a chef and Melody as a baker, but they had opened their own place together less than a year ago. Somehow, even owning a business that required them to report to work at 4 a.m., they seemed to have more free time than she did. In fact, it had been three weeks since she'd seen either of them in more than a drive-by at Bittersweet Café.

But that was the job. Long hours, late nights, and problem clients. When she'd taken the position in the crisis publicity division, she'd thought she was making the smart move; after all, most of her regular clients were in the middle of mini crises on a regular basis. Turned out it was less a matter of crises and more a matter of highly sensitive situations—she spent more time mitigating the negatives than accentuating the positives. It wasn't that she lied. Everything she publicized on her clients' behalf was 100 percent true. It was just that every fact was interpreted through the listener's bias; it was her job to make sure the bias leaned in her clients' favor. Like every criminal deserved a competent lawyer, she firmly believed that every public figure could use a brilliant publicist.

And just like every defense lawyer, she wished for once that she'd get a client who was innocent.

"That's why they pay you the big bucks, Ana," she murmured to herself. As if to punctuate that statement, she rose onto the five-inch heels of her favorite Louboutins, hoisted her Prada handbag over her shoulder, and prepared to make her way down to the parking garage where her leased company car—a shiny Mercedes-Benz SUV—waited for her. All the symbols of her success. All items that, once upon a time, she'd thought she needed in order to prove herself.

And not for the first time, she wondered if it was a hollow victory.

*   *   *

Ana didn't have time to go home and change before her dinner meeting at the high-end steak house, so at the last minute, she made a stop in the ladies' room to freshen up her makeup from the case she kept in her tote. A few bobby pins secured her thick black hair into a sophisticated French twist. Fortunately, the office dress code was business—the unspoken understanding among the women that it also meant both sophisticated and stylish—so her black peplum suit and bow-necked silk blouse would fit right into the ritzy surroundings.

She made it the handful of blocks from her office building in just a few minutes and handed her vehicle over to the valet at eight on the dot. Then she marched inside to the hostess desk. "Christopher Mason's party?"

"Right this way." The hostess smiled at Ana and led her through the sprawling dining room to where a man sat at a table with two women.

Two very young women.

"Mr. Mason?" Ana asked, inwardly hoping he would answer in the negative, even though she'd already seen his photo and knew he was the one she was meeting.

"You must be Analyn." He rose with a blinding smile and shook her hand, then gestured to the empty chair on his right. "I would like you to meet my friends Catelyn and Rebecca."

Ana looked over the "friends" surreptitiously. They were barely twenty, slathered in cosmetics, and squeezed into cheap polyester cocktail dresses that showed off both leg and cleavage. Everything about them screamed *escort*.

A waitress came to their table then to take their drink orders.

"Double Manhattan on the rocks," Mason said immediately, flashing that smile for the waitress again.

"Sparkling water for me," Ana said. When the waitress looked at the girls, she said, "Them too."

Only a quick second glance in the girls' direction betrayed the waitress's curiosity, but she smiled and nodded and hustled off to get their drinks. When Ana glanced at Mason, he was studying her beneath lowered lids, a half smile on his lips. So that's what this was about. A test. Or better yet, a statement. No wonder Morgan had resorted to deception to get rid of him, and why they'd been hired by the senator from Colorado to babysit his son. She was trying to decide on a response when a cell phone rang.

Mason fished his phone from his jacket's breast pocket and glanced at the screen. "Excuse me a moment." He answered the phone and strode toward the front entrance, his voice carrying through the din of conversations.

Ana fixed a stern glare on the girls. "How old are you two?"

Rebecca lifted her chin. "I'm a sophomore at CU."

"Studying what?"

"I'm still undeclared."

Ana rapid-fired at Catelyn, "And you? What's your major?"

Catelyn averted her eyes. "I don't have one yet."

Fabulous. She probably wasn't out of high school. Ana felt a sudden rush of pity for them. Not even twenty, but working in such an unsavory business. "You two need to go. Now. Before he returns."

"But we didn't get paid—" Catelyn began before Rebecca hastily shushed her.

"Come on, our night's over." Rebecca picked up her handbag and grabbed Catelyn's arm.

"Don't stop, even if he talks to you," Ana warned, "or my next call is going to be to your parents."

The older girl didn't look fazed, but the terrified look on the younger one's face as Rebecca hustled her out of the restaurant told Ana all she needed to know. Good. Did Catelyn have any idea what she'd almost gotten herself into? How this could have turned out if it wasn't all a stunt to get a rise out of his new publicist?

"Where are they going?" Mason demanded as he approached the table. His voice caused the patrons at surrounding tables to turn in his direction.

"Home." Ana gestured placidly to the seat opposite her. "Sit down, Mr. Mason."

He scowled at her, but he sat.

"Let me make one thing clear. While I'm your publicist, there will be no more escorts or Tinder dates or anything that even smacks of sexual misconduct. We just need to get you through the next month without doing anything to disgrace your family name. Once you're no longer my responsibility, you can do whatever you want."

"Wait a second. You work for me—"

"No, Mr. Mason. I work for your father. A man who will be very displeased to find you spending time with underage escorts who should be home studying for their chemistry finals."

Mason looked like he was about to argue, but she stilled him with a look. "Now that all the children are out of the room, I'm going to buy you an excellent meal and we're going to discuss the ground rules for our business relationship. Which, by the way, does not include after-hours calls unless you're in jail, about to be put in jail, or imminently facing a TV crew."

He cracked a smile. "Morgan told you about that."

"Morgan is too polite to tell you that you're being an arrogant, juvenile tool."

"But you're not too polite?"

Ana knew her smile looked cold, if not downright predatory. It was a practiced expression she could drag out on cue. "I've been accused of many things, Mr. Mason, but that's not one of them." She glanced up and put on a much more welcoming smile. "Here comes our server with our drinks. If you don't mind the suggestion, they serve a delicious rib eye."

For the next two hours, Ana outlined her expectations for his behavior and went through the opportunities that she'd lined up for him earlier this evening—one, volunteering at the grand opening of a new free clothing store for the homeless in Five Points; and two, mentoring minority business owners through a new SBA program.

"You've got an undergrad degree from Harvard and an MBA from the London School of Economics. There's no reason for you to be currently unemployed. Play it my way, repair your reputation, and I'll have you in a six-figure consulting position by the end of the month."

Mason studied her, a glimmer of respect surfacing for the first time. "Okay. If you think you can do that, I'm on board."

"Good. I'll be in touch with the details on Monday. I fully expect this to be a pleasant and productive month."

They finished their meal and Ana paid, escaping out to the valet stand. Her car had just been brought around when a message from Lionel buzzed through her phone. How did dinner with the frat boy go?

Ana cracked a smile. Good. I put him on a short leash and appealed to his greed. He's going to be too busy to be trouble.

I knew you could do it. This is why I assigned you to this account and not Ryan.

Thank you for the confidence. I'll keep you posted.

Ana put her car in gear, preparing to pull into traffic. Then she stopped. She was supposed to head to Rachel's, where she'd normally spill all the ridiculous details about her latest ridiculous client. But suddenly she didn't have the heart for it. This whole situation made her feel dirty, as if managing the creep had somehow rubbed off on her. There was nothing funny about it.

She texted Rachel and Melody: Sorry, guys, I'm not going to make it. Rain check? I'm still coming to supper club tomorrow, no matter what.

Rachel: We understand.

Melody: Whew. That's good. I already ate your eclairs.

Ana smiled to herself and pulled into traffic for real this time, but the momentary surge of happiness didn't last. She'd been awake for eighteen hours already. Her eyes were practically crossed with exhaustion, and the balls of her feet ached from a full day in shoes that had been designed for looks and status, not comfort. By the time she pulled into the parking structure beneath her Lower Downtown condo building, she ached for nothing more than her soft bed. A shower could wait until morning. Heck, pajamas could wait until morning.

She rode the elevator up to the twelfth floor, made a beeline to her front door, and punched her code into the smart lock. It unlatched with a click and she pushed her way through with a sigh of relief.

Her oasis. Small by most standards, but spacious by LoDo's, it was twelve hundred square feet of elegant design and calming colors. Herringbone hardwood floors. Upholstery in velvet and satin. Muted antique oriental rugs. It might seem like it was orchestrated for show, but she rarely had guests, even her best friends. This was all for her own pleasure. It was just a shame she had so little time to enjoy it.

A flashing red light drew her attention to the marble-accented kitchen, and she dropped her bag beside the phone before dialing voice mail. She knew before the message began who it would

31

be—she only kept a home line because her mother refused to call her cell phone while she was at work. And she was always at work.

Flora Sanchez's familiar Manila-accented voice poured through the speaker in her usual combination of Filipino and English. "Ana, this is Mom. Can you call back? *Gusto ko malaman kung uuwi ka para sa* birthday *ng* Daddy *mo sa* May. *Da-dating din ang mga kapatid mo, gusto ka nilaang makita.*" *I want to know if you're coming home for your dad's birthday in May. Your sisters and brother will be here. They all want to see you.*

Ana deleted the message and dug in her bag for her planner. Under Monday's date, she jotted *Put in vacation request.* She had plenty of time to plan, since her dad's birthday was after Mason would no longer be her problem. She should be able to steal two days to fly home to Southern California for a birthday party. As soon as she confirmed her time off, she'd call her mom back and book her flight.

Then her eyes alighted on the grid at the bottom of her page—her daily habits. Everything from Scripture reading to making her bed to flossing her teeth. The only box left unchecked for today was *exercise*. Thanks to Mason, she'd missed the hot yoga class she'd scheduled before dinner.

It's late. Go to bed and do it tomorrow.

But that empty box glared at her, and she knew the blank space in an otherwise-filled week would eat at her. She hadn't achieved her toned, size-zero figure by skipping workouts just because she was tired.

She dragged herself to her bedroom with a deep sigh, traded her suit for a pair of shorts and a sports bra, and climbed onto the treadmill positioned in front of the wide-screen TV. She inserted the flat plastic key and pressed Start.

"Five miles, Ana. You can do this. It's only five miles."

And one more box checked to keep up her six-month streak. Just one more box for a perfect day.

Chapter Two

BRYAN SHAW HAD ALWAYS viewed Denver as a mid-tier city, smaller than the suburban sprawl of Los Angeles or the compact metropolis of New York, just large enough to offer the conveniences of urban life. But as he looked out the rear window of his Uber crawling through the gridlocked city, it felt as if he'd been catapulted into the distant future.

There were changes, of course. Development had sped along in his eight months away, building projects completed in his absence, others just beginning. But mostly it was his perspective that had changed. Colombia had crept into him—the countryside with its lush green foliage and relentless rainy season, the cities that were a shocking mix of old and new, the people with their welcoming attitudes and unhurried pace.

The city he'd grown up in felt slightly alien by contrast. But he couldn't deny it was good to be home.

"You can let me out here," he told his driver, pointing to the high-rise building ahead. The driver double-parked, something that would have elicited a barrage of horns in Bogotá, but here the traffic just flowed around them. "Thanks for the ride." He levered the door open and climbed out, dragging his battered nylon backpack with him.

The familiar marble foyer felt equally strange as he punched the Up button to call the elevator to the ground floor. What did it mean that his first stop after a long absence wasn't his home? What did it mean that he wasn't sure where home was even located?

Bryan rode the elevator up to the fifteenth floor, where he emerged and knocked at one of the four penthouse suites. A minute later, the door swung open to reveal a tall, dark-haired man about Bryan's age.

"Hey, Alex."

"Bryan?" Alex Kanin blinked at him, momentarily stunned. "You're back. Why didn't you call?"

"Sorry. Is Rachel here?"

"No, that's not what I meant. Come in." Alex swung the door wider, still seemingly stunned. Bryan dropped his bag on the polished concrete as Alex shut the door. And then his friend pounded him into a hug.

"Okay then," Bryan said, returning the gesture before carefully extricating himself. "It's nice to see you too, bro."

Alex laughed. He was Bryan's oldest friend, practically a brother, especially considering Alex had lived with the Shaws their senior year of high school while his parents taught at a university in Russia. He was maybe the only person who knew who Bryan truly was. Suddenly, his destination didn't seem so strange.

"Grab a seat," Alex said. "Want something to drink?"

"I'll take a pop if you have it." He settled himself onto the hard, modern sofa while Alex retrieved a can of Coke from his refrigerator. He tossed it to Bryan, then sat in the adjacent chair and waited.

When Bryan didn't volunteer anything, Alex said, "Are you going to make me drag it out of you? Where have you been?"

Bryan popped the top and took a long drink of his Coke

before answering. "Would it be too dramatic to say I met Jesus in Colombia?"

"Coming from you, a little."

Bryan turned the can around in his hand thoughtfully. "That's kind of what happened, though. God got my attention in the most dramatic way possible."

Alex just stared.

"Vivian came while I was climbing in Suesca, slept with me before she told me she was engaged to Luke Van Bakker, and then proceeded to almost kill herself on a route that was way out of her ability range. You're a writer. You can probably extrapolate what happened next."

"I can imagine Luke wasn't particularly forgiving of either of you."

"Enough to get Vivian home, I guess. Me . . . it didn't take him more than an hour to email the notice of termination."

"So what then? You became a yoga teacher in the mountains of Colombia? Joined a Benedictine monastery?"

"Not quite. I bought a coffee farm." Bryan enjoyed the look of disbelief that crossed Alex's face, the way he was trying to decide which question to ask first. He decided to end his friend's suspense. "You ever hear of Café Libertad?"

Alex shook his head.

"They help coca farmers transition to coffee. I originally signed on temporarily as a translator, but then . . ." Bryan broke off while he figured out how to explain the change that had begun inside him. "All that quiet, it gave me a lot of time to reflect on my life and how far I'd strayed from my values, from God. It's easy to creep away one step at a time . . . and then one day you realize you're calling yourself a Christian, but no one would ever be able to tell the difference."

Alex nodded thoughtfully. "What about climbing?"

"In the past now. I didn't plan on buying a coffee farm, by

the way. The owners were aging without family to take it over, and I didn't want the land to revert to cocaine production. So I bought it."

"So you're what? A coffee farmer? An importer?" Alex seemed like he was having a hard time wrapping his mind around the situation, and Bryan couldn't really blame him. The last time Alex had seen him, he'd been renting a room in a townhome with three other guys, month-to-month. The very idea of putting down roots or committing to anything more than a climbing clinic a few weeks ahead had been laughable.

Alex's expectant expression made him realize he hadn't answered the question. Not exactly. "The harvest will yield a few thousand pounds, and green coffee beans are a lot less lucrative than you'd think. We'd barely be breaking even if I wholesaled it."

"So what then?"

"I'm opening a roasting company."

Silence stretched a long moment, and then Alex cracked a smile. "You had me going there."

"It wasn't a joke. I just spent two months in Oregon learning how to roast. As soon as I get funding, I'm going to set up my operation. Hopefully before four thousand pounds of beans arrive on my parents' doorstep; I had to use them as my permanent address."

"I take it you haven't told them yet?"

Bryan shot Alex a look.

"Right. I would love to be able to help, but my money is all tied up in these condos. At least until we sell Rachel's place. Then we can pay off the loans for both units and start banking some cash."

"I would never ask you to do that anyway," Bryan said. And he wouldn't. He was already putting his entire life's savings at risk; he wasn't going to ask his best friend to do the same, especially in light of his impending marriage. "How is Rachel, by the way?"

Now Alex's face softened into a genuine smile. "She's good. Busy with Bittersweet Café, her and Melody."

"And planning a wedding?"

"Honestly, I'm not sure how much she's actually doing. As soon as we set a date, Melody and Ana completely took over. Which is well enough, because Rachel has expanded the Saturday Night Supper Club to a weekly event at the café. They're sold out through October."

"Impressive," Bryan said. He'd been at the café's opening, but that felt like a lifetime ago now. He chugged the rest of the soda and set the can on the table. "Well, no more stalling. I guess I should go tell my parents I'm back."

"Are you? Back?"

"Like it or not."

"Good. Then you can be my best man."

Bryan pushed himself off the sofa. "Naturally. I didn't realize that was in question. Wish me luck."

Alex walked him to the door. "Good luck. Hey, drop by the café for supper club tomorrow."

"I thought you said it was sold out?"

"Friends-and-family night last Saturday of the month. I'll even spring for your ticket since you're a broke small-business owner."

Bryan grinned. "Had I known it was that easy to get you to pick up the tab, I would have started a business years ago." He hoisted his backpack and opened the door. "Don't tell anyone but Rachel I'm back. I want to make a grand entrance." Before Alex could reply, he gave a salute and strode to the elevator.

That had been easier than he'd expected. Then again, Alex had always had his back. He wasn't so sure he would get the same reception from his parents.

*　　　*　　　*

Bryan grabbed his backpack from the backseat of his second Uber of the day and gave his driver a wave of thanks as he closed the door. Late-afternoon sunlight poured down on him, casting shadows across the brick pillars of the wrought-iron gate. When he'd left Colorado, it had been summer. Now, patches of snow clung to the wall in the shady spots, evidence of a winter that he'd missed and the newly minted spring that was about to start the process all over again. Eight months away. Eight months of climbing, making mistakes, and rebuilding his life into something new in Colombia and Portland. And now he stood just outside his parents' Capitol Hill mansion, preparing to beg for forgiveness, for both the silent absence and the things that had caused it.

In all the years he'd read about the Prodigal Son in the Bible, he'd never really cast himself in that role. He could only hope that his father was in a similarly forgiving mood.

Bryan punched his code into the keypad by the gate and waited for the click of the lock to admit him to the manicured grounds. He'd grown up here, but the 1920s behemoth hadn't always been a showplace—when his developer father and decorator mother had bought the property, the house had practically been crumbling to the ground. His earliest memories involved construction; he'd learned to write his ABCs in the layer of plaster dust that settled on every surface. Since then, Mitchell Shaw had become one of the biggest developers in Colorado and could easily afford a 10,000-square-foot estate in Cherry Creek, but they stayed here to demonstrate his dual commitment to preservation and revitalization.

His father wasn't in the habit of casting off things that held personal meaning.

He was just stalling now. Bryan squared his shoulders and

made his way up the circular drive, where he let himself in the front door. An empty foyer, punctuated by oriental rugs and a round table holding a flower arrangement, greeted him with silence.

"Mom? Dad?" he called. "Is anyone home?"

Nothing. And then the tap of footsteps in the upstairs hallway drew his attention to the staircase. His mother halted at the top of the steps, her expression as shocked as if she'd seen a ghost. "Bryan?"

"In the flesh."

She scrambled down the steps and threw herself at him, wrapping her arms around him so tightly he could barely breathe. "You have no idea how much I missed you. And now that I see you're alive and well, I'm going to kill you. Tagging me on Facebook every few weeks is not a replacement for a phone call!"

Bryan chuckled, even though he sensed it was not entirely a joke. "I missed you too, Mom. I'm sorry. I needed to get my head straight, and I couldn't call until I did."

"Then it must have been really skewed if it took you eight months to come home." She stepped back and studied him closely. "I never thought I would say it, but the beard suits you."

Bryan felt the bushy growth on his chin self-consciously. "Yeah, I haven't decided whether to keep it or not."

"I like it," Kathy said. "I don't, however, like the ponytail. You look homeless."

"I kind of am, Mom. I let the townhome go while I was gone. Not even really sure where my stuff is, except for my climbing gear. I don't suppose you might let me stay here for a while?"

"Do you have to ask?" Kathy tipped her head in the direction of the kitchen. "Come get something to eat. I'm going to call your father. He'll want to know you're back."

Bryan nodded uncomfortably and followed his mom

through the expansive living room into the equally large kitchen. Kathy bustled around, pulling bread from the pantry, deli meat from the drawer of the large Sub-Zero refrigerator. Only when she'd fixed an enormous sandwich and pushed it his way on a stoneware plate did she pick up the phone in the kitchen and dial his father.

"Mitchell, you need to come home. Bryan is back."

He couldn't hear his father's response, but the wide smile on Kathy's face made him think it wasn't negative. "I know," she said. "I'm feeding him in the meantime."

He bit into the sandwich, aware of his mom's eyes on him as she hung up, aware of all the questions lurking in her expression. She made it only a handful of minutes before she asked the only one that really mattered.

"Why?"

He carefully swallowed and put the sandwich down. "It's a long story, Mom, and I'd prefer to tell it to both of you together if you don't mind."

She nodded thoughtfully. "Did you hear that Alex is getting married?"

"I was there when he proposed, remember? He asked me to be his best man."

The key rattled in the front door, followed by heavy footsteps on the wood floor. His dad must have dropped everything and raced home. When Mitchell entered the kitchen, Bryan braced himself. But his father wordlessly crossed the room and pressed him into a bone-breaking hug.

"I'm so glad you're back, Son," he murmured, his voice sounding suspiciously husky.

Bryan pulled back before his own eyes could get misty. "I'm sorry, Dad. I had some things to figure out and I couldn't do it here." He looked between his parents. "Maybe you should take a seat."

Mitchell pulled up a stool beside Bryan at the island, and Kathy leaned against her husband so he could put his arm around her waist. Typical of his parents, presenting a united front.

Bryan cleared his throat. "I don't know where to begin."

"Start at the beginning," Kathy said with an encouraging smile.

The beginning. Not of this disappearance, but where his life had gone off the rails. "When I left the last time, almost four years ago, I had asked Vivian to marry me. She said no."

His parents exchanged a glance. This was something he'd never told them.

"I convinced myself I was over her. But you know what happened next. A lot of different women . . ." He trailed off, not wanting to go into detail about what they already suspected. "When I went to Colombia last year, I thought it would be good to go to Suesca and face those ghosts. Except Vivian saw my posts and came from Peru to see me.

"I thought she was back for me. And then she told me she was getting married. To Luke Van Bakker."

"Your sponsor?" Mitchell asked.

"Yes. I'm not going to lie—it was a kick in the gut. They'd been together for over a year, and he never saw fit to mention it to me. Anyway, I was done. I intended to leave Colombia, but she insisted on climbing La Bruja, and I wasn't willing to let anyone else belay for her. It went horribly wrong." He told them how she'd zippered off the rock, the injuries she'd sustained. "I didn't have any choice but to call Luke to get her home. He didn't take the fact we were together very well, and he basically fired me."

Silence from his parents, obviously unsure how to respond.

"In any case, a pro climber without a sponsor really isn't a pro. And Luke is vindictive. Once he figured out that Vivian and I had—" he cleared his throat—"hooked up, he made sure no one would take my phone calls. So I guess we can safely say my climbing career is over."

Mitchell sighed heavily. "I'm sorry, Son."

"No, you're not. You always told me that climbing was a short-term job, not a long-term plan, and you were right."

"Do you need money?" Kathy asked, ever the practical one.

Bryan laughed, but even he could hear the absence of humor. "I do, but not for the reason you think. I know you don't think I listened to anything you said, but I do have a business degree. I lived way below my means for years and invested every free cent. With the way the stock market has gone, I had a pretty big nest egg."

"Then why do you need money?" Kathy asked.

He looked between the two of them. "Because I bought a coffee farm in Colombia."

For once, the Shaws were stunned speechless. His mom regained her composure first. "What do you know about coffee?"

"Quite a lot, actually. I spent four months working alongside the farmers, learning how to plant, grow, pick, and process."

He filled them in on the mission of the importer he was working with, how his farm gave high-paying employment to local workers, how he was part of a co-op with other farms that would leverage their collective bargaining power to make a living wage in the region. "For the first time in years, growing coffee is more lucrative than cocaine. The entire region is being transformed because of Café Libertad."

Mitchell exhaled slowly. "That's a lot to take in. I'm proud of you for choosing a new direction and seeing it through. But I still don't understand why you're here if your farm is in Colombia."

"We don't yet produce enough green coffee beans to turn

a profit after expenses. So I'm importing my entire crop next month. I'm opening a roasting business."

Mitchell seemed to be weighing his words. "Do you realize how difficult that's going to be?"

"I do. I've spent the last two months working with a roaster in Oregon, learning the technique, studying his business model. There's no guarantee of success in anything, Dad. But I've got a great story to tell, and it's one I think people will respond to."

His father nodded slowly. "It seems you've thought this through. If you like, I'll take a look at your business plan."

"Thanks. That really wasn't meant to be a pitch, but I would appreciate a place to stay while I'm getting the business off the ground."

Kathy jumped in. "Of course. You don't even need to ask. Your old room is here any time you need it."

"Thank you." Bryan hopped off his stool to give them each a hug, then lifted his backpack. "If you don't mind, I'm going to unpack and then see if I can track down the stuff I left in the townhome."

He smiled and left the room, trying not to feel like a kid again as he returned to his childhood bedroom, trying even harder not to linger and overhear the inevitable conversations that would follow. His mom would be on his side, relieved that he'd turned from his "wild ways" and seemed to be focusing on having a normal life. His dad would be more skeptical, cite the business-failure figures, talk about how Bryan had shown no interest in business until his epiphany— all legitimate concerns. Both of them would wonder about the state of his faith.

The state of his faith? Shaky. The Prodigal Son story was a parable, an illustration of how God welcomed back the lost without holding their past wrongs against them. But what

Bryan really could have used right now was what came after the feast, from the lost son's perspective. The father was overjoyed, but no doubt the relatives sided with the older brother, maintaining their skepticism while rumors flew. How did the Prodigal earn back the trust of those who had written him off as a wastrel? How did he prove he'd truly changed and not just crawled home when he hit bottom?

More importantly, did the change actually stick?

Bryan climbed the stairs to his room, the first one on the left. It had been converted from his teen decor back to the elegant and traditional scheme of the rest of the house, but that didn't kill the memories. He shut the door and began unpacking the few possessions he'd lived the last nine months with: an extra pair of jeans, three shirts, some athletic wear, a mess of climbing gear. It now seemed ridiculous to have toted thirty pounds of webbing and cams and carabiners when he had no intention of ever setting hand or foot on a rock again. Maybe he just needed to bring it back with him to come full circle. Once he'd inventoried what was left of his gear in his car, still parked outside his parents' house where he'd left it, he would put it up for sale. Use it to fund equipment for the roastery. Move on to the next phase of his life.

He was about to take his pile of clothes down to the laundry room when a gentle knock came at the bedroom door. He opened it, expecting to see his mother, but his dad stood there instead.

"Can I come in for a minute?"

Bryan stood aside. "Of course."

Mitchell looked around the room as if it were somehow unfamiliar and then seated himself on the wingback chair near the door. "I owe you an apology."

Bryan cocked his head and sank down onto the edge of the bed. "For what?"

His dad sighed. "I knew you were going through something four years ago, but I never pushed. I didn't interfere. Maybe I should have."

"So my choices are your fault now?"

Mitchell looked at him in surprise. Bryan clasped his hands and leaned forward onto his knees. "I'm not sixteen years old, Dad. I've made my own decisions. Unfortunately, those decisions have landed me back at home. But that doesn't mean you bear any responsibility for my actions."

"But we raised you—"

"Right. You raised me. But it was my choice to pursue a climbing career. It was my choice to go off the rails after Vivian dumped me, and it was my choice to sleep with her when she came back. I'm basically reaping the consequences of that, just as you always warned me I would."

Mitchell stared at him, sadness the only emotion showing on his face. "I'm still sorry."

"I'm not." Bryan pushed himself up. "It wasn't until everything fell apart in Colombia that I took a good look at where I was headed. I'm turning thirty-six. I've been saying that climbing is my career, but it's really just been a placeholder, an excuse to live entirely for myself. Not for other people. Certainly not for God. And for what? I wasn't even all that happy.

"And then God put Café Libertad in my path, and I started to realize there might be something else for me out there. I just couldn't come back until I had it figured out. Until I could prove that I'd changed. I hope you understand that."

"I do." Mitchell rose and put his hand on Bryan's shoulder. "Whatever the reason, I'm glad you're back."

"Thanks, Dad."

Bryan watched as his father left the room, only then realizing what Mitchell hadn't said. He hadn't said anything about the viability of the business, hadn't offered his help. Which was fine. The last thing Bryan wanted to do was to run back to Mitchell Shaw for help as he embarked on the first real challenge of his adult life.

That didn't mean he wasn't going to need help, though. He might know about coffee farming and roasting now, but his college degree didn't mean that he knew anything about running a business. And he only had one shot to get this right.

Chapter Three

FOR TEN SECONDS after Ana opened her eyes, she was happy.

All too quickly, yesterday's twin nightmares crashed over her like breaking waves, sweeping away those fragile particles of contentment. She might have mitigated the client issue, but she wasn't naive enough to think that was the end of it. Mason had proven he did things merely to get a rise out of his publicists, and there was little chance he would stop at underage escorts.

For all the distaste she had for her new client, he wasn't her biggest problem. Rachel and Alex still didn't have a wedding venue, and every day she procrastinated was one day closer to potential disaster.

But venues didn't open at 7 a.m. on Saturday. Ana hauled herself out of bed, brushed her teeth, squeezed into a fresh set of gym clothes. A cup of tea and half a slice of toast later, she was headed out to her usual Saturday morning spin class. Gibson didn't feel like he'd done his job until he'd made someone puke, so the real breakfast could wait until she was done.

A little more than an hour later, Ana left the gym, sweat-drenched and jelly-legged, but unaccountably proud that she had not been the puker today. That honor had gone to a poor noob who didn't take the class's high-intensity warning seriously enough before booking his bike.

One task down, thirty-two to go.

She went home to shower and change, then sat down with a cup of coffee and her planner. First up was her Scripture reading and daily devotions—a book for busy women that was supposed to teach her how to surrender and breathe. She powered through the reading, but halfway through the reflection questions, the only thing she was reflecting on was the list of wedding venues waiting on her laptop. She stole looks at the dark screen every ten seconds until she finally gave up and put the devotional aside. She'd go back to it later after she'd dealt with this task. Even as she logged in, though, she knew it was probably a lost cause. What were the chances any halfway decent location would have cancellations at all, much less on the particular date they needed?

Three hours later, Ana had a spreadsheet with half the text grayed out, the other half with notations to call back the following week. She pinched the bridge of her nose for a long moment and then drained her coffee cup down to the cold dregs. It was useless. On Monday, she would call all the venues that hadn't responded, but she didn't have high hopes.

She had to tell Rachel. She wouldn't stop looking, but she needed both Rachel's and Alex's input to determine acceptable alternatives. She just hated the feeling that she'd somehow failed two of her favorite people in the world.

But since it was still hours until she could head to the restaurant for supper club, she clicked over to her email. Not surprisingly, she'd racked up dozens of messages since she left the office last night.

Despite his antics, Mason wasn't even her most pressing client. She was currently juggling several active files, one of which involved a scandal surrounding allegations of performance-enhancing drugs against one of Colorado's most beloved Olympians, downhill skier Beth Cordero. Beth hadn't even tried to deny the accusations—she'd only come to Massey-Coleman in an attempt to stop the media firestorm that had followed her admission of guilt.

Ana certainly didn't approve of cheating, but when she'd heard Beth's story, she couldn't help but feel a measure of sympathy. Her mom had been the legendary slalom athlete Jeanine Cordero, both her career and life cut short by cancer in her thirties, when Beth was just an infant. Beth's father, Denton, had been determined to make over his daughter in his dead wife's image and devoted himself to her career, even homeschooling her while she trained. On the surface, Beth said, everything seemed great, but in private Denny had been abusive and overbearing, punishing her for bad training sessions and cutting her off from any influences in her life that he deemed unproductive.

The picture the athlete painted was of a woman bullied and isolated, who had never experienced life outside of skiing. Never willing to risk getting sued for slander, the firm had done its research and corroborated the story, though Beth's family and friends refused to go on record about the abuse.

Now Ana's real work began. Some heartfelt press conferences had preserved Beth's endorsements for now. Ana's real job was to take the momentum and convert it into charity work and speaking engagements. By the time she was done, Beth Cordero would be a positive role model and spokesperson for women suffering emotional abuse. No one would even remember the revoked gold medal.

But first, Ana had to craft a pitch for the speakers' bureaus. She wrote a compelling biography for Beth and then moved on to several less time-sensitive projects she'd been putting off during regular work hours. When she finally glanced up, the clock told her it was already after six. She'd spent all day on the computer at her kitchen table. No wonder her eyelids felt like they were lined with sandpaper.

At least she got to spend the evening with her friends. She went to the bathroom to freshen up her makeup, then traded her T-shirt for a floral-printed chiffon button-down and slipped into a pair of bright-green pointy-toed flats. The cheerful patterns and colors made her smile. Spring kept threatening through bouts of snow; she was going to pretend that today's sunshine would stay. She transferred the contents of her purse into a more casual handbag, grabbed her keys, and headed downstairs for her car. She'd be early, purposely— better to tell Rachel the bad news in private.

Street parking on Old South Pearl in Platt Park was as bad as ever, cars lining the streets on both sides and down inter-secting roads. She circled the block twice without finding a space, then gave up and pulled into the crowded alley behind the building. Both Rachel's old Toyota and Melody's Jeep were parked there, where they'd likely been since four a.m. Even nine months after opening, her friends were still working fourteen-hour days.

Ana stepped out of her SUV, avoiding a greasy puddle that had formed in the potholed asphalt, and moved toward the back door. Unlocked. She pushed through, the heat from the kitchen hitting her immediately in contrast to the cool outside air. "Hello?"

Melody saw her first. "Ana!" She turned away from what she was doing—labeling large round containers with Sharpies on masking tape—and held her arms out for a hug. "I'm glad you came early. We could use some help setting the table. We're running behind tonight."

Ana flicked a glance to the range, where Rachel stirred something in a gigantic pot with a long-handled spoon. They could be behind or on time, but you'd never know from looking at Rachel; in the kitchen, she always had the same measured stance and unreadable game face.

"Hey, Ana." Rachel offered one arm for a sideways half hug before turning back to her pot. "Sorry, I can't leave the risotto. How are you?"

"Long, crummy week. I'm glad to see you guys." Ana inhaled deeply. "Something smells amazing. What are we having?"

"Braised lamb shanks over parmesan-mushroom risotto. My guy brought in some morels this morning, and there was no way I was going to pass them up."

"I'm hungry already. What can I do?"

Rachel nodded in the direction of the dining room. "Tables are set up and the plates and flatware are on the front counter. Mark folded the napkins before he left, so you can just put those on the plates."

"Sure thing." Ana backtracked and put her purse and her wool coat in the staff room, not much more than a closet in the back of the kitchen, and then headed out front to get the tables ready for guests.

To say that Bittersweet Café was her happy place was perhaps an understatement. In the last two years, Rachel had left behind her high-pressure executive chef job and Melody her dead-end position in a chain bakery, then decided to open their dream restaurant together. The way all the details had come together was downright magical; nowhere in Denver's history had a functional café and bakery materialized in under four months. But Ana had no doubt there had been a healthy measure of divine intervention in the situation. She could feel it in the mood and the atmosphere of this place. Light, welcoming, refreshing. It was no wonder they'd quickly developed a devoted following. They were already in the middle of plans to take over the vacant space in the strip mall beside them and expand to meet their ever-growing demand.

Ana couldn't be prouder.

If she were truthful, she was also a little jealous. She might be good at her job, and she was certainly well paid, but there was an allure to the idea of working with her best friends, being surrounded by delicious food and baked goods. Too bad she had absolutely no culinary talent. Her mom had made sure she could cook rice properly and prepare Filipino dishes like *adobong manok* and *kaldereta*, but her skills stopped there. Considering the fat and calorie content of those foods, she'd left her childhood meals behind in favor of an endless stream of grilled chicken or fish over salad.

The smaller two- and four-person tables had been pushed together into one large rectangle in the center of the main dining area, chairs set at each place. Stacks of square salad plates sat on the counter, along with bins of flatware. Ana did a quick count. Twelve tonight. Friends-and-family night tended to be smaller and quieter than the regular supper clubs, which were now running sixteen to twenty-four guests. Even that seemed a bit much to Rachel, but she had expanded the invitation list simply because she hated constantly turning people away.

Ana carried a stack of plates to the table and set one precisely in front of each chair, making sure the square edge of the dish was parallel to the edge of the table. Each piece of flatware was placed as carefully as the plate: two forks to the left, a knife and a spoon to the right, dessert fork horizontally above. She had to search a bit for the napkins, but she finally found them in a plastic bin behind the counter.

"Ana," Rachel called from the kitchen, "can you unlock the

front door and put out the private-party sign? Alex just texted me. He's looking for parking."

"Sure," she called back. She found the chalkboard A-frame sign beside the counter, flipped the lock on the door, and carried the board out onto the sidewalk. Someone—Melody, most likely—had hand-lettered the message *Closed for private party. Visit us tomorrow beginning at 6 a.m.* They were always closed in the evening, but a full house and an open door had a tendency to attract the curious.

Ana was surveying the table, trying to decide what it needed, when the bell on the front door jingled. She turned, a greeting for Alex on her lips, then froze.

Alex wasn't alone.

"You're back." It was a dumb, obvious thing to say, but as she looked over Bryan Shaw, she wasn't sure she'd have recognized him on the street. His usually short hair was shoulder-length, now pulled back in a ponytail, his typically clean-shaven face covered by a short beard. It was Bryan, but not.

"Hey, Ana." He approached her slowly with a smile, and they did that awkward thing where they tried to figure out whether a handshake or hug would be more appropriate. Apparently, he voted hug, because before she could decide for herself, his arms were around her. She gave him a squeeze back, inhaling deeply and then wishing she hadn't when the whiff of his familiar cologne put a tremor in her middle. "When did you get back in town?"

"So, I'm just going to go say hi to Rachel," Alex said, "since no one has noticed me anyway . . ."

Ana laughed, and a flush heated her cheeks. "Sorry, Alex. I promise, if you disappear without a trace for eight months, I will give you the same greeting."

"I'm holding you to that." Alex looked between both of them with a smile and then pushed into the kitchen.

Bryan watched his friend go with a self-conscious laugh. "I got back yesterday. I asked Alex not to say anything because I wanted to make a grand entrance."

"Then you're about a half hour too early."

He gave her his trademark half smile. "No, I'm not."

Ana let out a laugh. "Whew. For a second there, I thought you'd come back from Colombia a different person. Nice to see the Bryan I know is still in there."

Bryan looked inexplicably pained by the statement, but he shifted back on his heels and crossed his arms over his chest. "You look good, Ana. How have you been? Still saving the world one publicity crisis at a time?"

Ana leaned back against the edge of the counter, bracing her hands beside her. "More like saving people from their own stupidity one publicity crisis at a time. You remember that coffee shop in Five Points with the image problem?"

"The one that had to close because of their insensitive sign? I actually saw it on *Westword* while I was gone."

Ana shook her head. "No, the other one."

"What other one?"

"Exactly."

Bryan threw his head back and laughed. "I missed you. I missed all of you, in fact."

She let the pleasure of the words wash over her for a moment before she shut down the feeling with methodical brutality. It had always been like this between her and Bryan. A little flirtation, a little mutual appreciation, always dancing around the fact that whatever they might think or feel about each other, they'd never act on it. It was one thing to bring new people into their group—Alex had become part of it, as had Melody's boyfriend, Justin—but she and Bryan were owed equal loyalty from everyone else. Should they get together and it not work out, it would make things hopelessly awkward.

Had they learned nothing from watching *Friends*? The last few seasons, the plotline between Rachel Green and Ross Geller had been downright painful to witness.

Ana gestured to the table. "Come have a seat and tell me all about it. Unless you want to wait until everyone gets here."

The door chimed before the words were fully out of her mouth.

"Tell us what when everyone gets here?"

Ana laughed as Melody's impossibly good-looking pilot boyfriend entered the café. "Hi, Justin. Come on in. Melody's in the kitchen."

Justin smiled at Ana; then his eyes fell on Bryan. He extended a hand. "You're back."

"Appears so."

"Good trip?"

"I'm not sure I'd use the word *good*, but it was definitely illuminating." Bryan's expression became pensive. "No, I take that back. It was good. I'm just glad to be home."

Ana nodded thoughtfully, sensing there was much more to this story than he was letting on, but she didn't have time to ask before the door dinged and another group of supper club guests arrived at the café. Only then did she realize she'd missed her window to tell Rachel privately about the wedding venue problem.

*   *   *

Bryan hadn't expected to see Ana at the supper club, which was somewhat ridiculous. She, Rachel, and Melody had been friends for years, rarely separated during their time off. Or at least that had been the case until recently. Rachel had Alex, with a wedding looming on the horizon. Melody had Justin, apparently—though before Bryan had left town, they'd broken up and Justin had moved to Florida to run a charter aviation business he'd purchased. He still wasn't quite sure what had happened, other than the fact that Justin was here.

But Ana . . .

He'd been interested since he met her at Alex's barbecue almost two years ago, and not in the way that he had been interested in most women. She was interest*ing:* tough, abrupt, funny. Didn't take his flirting too seriously, dished it right back in a way that said she saw through the act. And while there was unmistakable chemistry between them, she was just as reluctant as he was to see where things might go.

Back then, it had been because he knew she wasn't the type to go for a casual hookup, and he'd been pretty sure Alex would destroy him if he slept with her and then broke up with her. Now, it was for a totally different reason. He was all too aware of his faults, all too aware of how easy it had been to abandon his values when he'd gotten his heart broken. Anything he had with a woman from here on out had to be a real relationship, something he was pretty sure he'd forgotten how to do since Vivian. Ana could not be his trial attempt at getting back on the straight and narrow.

Fortunately, the repeated chime of the front-door bell interrupted the questions he saw lingering in Ana's eyes and turned their attention to greeting the stream of new guests. There was Dina, Alex's younger sister, beautiful, tattooed, and pierced— also with a perennial crush on him that he was careful not to stoke. She was a full ten years younger than them and far more innocent than her appearance suggested. Also brilliant, a bona fide Mensa-level genius, but that was something she kept carefully hidden from everyone but those who knew her well. She'd brought along her friend Danielle, an equally pretty Latina who was every bit as outgoing as Dina herself.

Then came Andrew, a tall blond man with strong Nordic features and a lingering air of arrogance, along with a plain, dark-haired woman trailing behind. Bryan sized Andrew up as he shook his hand. "I don't think we've met."

"I used to be Rachel's sous-chef at Paisley. I took over for her for a while after she left."

"Only for a while?"

"Paisley closed late last year. You didn't hear that?"

Bryan couldn't keep the surprise from his face. When Rachel had been in charge, the Larimer Square restaurant had been a rising star, garnering stellar reviews and constant buzz . . . until a social media scandal caused her partners to fire her. He'd bet they were regretting that move now. "No, I've been in South America for most of the last year. I'm sorry to hear that."

"I'm not," Andrew said. "What Maurice and Dan did to Rachel was lousy. I felt bad taking the spot, but I had to make a living."

Bryan's attention moved to the woman. She held her hand out and smiled. "I'm Andrew's wife, Laura."

"Nice to meet you, Laura." He instantly changed his opinion of her. She had ordinary features, but a look of undeniable intelligence. He could see she was sizing him up much like he'd done to Andrew a moment ago.

"So, what are you doing now if Paisley's closed?" He shifted his gaze back to Andrew.

"I'm a corporate chef. I work for a food conglomerate, developing recipes using their products."

"That sounds . . . interesting," Bryan said politely.

"It's okay."

"He hates it," Laura said flatly. "I've been trying to convince him to go back to restaurant cooking, but he's stubborn. Thought he had to give it up for me when we got married."

"I make a lot more doing what I do now, and I'm home evenings and weekends."

Laura rolled her eyes. "But back then you were actually happy."

Bryan repressed his smile and excused himself before pushing through to the kitchen. Laura really was the perfect chef's spouse—most lobbied for their significant others to take corporate positions so they could have more time together.

Rachel was stirring and slicing, completely focused, while Melody tossed a salad in a gigantic stainless-steel bowl.

"Can I help?"

Melody's eyes widened. "Bryan? You're back!" She set down the salad and went to hug him, but it was mostly wrists as she held her dressing-coated fingers out of the way. "No one told me!"

"I asked Alex to keep it a secret."

"Hi, Bryan." Rachel smiled, more subdued . . . but then again, his appearance came as no surprise to her. "Good to see you. We've missed you."

"Thanks, Rach. I just talked to Andrew. I had no idea Paisley closed!"

She nodded. "In November. It's kind of sad, after all the work I put into that place. Is it bad that I felt a little vindicated that it went under without me?"

"Probably." Bryan grinned, and she chuckled. "I don't blame you, though. I'd say it's nothing less than they deserve."

"I feel sorry for my staff. Fortunately, there's a massive shortage of line cooks in Denver, so I'm sure they didn't have any trouble finding positions. I just happen to know I was paying more than everyone but the most exclusive restaurants. Part of my employee-retention policy."

"Which is why you were so successful, I'm sure. That and your amazing cooking."

Rachel smiled. "I've already said I'm glad you're back, Bryan. You don't have to suck up."

"I'm just hoping you're still going to let your husband come out and play after you're married." He sent a smirk toward where Alex leaned against the wall and slung an arm around Rachel's shoulder. "What can I do to help? If I'm sucking up, you should take full advantage."

She inclined her head toward Melody's station. "As soon as she puts the salad in serving bowls, you can put them on the table for me. And fill water glasses. There's a couple pitchers of ice water waiting over there."

"It would be my pleasure, Chef." Bryan dropped his arm and retrieved the water pitchers, then pushed through the door back into the dining room. He carefully filled the water glasses, pouring from the side to fill them with ice, then from the spout to top off each glass with water.

"You look like you've done that more than once," Ana observed.

"I used to wait tables in college."

"Really? I wouldn't have thought you needed to work your way through school."

"I didn't, at least not how you mean. But my parents were pretty clear that my climbing trips and my extracurricular activities were on my own dime. And I made a killing in tips."

"I bet you did."

Bryan sent her a curious look, wondering about the subtext to that statement, but Ana's face didn't give anything away. She had the best poker face of anyone he'd ever seen, hands down. No wonder she was such a good publicist.

Alex came through holding two big white ceramic bowls filled with salad. "You're making me look bad, Bryan. Rachel put me to work." He set them down on the table and backed off. Ana stepped forward and arranged them so each was equidistant from the plates surrounding it.

Bryan and Alex stared at her. She shrugged. "What? Rachel would have done the same thing."

"Probably true," Alex said.

The door dinged once more and admitted an elegant brunette followed by a tall man with a shock of red hair. "Sorry we're late," the woman announced.

Bryan didn't recognize her until Alex said, "You're right on time, Camille. Come on in. I think you know everyone?"

Ah, Camille. She used to be the front-of-house manager at Paisley and was probably the closest thing Rachel had had to a work friend. If he recalled correctly, Camille had dated Andrew at one point. That could make tonight interesting.

But she greeted her old flame with a friendly smile and hug and then made the rounds introducing her boyfriend, Chuck. When she got to Bryan, she shook his hand. "Nice to see you again."

"Nice to see you too." He shook her boyfriend's hand before turning his attention back to her. "What are you doing now?"

"Insurance."

Bryan blinked.

"I know, it's boring, but it's stable and it pays well." She shrugged. "Couldn't stay in the industry forever, I guess."

It looked like everyone had moved on except him, even Andrew and Camille. But that wasn't really true. He'd moved on in a big way, quitting climbing and buying a coffee farm. He was simply in a holding pattern until he collected the funds to open his roasting business. Which needed to be soon—the timeline in his head, ticking down to his bean delivery, had two fewer days left on it, just since he'd been back in Denver.

Alex disappeared into the kitchen and reappeared a moment later. "Since everyone's here, we can all take seats."

They shuffled into place. Bryan attempted to anticipate where everyone was going to sit so he'd end up near Ana, but they still landed on opposite ends of the table and he couldn't reshuffle without drawing too much attention to himself.

Melody came out first, bearing three baskets of bread, which she staggered with Ana's perfectly placed salad bowls, putting them down with just as much precision as her friend. So maybe they were all perfectionists when it came to table settings. She took a seat at the end of the table, and then Rachel came to stand behind the free chair at the head.

"Welcome, friends. I'm so glad you could all join us tonight. We're starting with a mesclun salad and fresh sourdough bread. Then we're moving on to a braised lamb chop over parmesan risotto. This is one of the few times that I decided to do a plated meal rather than family style, so I'll go in the back and get them going while you enjoy the salad."

"Oh, join us, Rachel," Dina said. "We hate to eat without you."

"Don't worry, I'm not going to miss the lamb chops. I'll be back in a few minutes."

Conversation hummed around the table as baskets and bowls were passed and the group helped themselves to the first course, but it was only light and meaningless. They were just finishing their salads when Rachel poked her head out of the kitchen.

It was a signal, apparently, because Melody immediately rose and began busing their dirty dishes, stacking them in a precarious balance on one arm. As soon as the table was clear, Rachel appeared with the first of the plates.

The food was beautifully arranged as always, its aroma making Bryan's stomach rumble even though he was already half-full from salad and bread. Melody helped Rachel put the dishes down, and everyone had a plate in front of them in surprisingly little time.

Bryan wasted no time attacking his, closing his eyes in happiness at the first bite of lamb. Colombian food had been good, hearty and flavorful. But he'd missed his friend's cooking and his favorite Denver restaurants. It was a different world for sure.

Ana was watching him in a way that made him think she'd read his mind and gave him a small smile. "So, are you going to tell us where you've been and what you've been doing? Or are you going to make us wait until dessert?"

"Honestly, I hadn't thought much past the lamb. It's amazing, Rachel. Thanks for letting me slip in at the last minute."

Rachel smiled her acknowledgment, and everyone at the table echoed his thoughts, but from the eyes fixed on him, he knew he wouldn't get to enjoy his meal until he explained.

Might as well be blunt. "I bought a coffee farm in Colombia." He went through the whole story for what felt like the dozenth time, though he left out the loss of his sponsorship and the situation with Vivian, of course. Then he went on to the real kicker. "I'm going to open a roasting business here in Colorado. But before I can, I'm looking for funding to help me get set up. Most of my assets are sunk into the farm itself."

Ana was the first to speak up. "Your dad wouldn't help?"

"He's looking over a proposal, but he's pretty risk averse, even if it's his own son." Bryan paused. "*Especially* when it's his own son. And I'd rather have an outside partner if I can manage it. Family and business usually don't mix."

"Any leads?" Alex asked.

Bryan took a bite of the risotto and almost got too distracted to continue. It was perfect. "I have a couple of friends that I'm going to approach. We'll see what happens." *Friends* might be overstating it a little bit. *Acquaintances* was probably a better word. But Denver wasn't a large city, and considering who his father was, he had a pretty good idea of who might invest and who wouldn't.

"What's the business going to be called?" Melody asked.

"The farm is called Flor de Oro, but nothing has really stuck yet for the roastery."

Guests began throwing out potential names, but once again

he felt Ana's eyes on him, assessing. Or maybe it just seemed that way to him. He hadn't expected to feel this aware of her presence in the room. Apparently, time and distance hadn't dimmed his attraction to her.

When the main course was finished and all plates were cleared, Melody brought out their dessert: strawberry custard tarts. "We'd normally have specialty coffee to serve, but our barista, Mark, had an emergency. We do have some regular drip, and it's pretty good if I do say so myself."

"I can pull shots," Ana said.

Now everyone looked at her, including Rachel and Melody. "What?"

"I didn't know you knew anything about coffee," Bryan said.

She gave him a slight smile. "You know very little about me." She rose from her seat. "What does everyone want?"

"You don't have to do that, Ana," Rachel said quickly. "Sit down and enjoy dessert. Black coffee will go well with the tarts anyway."

The others murmured their agreement, and Ana sank back into her seat and picked up her dessert fork. But Bryan's curiosity was piqued. Ana was perhaps the most professional, focused person he knew besides his own dad. When had she learned how to pull espresso shots?

He barely kept the questions to himself until the supper was over, and he purposely lingered until everyone but the girls, their boyfriends, and Ana were left. He moved to Ana's side. "I don't suppose the offer is still open? I wouldn't mind a cortado right now."

Ana studied him for a second. "You just want to see if I can really do it."

"Maybe."

"Well, I can, but it's not worth getting the machine dirty for one shot. Another time, maybe."

"I'll hold you to that. How did you learn all this anyway?"

Ana shrugged. "Like most people did. Needed a job with flexible hours. I was a decent barista and made good tips."

"What else do you know about coffee?"

"I was an assistant manager, so I know a little about running a shop. A bit about flavor and bean selection, but little about the actual mechanics of the roasting. Why?"

Bryan hadn't even fully formulated why he was asking, but it came out of his mouth all the same. "When I get the business up and running, I'm going to need a sales manager. Someone who understands business and marketing and publicity, and has some coffee experience too, so it all sounds natural. I don't suppose that's something you'd be interested in?"

She seemed to be choosing her words carefully. "I'm flattered that you'd ask. But I like my job—I'm good at my job— and I don't intend on leaving it anytime soon." Her eyes took on a mischievous twinkle. "Besides, you couldn't afford me."

He laughed. "Probably not. Would you ever consider being a consultant?"

"I might consider it." She gave him a secretive smile. "Good night, Bryan."

She slipped into the kitchen, ostensibly to say goodbye, but she never came back. Bryan sat down in one of the vacated seats, his mind buzzing. Until now he hadn't really thought about it, but he did need an operations manager. He would be completely consumed with the importing and the roasting. He hadn't given much consideration to everything else that would need to be done to actually sell his beans and make a profit. Messaging, packaging, sales and distribution. Suddenly, the month that he'd given himself to find a place seemed ridiculously naive. If he didn't have the other elements in place, he'd be hemorrhaging money while he figured it all out. And that was the dumbest business move he could make.

He absolutely needed help. And now he was pretty certain that Ana was the one to give it.

*　　*　　*

Ana slipped back into the kitchen, a smile lingering on her face. Seeing Bryan had been a surprise, but at least it was a pleasant one. He seemed different after his long absence. There were still glimpses of that flirtatious nature, but it was tempered somehow. Was it just the responsibility he felt, buying a farm in Colombia? Or was it something else? Alex had said Bryan only disappeared when he had trouble with a woman, but to her knowledge, he hadn't been seeing anyone when he left. Not that she'd have any reason to know for sure.

"I see that smile," Melody said from where she was cleaning up her bench. "Don't try to hide it. You were glad to see Bryan."

"I was, actually." She paused. "He asked me to work for him."

"Really?" Rachel's eyebrows lifted. "That's a new one. What did you say?"

"I told him he couldn't afford me. I'll help him out a little, though. At least with the paperwork." She paused. "Rachel, I need to talk to you for a minute."

At the serious tone, Rachel stopped what she was doing and turned. "What is it?"

Better to just have out with it. "The venue you and Alex chose isn't available. They double-booked."

Rachel blinked. "How could that happen?"

"Calendar snafu, apparently. I'm so sorry, Rachel. I feel responsible."

"Why? You're not the one who double-booked the venue."

"Yeah, but I pushed you toward that one when there were other spots still available . . ."

"Stop." Rachel dropped her towel and moved to rest both

hands on Ana's shoulders. "Both Alex and I agreed that was the perfect place. We asked you to book it, and if you'll recall, *we're* the ones who signed the contract."

Ana exhaled. She should have known that always-calm Rachel would react this way. "I'm still looking for alternatives. I'm halfway through my list with no luck, but something has to turn up."

"It will." Rachel dropped her hands and went back to wiping down her station. "We'll figure out something."

"What about the lodge in Silverlark where Justin took me last year?" Melody suggested. "That place is gorgeous and it can hold tons of people."

Rachel considered for a moment. "That's an option. But it's pretty far, isn't it? Everyone would have to drive, or we'd have to charter buses to take them up there."

"That could be fun," Melody said.

"I'll make a note," Ana said. "Don't talk to Justin yet, though. A venue in Denver would be preferred, especially because of the out-of-town guests."

Melody made a zip motion across her lips and winked at Ana as if to say *Told you she wouldn't freak*. Ana still wasn't sure how Rachel managed to stay so calm. Had it been her wedding, she'd be panicked. It wasn't even her wedding and she was still panicked.

"Did I tell you we're getting ready to put my house on the market?" Rachel said suddenly. "Alex is coming over tomorrow night to help me paint. We're going to try to get it up in May. With any luck, we'll get an offer right away and be able to close escrow right after the wedding."

"That's great, Rachel," Ana said. "Are you going to miss your place?"

She paused to consider. "Maybe a little. It's the first house I ever actually owned. The first time I had a salary that could support a mortgage. But Alex's place is amazing and it would be silly to give it up to move into mine."

"But his only has one bedroom," Melody said. "What happens when there's little baby Kanins running around?"

"We thought maybe we'd remodel. The condo is big enough to add another bedroom. The living area is cavernous."

Melody gasped. "You *have* thought about it then!"

"Not right away, of course. But yeah. I mean, he's turning thirty-six. I'm turning thirty-two. We've got some time, but not a lot of time."

Melody sighed happily. "Rachel as a mom. I can just picture it. Your kids are going to be flat-out gorgeous. Won't they, Ana?"

"Without a doubt." Ana smiled, but inwardly she couldn't help but feel a stab of envy. Rachel was getting married soon and potentially having kids. Melody was happily in a relationship with a great guy. And she . . . well, her night out with Christopher Mason had been better than some of her recent dates. "Next thing we know, it'll be you and Justin."

"What about me?" Justin pushed through the door into the kitchen and went straight to Melody, wrapping his arms around her waist from behind and planting a kiss on her cheek. "Are you almost ready to go?"

"In a couple of minutes. I'll meet you out front."

Justin seemed to realize that he was interrupting something and took the hint. He kissed her once more and returned to the front of the house.

Ana and Rachel stared expectantly, but Melody just shrugged. "I'm trying not to get ahead of myself. He's back in Colorado and he lives nearby . . . That's good enough for now."

"How does he like the new job?" Rachel asked. "I keep forgetting to ask him."

"It's good. He likes having a regular route and he's home every night by seven. It beats his AvionElite schedule."

When Melody and Justin met, he had been a pilot for a fractional company that sold shares of private jets, which meant he was gone several weeks out of the month. He'd been in the process of buying his dream charter business, but its location in Florida made the romance look nearly impossible. After a lot of heartache, he'd taken a job with Mountain State Airways, a commuter airline that flew between Colorado Springs, Denver, Grand Junction, and Salt Lake City. He and Melody might not be talking marriage, but the fact he had come back was a statement of commitment.

More commitment than Ana had ever been able to elicit from a man.

She straightened abruptly and smiled at her friends. "I better go now. I'm going to check into some new venues for your wedding, Rachel, and I'll let you know what I come up with."

Rachel hugged her hard. "Thanks, Ana. I really appreciate you doing this."

"Of course." She shifted to give Melody a hug goodbye too, then dug her keys from her purse. "Are we still coming over for dinner on Wednesday?"

Rachel grimaced. "I'm sorry. I forgot Alex and I are going to his parents' house that night."

"Wow," Melody said. "This isn't the first time, right?"

"No, but it's been a while."

"Not a problem," Ana said. "Let me know if you reschedule." She threw one last smile in their direction, strode out the back door, and unlocked the driver's side of her black Mercedes.

Where she sat, in the dark, feeling unaccountably lonely.

No, not lonely. Left out. Left behind.

Which was stupid. After all, hadn't she always been the hard-charging one? The career-oriented one? It wasn't as if she didn't have a social life. She dated. A lot. It was just that none of those dates had ended in something lasting like Rachel's and

Melody's relationships. All the guys she met were either too self-absorbed or too needy. Where were the normal ones who were happy to spend some free time together but otherwise allowed her to have her own life?

But it wasn't just that. It was that in Rachel and Melody finding their happily-ever-afters and their business together, they'd become a tight little unit of two. It wasn't intentional, of course, and it was as much Ana's fault as theirs. Hadn't she been the one to throw them over in favor of her new problem client last night?

She cranked the key in the ignition and the motor purred to life, nearly silent in the cabin of the luxury behemoth. It was completely ungrateful to want more than she already had; it was downright spiteful to resent her friends' happiness. She sent a prayer of apology skyward, crossed herself automatically, and backed out of the narrow parking spot.

She was just unsettled because of all the unknowns in her life right now. The new client, the wedding venue. Once she got those things figured out, she'd be feeling like her old self once more.

Chapter Four

"SO WHAT DO YOU THINK?" Bryan turned off the ignition of his car and peered through the windshield at the building on the opposite side of the street. It was constructed of old red brick, as most of the neighborhood's buildings were, with a peeling white metal sign above. "It used to be a ketchup factory."

Alex leaned forward in the passenger seat to take it in. "That makes sense. Because it looks like it's either being held together by ketchup or rust. Maybe a mixture of both."

Bryan laughed as he opened the door. "Don't judge it until you see it. The inside is better."

Alex didn't look convinced, but he climbed out and stood next to Bryan while they waited for traffic to clear enough to cross to the other side. Bryan pulled a key out of his pocket and fitted it into the glass door on the right side of the roll-up warehouse door.

"You have a key? You already rented it?"

The lock opened with a smart click, but the door itself took a little yank to clear the metal doorframe. "No, but the listing agent is a friend of my dad's, so he said he'd trust me with it. I told him I'd make a decision by the end of the week."

"You still don't have any money," Alex said.

"Don't bother me with irrelevant matters like that." Bryan gestured for Alex to enter first, then followed him in and locked the door behind them.

The office area was spacious but dingy, with threadbare blue commercial flooring and white walls that looked to be nothing more than drywall screwed into the original brick. A grayish acoustical tile ceiling added to the depressing feel of the space. "I'd rip down the drywall, pull up the carpet, clean up the floors. Bring in some industrial furniture and shelving to hold sample bags. All we really need is a place to meet customers should they come by the roastery."

Alex looked around, nodding slowly. "It's not the worst. It has potential. I'm reserving judgment."

"Good, because this is the part you have to see." Bryan led Alex into what had been the warehouse and appreciated the shocked look that came over his friend's face.

It was big, at least five thousand square feet, with soaring twenty-foot ceilings and old transom windows atop the high brick walls. Ductwork snaked across the ceiling overhead.

"What would you do with all this space?"

"I'm glad you asked." Bryan moved to an oddly shaped jog in the space behind the office. "I was thinking about closing this off to be a cupping room. I'd put a sample roaster in there, so we could hold cuppings for coffee shop owners and distributors to taste our different roasts. If we open it up from the office, it could stay closed off from the main roasting area."

He moved on and swept a hand toward the back. "This area here we would build out and insulate to store our beans. Humidity and climate have a major effect on the roast. The goal would be to keep it at a constant level year-round. We're not going to have a huge crop yield, so I'm certainly not going to risk ruining what we have. And once we get going, I'll probably need to buy beans from other farms. It will allow me to expand our offerings beyond the variety that I grow."

"You do know a lot about coffee." Alex seemed a little surprised, and Bryan tried not to be hurt that his best friend had underestimated him.

"I spent the better part of the last year figuring this stuff out. I know you think I'm a screwup, Alex—"

"I don't—"

"Yes, you do. But you'll remember I actually do have a business degree—magna cum laude, in fact. I'm smart enough to do this. And determined. What else do I need?"

Alex threw him a sidelong glance. "Money?"

Bryan laughed. "Well, there is that. But I have a plan."

"And what's that? Besides hiring Ana to do all the work."

"I'm going to pretend you didn't say that." Bryan settled on the edge of an abandoned table, ignoring the fact it was covered in dust and he'd now have a dust print on the seat of his athletic pants. "I've done a lot of favors over the years. All those people who say they owe me one? I'm calling them in."

Alex didn't look convinced. "You're calling in favors."

"They were big favors, bro."

"Well, that may be. But landlords don't tend to take payment in favors."

"They do when they're your dad."

Alex looked shocked. "What?"

Bryan laughed. "My dad owns this building. Why do you think the agent let me have the key? I'm going to rent it from him, but at a reduced rate. It's been sitting vacant for over two years and costing him money in upkeep and security. He offered to give me the space cheap until I broke even, but I need to build it out and furnish it." It hadn't been quite as easy as he'd made it sound. Bryan had laid out an entire business plan and his projected earnings report based on a conservative expected yield on his farm, low initial overhead, and a 35 percent profit margin. Mitchell had point-blank told him that it was a bad risk to lend him money, but if he was going forward with it, he'd give him the building at a quarter of the going occupancy rate. For a self-made man who didn't believe in coddling his son, it was a significant show of support.

Alex was nodding slowly. "That's really decent of him. Low risk on his part, but it cuts a big part of your overhead."

"The advantages of living with a real estate mogul." Bryan pushed himself up off the table, dusted his butt off, and jerked his head toward the office door.

"How's that working out, by the way?"

"Weird." It was nice in a way. He hadn't lived at home since he was eighteen, and now that he was back, however temporarily, his mother was cooking for him and plying him with her baked goods. His father, on the other hand, kept giving him searching looks that he couldn't quite interpret. "I really need to make this work so I can get my own place again."

"Cramping your style, huh?"

"No style to cramp these days." Bryan flipped off the lights as they went, then opened the front door and locked up behind them. The noise from the highway that had been barely perceptible a minute before washed over them. "I'm done with women. For a while at least."

"Why?"

Bryan glanced at Alex before he darted across the street in the gap of traffic, his friend following. "You know why."

"Tell me."

He unlocked his car door and climbed in, the seal shutting out the noise again. The time it took for Alex to get to the passenger side allowed him to order his thoughts. "Because no one is Vivian. And she pretty much destroyed me twice. I'm not willing to do that to someone else. I need to get my head on straight without a woman around."

A smile rose to Alex's lips. "Even Ana? You guys seemed pretty close at the supper club on Saturday."

"Especially Ana. That whole thing would go wrong in a hurry."

"Why? Because she would expect too much from you?" Alex must be in a pushy mood today because he never leaned this hard when it came to women. Definitely not when it came to innermost feelings. His former career as a psychologist was showing.

"Because she would expect exactly what she should, and I would screw it up. And lose all of my friends in the process. I don't know if you've noticed, but you and the girls are pretty much all I have left these days." Bryan cranked the ignition, put the car in gear, and then rolled down the windows, effectively shutting off conversation. That was enough honesty for one day.

Of course, Alex didn't seem to agree. "I think you're selling yourself short, as usual. But this plan of yours seems like a good one."

"Really?" Bryan took his eyes off the road briefly to assess Alex's expression.

"Really. The last time I saw you throw yourself into something this thoroughly, you were junior world champion the following year."

"Yeah, but you saw how my climbing career turned out in the end."

"Just don't sleep with the fiancée of your investor and then throw her off the side of your building, and you'll be okay."

Bryan whipped his head toward his friend. "I can't believe you just said that."

"Why? It's just good business practice."

Bryan snorted in response, and then the laughter came,

pouring out of him along with tears from his eyes until he could barely see where he was driving. Oh, it had been a long time since he'd laughed like that. "You don't pull punches, do you?"

Alex grinned and Bryan swiped a hand across his face, still chuckling. He owed Alex one for that. What had happened in Suesca had taken up a good part of his brain, blowing up to gargantuan proportions in his mind. He'd received an email from Vivian a month ago saying that she'd made a full recovery, even though she wasn't keen on climbing again, and Luke had taken her back. No apology, no blame for Bryan. Just water under the bridge.

He needed to start thinking of it like that. If God had truly forgiven him, at some point he needed to forgive himself and move on. He smiled to himself at Alex's bald-faced statement. That's why he needed to be back home with his best friend. After all, if you couldn't joke about the event that broke your heart and ruined your career, what exactly could you joke about?

Chapter Five

ANA CLIMBED OUT of her car and immediately wished that she'd changed her shoes before she'd made the drive. Her heels sank two inches into the soft dirt beside her vehicle, probably staining the cream-colored leather, the gravel no doubt leaving little scrape marks on the stilettos. Had she known she would be taking the road less traveled today, she wouldn't have worn her second-favorite pair of pumps.

It had started with arriving early in the office to get some work done, followed by surreptitious phone calls to the remainder of her venue list, all of which had been booked. Then a coworker opened up a long flat box at the desk next to her and brought out the most beautiful arrangement of flowers.

"Where did those come from?" Ana had asked, enchanted.

"Larkspur Flower Farm," the coworker had said. "Their Instagram is amazing. They're local but they ship all over the country."

Which of course had ended in an Instagram stalking session revealing that Larkspur Flower Farm was less than an hour from Denver, on a gorgeous, sprawling piece of land. It was like an organic butter commercial or something, where the sweeping green landscape was intended to show how natural and untainted their animals were. Rachel would love it, given the fact that all her produce came from local places. Maybe she'd want to bring in some flower bunches to sell in the . . .

Ana gasped. Not flowers for the café. Flowers for the wedding. A *venue* for the wedding. With trembling hands, she'd looked up the phone number of the business and then dialed on her cell phone. A woman answered on the first ring.

"This is Analyn Sanchez with the Massey-Coleman Group. I'm looking for an unusual venue for an upcoming event, and I've fallen absolutely in love with the photos on your Instagram feed. Do you ever hold events on your property?"

She never had, but she was open to the idea, which was what had led Ana forty miles south of Denver—the middle of nowhere—wearing a silk-blend suit and five-hundred-dollar shoes in the mud.

Before she could finish imagining the damage to her pumps, the door to an enormous greenhouse opened and a woman about Ana's age emerged. She wore jeans and a flannel shirt open over a Led Zeppelin concert tee, her burgundy-streaked hair piled into a bun on top of her head. She carried a pair of sizable garden shears, and Ana couldn't tell whether she'd been pruning something in the greenhouse or if they were meant for protection.

"Hello!" Ana called, stepping away and shoving the door of her SUV closed. "You must be Darcy."

"That I am. You must be Analyn." When she got close enough to stick out her hand, Ana realized Darcy was at least a decade older than she'd first thought, if not more. She smiled and her eyes crinkled up around the corners. "I have to say, your call surprised me. You want to hold an event all the way out here?"

Ana filled her lungs with fresh air and looked around. Much of the land was still barren this early in the season, but she knew from the photos that it would be alive with all sorts of wildflowers and cultivars in less than a month. "It's actually for a friend's wedding. She's a chef, emphasis on fresh and locavore, and I think this would be absolutely perfect for her."

Darcy nodded thoughtfully. "Why don't you come with me? I've got a pair of boots you can borrow and then I'll show you around the property."

"That would be great." Ana's laugh left on an exhale as she picked her way through the damp gravel lot toward the main house. "I was so excited when you said you'd consider it, I didn't even stop at home for a change of clothes."

"Well, I don't recommend heels for your wedding guests. In fact, if we're talking summer, they might be better off in casual clothes. Afternoon rain can get everything pretty muddy." She led Ana to the farmhouse, a freshly painted white wood structure, and opened the door into what was no doubt a mudroom, from the look of several pairs of galoshes lined up on the tile floor. This was a true working farm that someone—Ana assumed Darcy—lived and worked on.

Darcy plucked out a pair of bright-red galoshes and handed them to Ana. "These will be big, but they're better than ruining your heels. You can leave your shoes here. They're safe as long as we take Donald with us."

"Donald?" Ana asked, but her question was answered when Darcy stuck two fingers in her mouth and whistled. Immediately, a huge, mud-spattered golden retriever appeared from around the house and bounded toward them.

The dog made a beeline for Ana's trousers, but Darcy stopped him short with a cluck of her tongue. "Heel, Donald. With me." He skidded to a stop and circled to her side, tail wagging madly.

"Good dog you have there," Ana said.

"Well, he's a better companion than a guard dog, that's for sure." Darcy chuckled and began walking across the wide gravel lot. "Since you called, I've been thinking about locations for the wedding. There's an old garden that dates back to the original construction of the house. It could be a good place for taking vows, if we positioned the chairs in a semicircle around the outside . . ."

They rounded the house and Ana gasped. It was a fairy-tale garden, or it would be when it was in full bloom. The tiny space, marked off by a low stone wall, showed the signs of summer, green creeping vines beginning to poke from the ground and crawl up the collection of peeling white trellises. At the farthest end was an arch; if she wasn't mistaken, the bushes around it were climbing roses. "Do you think those will be filled out by mid-June?" Ana asked.

"Depending on the rain and the weather, possibly. We can always add some cut greenery or potted trees to make up for them." Darcy shrugged. "It's Colorado. We could have snow in June that kills the buds. But I figured the arch would be an ideal place to get married since there's already a little stone aisle to walk down."

Ana pulled out her phone and snapped several photos of the garden, not trusting her memory to properly convey the size and layout to Rachel. "Where could we set up tables for the reception?"

"It depends." Darcy gestured again and Ana clomped after her, curling her toes in the boots so they didn't slide off her feet while she walked. The advantage of being a size five was that you could buy great shoes on clearance. The disadvantage was that almost no one had anything you could borrow.

"If the weather is good," Darcy continued, "you could set up tables out here in front of the fields, in view of all the flowers.

You'd need to bring in lighting and heat, though. This is the first time I've thought about hosting an event here, so I don't have any of that in place. Pretty much what you see is what you get."

Ana nodded thoughtfully and took several more photos, using her sketch app to mark the area where Darcy had suggested they set up. It could be perfect. Hadn't Rachel once said that she wanted a simple backyard wedding with lights and flowers? This was a little bit more in depth, but it solved the problem of what to do with a hundred and fifty guests.

"What about if the weather is bad?"

"I've been thinking about that. Follow me." Darcy turned on her heel and began walking down a gentle slope toward a cluster of outbuildings. She led Ana straight to a big white barn and pulled one of the creaking doors open.

Ana coughed at the cloud of dust that enveloped her when she stepped inside. It was . . . a barn. Big, empty, with an unused hayloft above. Right now, it housed only a green John Deere tractor and a bunch of hand tools.

But it was big enough to hold hundreds of people if they arranged the tables right . . . and she'd bet that Melody could do something amazing with lights and decor strung from the rafters.

Ana nodded slowly. "Lots of possibilities. What are you thinking for a rental fee?"

Darcy named a price that was less than half of what they'd been paying the event center.

"Did I hear that right?"

Darcy shrugged. "You're just paying for the space. You'll need to bring in everything else yourself. So really, I wouldn't want to charge any more than that."

Ana took several more photos of the barn and then held her hand out to shake Darcy's. "Let me show these to Rachel and we'll get back to you. Thanks so much for taking time to consider it."

Darcy nodded placidly and gestured to Ana's borrowed boots. "Think you might want to switch out your shoes first . . ."

Ana laughed and followed Darcy back to the farmhouse, where she swapped her boots for her heels and then gingerly picked her way out to her now-muddy SUV. Once ensconced in the quiet interior, she pulled out her phone and dialed Melody. It rang several times and then went to voice mail. She was probably elbow-deep in bread dough right now.

"Melody, it's Ana. I think I have a solution for Rachel's wedding. I'm going to text you some photos now."

She sat there for several minutes, picking the best of her photos and sending them to Melody. The baker was very visual—once she'd seen the space, she'd be mentally designing it. Then Ana could figure out how much it would cost to decorate and furnish to Melody's specifications, and they could present it to Alex and Rachel.

For the first time in days, a tiny portion of her worry lifted. It might not be her fault, but she'd volunteered to help organize this event, so that made it her responsibility. And she wasn't going to sleep until she had the problem completely solved.

Not that she slept anyway.

The sun was just dropping behind the horizon when she pulled back onto the highway and headed north to Denver . . . and found herself smack in the middle of a traffic jam. Despite the constant talk about widening and expanding I-25 south of the city, the work never actually materialized, which meant a single accident could cause gridlock. Ana took a deep breath, held it in for a count of four, and then blew it out in a long exhale. Despite what her yoga teacher said, it didn't help with her stress levels. She checked her watch. At this rate, it would take her forever to get home.

Her phone rang through the speakers of her car. She answered it with a button press. "Analyn Sanchez."

"Well, well, no need to be so formal."

Ana's tone softened. "Hey, Mel. Did you get my photos?"

"I did! That place is gorgeous! I can just imagine . . . well, I've got ideas already. It's all I can do not to dump the cleanup on Talia and get to work sketching."

"You won't do that. You're too responsible now that you're a business owner."

"You're right, but I thought about it. Where are you now? We could draw it out together."

"Stuck on the interstate. Accident south of Castle Rock. I can drop by your apartment when I make it back to Denver, though."

"Justin and I have dinner plans later. I might not be there. How about tomorrow afternoon?"

"Sure. Just let me know." Ana kept her voice light, without anything to communicate the pang of . . . something . . . that surfaced in her chest. She didn't blame Melody for wanting to spend time with her boyfriend. But once more, the sensation of being left behind overwhelmed her. Before, they'd been three single women trying to make their way in the world together. And now that Rachel and Melody had significant others, they didn't need her anymore.

No, that was ridiculous. Of course they needed her. Who did they call anytime they had an unsolvable problem? When they needed business advice? When they needed a reliable Denver contact in any industry?

They just didn't need her for personal advice. They had Alex and Justin for that. Partners.

Ana dropped her head back against the seat of her car, fighting something she could only call self-pity.

No. She wasn't that person. Not anymore. She didn't sit back and let things happen to her, feel bad about how things

turned out. She took control of matters. Right now, those matters just might not include a man. She felt like she'd exhausted
every dating option in Denver, including online, blind dates,
setups, and the never-successful bar scene. Heck, she'd even
tried dating guys she'd met at her *two* churches, and that
hadn't gone any better.

It was beginning to feel like she was destined to be alone.

She knew she shouldn't let it bother her. The Bible talked
about the blessings of singleness and the troubles one faced
when married. But right now, her single status didn't feel like
a gift or a bullet dodged. It just felt lonely.

Though it was harder to feel lonely when you were busy.
By the time the traffic finally loosened up—and then slowed
again approaching downtown—she'd dictated a full list of
tasks to her calendar. The only thing she'd leave to Rachel was
food. Now that their original venue, chosen as much for the
chef as the location, was unavailable, Rachel was going to have
strong opinions about a replacement. Maybe she'd be able to
call in one of her culinary contacts to help.

Ana was feeling significantly better when she finally pulled
into her garage at a quarter past nine, having spent almost four
hours on the road this evening. Even with her comfy seats, her
back and legs ached from the inactivity. She could crank out a
few miles on the treadmill to work out the kinks and figure out
something light for dinner . . .

Her phone rang. She let out a sigh before answering.

The panicked voice on the other end snapped her to attention.

"Slow down. What happened?" Her stomach sank as the
details seeped in. "Call 911. I'll be right there."

Chapter Six

ANA FOUND PARKING down the street from the Stafford Hotel and slammed the door, clicking the lock button on her key fob as she hit the sidewalk at a near run. She blew through the opulently decorated lobby, waving away offers of assistance from employees and going straight to the elevator banks. She punched the Up arrow a handful of times, as if her urgency would somehow get the elevator there faster. Her stomach cramped at the idea of what she might find above. Emergency services were slow tonight if she'd gotten here before the ambulance.

Mercifully, the car arrived with a ding and the doors slid open. Inside, she hit the Door Close button so the approaching family with loads of suitcases couldn't get on with her. It was a jerk move, but the last thing she wanted right now was to be held up by a Dora the Explorer roller bag.

When the elevator deposited her on the top floor that held the VIP suites, Ana went straight to the door ahead of the elevator and knocked sharply. "It's Analyn Sanchez. Open up."

Immediately, the door opened to a disheveled man in a suit, all too familiar . . . Christopher Mason.

"What's going on? Why aren't the paramedics here?"

Mason ran his fingers through his hair. "I didn't call them."

"You didn't . . . what?"

"It's okay, though. I called a doctor I could trust. He'll be here any minute." He looked at her with worried eyes, the usual arrogance stripped away. "You said to stay out of the media. You don't think calling 911 is going to attract attention?"

Ana pushed past him. She had indeed said that, but that didn't mean withholding medical attention from someone who needed it. "Where is she?"

He pointed to the bedroom.

Ana's stomach gave another heave of anxiety as she moved silently across the plush carpet to the double doors that separated the living space of the suite from the bedroom. There on rumpled sheets sprawled a woman, dressed in a skimpy cocktail dress, the straps fallen off her shoulders. No, scratch that. Not a woman. A girl. She couldn't be more than eighteen, if even that. And she was unconscious.

It didn't take much to figure out why. The low table in the seating area held drug paraphernalia and what Ana could only guess was heroin. She rushed to the girl's side and pressed her fingers to her neck. Finally, she found a pulse, weak but present.

Ana pulled out her cell phone and began to dial 911, but Mason jerked it out of her hand before she could finish dialing. "You can't do that."

"She needs emergency medical attention, an ambulance. Not some concierge doctor."

Mason's expression hardened. "You will not call 911. This is why we hired you. To take care of problems like this."

Had she thought that he looked concerned earlier? Not

for his date's well-being. Probably for his own reputation and what Daddy would say if he was caught shooting heroin with an underage girl.

"You hired me to fix your mistakes in the media after they came to light. Not to cover up a crime. I can't. I won't."

"Then you won't have a job tomorrow."

Disgust coiled through her. She'd just thought he was a provocateur. But now there was no question that he was the bottom-feeder the media made him out to be. No wonder his father had paid through the nose to get him a minder. He really thought she was going to put her job above someone's life? Ana didn't know all that much about drug overdoses, but from what she saw, the girl probably didn't have a lot of time.

She held Mason's gaze with one she was sure was equally hard and held out her hand. Reluctantly, he placed her phone in it.

"You're on your own this time. I was never here. And I hope for her sake that the doctor gets here soon."

"Analyn—"

"Save it, Mason. This is your mess. You clean it up."

Without a backward look, she strode from the suite and closed the door carefully behind her. She got on the elevator and rode down stiffly, not looking at her own reflection in the mirrored walls. She wasn't sure that she would like what she saw.

She managed to hold on to her composure through the lobby, but as soon as she hit the sidewalk in the cold air outside, she had her phone in hand, dialing.

"911, what's your emergency?"

"Potential drug overdose at the Stafford Hotel, suite 1901. Please come quickly. She's breathing and she has a pulse, but I don't know for how long." Ana clicked off the line before they could ask for any identifying information. Contrary to popular belief, emergency services had no way of tracking the origin of the call, so it would never get traced back to her. But at least she had done what she could. It was all out of her hands now and in God's. The girl's health, Mason's fate, her job.

She went back to her car, hearing the first whine of sirens in the distance, then dropped her head onto her steering wheel with a long exhalation. "Please," she whispered, not even entirely sure what she was asking.

As if it were a direct answer to her inarticulate prayer, a fire truck pulled up in front of the hotel in a spin of red lights, followed almost immediately by the paramedics. She watched as firemen and EMTs rushed into the building with their bags.

She texted Melody and Rachel: I need you guys tonight. I just tanked my career. Bring something sweet.

Melody came back first: Be there in 30.

Then Rachel: Finishing up dinner with Alex. Be there in a few.

Ana let out a breath, the angst she'd felt earlier evaporating. They might be busy with their lives, but they still had her back. She could almost believe everything would be okay. Except Mason's threat might very well be the reality. He'd call his daddy, and Daddy would get her fired. It was only a matter of time.

She made it out of her car just in time to vomit on the street and on the tips of her expensive patent-leather shoes.

*　　*　　*

Tuesday dawned with dread and another stomachache, but it was hard to tell if that was because of Ana's anxiety or the sugary dessert that Rachel and Melody had brought over. They must have had a sixth sense about Ana's panic—for her, job crisis was at least twice as bad as a breakup—because they'd come prepared for the worst with Melody's butterscotch blondie bars, homemade caramel sauce, and vanilla bean ice cream. It was one of the bakery's specialties, taken from Melody's grandmother's signature recipe, and it made Ana think Melody had gone back to Bittersweet Café for provisions on the way.

A gigantic blondie sundae and a lot of conversation later, she'd finally made peace with whatever was going to happen. Rachel and Melody reassured her that she had done the right thing and anything that happened from here was not her fault. The only question was whether the fallout would be bad enough to blackball her from other firms in Denver. She hadn't thought so. This would be more a matter of dereliction of duty; that sort of thing normally didn't come with vindictiveness.

This morning, she wasn't so sure.

She dressed in her most professional suit, aware that she looked more like a high-powered litigator than a publicist, but she wasn't in the mood for friendly and approachable. Slim-cut black jacket with matching pencil skirt, blood-red silk blouse with a deep-V shawl collar, black patent Louboutins with their bloody slash of a crimson sole. For good measure, she clasped on a diamond solitaire necklace that lay precisely at her collarbone, the only piece of fine jewelry she'd ever bought herself, acquired after her promotion to the crisis management division. It had cost her an insane chunk of her equally insane new salary. She still didn't know why she'd done it. Maybe just because she could.

"Whatever happens, God will take care of me," she whispered to herself, fingering the necklace. "I did the right thing."

She held on to that thought all the way into the office, up the elevator, until her foot touched the carpeting on the floor of their office. She knew it wasn't good the moment she saw her assistant Daphne's expression.

She dropped her bag beneath the desk and settled into her chair, making her expression impassive as she logged into her computer. Daphne drifted over to the corner of her desk, clutching a stack of paperwork.

"How bad is it?" Ana asked without looking up.

"He's been in there since I got here. He looks like a windmill."

That could be good or bad. When Lionel was arguing with someone, his hands and arms started gesticulating wildly . . . which she hoped meant that he was fighting for her. Placid resignation would make her more worried.

"He asked to see me yet?"

"As soon as you got in."

Ana sighed and dropped her head forward. "Okay. I'll be right back. I hope."

"Good luck." Daphne's eyebrows drew together, furrowing her pale forehead beneath her strawberry-blonde hair. She'd been Ana's assistant for almost eighteen months after Ana had rescued her from Ryan, who seemed to think she was his personal slave. She had to be wondering what was going to happen to her if this all went bad for Ana.

Amazing how things could turn so quickly. Five days ago, she was being called into Lionel's office to take over this account; now she could be going in there to get fired.

She paused at the door and rapped on the glass divider. "You wanted to see me?"

"Come in, Ana." Lionel's face looked serious, but he wasn't angry, at least. "Close the door behind you."

Uh-oh. She shut the glass door and then seated herself in one of the chairs across from his desk.

"First of all, I wanted to say, you did the right thing."

Ana froze, momentarily speechless.

A tiny smile surfaced on Lionel's face. "The girl is going to be okay. And I do mean girl. She was sixteen."

A wave of shock and revulsion passed through her. "I had to call. He said he'd called a doctor, but I had no way of knowing if that was true. If I didn't and something had happened to her, I would have been responsible."

"Like I said, you did the right thing. But that doesn't mean there aren't consequences." He folded his hands atop the table and studied her carefully. "Tell me the truth. Was it you who called the media?"

Ana stared at him blankly. "Media?"

Lionel clicked on the television on one side of his office and selected a DVR recording. The video had been shot outside the hotel, showing the emergency vehicles and several news vans.

"No! I didn't have any idea. I only stayed long enough to make sure the ambulance got there." Ana pressed a hand to her mouth for a long second. "Did they have Mason's name?"

"Oh, they had Mason's name and the girl's too. I don't need to tell you that it's bad. I've spent half my morning on the phone with Clark Mason, but he's been told there's no possible way he'll be named to the cabinet position after this."

"Christopher Mason probably did it himself," Ana said. "Figured if he was going down, he was taking his dad down with him."

"That's my thought as well, but Clark remains convinced it's my office that leaked the information. To what end, I can't possibly imagine, since confidentiality is our most closely-held value, but he's not being reasonable. He's demanding that I fire you."

Ana had known it was a strong possibility, but up until now, she hadn't really believed it was going to happen. She drew in a deep breath to mitigate the wave of nausea. "I'll go pack my desk, then."

"You should pack your desk, but I'm not firing you."

Ana looked up. "What?"

"I have to do something, Ana, but I know very well you're not the one who put this whole thing in motion. I blame myself.

I should have never taken the account." Lionel rubbed his hand across his short-cropped hair, and for the first time, she saw how much of a toll the job had taken on him. "I'm the one who brought you to Denver. Back in San Francisco, I knew you had an uncanny knack for this work, and I knew you were going to be a great asset to this company. I still believe that."

"I don't understand."

"You're going on leave. You've got six weeks of accumulated vacation time. I think another ten weeks of paid leave should allow the whole thing to blow over."

She stared at him. "You're going to pay me to not work."

"I'm going to pay you to be scarce so I don't have to answer difficult questions. Clark Mason is no doubt going to be talking about you, but I managed to convince him not to take the firm under. I'm sorry to say you get to be the sacrificial lamb."

"But my reputation . . ."

"Will be intact." Lionel smiled sardonically. "Really, Ana, the attention span of the public is short enough that even were you mentioned in the news, no one would remember you by the time you came back. Granted, I don't think we're going to have you working with any more politicians, but that probably won't break your heart."

"I don't know what to say."

"'Thank you, Lionel' would be a good start. You're getting a four-month vacation and then you can come back like nothing happened." He looked at her closely. "And to be honest, I don't think this is the worst thing for you."

"What am I going to do?"

"What everyone else does on vacation. Go to Hawaii. Get a cabin in the mountains and hike for a few weeks. I don't know. What do you like to do outside of work?"

Ana stared at him blankly. It had been so long since she'd

had anything else in her life, she had no idea how to answer that question. When she said as much, he laughed.

"Now I know I'm doing the right thing. Go have some fun, Ana. It's past time you had a life. Figure out who you are besides an impeccably dressed spokesperson for very bad people."

Ana gaped at him.

"I don't have any illusions about what we do here," he said softly. "But it's a living. And no matter how misguided or downright awful some of our clients are, I don't think they really deserve the media feeding frenzy that would occur without us. Or maybe they do, but their families certainly don't." He stood. "Go. Have fun. Rediscover life outside of these four walls."

Ana rose too. "What about Daphne? Will she go back to Ryan?"

"I'll probably make her a floater until you get back. But she will remain your assistant."

"Thank you, Lionel."

"I'm sorry, Ana. I wouldn't have given him to you if I thought it would turn out like this. Your clients are going to miss you."

Ana nodded and turned, leaving the office far more ambivalently than she had entered it. She wasn't getting fired, not really. In fact, she was practically being rewarded with extra vacation time until the situation blew over, after which she could quietly get back to work.

So why did it still feel like a punishment?

"What did he say?" Daphne hissed, falling into step with her back to her desk.

"I'm on leave for four months." Ana opened her top desk drawer and began moving the personal items to her bag—lip gloss, hand cream, feminine products—and then took the single framed photo of her family and shoved it in as well. "You'll be a floating assistant in the office until I come back."

"You *are* coming back, right?"

Ana looked at Daphne curiously. "Of course I'm coming back. What else would I do?"

Daphne chewed her lip, still looking worried. "Well, enjoy your . . . leave . . . I guess? I mean, you really could use some time off. You haven't taken a vacation since I started working here."

Ana just smiled in return and made one last pass through her desk. For someone who practically lived here, there was very little to identify it as hers. She looked back at the still-hovering Daphne, then impulsively hugged her. "Thanks, Daphne."

"For what?"

"For everything. I'll be back. I promise. You know how to get ahold of me if you need me."

Ana took one last look around the office, aware that all the other publicists were attempting to see what was going on without looking like they were interested. Lionel could explain. Or not, and she'd surprise them all when she walked through the door sixteen weeks from today.

Sixteen weeks. That sounded a lot more intimidating than four months. She rode the elevator down, feeling almost like she was floating. No, not floating. Unanchored.

She'd been in this office every weekday and most weekends for the last seven years. She finally had the time and freedom to do whatever she wanted. And thanks to the fact she was on paid leave, the money to accomplish it.

The only problem was, she had absolutely no idea what that was.

Chapter Seven

"I . . . DON'T . . . UNDERSTAND. Why . . . not?" Alex's words came out in gasps, punctuated by the tap of his running shoes on the cement steps.

Bryan laughed and glanced at his friend. "Slacking while I was gone, huh? There was a day when you could have held a whole conversation doing this." He sent a smirk at Alex and took the wide upward steps of the Red Rocks Amphitheatre at an even quicker pace.

It became clear that Alex wasn't going to play the game, though, and Bryan immediately outdistanced him, taking the upward climb as quickly as he could, passing other exercisers who were doing the same thing. Fine. When they moved more slowly, Alex could talk, and right now he was asking questions Bryan wasn't interested in answering.

He made it to the top a full thirty seconds before Alex and took the opportunity to stretch his quads and calves while looking out across the spectacular view. Nestled into the foothills of Morrison on the western edge of Denver, the amphitheater was carved out of the jutting red rocks that gave it its name, affording a spectacular view of the city and the plains beyond.

Straight ahead were the clusters of high-rises that indicated downtown; to the right, a smaller grouping that was the Denver Tech Center, houses and streets and buildings painting the landscape between.

Alex hit the top step and doubled over, panting. "Okay, you might be right. I've been slacking. But in my defense, it's just my conditioning. I've still been climbing. Which is why I want to know why you're not."

"I told you. I left that all behind me."

"And I still don't believe you. Just because you don't have a sponsorship, just because you aren't competing, doesn't mean you stop climbing. Most retired climbers can't keep themselves off the rock."

"Maybe it's not as hard to stay away for me. I've got a business to build." A business that was getting a ridiculously slow start. He had the space. He actually had enough savings that he'd started the build-out. But as far as the equipment to roast the beans? He was still short by thousands. The roaster he was looking at ran nearly twenty thousand dollars, with another five for a sample roaster. That didn't even include the afterburner and other emissions equipment he needed to meet Denver's air quality requirements. He might be able to find used equipment, but he'd hoped to make it easier on himself by buying the same drum roaster he'd learned on in Oregon. That way he'd only be adjusting to the difference in beans and not the difference in equipment performance. It had seemed like a good idea at the time, but that was before he was thirty-five grand short.

"Where'd you go?" Alex studied him carefully. "There's more going on here than you're telling me, isn't there?"

Bryan clapped him on the shoulder. "You give me too much credit. I'm not that complex. Just worrying about money."

"Your dad—"

"Has done plenty. I just need to find someone who's willing to lend me the money in return for an equity stake in the business."

"You sure you want to go that route? I know you don't like the idea of bank debt, but you'd retain your entire share of the company."

"But the bank wants to be repaid no matter what happens to the company." Bryan grinned at Alex. "Trust me, I can find the money."

"Then what's holding you up?"

What was holding him up? His beans were going to arrive in two weeks. Besides finding someplace to put them, he hadn't made much progress. Part of it was the fact that the learning curve going from a professional climber to a business owner was pretty steep. Sure, he had a business degree, but most of what he'd learned in college was theoretical. Putting it into practice and knowing he was doing the right thing was another matter entirely. He needed someone to help.

"Ana!"

That was some impressive mind-reading from Alex. "I already asked Ana, remember? She said she might be able to consult on marketing, but she's busy with her full-time—"

"No, I mean, there's Ana." Alex pointed to a dark-haired figure at the bottom of the steps. Or she had been at the bottom of the steps. She was charging up the wide platforms with determination, her black ponytail bobbing with every step.

"What's she doing here? She's not the type to ditch work to exercise."

"I'm not so sure I'd agree with that assessment," Alex said. "But didn't you hear? She lost her job."

Bryan's eyebrows flew up.

"Well, not lost exactly. Put on leave for political reasons. Very political from what I heard."

"Ah, that whole senator's-son drama?" Bryan had caught a little snippet of the situation on the news, but he hadn't paid much attention. His opinion of politicians was sufficiently low that nothing they or their families did would change it much.

"Supposedly. She's been out since last week. Rachel says she's going stir-crazy."

"Is that right?" Bryan watched her thoughtfully as she continued her upward charge. She was sharp and aggressive, just the type of person he could use on his side. And now that she had some spare time . . .

Though honestly, her intelligence wasn't what had his attention at the moment; that had much more to do with the brightly colored running tights and sports bra that showed off her toned body and a flat expanse of abs. But he'd always been attracted to her, and her work situation didn't affect the reason he stayed away. It did, however, make it far more likely that she'd be willing to help him.

She finally reached the top, only slightly out of breath. "Hey! I thought that was you. I saw your car in the lot." She was speaking to Alex but looking at Bryan, probably the reason for Alex's amused chuckle.

"I just heard what happened at work. I'm sorry."

"Yeah, well . . ." She wiped her sweaty forehead with a glistening arm, and slay him if it wasn't one of the sexiest things he'd seen in a long time. Nope. Not going there. She took a drink from the water bottle clutched in her right hand. "Who would have thought we'd almost hit eighty in April?"

"Denver," Bryan said with a shrug and Ana smiled in agreement. He swiftly moved on. "Are you just starting or finishing your workout?"

"Depends." A sparkle surfaced in her eyes, directed toward him. "You game for another couple of rounds?"

"You're on."

"How about you, Alex?"

Alex looked between the two of them. "I'm done, but you can stay if you want. Ana, you mind dropping Bryan home?"

Ana nodded. "Not at all. If that's okay with you, Bryan."

"Yeah, I'd appreciate it." The three of them started down the stairs slowly, but Bryan had a distinct sense of Alex's self-satisfaction. Nice. His friend might think he was doing him a favor, but he was just putting him in the path of temptation.

Ah well, he'd resisted this long; it wasn't like a couple of rounds of steps were going to make any difference.

At the bottom, Alex gave a salute. "See you later, Ana. Bryan."

She waved back with a smile, but part of her was already focused on the steps again. There apparently wasn't anything she didn't give her full attention. That was something he could get on board with, especially if he was the object of her attention.

Maybe this was going to be more difficult than he thought.

There was no way Ana could win a race against him, though, and she must have known that when she'd thrown out the challenge. She barely topped five foot one; he had a full ten inches on her. For a moment, he considered letting her win, but he knew that would irritate her more than losing. Besides, he wasn't the type to throw a race because of a girl.

"Ready?" Ana asked, sending him a challenging look.

"Go!" he said, and they were off.

He quickly outpaced her, first just by a step, then several, then a large section of the steps. When he hit the top, he turned, panting, and saw she was still at the quarter mark, still taking the steps at a steady, almost unhurried pace. Had she thrown out the challenge to see him kill himself? He grinned. If she had, his respect for her went up a notch. He'd always known she was tough, but there was something particularly attractive about that evil streak.

She reached the top, barely out of breath, and checked her pulse rate on the fitness watch. "You beat me."

"As you knew I would."

"I wanted to see if you were going to throw it for me." She worked a kink out of her neck and pulled one arm across her chest to stretch out her shoulders. He averted his eyes from the glimpse of cleavage displayed above the neckline of her sports bra. Definitely not letting his mind go there. But she was moving on. "I was thinking about hiking the Trading Post Trail. It's only about a mile and a half, but it's a nice cooldown. What do you think?"

"I'm game." He started down the stairs beside her, their pace slower this time, and threw her a smile. "A mile-and-a-half hike is a cooldown?"

"To me it is." She smiled too but didn't look at him, focusing instead on the steps ahead of them. They'd known each other for two years, but thanks to Alex, this might be the first time they'd ever been alone together.

A warm breeze caught them on the way down, drying sweat and giving a moment's relief from the surprisingly hot April sun. At the bottom of the amphitheater stairs, there was still the long walk down the cement switchbacks, then down the hill to the parking lot, which also served as the trailhead. Only when they'd traversed the whole descent in comfortable silence did Bryan broach the subject he'd been wanting to mention from the moment he'd seen her.

"Weird coincidence that we'd all be here today."

"Not really." She flicked her gaze up to his face. "Rachel told me you and Alex would be here. I was hoping to run into you."

"Oh yeah?" He'd like to say that all he felt was curiosity at that revelation, but that would be a complete lie. "Why's that?"

"Obviously you heard what happened with my job."

"I did. I'm sorry, Ana. Sounds like you got a raw deal."

She shrugged. "My boss did what he had to do to keep a client without losing me. Do you know that I was one of the first people he hired when he opened his firm? I came from San Francisco for this job."

"At least you get a vacation out of it. Most people would love to be in your position."

"Except other publicists are taking over my clients and forming relationships with them. Most likely they won't come back to me in four months. I'm going to have to build my roster from scratch. Which I can do—" she paused and wiped her arm across her forehead again, a stalling gesture—"but it's going to be a lot of work."

Bryan hadn't thought of it like that. She'd been trying to do the right thing, and she'd gotten her clients taken away from her. That didn't seem right. "You have anything you've always wanted to do? Play the guitar? Take up needlepoint?"

"You'd think so, wouldn't you? But no. Honestly, it's only been a week and it's killing me. I'm bored out of my mind."

"Well, I have a coffee company that needs help getting off the ground. The offer's still open. The plea, really, because I could use your help much more than you need mine."

"I was hoping you'd say that." Ana finally focused on him. "What still needs to be done?"

"Pretty much everything." He filled her in on the space he was renting from his dad and the progress on the build-out. "My beans arrive in two weeks. Problem is, I don't have any money for the equipment. I need to find someone to invest in the company to even have a company. And that's a tough sell when we haven't made a cent."

"You're 'pre-revenue,'" Ana said, putting the words in air quotes. She gestured with her head to break off from the paved path down to the soft dirt that wound around the large red rock formations and into a meadow. "You have a business plan? Sales projections? An idea of your overhead?"

"Of course."

"Then you don't have *nothing*. You have any leads on investors?"

Bryan rubbed his chin thoughtfully, still surprised to find a beard there. He kept thinking he was going to shave it, but stopped each time before he went through with it. "As a matter of fact, I got invited to an engagement party tonight at the Oracle. The guy getting married owes me some big favors."

"He have the bank account to pay off those favors?"

Bryan nodded.

"Great. What time should I be ready?"

Bryan blinked at her. "You're coming?"

"Of course I'm coming. At very least, you need a wingman . . . er, woman. And I can be very persuasive."

I bet. "In that case, I could pick you up at eight thirty. We don't want to be there before the alcohol starts flowing, but we need to get to them before they're too drunk to remember what they agreed to."

Ana nodded as if that was a perfectly reasonable statement. He'd gotten the impression that her clients had been the bad boys—and girls—of pretty much every industry in Denver, but now he wondered how much of their behavior she'd had to witness herself. Besides being called to the drug overdose of an underage escort.

Probably a lot.

And to his shame, he realized that up until recently, he'd probably had a lot more in common with them than he had with her.

"Anything I need to know? I don't like going in cold."

She was serious about this. "Maybe we should define your role here before we go in there tonight."

She waved a hand. "Call me your advisor."

"And what do you expect to get out of this arrangement?" He couldn't help it: the words came out more flirtatious than businesslike.

She drilled him with look. "A share of the profits, of course. But as they're advisory shares, let me prove my worth and then we can discuss my percentage. I don't bring any value, you don't pay me anything."

"That seems . . ." Pretty typical for an advisor, but generous coming from an average person. Then again, she was on leave from a job that paid a salary well into six figures. At least that's what he assumed from her LoDo address and the new leased Mercedes every two years. She didn't need the money, just something to do.

"How can I pass up that offer?" He stopped abruptly and put his hand on her shoulder to stay her progress as well. "Look. A bald eagle."

She followed his gaze to where a huge raptor circled above them, no doubt looking for snakes and rodents for its lunch. A smile came to her face and she cupped a hand over her eyes to shade them from the sun. "It's beautiful."

"There are several breeding pairs that nest at Castlewood Canyon, where Alex and I used to climb. Some of the routes are closed so no one disturbs them. Of course, there's also plenty of turkey vultures and hawks, which aren't quite as glamorous."

Ana started walking again, but she hadn't missed the comment buried in his wildlife ramblings. "Used to climb?"

"Yeah."

"You want to talk about it?"

"Not really."

She nodded thoughtfully, but she didn't press. He figured that only got him off the hook for today. She wasn't the type to let something go when she was curious. And why wouldn't she be curious? Before he left, climbing had been his life. Now he wouldn't set hand or foot on a rock. That wasn't a normal reaction to a disaster that had befallen someone else.

But then, his abandonment of his former career had nothing to do with Vivian's fall at Suesca. It had to do with the catastrophe that was his life, everything that had led him up to that point. He'd left that part of himself in Colombia, hopefully never to be seen again. His rebirth was more than just spiritual; it was a desperately needed whole-life overhaul.

"So, what's the dress code for tonight?"

"Club wear, I guess. I don't know. I'll wear jeans."

"That's very helpful, thanks."

"You're asking a man what you should wear to a club? You're far more qualified to answer that question than I am."

"And you know your friends better than I do." When he just gave her a blank look, she waved her hand. "Oh, never mind. I'll figure it out. Tell me more about this coffee of yours."

That he had no problem talking about. It was the easiest part of this venture, the story behind the organization and his farm in particular. The owners had started out growing coffee years ago, but during the early nineties and then again in 2001, the wholesale cost of coffee plummeted and they'd sold off more and more of their farmland to neighbors who were growing coca for the local cartel. Eventually, they'd seen that the only way they were going to survive without having to sell the family farmlands was to grow coca as well. But it had never sat well with them, especially when their only son left the farm, ended up working for the cartel, and was killed in an altercation with government forces who were trying to encroach on the cartels' territory.

Café Libertad had essentially offered a way to get their revenge all these years against the drug runners, or at least to assuage their conscience in working to supply the people responsible for their son's death. In the five years since they'd started producing a coffee crop again, the farm's soil had proven somehow unusual and yielded a coffee that had been rated between eighty-eight and ninety-six points.

But eventually they found themselves in their seventies, past ready to retire but with no one to pass the farmland on to, leaving a good chance their land would get swallowed up by the neighboring coca plantation against their wishes. Which was where Bryan had come in.

Yes, he owned a coffee farm in Colombia that bordered coca fields. There was a sentence he'd never expected to say aloud.

"The thing is, these farmers are practically slaves to the cartel. The only reason they've been able to escape its control is because of all the conflict with government forces. Coffee gets them out of the middle of the fighting, gives them a sustainable livelihood, and allows them to band together with others like them. In numbers, they have a voice. The co-op lets them negotiate higher prices from wholesalers, brand the region."

"But you're not part of that?" Ana asked. "You're bringing in beans for your own use."

"Because it doesn't cost me anything, in the sense that I already own them. Over time, though, I'm going to need more than my farm can supply. And I'm hoping I can get those beans from co-op members. After all, I'm basing my story on the redemption of these coca farmers, drugs to beans. I can't buy them from just anywhere and feel good about it."

"The redemption angle is really compelling. We can do something with that."

He threw her a sidelong glance. "It's not just a story. It's as much my second chance as theirs. I've been so unanchored, it feels like my opportunity to have something solid for a change. Lasting."

Ana stopped walking as if she were surprised by his transparency. For good reason. He was used to glossing over real feelings with humor or flirtation.

And then she said slowly, "Solid . . . like . . . solid ground. Solid *grounds*. The Solid Grounds Coffee Company?"

"The Solid Grounds Coffee Company." He tried the sound of it on his tongue. "Just enough humor. Just enough meaning. I like it."

"Good. Me too." She socked him in the arm, surprisingly hard for such a small woman. "You've got yourself a business name."

"Solid Grounds," he repeated to himself. "I guess you're earning your advisory shares in the business already."

"It's not a business yet. It's an idea. But after tonight . . . who knows?" She picked up her pace. "In which case, we should probably get back. I've got things to do before we go out. Can you email me the business plan when you get home? I want to have an idea what I'm talking about."

Bryan fell into step with her. "Of course I can. Thanks, Ana. I don't need to tell you I needed the help."

She seemed surprised, but at what, he couldn't guess. "Don't thank me yet. Right now, I'm just a friend. But when I've got a stake in the company, you'll see an entirely different me." Her expression turned wicked again, and he found himself hoping her words were true.

Chapter Eight

"You're going out with Bryan?"

Ana stopped short at Rachel's words and looked up from the muffin she was eating. "I'm not going *out* with him. I'm going to an engagement party with him to talk to potential investors. There's a difference."

Melody chimed in from her workbench, where she was scoring an assembly line of unbaked bread. "Maybe to you there is, but I can practically guarantee that he's not thinking of it that way. Bryan's the kind of guy who likes to mix business and pleasure."

"I don't think so," Ana said resolutely, though her stomach gave a little jolt of nervousness at the words. At least she thought it was nervousness. Surely it wasn't anticipation. "Mostly, I want to see if there's any truth to these claims that his friends will pay back his favors in cash. What kind of favors could they be anyway?"

"Hard to tell," Rachel said. "From what Alex says, he's always been the guy who can run in any circle. Climbers or investment bankers, doesn't really matter to him. And thanks to his dad, he has all sorts of contacts. It's just surprising that he hasn't taken advantage of it until now."

"I guess it hasn't really mattered to him until now," Ana said, polishing off the rest of the muffin.

Melody looked at her closely. "You're sure you're okay with this?"

"Yeah. Why wouldn't I be?"

"Because that's the first muffin I've seen you eat in like . . . ever. You always say they're tasty little fat bombs that are going to cost you a thousand squats the next day. And we all know how much you like squats."

Ana made a face. "Maybe I felt like it. I ran the stairs at Red Rocks today. That had to burn a thousand calories. Alex and Bryan seriously do that once a week?"

"Used to, until Bryan disappeared," Rachel said. "Did he say anything about that?"

"No. I asked about the climbing, but he didn't want to talk about it." Ana paused and cocked a hip against the wall. "Have you guys noticed anything different about him?"

"You mean the beard?" Melody asked. "I don't know about you, but I kind of like it. It makes him look like a hipster mountaineer."

"No, I don't mean the beard." Secretly, Ana had wanted to hold him down and shave it off since she'd first seen him. He was a good-looking guy; he didn't need to hide behind all that hair. "I mean . . . he's subdued. You know, he was always the life of the party. Flirtatious. Maybe even a bit inappropriate, but not in a creepy way."

"He had a come-to-Jesus moment," Rachel said. "What happened to Vivian woke him up, I guess. And the coffee co-op is a Christian organization. Sounds like the farmers aren't the only ones who got the gospel down there."

"Maybe." Ana still wasn't convinced his sudden personality

change was due solely to a spiritual awakening. There was something odd about his refusal to climb when it had been part of his life for almost twenty-five years. "What's the deal with Vivian?"

"Why all the interest about Bryan and his personal life?" Melody asked, a smile in her voice.

"If I'm working with him, I want to know what I'm dealing with. Besides, isn't he the guy who never commits? A new girl every week?"

Rachel lowered her voice, though there was no one else present. "I asked Alex the same thing a while back. Apparently, he was head over heels for this woman. Even asked her to marry him, very publicly, and she said no. He wouldn't say her name aloud for three years. And then suddenly they end up in Colombia, climbing together? Something big must have happened. Alex wouldn't tell me because he thought Bryan wouldn't want us to know."

"But you have your suspicions."

"I wouldn't speculate. I know Bryan seems like an open book, but he's actually pretty private. We spend a fair amount of time with him and I still don't know much about him."

Interesting. Ana just nodded, filing away that information for future reference. Maybe what seemed out of character to her wasn't really out of character . . . she just didn't actually know who he was.

She wasn't sure it was such a good idea to be intrigued by him, though. She'd made a living out of reading people's weaknesses and bolstering their strengths, but she'd written him off as a two-dimensional player. Add in some depth, and he suddenly became someone to figure out.

"Regardless, tonight should be interesting." She ignored the knowing looks her friends sent her way and threw her muffin wrapper in the trash by the back door. "I'll text you guys and let you know how it goes. Fingers crossed this isn't just a waste of a night with a bunch of overage frat boys."

But if what they were saying about Bryan was true, and she'd really underestimated him, it might be just what he said. And if that were the case, she was determined to walk out of the club with an investor.

*   *   *

Ana spent the rest of the afternoon looking over the business plan Bryan had emailed her, and she had to admit she was impressed. It looked like he'd done his homework. He had no illusions over the difficulty of this business, including its high costs, seasonal variability, and low margins.

There was even a provision in there for a portion of the proceeds—once there was a profit—to be set aside for school ventures in South America for farmers' kids.

That didn't fit the picture she'd formed of him.

But good intentions were one thing; being able to execute them was another. Right now, he had the advantage of low raw material costs, because he owned the farm and just had to pay a cut to the importer. His space was cheap. And it all meant nothing unless he could raise thirty-five thousand dollars for roasting and packaging equipment.

"What did I get myself into?" Ana murmured as she rose from her kitchen table and moved into her bedroom. She began flipping through the clothing options in her huge walk-in closet, bypassing her professional suits and slacks before selecting a favorite pair of dark-blue skinny jeans. After a moment, she chose a ruffled pink silk blouse and a buttery black leather jacket. High-heeled peep-toe booties for the shoes, for sure. It projected just the image she wanted now: pretty but tough, stylish but smart. From experience, she knew if she walked in wearing a skirt, she'd be fending off advances from every drunk idiot all night. Apparently showing even a little skin made her look like she was after a hookup.

An hour later, showered, her hair pulled back in a sleek ponytail, makeup done flawlessly with a collection of expensive cosmetics that inhabited their own cabinet in her bathroom, she was ready to go. She clasped a bracelet watch around her wrist, added the crucifix that her mother had given her at her confirmation, and dabbed on one more coat of gloss.

She glanced at the watch—8:25. Bryan would be here any minute. She found herself pacing the length of her living room. Why was she so nervous? This was neither a date nor a business meeting. It was a . . .

. . . long shot. She sighed. Bryan better have read his friends right. Her feet already ached from the booties, and she hated to waste an evening of high heels on a lost cause.

At 8:28, a knock sounded at her door. She opened it without looking through the peephole. The doorman would have vetted him before he came up anyway; she'd given instructions long ago that no one but Rachel, Melody, and now Bryan be let up without calling first.

"Hey," she said, stepping back to let him in. "You're on time."

"By my watch, I'm early." He gave her a once-over, but it was friendlier than she might have expected. "You look great. You sure you want to look that good? You're going to be fending off drunk idiots all night."

She laughed. He'd chosen the exact words she'd thought earlier. "I think I can handle myself. Besides, you're there to run interference. You clean up nice, by the way."

More than nice, if she was being honest. She'd always admired his athletic build in a distant sort of way—no bulky gym muscles, rather lean and wiry, deceptively strong. A fine-gauge sweater clung just enough to his upper body to show he

was in shape, not enough to make him look like he was trying to show it off. Casually relaxed jeans cuffed at somewhat-
battered ankle boots. He was the epitome of good-looking
without trying too hard.

And he'd shaved.

She turned away to grab her handbag. "Don't take this the
wrong way, but I'm glad you finally got rid of the animal hanging out on your chin."

"How could I possibly take that the wrong way?" He was
grinning when she turned around, and he ran a hand across his
clean-shaven jaw. "I figured it was time when some guy offered
me half a sandwich on the street."

Ana chuckled. "I guess so. Ready to go?"

"Sure." He opened the door and stepped out before her,
then stood back to allow her to lock it. All the way down the
hall to the elevator, he kept his distance, and inside he stood
back a respectable several paces.

However, he did open her car door when he led her to his
little black hatchback parked on the street and closed it behind
her when she climbed in. Once settled into the driver's seat,
he grimaced. "Maybe I should have had you drive. Sorry about
the car."

She glanced around and shrugged. It was old but clean—
more than clean, recently detailed. She could still smell traces
of the air freshener they'd used. "It's fine. Easier to park in
the Highlands anyway. The Benz is a monster. I just drive it
because it's intimidating."

"That's important to you?" he asked when he pulled away
from the curb into light evening traffic. "Being intimidating,
I mean?"

Ana thought for a second how to explain it. "I deal with a lot
of people who don't look at me as a human being. I'm a machine
or a tool or a means to their end. But every once in a while, I

have a client who tries to get too personal, and then, yes, intimidating is important to me. You don't mess with a woman in a power suit and a massive black Mercedes." A smile came to her lips. "It's psychology. Silly, but it works."

"Always?"

She sobered. "Not always." Being a five-foot-one Asian woman, even in five-inch heels, came with its own set of challenges.

He was darting looks at her, as if she'd surprised him. That made two of them. For the second time today, she realized they'd hardly spent any time together alone. They barely knew each other. They shouldn't be surprised to find out unexpected things.

He cleared his throat. "So, a little background that you might need to know about the people you're going to meet tonight."

He proceeded to run through half a dozen names, which Ana tried to commit to memory along with their stories: how he'd met them, what they did, how likely they were to invest, how they owed him. She'd thought he'd meant youthful, joking sorts of debts, but these were some serious favors. One guy was a friend from college; Bryan had bailed him out of jail when he got arrested for a bar fight. The hothead was now a venture capitalist. Another had been an aspiring architect just out of his master's program, finding it impossible to get a job when the housing bubble burst in Denver; Bryan had pitched his portfolio to his dad, got him a job with Shaw Associates, and now he was designing a multimillion-dollar development in Sun Valley.

"And the pièce de résistance . . . the couple we're celebrating tonight? I introduced them."

Ana smiled. "How much is nostalgia and gratitude worth to him?"

"Hopefully a lot. He's a TV producer. His fiancée, Margot, was a college friend of Alex's and mine."

"Wait." Ana racked her brain. "I know them. Sort of. Weren't they at the very first supper club that Alex and Rachel put on?"

"I think they were," Bryan said. "He didn't have the money to invest in a restaurant back then, but I'm also not asking nearly as much as Rachel was. Regardless, I kind of have to make an appearance at the engagement party."

Ana smiled and shook her head. "You've got some pretty far-reaching connections for a climber. How did that happen?"

She didn't miss the flinch when she mentioned his old profession, but he quickly smoothed it over. "My parents, remember? I grew up attending all these events and galas and dinner parties. Sometimes my dad's associates would bring their kids along and we'd eat pizza and play foosball in the basement while the adults talked. A lot of them grew up to be influential, as you might guess." Bryan shrugged. "I kept up with most of them over the years."

Now she was even more nervous. Childhood friends who owed him favors? That could go either way.

The tiny car slid through the dark night, the pulse of rock music on the radio just low enough that she couldn't make out the words. He finally found parking on a side street a few blocks from their destination. "Hope you don't mind a little walk in those heels."

"Not at all," she said, even though her toes already ached at the prospect. She let herself out of the car so he wouldn't open the door for her again, pleased that he just waited at the back for her and then fell into step with her on the sidewalk. No attempt to take her arm, no sign that he thought this was a date.

At least she thought she was pleased.

Chapter Nine

BRYAN KEPT HIS DISTANCE on the sidewalk as they traversed the two blocks to the club, but he couldn't stop himself from stealing surreptitious looks at Ana while they walked. Repeating *this is just business, this is just business* to himself with every stride.

Ana was stunning. Well, she was always stunning, even—or especially—sweaty in workout clothes, but made-up for the evening, she was hard to look away from. He'd be willing to bet that every man in the club would have his eyes on her at one point or another, which could definitely work in their favor. It also meant that he wasn't going to leave her side all night. Never mind the fact that the only parts of her body left exposed were her collarbone and her pink-painted toenails. Those jeans were enough to make any man stupid, especially ones who weren't determined to keep their less-than-honorable impulses in check. But she looked tough enough that they would take no for an answer when she blew them off. At least he hoped she'd blow them off. There was no way he was bringing her there and letting her leave with someone else.

Now where had that thought come from? Even if that were

her intention—and he was fairly certain it wasn't—he had no claim over her. No right to tell her what to do.

"What's wrong?" Ana asked.

Add *perceptive* to the list. "Nothing's wrong. Just thinking."

She didn't look convinced, but she didn't say anything else. And then they were approaching the club and she couldn't. They bypassed the long line snaking down the sidewalk and went straight to the doorman. He checked Bryan's name against the list and let him in immediately. Ana would be a no-brainer even if she weren't with him. He noticed the waiting guys checking her out and pushed down the sudden murderous impulse that flooded him.

Which he had a feeling he was going to do a lot tonight.

Then they were enveloped in a crush of people, surrounded by pulsating music. Why Roger and Margot had picked this place for the engagement party, he wasn't sure. It was more of a high-end bar than a club—at least a dance club—and you could barely have a conversation without shouting. Or getting close and whispering, which he suspected was more of the point.

From across the room, Roger caught sight of Bryan and signaled him with the beer bottle in his hand. He looked like he'd come directly from work, but he'd lost the jacket and tie and was already looking a little rumpled from the hot, humid atmosphere. Bryan was even beginning to regret his thin knit. Ana must be sweltering.

"There's Roger," he said, bending to her ear and pitching his voice low. "I don't see Margot, though. She's probably off with her girls."

Ana grabbed his arm to get him to stop and then stretched up to his ear. A little shiver ran down the side of his body at her touch. "Which one of them has the wandering eyes?"

He frowned. "What?"

"This isn't an engagement party if they've been engaged for

two years. It's a combined bachelor/bachelorette party. Who doesn't trust whom?"

She'd picked up on something in thirty seconds that had never occurred to him. "I don't know, actually. But I bet you'll tell me by the end of the night."

"Won't even take me that long," she said, that wicked twinkle coming back. "Introduce me."

Bryan did as she asked. Ana smiled and said all the right things. Yes, she'd tagged along tonight. No, they weren't a couple, just friends. Plus, they were working together on their new venture. What new venture? Oh, better to let Bryan tell him about that. She worked the conversation so brilliantly that he slipped into the opening she left him without thought. He faltered when she made her exit, but the quick look she sent back threatened violence if he walked away from the beautiful segue she'd left him. She could take care of herself, all right.

"So, tell me again what you're doing?" Roger said.

Bryan started at the beginning, talked about the co-op and the farm he'd bought. He was halfway through his spiel when Roger started laughing. "What happened to you, man? Did you join the Hare Krishnas or something while you were down there?"

For the first time, Bryan realized that his friend's fiancé was already a little drunk. "I don't understand."

"You really expect me to think you suddenly grew a conscience, that you care about the global good?" Roger took a swig of his beer and then signaled the bartender for another one. "Tell me the truth. It's because of the chick."

"The *chick* is a good friend of mine," Bryan said, keeping his tone casual. "I brought her on to help because she has a background in marketing, which I most certainly don't have."

"C'mon. You want me to believe *you* aren't hitting that? She's just your type."

Bryan ground his teeth together. The only thing that stayed his retort was the realization that he had earned that reputation. That he *had* been the kind of man Roger was expecting now. He clapped him on the shoulder. "I'm going to go say hi to a few people. Congratulations on your upcoming marriage. I'm sure you'll be very happy."

He blew out his breath and wove his way through the crowd to where Ana was standing talking to a couple. She brightened when she saw him and sent him a questioning look. He shook his head slightly. Her enthusiasm dimmed but she still smiled. "Bryan! There you are. I was wondering where you'd disappeared to."

"Hey, Bryan, I didn't know you were back." The man, Robert Boykin, held out his hand and used it to pull Bryan into a back-pounding hug. "Nice to see you."

"You too, Bobby Boy." Bryan grinned, throwing out the hated elementary school nickname. "You look good. Still at Kramer and Associates?"

"Nah, I went out on my own a couple of years ago." He turned to the attractive redhead beside him. "I don't think you've met my wife, Roberta?"

Bryan paused. "Robert and Roberta?"

"Robert and Bobbi, actually." She gave a helpless laugh as she shook Bryan's hand. "You can't help who you fall in love with."

"Apparently not. Bob and Bobbi Boykin." The grin came back. "You two have any kids?"

"One," Bobby—er, Robert—said. "A little girl, turned two last week."

"And I promise, her name is no variation of Bob. We named her Lily."

"Good call." Bryan turned to Ana. "You've obviously met my friend and business advisor, Ana?"

"She was just telling us about your new business," Bobbi

said. "Sounds interesting. I had no idea that farmers were converting from cocaine to coffee."

Robert lifted his eyebrows. "And I had no idea you were interested in anything like this. Quite a departure from your climbing career, isn't it?"

Quite a change from caring about no one but himself, he meant. "Yeah, I'm getting that a lot, actually. But we all change, hopefully for the better. I seem to remember a time when you swore you would be single forever, Robert."

His friend laughed. "Well, it was beginning to feel like that. But when you meet the right person, you know."

"Do you?" Bryan said, without thinking. At their surprised looks—Ana's included—he smiled. "I guess you do. The fact I can ask the question just shows I haven't found her yet."

"Oh." Bobbi's eyes flicked to Ana. They obviously hadn't believed it when he said they were just friends and business associates.

"I'm going to get a drink," Ana said. "You want anything?"

"You don't need to do that. I'll get them."

"We can go together." She turned to the couple and held out her hand. "It was truly a pleasure meeting you. Will you be around here for a while? I'd love to talk more and hear about that adorable daughter of yours."

"I'd love that," Bobbi said genuinely. "We probably won't stay long, though. Not really into this scene these days."

"I hear you," Ana said with sympathy. "It's a sign we're getting old. We like to be able to hear each other talk."

Bryan shook hands with them as well and let Ana steer him back to the bar. "You're impressive to watch."

"They're nice people. I enjoyed meeting them. But they're not investors."

"You don't think so? She's carrying a Prada purse, and unless I miss my mark, he's wearing a Rolex."

"The purse is four seasons old and the Rolex is fake," she said. "They want to get home so they don't have to pay the babysitter extra."

Ouch. He glanced back at the couple, who were having an intense conversation under their breath, about what, he couldn't guess. Ana probably could, though.

"What about you? The happy groom have anything interesting to say?"

"Just that he doesn't believe I've suddenly grown a conscience."

Ana grimaced. "Sorry. That's the problem with old friends. They have long memories."

Something in the tone of her voice made him think she wasn't talking about him now, but before he could explore that idea further, he caught sight of a familiar man making his way from the pool tables in their direction.

"What? What's wrong?" Ana had picked up on his tension, apparently, and she tried to look in that direction, but he grabbed her arm.

"Let's just say I didn't think Adrian would be here tonight."

Ana leaned forward to take her drink from the bartender and casually took a sip as she looked around. "He looks ticked. What did you do to the guy?"

"Dated his sister. And dumped her. Quickly."

"Oh." Ana seemed to read the subtext of the statement, and her expression shifted to one of wariness. "What do you want to do?"

"Other than go back in time? Not sure there's anything I can do. Just brace yourself."

Adrian approached, a beer bottle clutched in his hand, but there was nothing in his expression that said it wasn't his first. "You're back."

Bryan met his eyes directly. "I am."

"Too bad. Amy will be sorry to hear that."

"About that—" Bryan began, even though he didn't know what he could say that would make it any better. It had been a mistake? Everyone knew that. That they'd both been drunk, and Bryan had assumed she was looking for a one-night stand like he was? No, that wouldn't help.

"I don't think we've met. I'm Ana." She inserted herself between them and held out her hand.

His eyes flicked down to her, and his expression softened a little. "I'm Adrian."

"It's a pleasure. I don't suppose you're up to another game? I've been thinking I should finally play pool, but I haven't gotten up the courage to break up your little crew over there."

"Your boyfriend would be okay with that?" His eyes flicked to Bryan and hardened again.

"Oh, he's not my boyfriend," she said airily. "We work together and he gave me a ride. What do you say? Got time for a game or two?"

"Sure." He cocked his head and Ana followed, strutting toward the table with him.

Bryan watched, his throat tight, as Adrian helped her choose a cue from the rack by the pool table and then cleared everyone else away. "What are you playing at here, Ana?" he murmured.

Adrian wasn't a bad guy, despite the homicidal way he was looking at Bryan. He'd been another college friend, albeit a couple of years behind him. Bryan just hadn't realized he had such a long memory or a vengeful streak. Probably wouldn't have stopped him from taking Amy home, but he might have waited longer to disabuse her of her mistaken romantic notions.

Man, he'd been a creep. Maybe he deserved to lose everything in repayment for his actions.

But the farmers and the coffee pickers on his farm didn't deserve to lose their salary or be forced back into an industry that harmed their region, their families. And he knew all too well that the farm wasn't going to be sustainable for him unless he could roast and sell the beans at a profit. He needed to make this work. Which meant that he needed to circulate and reconnect with old friends and contacts.

Except he couldn't do anything but sit on this barstool and stare at the pool table, where Ana was laughing at something Adrian had said. He was behind her, showing her how to line up a shot, his body just close enough to make a statement. No, an offer. One that, if Bryan was judging from Ana's body language, wasn't altogether unwelcome.

Bryan turned away. He was wrong. He couldn't watch this, not when the sight of Ana looking up at Adrian filled him with cold fury.

Not when he knew he had no right to feel that way.

*   *   *

Ana had Adrian pegged before they got to the pool table. He was handsome, bordering on beautiful, and he knew it. Gym-rat physique, close-cropped dark hair, and bronzed Latin looks, pretty much the opposite of Bryan, though she wasn't sure why that thought would occur to her now. And for all his playacting, his irritation over what had happened with his sister was long gone. It was merely posturing, part of Adrian's tough exterior, and she could tell right now he was a lover, not a fighter.

Or at least he thought of himself that way.

"So tell me, Adrian, what do you do?" she asked, letting him lead her to the pool table.

"I'm in venture capital," he said.

"No kidding." She didn't need to pretend interest. When

she'd drawn him away from Bryan, she'd just been trying to defuse the situation, but it couldn't have worked out better had she planned it. "I'm not sure I've ever met a venture capitalist before. What do you specialize in?"

"Manufacturing, mostly. Just invested in a little Paleo foods start-up out of Broomfield. Velocity Organics. You heard of them?"

Bingo. This was their whale. "Really? They're going to be huge. The next big thing. I've heard whispers that Starbucks is thinking about buying them."

"And if they do, we'll cash in big time."

"That's impressive. I know you're probably a good judge of business ideas, but it's still a bit of a gamble, isn't it?"

"What can I say? I'm a risk taker." He flashed her a set of straight white teeth, and she barely kept herself from rolling her eyes even while a plan formed in her mind. He'd assumed that her statement earlier meant she couldn't play pool, so she went with it, letting him help her choose a pool cue and show her how to line up the shots. She took her time, hitting a few good ones, letting some others spin purposely off-angle. At the end, she'd only sunk three of her balls, but Adrian was still looking pretty proud of his victory.

"I feel like I'm starting to get this," she said. "I think I might even beat you the next round."

Adrian sidled close to her. "You think so, huh?"

"I do." She looked up at him, letting a smile play at the corners of her mouth. "Why don't we put a wager on it?"

He dipped his head closer to her, getting into her personal space. If she were the least bit interested in him, she'd have flutters in her stomach right now. As it was, she just wanted to back up. "What do you intend to wager?"

"Well, I've got a stake in a company that could use venture capital."

Something sharp glinted in his eyes, as if he smelled a setup. "You don't say."

"I do say. And it's something that would fit right into your portfolio."

"You're asking for what? An investment?"

"Not an investment. Just a meeting with you and your partners. I've got an advisory share in this business, and between you and me, I wouldn't bother if I didn't think I could make money. But we need start-up capital."

He stepped back, his expression closing. "I don't mix business with pleasure. And I know a hustle when I see one."

Yeah, she was kind of thinking he might. "So? What do you have to lose but an hour of your time? Unless you're not confident in your pool skills. They looked pretty good to me, but then again, you haven't seen what I've got."

A smile returned to his face. "Okay. But I can't be the only one risking something. You win, I give you and your business partner a meeting. I win, you go on a date with me."

"Now that doesn't seem equitable," she said, a teasing note in her voice.

"Those are my terms."

She held those dark eyes with her own and then gave a little nod. "You're on. I'll even let you break."

He grabbed the square of chalk and twisted it viciously onto the tip of his cue. A glint of determination showed in his eyes. Now she knew she'd read him right. Arrogant, in constant need of challenge, a chance to prove himself. He must know now that her novice act had been a put-on, but he was sure enough in his skills to pit them against whatever she might bring to the table. Or maybe he just thought women couldn't play pool. Either way, it was irrelevant. She wasn't going out on a date with this guy, and they needed that meeting.

She set up the table and then shoved the rack beneath it.

As she stood back, her eyes automatically wandered to where she'd left Bryan at the bar. He was gone. Great. Hopefully he hadn't decided to take off without her. Surely he could guess what she was doing here.

"One ball, corner pocket," Adrian said, then proceeded to sink it with precision. No hesitation, just the confidence of a man who had spent way too much time at the table. He proceeded to sink the next three with the same directness.

And then on his fifth shot, he hit the cue ball just off-center, enough to alter its spin. The five ball hit the edge of the pocket and veered off. Adrian swore under his breath.

Ana didn't bother to flirt or console. They both knew this was no longer anything personal. She chalked her cue, moved to find her position, and sank her first ball with every bit of the precision he'd shown. She glanced up at him, hoping to catch a glimmer of realization of the trouble he was in, but his eyes were fixed firmly on her backside. She straightened and sighed. So maybe this was a little personal.

Too bad for him, she'd spent an entire year of her life in dive bars, killing time by playing pool. One after another, she called her shots and sank each ball in order. Some rammed into the back of the pocket with authority; others took their soft, precisely determined trajectory around the table. She couldn't help looking up triumphantly at Adrian as she lined up her eighth and final shot, an easy straight shot into the side pocket. But instead of Adrian's face she glimpsed Bryan just beyond his shoulder, his eyes fixed on her, his brow furrowed. If she didn't know better, she'd think he looked angry.

Or jealous.

She blew out her breath at the sudden flip-flop of her stomach.

"What's wrong? Feeling the pressure?" Adrian taunted, his handsome face lighting up with amusement.

Not anymore. She lined up the shot, pulled back the stick, and just barely tapped the cue ball to the eight ball. It placidly rolled and dropped in the pocket.

Ana allowed herself a smile before she straightened her face and turned. Adrian was standing directly behind her, a grudging smile on his face. And between the tips of his first two fingers, a business card.

"Fair is fair," he said. "Call me tomorrow and we'll set something up."

Ana plucked the card from his fingertips and tucked it into her pocket. "Thank you. I'll look forward to that."

He stepped a bit closer and bent down. "You sure I can't convince you of that date anyway? There's a great new place that opened up near Union Station last week."

Ana peeped up at him through her lashes and gave what she hoped looked like a secretive smile. "I'll think about it. Thanks for the game."

She gathered her purse and strode toward Bryan. "That was fun. Are you ready to go?"

He studied her for a long moment. "You sure you don't want to stay?"

"No, I got what I came for. Let's go. This music is giving me a headache."

Bryan followed her through the club to the exit, close enough that she could sense his presence. She could almost feel the tension pouring off him. What did he have to be tense about? Other than the fact his so-called friends were kind of jerks?

They walked a safe distance apart on the sidewalk, not talking, Ana's arms wrapped around herself against the chilly night, Bryan's hands thrust in his pockets. Only when they got back to the car did he finally speak.

"I had no idea you could play pool," he said.

"There's a lot you don't know about me." The adrenaline of the challenge, the energy from being "on," suddenly drained from her body and all she felt was weariness. "But we got what we came for."

"That's what you said, but from my perspective it was a big bust."

"I thought we went to see your friends."

"*Friends* might have been overstating things."

"Frenemies?"

"Guys don't have frenemies." The thundercloud was fading from his expression. "You know, Adrian really isn't a bad guy. The fact he cares that much about his sister proves it."

"He's over it," Ana said. "Besides, I'm not interested in anything but his business sense and his company's pockets." She pulled the card from her pocket and handed it to him. "I'm supposed to call him tomorrow. He'll take our pitch. Or more accurately, *my* pitch."

Bryan studied the card. "I don't understand. You looked pretty cozy over there."

"Just business." She took the card back and slipped it into her purse. "I played him for it. He's a gambler. He saw the hustle coming and played me anyway."

Bryan nodded and put the car in gear. After they'd pulled onto the street, he said, "So I should let you take the lead on this?"

"For now. I've got his attention, and this fits really nicely within his portfolio. We don't want him to get distracted by animosity toward you. Or the burden of pretending he's still mad. Like I said, he's just yanking your chain."

"How do you know that?"

"I told you, I read people for a living." She pressed a hand to her mouth to suppress a yawn. Why was she so tired all of a sudden?

Another long stretch of silence and Bryan asked, "Where *did* you learn to play like that?"

Ana licked her lips and stared out the window, sorting through plausible answers. In the end, she decided to just be honest.

"You're not the only one with a past you'd like to forget."

Chapter Ten

Ana should have woken still glowing in the aftermath of her victory, but the only thing she felt was a vague sense of unease. She couldn't place it immediately. She was used to waking stressed, her mind instantly going to the challenges of her day, but this was something different. It felt suspiciously like shame.

Except she had nothing to feel ashamed about. It had been a successful evening. She'd beaten a guy at his own game, literally, and now they had a chance to get the funding that Bryan needed to make Solid Grounds a success. Or a real business, at least. There was still the question of four thousand pounds of beans in transit from Colombia and nothing to roast them with.

Enough navel-gazing. She didn't have the time or the patience to mine the reason behind every weird feeling that flitted through her body. She'd already slept far later than she was accustomed to—she placed the time at 8 a.m. from the sunlight streaming through the window before she ever looked at the clock. That meant not only had she missed her chance for spin class, she'd missed Mass at Holy Ghost. Which also meant that she was going to have to dodge her mother's calls for another week so she didn't have to lie to her. She'd officially left the Catholic faith a long time ago, but being born Filipino in California made attending Mass more of a cultural expectation than any particular question of doctrine. So every Sunday she attended the same nondenominational church that her friends did; every Wednesday morning, she made her trek to the historic church in Lower Downtown. That way when her mom asked if she was going to Mass, she could honestly say yes.

Besides, there was something comforting about the ritual and pageantry of her youth. It was easy to feel disconnected here in Denver; the faster the city grew, the more anonymous it became, a Silicon Valley clone where everyone kept their heads down and worked long hours until they could escape to the Rockies on the weekend with their skis or mountain bikes. At least when she walked into the church, she got that feeling of connection to who she used to be, who she'd always been.

It was also a reminder of who she would never be again.

And there she was navel-gazing. She threw back the satiny cotton sheets, padded to her closet for her workout clothes, and swapped her nightgown for a pair of shorts and a sports bra. An hour on the treadmill was almost always better than therapy. And it would keep her from picking up the phone too early and calling Adrian. He'd said morning, but there was no need to look too eager. She should make him wonder how serious she'd been about the meeting after all.

She clicked on the large television opposite her treadmill and set it to the morning news, then programmed her route on the treadmill's screen. She'd been thinking about California, so she set it for part of the San Francisco Marathon course. The hills would wring every last bit of discomfort out of her body, and then she'd be too tired to analyze why she was still feeling weird about last night.

An hour later, she was climbing off the treadmill, her quads and calves burning. Another hour after that, she was showered, made-up, and dressed presentably in her casual uniform of skinny jeans, a button-down blouse, and her favorite pointy-toed flats. Now she was ready for a phone call. She settled at the kitchen table with her planner, her cell phone, and that heavy vellum business card.

Adrian picked up on the third ring, his voice warm and deep. "Ana. You called. I was wondering if you would."

Ana smiled so the expression would transmit through the line in her voice. "Then you don't know me all that well. I always follow up when there's money on the line."

"You're right. I don't know you at all. But I'd like to remedy that. Have you considered my offer?"

"Of a meeting? Of course. I'd like to set one up at your earliest convenience."

"That's not what I meant."

Ana let the pause stretch for a moment, then softened her voice. "I don't mix business with pleasure either. So let's deal with the matter at hand, and the other . . . well, I'll think about it."

"Depending on the outcome of the meeting?"

"No, depending on how much you irritate me during the negotiations."

He laughed again. There was apparently no putting this guy off. "I've got an opening on Tuesday morning. Ten o'clock. Can you make it?"

"We'll be there."

"We?"

"Myself and Bryan Shaw."

A long pause, this time on his side. "I was afraid you were going to say that."

This was where the whole thing could fall apart. She chose her words carefully. "I'm curious how long you're going to keep up the pretense about being mad over your sister."

"He told you that?"

"He had no reason not to. I told you: we're friends and we work together. But I also know that you just like needling him when you see him."

"I don't like the guy."

"You don't have to like the guy. He's going to make you a lot of money."

Now she could hear his smile through the line. "Okay then. Tuesday at ten."

"We'll see you then. I'm looking forward to it."

"Oh, so am I."

Ana clicked off the line and blew out her breath. That had gone just about as well as she expected, though it was far from perfect. In an ideal world, he would have asked her about this business so he could do his homework. The fact he didn't made her think he was just taking the meeting so he could see her again.

So why is that such a bad thing? He's good-looking, successful, probably a lot of fun. Never mind that she hadn't felt even a stirring of attraction beyond the general admiration of a pretty face. That didn't necessarily mean anything. She hadn't exactly been focused on romance when she was at the club, and she had the tendency to be pretty one-track when she had a mission. Last night, she'd definitely had a mission.

But there had been that odd little moment when she'd caught Bryan watching her, when she'd thought he looked jealous. Likely she'd misread that expression, but he'd clearly been troubled. Maybe he knew something about Adrian she didn't. He was smart enough to know that insulting a guy a woman was interested in often had the opposite effect from the one intended.

Only one way to find out. She dialed Bryan's number.

He picked up immediately, the sound of sawing and hammering in the background. "Good morning."

"Hey, Bryan. I have news. Where are you?"

"At the roastery. We're making progress. You should come by and see. Are you free?"

She was nothing but free. A week into her vacation, working out and watching TV was already getting old. "Address?"

He gave it to her and she scrawled it inside her planner. "I'll be there in twenty."

"I can't wait. See you then."

Ana clicked off, grabbed her purse, planner, and keys, and headed straight for the door.

Exactly twenty minutes later, she pulled up in front of the address he'd given her, squinting through the tinted passenger window. It was an old building in an unfashionable neighborhood, which made it perfect for a boho/hipster sort of business. She smiled to herself and circled the block one more time before she found street parking. That was something they'd have to address if they ever had guests—parking was something of a nightmare during the middle of the day due to the warehouses down the street. She hopped out of her car, locked it with the fob, then strode down the sidewalk to the building.

She could hear the construction noise through the open door, and she slipped in quietly so she could observe without being noticed. The small office space in the front was partially finished and empty of workmen except for one in a T-shirt, shorts, and a tool belt, hammering nails into planks of reclaimed wood on the back wall.

Scratch that . . . *Bryan* was standing on the ladder, hammering nails into planks of wood. She watched for a second as he fished a nail from between his lips, lined it up, and drove it into the wood with two strokes. Obviously he was no stranger to construction.

"Turns out you're a man of many talents," she said.

He whipped his head around in surprise, and then his expression melted into a smile. "You don't know everything about me," he teased, sending her words from last night back at her. He holstered the hammer and backed down the ladder to face her. "It's not even close to being done, but what do you think?"

Ana took a look around. It was hard to tell when it was just a brick box with a partially finished wood wall, but she nodded. "This is going to be the front office and retail space?"

"Exactly. We have a cupping room going up in the back. Come. I'll show you the rest."

He jerked his head toward the open doorway and led her into the cavernous warehouse. The beginnings of a massive room had been carved out, framed in wood, the drywall starting to go up on both sides of the walls, insulation peeping out between. "That's going to be bean storage. Controlling the temperature and humidity cuts down on the variability of the roast."

"You're anticipating storing a lot of beans?"

"Not at first. But the room has to be big enough to maneuver a pallet lift around."

This was a level of detail she was completely unfamiliar with—storage and warehousing and all the associated equipment. "Where's the cupping room?"

He led her a little farther back to where a second space was being framed out. "It doesn't look like much right now, but we're going to have a counter with barstools here and the sample roaster behind."

"Any ideas on the design?"

Bryan looked sheepish. "Actually, I was hoping we might be able to enlist Melody to help with that."

"She won't take too much convincing. Assuming you can get her away from the bakery long enough to help."

"That's what I was afraid of. Bittersweet Café seems to be going really well, doesn't it?"

"It's been extremely successful, and the supper club is helping bring in new customers all the time. They're expanding into the space next door. Did you know that?"

"I remember hearing something about that. What's the holdup?"

"Negotiations with the landlord over price. They assumed the lease from the old bakery, and so they're paying way below market value. Seems like he's trying to make it up by charging way more than market value on the spot next door. Rachel's letting him cool his heels right now. It's been nine months and he hasn't been able to fill it. He's got to break sometime."

"You two are a bit scary, you know that?" Bryan said it in an admiring way, and Ana couldn't help but smile.

"I'll take that as a compliment. Speaking of . . . we have a meeting with Adrian Valencia on Tuesday at 10 a.m."

His whole expression brightened. "You're amazing. But wait . . . *we*?"

"Yes, you and me."

Doubt surfaced in his face. "Are you sure that's such a good idea?"

"He's not mad over his sister anymore. He just doesn't like you."

"And that's better?"

Ana grinned. "I told him to get over it because you were going to make him a lot of money. You need to be there, Bryan. It's your company. It's your vision. And if he happens to make us an offer while we're there, it's your decision."

He still looked doubtful. "This isn't exactly my strength, Ana."

She squeezed his arm, momentarily distracted by the feel of muscle beneath her hand. He'd quit climbing, but he definitely hadn't let himself go. What was she going to say? Oh, right. "You underestimate yourself. You explained yourself quite well to me, and I'm a tough audience. I can help with the presentation, but I think it's better that you do the talking. Adrian needs to have confidence in the person who's actually running the company, especially considering your history together."

He ran a hand through his hair, looking suddenly young and unsure of himself. She'd never seen him anything but completely confident, and it threw her.

"Hey. What's with the sudden modesty? You have more confidence than anyone I know."

"Hasn't worked out so well for me so far, has it?" he muttered, almost to himself. To her, he looked up with surprising directness. "I've got a lot riding on this, Ana. I can't mess it up."

"You won't. We won't." She nudged him with her shoulder. "Come on. Let's go grab lunch and we'll form an attack plan."

"Okay, let me tell the guys I'm leaving." He unbuckled his tool belt and disappeared into the bean storage room for a moment, then returned. "I'll come back to check on their progress and finish the wood cladding."

Ana led him to where her car was parked down the street, soaking up the April sunshine as they walked. "So, construction?"

"Why is that so hard to believe?"

"I don't know. It just never seemed like your thing."

He shrugged. "It wasn't. But the Flor de Oro farm was pretty much falling down around us. It's not like here. You don't just call up a contractor. The workers and I did a lot of repairs to the farmhouse and the bunkhouses. To be fair, I got tired of falling through the floor of my bunk."

"You weren't living in the farmhouse?"

"Of course not. That's Edgar and Maria's place, and it will be for as long as they're alive. I'm not going to move seventy-somethings off their land just because I own it."

Ana sent him a curious look. He'd always been so funny and flippant that this heartfelt side of him was almost disconcerting. "That place really got into you."

"It was eye-opening. We have no idea, here. We live so removed from everything in cities." He shrugged. "I mean, I guess I've never exactly been on board with typical American consumerism, but when you live on a farm according to the rhythm of the seasons . . . it's different."

Ana nodded slowly. "I guess it would be."

"I want to do right by Edgar and Maria. They were kind to me at a time when I really needed kindness. I mean, I want to make my money back, of course." He laughed self-consciously. "Living with your parents is understandable when you're twenty. At thirty-six, it feels more like failure. But for once in my life, I'm connected to something."

His words stirred something in her she couldn't quite name. Wasn't that what she had been thinking this morning? About how disconnected she felt at times in Denver? There had to be something more than just work and friends, on endless repeat. When she glanced over at Bryan, she finally put a label on it. Kinship. Understanding. Maybe he'd felt the same vague emptiness that she'd woken up with and decided to do something about it.

"What do your parents think about this?" she asked, just to fill the silence.

"I think they're reserving judgment. My mom is the ultimate cheerleader, but I suspect my dad just thinks I'm a screwup."

"I don't think he believes that. Your parents are proud of what you've accomplished in your climbing career."

"Which I walked away from, without any backup." He stopped. "Wait. Wasn't that your car?"

Ana jolted to a stop and looked across the street, where her car indeed stood waiting. She would have walked right past it. Her cheeks heated. "Yeah. I guess I wasn't paying attention." She clicked the key fob, unlocking the doors with a chirp, and they dashed across the street.

When they were both settled in the car's luxurious interior, he asked, "Where to?"

"I was thinking Bittersweet. We can ask Melody about lending her design skills to the place."

"You move fast."

"Every day we waste is another day you're not earning back your investment. Don't worry, Bryan. I'll do everything in my power to make sure this isn't a bust. Assuming you can roast the beans, I'm pretty sure I can sell them."

He reached across and placed his hand over hers on the gearshift. "Thank you, Ana. I mean that."

She glanced down at his hand covering hers and then up into his eyes, her breath momentarily catching. "That's what friends are for."

*   *   *

The tension in the car was palpable, and it was all Bryan's fault. He jerked his hand back into his lap and cursed himself for not thinking. Ana had always been a bit touchy about people getting in her personal space; he'd known that about her from the start. She held it around her like a force field, making men in particular back off to a respectful distance. Which was why he'd been so surprised that she'd let Adrian get up beside her like he had last night. No matter what she said, she didn't do that lightly. She must be really interested.

Which was also why he was stupid for feeling this sudden

sense of closeness with her. He'd never been the type to let feelings hijack him, at least where anyone but Vivian was concerned. He was letting his fear of failure get to him, and his relief that he wasn't in this alone. If he wanted to keep Ana on board as his advisor—and he hoped his partner—he needed to keep things strictly businesslike.

He turned the conversation to something more on-topic. "So is this a PowerPoint kind of meeting? Should I be thinking about condensing the business down to slides?"

Ana seemed to be thinking. "It would be a good idea, even though I think this is the kind of meeting where you go in with copies of your business plan, revenue projections, and a story. Adrian is the type to get excited about a concept and how it fits into his portfolio of businesses. He told me all about this Paleo foods company he invested in, so I think we can definitely go with the virtue sell. He likes being on the right side of social and cultural issues."

"You got all that from a game of pool?" Bryan asked.

"I got all that from him trying to get me to go out with him," Ana said wryly.

"Did it work?"

"I'm still deciding." She said it so matter-of-factly, he wondered what kind of calculations it would take for the venture capitalist to get a yes. Did Ana have line charts in her head for this sort of thing, where the x axis was attractiveness and the y axis was time? A guy who was good-looking enough and persistent enough would finally get to take her out? Or did the labels say "money" and "success" or some other variant of what she might consider in a partner?

As if most women weren't a conundrum as it was, Ana had to go and be unlike any other woman he'd met. He wished Adrian luck; he'd need it.

In midday surface traffic, it didn't take long to reach Platt

Park, where Rachel and Melody's bakery was located, but it took almost as long to find parking on the intersecting streets. "We might need to wait for a table," Ana said. "Is that okay with you?"

"Of course." He hopped out of the SUV and waited for her to join him on the sidewalk as they walked toward Bittersweet. Sure enough, the line at the counter was just starting to burst out the door when they arrived.

"Didn't take long," he said, gesturing to the crowd. "The food's amazing, though."

"And the press has been good." Ana threw him a mischievous look. "Never underestimate the value of a good publicist."

"You did this?"

"No, they did this. I just helped get the word out. Call it a personal project."

He had a sudden feeling she'd done far more than she was letting on. "So Solid Grounds will benefit from the Analyn Sanchez special treatment?"

"Well, if your beans are any good, I know your first customer." She gestured to the counter, where the barista was pulling a shot for a coffee drink. "They've gone through three coffee suppliers since they opened. The one they're using now is good, but not locally roasted, so I know Rachel will be open to trying you out. And if it's successful, that means point-of-purchase bean sales."

The line crept forward and Ana continued. "There's also a handful of restaurants I've done publicity for that might be interested in featuring your coffee. And I do mean featuring. Like I said, local is a big deal around here."

Bryan looked down at his T-shirt, which bore a version of the Colorado state flag on the front, and grinned.

"Exactly. You'd never see Californians wearing their state flag on their chest. Only tourists."

"That's because everyone in California is from somewhere else," he said. "Coloradoans are rightly proud of our state."

They finally reached the counter and placed their order. Bryan opened his wallet, but Ana waved him off. "My treat. Consider it part of my advisory duties. It's a business lunch."

He considered arguing, but she looked determined, and a determined Ana always got what she wanted. He replaced it in his pocket and said, "Only if I buy next time."

"Deal," she said. "Grab the table tag?"

"Yes, ma'am."

They found two spots at the long counter-height table at the back, wedged in between some other business-lunchers, and Ana vanished into the kitchen without a word. Probably to tell Rachel and Melody they were there. Then she came back and plopped on her seat. "Melody said she'd come out in a bit. I might have also told them our table number."

"Special treatment, huh?"

Ana shrugged, but she was smiling that mysterious smile again. What was she thinking when she did that? It was as if she was perpetually amused by how she massaged the system. The way she could work a room was a thing of beauty; she'd definitely gone for the throat with Adrian. But she hadn't seemed nearly as pleased with herself last night. Why?

Their food only took a few minutes to come out, either a result of Rachel's extreme efficiency or the little nudge Ana had given when she disappeared back there. Either way, it looked delicious. Ana had ordered a spring salad that was chock-full of nuts and berries; Bryan had opted for the grilled tuna on olive bread, one of the house specialties. Fortunately, the food negated the necessity of speaking, and therefore wondering about subtext. Just as they were finishing, Melody appeared and plopped herself down on the recently vacated seat beside Ana.

Ana pressed her into a warm hug and brushed a smear of flour off Melody's cheek.

The baker laughed and smiled across the table at Bryan. "Hi there. Ana didn't tell me you were here too." She looked back at Ana with a lifted eyebrow.

Ana didn't even seem to notice. "We have something to ask you."

"Shoot. I only have a couple of minutes, though. Talia's covering for me, but we're slammed today. Every day, actually."

"That's great." Bryan glanced at Ana, who made a gesture that looked something like *hurry up*. "I showed Ana the roastery today. All the structural stuff is coming along, but I have no idea what to do with the cupping room and the front office. I was hoping you might be willing to use your design genius on my behalf."

"Design genius, huh? I like the sound of that." Melody grinned. "I need photos, though. I'm totally visual. If I can see what we're working with, I can start putting together some ideas for you. And I need the measurements, of course."

"I can actually help with that." He pulled his phone from his pocket and found the photos he'd taken when he was with Alex, then texted them to Melody. "And I'll email you the measurements later."

"Sounds good. I'm happy to help." She hopped off the chair and gave Ana one more hug before sending a significant look between them. "I'll see you tonight. I want to hear how everything is going."

"Sure thing." Ana appeared completely unperturbed by what Melody seemed to be insinuating. As soon as Melody was gone, she shot him a satisfied smile. "She was an easy sell."

"Melody's probably the most generous person I've ever met," Bryan said. "When you talk to her, please make sure she understands I'm paying her for her work."

"And she'll likely refuse it. But I'll tell her." Ana gathered her plate and her paper napkins, then slid off her seat. "Ready to go?"

"If you are." They tossed their trash, set their plates in the tubs near the trash cans, and emerged back onto the street. Whatever closeness he thought he'd imagined earlier was gone; she was all business.

Ana slid on her sunglasses. "You want me to drop you back at the space?"

"Please. We never did talk about the presentation, though. You free for dinner one of these nights?"

She sent him a look.

"I just thought dinner would be more convenient. I'm going to be working at the construction site until it's done, trying to save a little money on labor. There's that noodle shop on Seventeenth. They don't mind if you bring in your laptop and work while you eat."

"Oh." She pulled out her planner and checked her calendar quickly. "How about tomorrow night? That still gives us three days to polish before we meet with him on Tuesday."

"Works for me. Pick you up?"

"No, I'll meet you there. Seven?"

He nodded. "Sounds good to me. Thanks again, Ana. I do appreciate it."

"I know," she said lightly, then unlocked her car door and climbed in, clearly the end of the conversation.

Chapter Eleven

"YOU'RE GOING OUT WITH HIM *AGAIN*?"

Ana paused in her coffee-pouring to look at Melody. "No, I'm having a business dinner with him. That doesn't constitute going out."

"Who's paying?" Rachel asked, pulling a carton of vanilla ice cream from her old avocado-green freezer. At long last, they'd managed to put together a nonemergency girls' night at Rachel's house that they could all attend. Odd that now Ana was the one with the wide-open schedule and Rachel and Melody were the ones who had to squeeze her in.

"What's the deal with this arrangement anyway?" Melody took the ice cream from Rachel and began scooping little football-shaped dollops on top of the turtle brownies she'd made at the bakery for this very reason.

Ana finished pouring the coffee from the French press into three mugs and fixed them with varying degrees of cream and sugar, her own staying black. "Basically, I'm a business advisor. If we get this investment, we'll determine the valuation of the business and I'll get my equity share."

"So you're working for nothing unless he makes money," Melody said.

"I'm still getting paid at a job I'm not doing. I don't need another paycheck right now. Besides, he's a friend. It's not like I left you guys in the lurch when you opened Bittersweet or anything."

"No one's saying you did." Rachel handed the completed sundae to Ana, then took one for herself along with her cup of coffee. "Living room?"

"You guys didn't need as much help. Bryan's on a time crunch and a shoestring budget. But he's got a good story for marketing, and if the product is good, I think it could be successful." Ana took a spot in the lone armchair in Rachel's living room, positioning herself opposite the green velvet sofa and curling her bare feet up beneath her. "Besides, it gives me something to do."

"I knew you were missing work," Rachel said, settling on one end of the sofa. "How long exactly did you take off from doing anything work related?"

Ana frowned. "I don't know. A week maybe?"

Rachel held out her hand to Melody. "You owe me five bucks."

Melody sighed. "You're seriously going to collect on that?"

"Collect on what?" Ana looked between the two of them suspiciously.

"I bet Melody that you wouldn't last more than a week before you found some sort of job or side hustle to keep you busy. Sitting still isn't your strong suit."

"I don't know whether to be mad or to demand a cut," Ana said.

"Neither." Melody rummaged in her purse before coming up with a five-dollar bill, which she handed off to Rachel. "It's just the way you are. You hate being idle. But seriously . . . Bryan?"

"I know." Ana took a sip of her coffee. "I actually feel bad for underestimating him. Did you know he graduated magna cum laude with his business degree? Underneath all that Colorado casual is some brains. And honestly, I think he's a lot more thoughtful than I've given him credit for."

Melody and Rachel exchanged a glance.

Ana sighed. "Okay, enough with these meaningful glances. Just say what you want to say."

Another glance before Rachel realized what they were doing and grimaced. "Bryan has been interested in you romantically from the moment he saw you. Are you sure he's not just taking this as an opportunity to get close to you?"

"It doesn't matter if he is or not, because I'm not interested in him that way." Ana sipped her coffee, then realized her friends were staring at her. "What? I'm not."

"Feeling a little warm over there, liar?" Melody asked. "Because from where I'm sitting, your pants are on fire."

Ana sighed. "Fine. I'm attracted to him. I always have been. But it's a just a chemical thing. We can't control who gives us butterflies, but we can control our own stupid decisions. And he is most definitely not suitable for more than friendship or a business relationship."

"He gives her butterflies," Rachel said flatly to Melody, and they both looked at Ana with raised eyebrows.

"Oh, for heaven's sake." Ana uncrossed her legs and jumped up from her seat, almost upsetting her sundae. "If you're just going to jab me about Bryan all night, I might as well leave."

"No, don't do that, Ana." Melody managed to sound a little contrite. "We'll lay off. We just find your choice of entertainment on your time off a bit . . . interesting."

Ana paused and then sat back down, regretting her emotional outburst. She wasn't usually that touchy, but to be fair, it had been a pretty trying couple of weeks. "The thing is, guys, I think this business could be really exciting. I know there are some local roasters who are already getting beans from repurposed coca plantations, but to build a business completely from fair-trade, organic, redeemed farms . . . that's something I can sell." Come to think of it, there was a lot more they could do with the socially conscious angle than just the coca-to-coffee thing. She pulled up her phone and tapped a few ideas into her notes app. "If I could get Kenneth Lazarus on board . . ."

"Who's Kenneth Lazarus?" Melody asked at the same time Rachel said, "Oh, I love him!"

"Recently retired Rockies pitcher," Ana explained. "I didn't know you liked baseball, Rachel."

"Alex does. We watched the entire last season together. We're talking about getting season tickets one of these days. Turns out when I have time for sports, I actually kind of like them."

"Traitor," Melody said, and Rachel and Ana laughed. Melody's idea of sports was reading about lawn tennis or croquet in her extensive collection of classic novels.

"What about him, Ana?" Rachel asked.

"Well, he has that whole foundation teaching baseball to inner-city kids to keep them away from drugs. If we could do some sort of benefit, with Solid Grounds providing the coffee, it would be great publicity. The tie-in makes so much sense."

"That's the name of the company? Solid Grounds?" Rachel turned it over for a moment. "I love that. It fits so well."

In more ways than one. Bryan really seemed dedicated to the venture, determined to build something steady and lasting. She wouldn't be surprised if it had taken on a new layer of meaning for him as well.

"Anyway, this all hinges on us getting the funding, buying the equipment, and roasting the beans. I've done a little research, and it sounds like there are a lot of elements that go into making coffee good or not. The bean quality has a lot to do with it, but so does the skill of the roaster. You can make up for lower-grade beans, depending on the faults, if you're a good roaster, but even great beans won't meet their full potential if you don't know how to treat them."

"And you think Bryan has that level of skill?" Melody asked, a tinge of skepticism in her voice.

Ana quashed down a sudden swell of defensiveness. "I honestly have no idea. I hope so, or this whole thing is going to be a bust. I looked up the guy he learned from in Oregon and he's pretty much regarded as the father of the third-wave coffee movement, so I'd like to believe that Bryan knows what he's doing."

"Well, I should have some design ideas for him in two weeks," Melody said. "I just need the dimensions of the space so I can draw it out. Speaking of . . . What did you think about the sketches I sent you last night, Rachel?"

"I got busy with the deliveries and totally forgot to tell you. They're amazing. Ana, did you see these?" Rachel pulled out her phone and brought up her photo gallery, then passed it to Ana.

"These are for the farm?" Ana scrolled through the sketches. Melody's vision was beautiful and magical, and yet they still had the stripped-down industrial vibe that Ana had come to associate with Rachel's minimalist taste. Rustic wooden tables, old-fashioned metal folding chairs, earthenware place settings with a mix of textures and colors. "It's like supper club, wedding edition!"

Rachel laughed. "I never thought of it that way, but that's exactly right. I love it."

"These are fantastic, Mel," Ana said softly, feeling a pang at the realization that once again, she hadn't been included. "What do you need me to do?"

"I've already ordered the rentals for the tables and chairs," Melody said. "If you can just help me with the coordination of the rest of the decor, I think we'll be good. Rachel has the food thing in hand."

"Caleb Sutter agreed to cater," Rachel said.

"No! Seriously?" Caleb Sutter was perhaps the hottest chef in Denver—a spot that would rightly be Rachel's had she not decided to step out of the fine dining space in favor of Bittersweet—and currently had two of the most celebrated restaurants in the city. He'd also been one of the chefs who had abandoned her in her hour of need, not wanting to hitch his own career to hers.

Rachel nodded slowly. "He's had this farm concept in the works for a while, and with the success of the Saturday Night Supper Club, he wants to start his own down at his farm. My wedding is going to be something of a proof of concept for him. I gave him free rein, of course . . ."

"Of course." Ana shook her head. "This is going to be amazing, Rachel. The event of the year."

"Even better, I got my dress back from the seamstress today. Do you want to see the finished version? The sample you saw doesn't really do it justice."

Melody and Ana stared at her. "Um, yes," they said in unison.

Rachel laughed. "Stay here. I'll bring it out."

As soon as she left the room, Ana looked at Melody and said, "I can't believe she didn't lead with that. It's all about the dress."

"Not for Rachel. It's all about the food and the place settings. I had to remind her that you couldn't buy a wedding dress off the rack."

"Well, you could, but you shouldn't. What's taking her so long? I thought she was just bringing it out."

Rachel appeared in the doorway then, and they gasped. She wasn't carrying the dress, but wearing it, a simple confection of draped white silk muslin with a deep-V halter.

Ana rose to her feet. "Rachel, that's stunning."

"I never expected to go for couture, but I couldn't help myself with this one." She gave a little twirl, showing that the halter straps crisscrossed over the back and then tied in front again as a belt. "And look, it has pockets!"

"Hallelujah," Melody said. "A designer finally figured out that brides need pockets." She pressed her hands to her mouth, tears forming in her eyes.

"Oh, Mel, don't cry." Rachel rushed to her and put her arms around her. "I didn't mean to make you feel bad."

"You didn't!" Melody squeezed her and then backed away. "You're just such a beautiful bride."

Rachel sank down onto the sofa, just inches from where Melody had left her chocolate-covered dessert. Ana cringed and swooped it out of the way before it had a chance to tip. "Are you sure that's all it is?"

"Of course," Melody said brightly. "And now I know how I'm going to tweak the design of the place settings to match the dress. It's going to be beautiful."

Rachel looked like she wanted to argue more, but Melody's posture said she just wanted to drop the subject. Ana jumped in. "Remind me what kind of flowers you selected, Rachel?"

"Well, I'd picked roses and lilies, but that was before we had the farm setting. I mean, we're going to be on a flower farm. Do you think Darcy would do my flowers?"

"I think she would be delighted to do your bouquet and arrangements," Ana said.

Melody jumped in. "What about your deposit for the other florist?"

"I'll take care of that," Ana said. "If we agree to do some business with them next year, I'm sure . . ." She broke off when she realized she no longer had any influence over what Massey-Coleman did. As far as the other publicists were concerned, she was all but fired. It was going to come as a huge surprise when she showed up in fifteen weeks and got back to work.

"It's okay," Rachel said. "He can keep the deposit. It's my fault that I made the change. I just think there's a poetic symmetry about having the flowers done where the wedding is being held."

"Woo, poetic symmetry," Melody said. "Someone's getting all romantic."

Rachel rolled her eyes and got to her feet. "I should get out of this before I mess it up. You really like it?"

"It's gorgeous," Ana said softly. "You make the most beautiful bride. Alex is going to feel like the luckiest man on earth."

Rachel repressed her smile, but happiness practically seeped from her pores, giving her the bride-to-be glow that countless cosmetic manufacturers attempted to bottle. "I'll be right back."

As soon as Rachel left the room, Ana turned on Melody. "Okay, what's up?"

"Why would you say anything's up?"

Ana made a face. "Melody, I know when you're hiding something. Those tears didn't have anything to do with Rachel's dress." She sat down on the sofa next to her. "You can tell me. I won't tell Rachel if you don't want me to." Then a thought hit her. "It isn't Justin, is it?"

"No! At least not in the way you think." Melody glanced nervously toward Rachel's bedroom and lowered her voice. "The charter isn't doing so well in Florida."

Ana's hand moved to her mouth. "Oh no. Justin's dad isn't working out?"

Melody shook her head. "He's great with the pilots, but not so much with the office staff. Monica quit, and she was the backbone of the company's sales and marketing efforts. Justin is worried he's going to need to go out there and get things in hand."

"Oh, Melody. What will you do?"

"I don't know. No, that's not right. I do know. I love him, Ana. If he goes, I'm going with him."

"And you'd be leaving Bittersweet."

Melody nodded. "Neither of us want to leave. Justin loves his job at Mountain State, but he'd have a similar schedule and more freedom if he took the charter over. And Rachel and Alex can afford to buy me out."

Ana sat back on the sofa, feeling like the wind had been taken out of her. She already felt like she was losing Rachel to Alex. If Melody moved away, they'd be losing her for real. No more late-night dessert meetings. They could still have phone calls and out-of-control group texts, but it wasn't the same as being here together.

"On the upside," Melody murmured, "Justin technically owns several planes. I could probably convince him to fly me here for a girls' weekend every couple of months . . ."

"Well, there is that." Ana took herself in hand and hugged Melody hard. "You need to do what's best for you and Justin. You may not be married yet, but we all know you're going to get there."

"He's already starting to get antsy," she said. "And so am I."

"Get thee to a chapel, then," Ana said with a laugh. Melody was a commitment girl at heart, and she was determined to make it to her wedding night before they slept together. But the heat between her and Justin was practically searing, so it couldn't be easy, especially since they'd decided to date for a minimum of a year before they started talking about marriage. Which, by Ana's calculations, was already up.

And even that thought made Ana feel like a loser. She hadn't met a guy who wanted to wait until the second date, let alone until marriage. Modern dating when you were a thirtysomething Christian woman was beginning to feel downright laughable.

Rachel came back, dressed again in her jeans and T-shirt, and looked between them. "What did I miss?"

"Nothing. Just trying to figure out a way to fix the bouquet toss so Melody can catch it." Ana winked at Melody and moved back to her position in the chair, where her ice cream had melted into a pool over the brownie.

"Is that a possibility?" Rachel asked. "Are you really talking about it?"

"We've been talking about it," Melody said. "But I don't want to rush things."

"You've known each other over a year," Rachel said. "That doesn't sound like rushing things."

"And once more, the happily engaged wants everyone else to join in holy matrimony," Melody said, sounding almost like she was quoting out of one of her books. "We need to get you married first. Now, I was thinking . . ."

As Melody detailed more ideas for the wedding venue, Ana listened with half an ear, only contributing when a question was sent in her direction. It was impossible not to look at her two blissfully coupled friends and wonder, if they'd found love, why couldn't she? What was so wrong with her that good men flew from her like mosquitoes from a citronella torch at a barbecue?

No, she knew what. Her mother gave her a list of reasons every time she went home: too independent, too assertive, too opinionated. Too wealthy, even though she was more likely to call herself upwardly mobile. And next month, when she returned home alone for her father's birthday, she would again prove everything they'd always thought about her was true.

Chapter Twelve

BRYAN SHOWED UP at the noodle place at ten minutes to seven, his laptop clutched under his arm, and proceeded to stake out the dining room until the corner booth he wanted was free. The place bustled, but they didn't seem to mind people camping out there to work; most of the turnover was at the long communal counters, where customers slurped bowls of pho garnished with huge sprigs of Thai basil and bean sprouts, holding conversation above a noise level just short of a roar.

It was the very reason he'd suggested the place. It was about as far from a date location as one could get, and the way Ana had balked at seeing him again made him think she still doubted his intentions in spending time with her.

Maybe there was an element of truth in that, hence the more secluded corner table, but the larger reason was that they'd have to be able to communicate to get this presentation hammered out in time for their meeting.

Finally, the trio sitting in the corner got up, and Bryan hovered just out of range until the busboy came to clear their plates and wipe down the table. Then he descended on the booth and booted up his laptop.

"Hey, thanks for getting a seat. I thought we were going to have to wait."

Bryan lifted his head from his notes to find Ana standing there in jeans and a casual blazer, a tote bag slung over her shoulder. Tonight, she had her long black hair twisted up on her head with a clip, a few short tendrils falling free around her nearly makeup-free face. Without the war paint, she looked young and approachable. He figured he should take it as a good sign if she was letting him see her as she really was.

"Can I sit down?" she prompted with an amused smile, and he hastily slid over to make room for her. "Have you ordered yet?"

"No, I was waiting for you." He pushed a paper menu her direction, but she didn't open it.

"I always get the same thing. *Phở bò viên*."

"I never pegged you as a meatball girl. I'm partial to the *phở tái nam* myself." He grinned at her surprised look. "What?"

She held up her hands. "Nothing. It's just that pho has been a thing forever where I grew up. It's only recently gotten fashionable here. Denverites usually aren't that familiar."

"I feel like you just called us provincial or something." But he smiled so she knew he was kidding.

The server came to their table and took their order, and then Ana reached into her bag for a tablet with an attached keyboard. "Do you want to show me what you've got so far?"

Bryan nodded. So they were getting down to business. "Not very much, honestly. I've just pulled out what I think are our biggest selling points and differentiating factors from our competitors."

She leaned a little closer to see his laptop screen, giving him a whiff of an expensive perfume, a mix of florals that he couldn't place. He settled back in his seat so he wouldn't be tempted to inhale more deeply. He could only imagine what she would do if she caught him trying to sniff her.

"I think this is a good start, actually. Why don't we do this . . ."

By the time their steaming bowls of noodle soup arrived at the table, they had the beginnings of an outline put together, pulling figures from his business plan and market-positioning details from Ana's work. She'd apparently done a fair bit of research already; regardless of how this meeting turned out, she was proving her value. They paused and pushed back their laptops long enough to slurp soup from deep spoons and dig out long strands of rice noodles with chopsticks.

Taking the usual flirtation out of their interactions meant that Bryan felt far more comfortable than he ever had around her. He liked her, he realized. She was smart, funny, had something to say on just about every topic, and she knew how to keep a conversation going naturally. Or maybe that was just because they had a lot more in common than he'd thought.

"How did you ever get to the Philippines?" she asked when he revealed that he'd gone there about ten years ago.

"A friend arranged the trip. You know climbers are always seeking out new routes and new locations. It was beautiful. There are some good climbs if you love limestone. I'll admit I was happy to get back home to some granite after two weeks."

"Where exactly were you?"

"Iloilo and then Cantabaco. That's in the Visayas, right?"

Ana nodded and reached for her water glass. "On different islands, but yeah. I have relatives there. My parents are both from Manila, but Mom has cousins in Toledo, which is close to Cantabaco."

"It's gorgeous. Honestly, I wouldn't mind going back just for a vacation. I've been to Hawaii, but the beaches in the Philippines just blow it out of the water. No pun intended."

Ana sent him a smile, clearly pleased by the praise of her parents' homeland. "You could always go back to climb while you're there."

He shook his head.

"Why not? I don't understand why you're refusing to climb. It was more than half your life, Bryan. It's not like you can just turn that part of yourself off."

"I can," he said, "and I have. I've moved on. And I'm not really sure why you're so fixated on it."

Ana held her hands up, looking a little offended. "Fine. I was just trying to help. I thought that's what friends do."

Bryan cringed. The last thing he needed was to alienate her. "I'm sorry. I didn't mean to snap at you. Just, please, try to respect the fact I don't want to talk about it."

She studied him for a long minute, then nodded. "Okay." She began gathering up her things and shoved her tablet back in her shoulder bag. "I'll email you my notes when I get home. You're sure you're comfortable with all of this?"

"Of course," he said, though he was nothing of the sort. "I'll run through the deck a few times before the meeting."

"Just not too much. You don't want it to sound canned."

"Yes, ma'am."

Ana actually flushed. "I'm sorry. This is your business. You'll do great." She slid out of the booth and hovered uncertainly at the edge of the table. "Thanks for dinner."

"Thanks for the help." He watched as she nodded, then turned on her heel and strode from the restaurant. Only then did he let the sigh escape his lips. Just when things got comfortable, he was back to feeling like he was walking on eggshells with her. They were friends, yes, but they weren't close friends. Then again, maybe this was the way Ana showed concern; she had started some serious drama the first time Melody brought Justin to the supper club. Her motivation might have been worry for Melody, but she didn't seem to know when to stop digging.

He needed her to have full confidence in his ability to make this business a success, and to do that, he needed to project certainty. Neither she nor their potential investor needed to know that the last time he'd been absolutely sure about anything was twenty seconds before Vivian plummeted from that crag, ending both of their careers and everything he thought he'd known about his own future.

Chapter Thirteen

ANA WAS NERVOUS.

She couldn't remember the last time she was nervous, certainly not over business. Anxious, maybe; annoyed, frequently . . . but nervous was a new and entirely different sensation for her.

Which made no sense. Over the last several days, she and Bryan had spent hours on the phone and their laptops, finetuning the details, making sure they were prepared for every single eventuality. And she couldn't help but admit that he had a good handle on the presentation. He was smart—far more intelligent than she'd once given him credit for—and he was passionate. But she had still helped shape the pitch, tailoring it to what she knew of Adrian. It was one thing to stake her own career on her instincts. It was another to hinge Bryan's second chance on them.

Please, Jesus, make this go well. Don't let me let Bryan down.

She exhaled the prayer, pushed down her doubts, and sifted through her expansive closet, choosing and discarding half a dozen outfits before she settled on her go-to power combination again: black suit, red blouse, black pumps. It never steered her wrong, and she needed the confidence that came from a bold color and five-inch heels. Maybe it hadn't done her any good the day she'd been fired—put on leave—but no outfit in the world could have changed the direction of that fiasco.

Made-up, adorned with her solitaire necklace and her favorite diamond stud earrings, she grabbed her tote bag containing her laptop, notes, and a hard copy of Bryan's presentation and made her way down to her car. Ten minutes later, she was pulling into the drive of the Shaws' 1920s Capitol Hill mansion. He might not like living at home, but in a house this size, she'd bet he barely saw his parents.

He must have been looking for her, because before she could even get out of the car, the front door opened and Bryan emerged. She did a double-take, her stomach doing an odd little leap. She'd legitimately never seen him in anything dressier than jeans and a sweater, and the other night at the club had been the first time she'd realized he owned anything more formal than T-shirts.

Which was why she barely recognized the man coming toward her car, clean-shaven, the ponytail gone. He'd covered his trim physique in a stylish slim-cut suit in a dark pinstripe and paired it with a not-quite-conservative tie. When he pulled open the car door and climbed into the passenger seat, she got a glimpse of baby-blue socks decorated with scarf-wearing llamas above his dress shoes. Basically, about as on-trend for the millennial businessman as you could get.

"What?" he asked, noticing her attention. "Do I look okay? Should I have worn something else?"

"No," she finally managed. "You look fine. Good, I mean."

He smoothed down his tie and let out a breath, and she realized he was as nervous as she was. "Thanks. If you hadn't guessed, I don't have much use for suits. I had to go shopping."

"The horror," Ana quipped, and she caught his smile out of the corner of her eye as she started down the other side of the circular drive. "If it's any consolation, you look perfect for this meeting. And you wear the suit well; it doesn't wear you."

"I'm not sure I understand what that means."

"You can put some guys in a suit, but they never carry themselves in a way that makes you believe they belong in it."

"Must have been all the practice I put in with my parents' galas. I've been wearing a tux since I was nine."

"And you hated it?"

"Not really." He settled back into the seat. "Mostly I hated having to be on my best behavior. The tuxedo was just details."

Ana laughed. "You may know this since Adrian is your friend—"

"Acquaintance."

Ana dipped her head. "Acquaintance. But he's something of an aspiring mountaineer."

"Oh yeah?"

"He's two peaks away from climbing all the fourteeners in Colorado. I found an interview with him in a local paper."

"That's hiking, not climbing," Bryan said automatically. When she shot him a look, he conceded, "But it is a point of common interest. I get it."

"He is also on the board of a charity that helps kids coming out of juvenile detention develop life and job skills."

Now she could hear a grudging bit of admiration in Bryan's voice. "He's not just a money-hungry suit, you're telling me?"

"I'm saying there's something about this idea that will resonate with him and how he sees himself. Play to that, don't say anything stupid, and I think we've got this in the bag."

"You know, Ana, I'm not completely socially inept."

She flushed. "I know you aren't. But you have the habit of speaking your mind, and I just wanted to remind you—"

THE SOLID GROUNDS COFFEE COMPANY

"That this is not that time. Gotcha." He reached for her and squeezed her forearm quickly. "Don't worry. We've got this. I think you might be more nervous than I am."

"I think you're right. I feel responsible for this meeting, so I really want it to work out."

"Whether or not it does, I'm grateful for your help. Truly."

She braked at a stoplight and glanced over at him. He was looking at her in a way that made something hard in her middle melt: gratitude and something else she couldn't name. Didn't want to name. Now was not the time to think about this. Now was the time to think about business. Game face on.

They reached Adrian's Lower Downtown office building in record time, and Ana pulled into the parking structure beneath the offices. They climbed out, and Ana smoothed her suit, letting out a long, steadying breath. "Now or never."

Bryan nudged her with his elbow. "C'mon. Let's do this."

Adrian's firm, Compeer Capital, was located on the eighth floor of the building, a rigidly professional office with a large glass door and decor bordering on stuffy. All except the art, which Ana didn't recognize except to know that it was original and expensive. There was no shortage of cash here for sure. Bryan gave their names to the perfectly coiffed receptionist at the front desk and then stepped back to admire the art.

"Marcus Lee," he murmured.

She came up beside him. "How do you know?"

"My parents bought one of his paintings at a charity auction." He cast her a quick look, the corner of his mouth lifting. "Personally, I think it's one of the ugliest things I've ever seen."

Ana studied the splash of oranges and yellows. "They're power colors. Pretty sure they picked the painting solely for that reason."

"Well, that's telling, isn't it?" He smiled down at her, and the nerves dissipated. They were in this together. And they were going to walk out of this building with the money he needed for his equipment.

"Bryan, Ana." Adrian's voice boomed out behind them and they turned. Adrian strode toward them, his hand outstretched, and they each shook it. He was dressed as formally as they were, in a navy-blue suit and power tie. Another man who wore it well, but this one clearly knew it.

"Thanks for seeing us," Ana said.

"It's my pleasure. Follow me. We've got the conference room." He turned and led them behind the reception desk to a long hall with glassed-in offices, all filled by men—and precious few women—on their phones or glued to their computers. At the end, he made a sharp right and led them into a large conference room with an oval table and an expansive view of downtown Denver from the floor-to-ceiling windows. He took a seat on one side of the table with his back to the view and gestured for them to take chairs opposite.

"Are we waiting for your associates?" Ana said, slipping herself into the large leather seat.

Adrian unbuttoned his jacket and leaned back in the chair. "No, it's just me. To be honest, your business is just too small for Compeer to be interested. It's not investable."

"Then why are we here?" Bryan asked, his tone neutral. "Other than Ana's pool skills?"

A smile flitted across Adrian's face. "Because I think you have an interesting idea. And because I've acted as an angel investor for more than one start-up, and this concept fits nicely into my portfolio."

"I'd hoped you were going to say that," Ana said. "Given your interest in Velocity, it seemed to be right in your wheelhouse."

Adrian focused on Ana, his gaze barely flicking to Bryan. "So tell me, what do you have for me?"

Bryan pulled out his laptop and opened to his presentation.

He'd planned on projecting it to the conference room screen, but since it was just the three of them, he swiveled it around so Adrian could view his pitch deck. He started with the cover slide that had a stock coffee photo and the preliminary tagline Ana had come up with, then flicked over to the photo of Flor de Oro's previous owners that he'd taken before he left, their wrinkled faces creased into smiles.

"This is Edgar and Maria Hernández, the third generation of Hernándezes to live and work on the Flor de Oro farm near Manizales, Colombia." Bryan went into the story he'd told Ana and the supper club, about how they had been forced to switch from their family's traditional coffee crops to growing coca in order to keep their farm solvent. Through the whole story, Adrian's expression remained unreadable, even when Bryan detailed how their son had been killed because of his involvement with the cartels.

"Café Libertad helped them make the transition back to coffee. However, they're getting to where they can no longer manage the farm themselves, which is where I came in. I'm currently the sole owner and a farmer-member of the Café Libertad co-op, which has more than twenty-five farms in that region alone. The advantage to owning the farm from which we're sourcing our beans is that it gives us control over the quality of our supply as well as significantly decreasing the variable costs."

Bryan clicked through his deck as he outlined the numbers, from expected overhead costs to revenue projections. Adrian threw back his own set of questions, which Bryan answered smoothly and confidently. Then Adrian glanced at Ana. "And what's your role in this venture?"

"I'm an advisor. My job is to work with distribution channels for the finished product along with coordinating our marketing and messaging. As you probably already know, I'm currently a publicist for Massey-Coleman. I hold a degree in communication and media studies from USC as well as an MBA from Berkeley."

"That's very impressive," Adrian murmured, his eyes staying on Ana for just a touch too long. Then he looked back to Bryan. "I'm going to go out on a limb for you. Assuming everything is in line, I'd be willing to invest fifty thousand dollars for equipment and packaging, but I want a 50 percent stake in the company."

"No," Bryan said flatly.

Ana glanced at him. "You're putting the valuation at a hundred thousand dollars. That's a bit shortsighted."

"That's generous," Adrian said. "As you well know, the coffee business is extremely competitive. Your entire concept is based on the social-responsibility angle, but your supply is small. If you don't have beans from former coca plantations, you don't have a business. And agriculture in general is risky."

Ana chose her words carefully. "Given Bryan has already made a significant investment, I don't think that's something we're willing to do."

Adrian shrugged. "That's my offer."

Bryan's gaze never left Adrian's face. "I'm asking fifty thousand for 15 percent."

Adrian smiled. "This isn't *Shark Tank*, Bryan. We're not negotiating here. I'm largely doing this as a favor, and given our history, I think that's more than generous."

"You're doing this because you like the story behind the company, and you like what it says about you if you invest in it." Bryan cocked his head. "If I'm not mistaken, your family is from Venezuela; isn't that right?"

Adrian looked taken aback.

"Last time I checked, Venezuela was the main route for trafficking cocaine from Colombia to the rest of the world, particularly Europe. In fact, the American crackdown on the

Colombian cartels and the Venezuelan government's lack of interest in the antidrug campaign—and corruption, of course—has resulted in a large number of traffickers moving into the region. I'll be the first to admit that I don't fully understand the political situation in Venezuela, but I have to imagine that the massive amount of money being fed in by Colombian cartels has to be contributing to the human rights situation in your country. Or rather, your parents' country, since you were born here."

A smile returned to Adrian's face. "You did your homework."

"Of course I did." Bryan held his gaze. "So this may be business, but I also know it's personal."

Adrian's attention flicked to Ana. "And here I thought you were the one to watch out for."

She just lifted a shoulder in response.

Adrian considered for a long moment, then licked his lips. "Thirty percent. I've got no guarantee that I'll ever see a return on this business, and sentimentality only goes so far when it's my own money on the line."

Bryan glanced at Ana, and she gave him her imperceptible nod of agreement. It wasn't the deal that she'd hoped to get, but for a small operation like theirs, it was reasonable. And regardless of what happened with the roasting business, it was still Bryan's farm.

"You have a deal," Bryan said.

The three of them rose, and Adrian shook their hands. "Send over your due diligence package and I'll get started on it right away. If everything checks out, you should have your money in a few weeks."

They moved into the hallway, but when Bryan started toward the reception area, Adrian held Ana back. "If you'll give us just a moment, Bryan, I'd like to have a word with Ana."

Ana gave a nod of assent, and Bryan paused at the end of

the hallway out of earshot. He didn't look particularly pleased. Ana turned to Adrian expectantly.

"Now that we've gotten the business out of the way, what are you doing for dinner on Friday?"

Ana blinked at him. "Why?"

He smiled. "Because I'm busy tomorrow and Thursday, and Saturday is too far away."

Despite herself, Ana felt a smile come to her lips. "I mean, why are you being so persistent?"

Adrian shrugged and thrust his hands into his pockets. "I like you. You're smart, you're beautiful, and you play a mean game of pool."

Ana worried her lip with her teeth and unconsciously glanced down the hallway at Bryan, who was staring at them with a slight frown on his face.

"Ah, I see. I'm sorry, I thought you said you two were just friends." Adrian held up his hands. "I didn't mean to step on any toes here, especially when we may be in business together."

She snapped her attention back to Adrian. "No, it's not that. We really are just friends. It's just that . . ." She took a breath and realized she really didn't have any reason to say no. He might have come off as arrogant at the club the other night, but she was beginning to think he really wasn't a bad guy. It also occurred to her that he might be doing this to get back at Bryan, but that was silly considering Bryan had no interest in her besides her help in his business.

"Okay," she said finally. "You have my number."

He smiled, and Ana had to admit it was a nice smile. "I'll call you later this week then."

"Okay," she said again. "We can let ourselves out. No need to walk us."

She turned on her heel and walked toward Bryan, who was now looking at her expectantly. "What was that all about?"

Ana took a deep breath. "He asked me out."

"Now? What did you say?"

She shrugged as if it didn't matter. "I said yes."

"He didn't imply that if you didn't—"

"No, not at all." Ana hiked her bag higher on her shoulder. "Can we just go now?"

Bryan nodded, but there was a tightness in his jaw that implied he didn't quite believe her. He should know her better than that. She might work situations to her advantage, but there was no way she was going to date someone just to make sure a deal went through. In fact, that whole idea was insulting.

But when they climbed into her SUV and Bryan still remained silent, something else occurred to her. Maybe he didn't disapprove because he thought it was related to their deal; maybe he disapproved because it wasn't.

Chapter Fourteen

"WHAT'S YOUR PROBLEM TODAY?" Alex glanced at Bryan in the gym's weight room mirror as he slid weights onto the end of a barbell.

Bryan settled on the edge of a weight bench with a dumbbell and positioned himself for his next set of bicep curls. "I don't have a problem. Everything's great. Why do you ask?"

Alex shrugged. "No reason. You're just attacking the weights like you have something to prove."

"I'm not climbing, so I need to amp up my routine." Bryan gritted his teeth and adjusted his grip on the dumbbell as he curled it toward his face. It was heavier than he usually worked with—quite a bit heavier. Most climbers stuck with light weights and lots of fast reps, if they lifted at all, building strength without adding more mass they'd have to carry up a pitch. But since he didn't plan on putting himself a hundred feet up the side of a mountain anymore, it was fine if he bulked up a little. Preferable even. There was a reason guys like Adrian spent half their free time at the gym.

Alex decided to let the question be, starting his own set of dead lifts and leaving Bryan's mind to wander when he should be focusing on his form. No matter what he might say to Alex, he was in a bad mood. And he had no reason to be in a bad mood. They'd sent over the paperwork to Adrian, and in a show of faith that the deal would go through, he'd begun looking online for used versions of the drum roaster he wanted to use in his facility. He'd found one that was less than a year old in Missouri, and the guy was willing to ship. There was just the question of whether or not he trusted the description, or if it was worth it to fly to St. Louis and drive it back himself. He was leaning toward the latter.

The sample roaster was both easier and less satisfying; he couldn't find any sign of the one he wanted used, so he was going to have to buy new. Four thousand dollars gone with a click of the mouse. It was necessary, though; each batch of new beans had to be sampled and evaluated before it could be roasted and sold to consumers.

Assuming he could actually do what he said he could do. It wasn't as if he had a lifetime of roasting experience. Those two months had been intense, but it still left room for a lot of trial and error on his end.

"Bryan?"

He looked up and realized that he had stopped and was staring blindly into the mirror. "Yeah. I think I'm done today. Too much on my mind."

"Business or personal?"

Bryan stood and returned his weights to the rack. "You can put away your shrink hat today. I'm not in the mood."

"Personal then." Alex grinned. "This doesn't have anything to do with the fact that Ana is going out with that venture capital guy tonight, does it?"

"Why should I care?" Bryan growled.

"I didn't say you did. It was just a question." But Alex's

repressed smile said he knew exactly where his friend's foul mood was coming from and was amused by it.

It was irritating when he was right.

Worse yet that Bryan couldn't do anything about it. He and Ana were friends. Only friends. It didn't matter that there was a spark of interest or chemistry or whatever you wanted to call it any time they were in the same room. Now that they were working together, their flirtation had turned to solid camaraderie. Which meant that he had absolutely no way of knowing what she was thinking because all their interactions had to be completely professional.

Bryan snatched up his towel as he stood and wiped down the bench. "I'm going to hit the showers. I'll give you a call later."

Alex nodded and gave a salute of goodbye, then moved on to his next set of dead lifts. Bryan exited the weight room and paused outside in the cavernous climbing arena. There were indoor walls of varying difficulty, littered with climbers of all ability levels. He watched for a moment, then shook his head and brushed by down the hallway to the locker rooms. Maybe he should have found another gym, one that didn't cater to Denver's climbers and extreme athletes, but he'd been coming here for years. Besides, he was paid up through the end of the year, and now especially he couldn't afford to waste money, not if he ever wanted to get out of his parents' house. It wasn't like he was tempted by the walls. They were just an unwelcome reminder of a part of his life that was over.

He found his locker inside the bare-bones locker room and spun the dial before entering his combination. He'd moved on. Just like Vivian had moved on. He'd expected a pang of resentment or even envy at what she and Luke had, but instead he felt regret. Regret that he'd made bad decisions. Regret that he'd held on to her memory for so long and caused both himself and a string of women even more remorse. Regret that he hadn't been more insistent about safety on Vivian's climb; even if it was her mistake, he was her teacher.

What he didn't feel now was desire for her. She'd broken his heart twice, broken his life along with it the second time around. All he felt was relief that she was gone for good.

*　　*　　*

"Which do you think? This one or this one?" Ana held up two different outfits, one after another, in front of her and waited for Rachel and Melody's reaction.

"Neither of them." Melody uncrossed her legs where she was sitting at the foot of Ana's bed and hopped off onto the thick rug. It was a rare night that her friends actually came to her rather than the other way around, but she was feeling unexpectedly ambivalent about this date with Adrian. She needed her girls for support.

Melody pushed past her into the closet and came out with a flirty black slip dress. "This one."

"No, not that one. It's way too sexy for a first date."

"Since when is that an issue?" Melody countered.

"I agree with Ana," Rachel said. She'd largely stayed silent through this whole process, taking as little interest in fashion as Ana normally did in cooking, but now Ana was grateful for the backup. "She hasn't decided if she even likes this guy, so she's not going to wear something sexy."

Melody sighed and put the dress back. "Fine. But you're not wearing that potato sack."

"It's Chanel!" Ana exclaimed, looking at the sheath dress.

"You're not going for shock and awe here, Ana. You're going for approachable."

Rachel grinned. "She kicked his butt at pool and hustled a meeting out of him. The approachable ship has sailed."

"You two are impossible." Melody sighed and went back to the closet. "Okay, how about this?" She came out with a pair of artistically ripped jeans and a cross-front sweater. It was one of Ana's favorite tops, actually; loose-fitting and just low-cut enough to give a glimpse of cleavage without being indecent. "Throw on a pair of ivory heels and you're done."

"Fine. Let's just hope he doesn't show up in a suit."

"He won't," Rachel said. "The Cellar is upscale casual. He'll be appropriately dressed."

"How do you know?" Ana asked.

Melody cocked her head. "You're really nervous about this one, aren't you? This guy must be special."

"He's just a guy. I mean, a really good-looking guy, but a guy all the same. I'm not even sure if there are sparks yet." Ana took the hangers from Melody and retreated into her bathroom, where she took off her robe and hopped herself into the stretchy, tight-fitting jeans. She pulled the sweater on, then appeared back in the doorway. "Good?"

"Perfect. Just need some jewelry." Melody rummaged through Ana's jewelry chest and pulled out a couple of bangles and a pair of long, delicate earrings. "Here. You're all set."

Ana put them on and took a look in the mirror. "Okay. I think I'm ready. Grab me the ivory clutch and my white snakeskin Manolos, will you?"

Melody retrieved the items, giddy at getting to play in Ana's closet, and plopped them on the bed. "I'm almost jealous. I miss this first-date thing."

"Oh, please," Ana said, sliding her feet into the heels. "Justin is perfect. I've never seen you so happy."

"That's true, but we're already in the established-relationship phase. I miss the butterflies."

"More kissing," Rachel said.

Melody laughed. "Trust me, there is *plenty* of kissing going on. But you know, as romantic as candlelit dinners in bare feet can be, I liked that first-date anticipation. The excitement of a new relationship."

Ana touched up her lipstick and dropped it into her clutch, stuffing in her wallet while she was at it. "No relationship, just a date. And on that note, I have to go."

"Isn't he picking you up?" Melody asked. "I was hoping to get a peek."

"Meeting him in the lobby. Guys don't get the condo number until at least a month in." She drilled them with a stare. "And no hanging out to get a glimpse."

"Okay, okay. We're going, we promise." Melody gathered her purse and nodded for Rachel to come with her. "Text us the minute you get home."

"I will." Ana hugged her friends goodbye and saw them to the front door, then unplugged her cell phone from where it was charging on the counter. It rang almost immediately, as if it were waiting to be picked up.

"Hey." Bryan's voice, warm and familiar, came through the handset, bringing a smile to her face.

"Hey! I didn't expect you. It came up as a private number."

"Oh, sorry. My phone is dead so I called from the home line. Am I interrupting anything?"

Ana checked her watch. Still five minutes until seven. "I've got a couple minutes. What's up?"

"I am heading to Missouri on Monday to look at a drum roaster. Do you want to come?"

Ana blinked. "Uh, like a road trip?"

"Exactly like a road trip. Fly out early on Monday, stay overnight in St. Louis, drive the equipment back on Tuesday."

Two days with Bryan. Two days alone, with an overnight. Separate rooms, of course, but still . . . Then she focused on the more important part of the statement. "Wait, did you hear from Adrian?"

"He emailed me this afternoon, said the paperwork was on its way to his lawyer. We should have the funds on Monday."

A beep came through on her phone and she pulled it away to check the preview screen. A text from Adrian: he had arrived and was waiting for her in the lobby.

"Wow. That's great news. That was fast. Let me think about it and get back to you, okay?"

"Okay. Call me tomorrow."

Ana said her goodbye and hung up the phone, holding it for a long moment before she dropped it into her bag. That was . . . odd. Not just the invitation, but the timing. He knew she was going out with Adrian tonight. Had he wanted to be the one to break the news that the deal was going through ahead of schedule? Or was he just nervous about spending a chunk of not-yet-verified change on a roaster?

She was still turning over the matter in her head when she rode down the elevator and emerged into the lobby. Adrian stood there in the corner, hands in his pockets, looking out the window. Rachel had been right: he was wearing slacks, but with an untucked button-down and a pair of very expensive shoes. Just dressy enough for a date, just casual enough for their destination. He turned at the sound of her heels clicking across the marble floor and smiled.

Well. He was definitely handsome, she'd give him that.

He approached her and leaned down to kiss her cheek in greeting, giving her a whiff of a recognizable, high-end cologne. "Are you ready to go?"

"Sure." She waved goodbye to the doorman as she preceded Adrian out the glass doors to the busy LoDo street.

"I'm just down there." He pointed to a black Tesla Model S

parked down the street, and Ana almost laughed. Of course he drove a $130,000 electric car. She shouldn't have expected anything less. At least her instincts about him were right—the virtue play had definitely been the right one. He probably bought wind energy credits for his house to offset his electricity usage.

He opened her door for her, and she climbed into the sleek, leather-scented interior. When he joined her, she half expected him to start talking about the car, but instead he shifted directly to the restaurant. "Have you been to the Cellar?"

"I haven't, actually. I've been so busy, I haven't been out in ages. Besides, it just opened last month. Reservations have been impossible to get."

He smiled. Ah, there it was. It wasn't the restaurant that was meant to impress, but his connections.

The restaurant itself was moody and dim, modeled after a wine cellar with brick walls and rustic furnishings. Candles at each table. Ana began to feel uneasy as they were led to a two-top in the back corner, private and romantic. The host held out the chair for her and draped her napkin into her lap, while Adrian seated himself to her left.

"What do you think?" he asked, looking suddenly eager to please.

"It's nice," she said. "Interesting ambience. What kind of food again?"

"Rustic continental, I think. I hope you don't mind. I took the liberty of ordering us the tasting menu in advance."

"That's fine."

"Tell me, Ana, how did you end up in publicity? I understand the media studies, but not the MBA."

So Ana gave him the rundown of how she'd made her way to Denver: she'd stayed close for her undergraduate studies so she could live at home, then gone to Berkeley because of their stellar MBA program. She didn't say that she'd lived with her

Aunt Belen the whole time to save money, both in college and after. She'd gone to work for a boutique publicity firm in San Francisco, where she'd worked for several years.

"That's actually how I met Melody," she said, before realizing that Adrian had no idea who Melody was. "One of my best friends. She's a pastry chef. She and my other friend Rachel own Bittersweet Café on Old South Pearl."

"Ah, I've been in there before. Good croissants."

Ana smiled. "They're Melody's specialty. Anyway, it was total coincidence; we met through a mutual acquaintance at a party. We became friends, and when she mentioned she was thinking about moving back home to Denver, I thought it sounded like a good time for a change since my boss was refusing to promote me. I hired on with Massey-Coleman and the rest is history."

"Except for the leave of absence part."

"Oh yes." Ana took a drink of water. "That was just politics. I go back in thirteen weeks."

"You seem pretty confident."

"Why wouldn't I be?"

Adrian shrugged. "I don't know. Call me cynical, but I've seen too many of these temporary leaves turn permanent. It's hard to jump back in."

It was exactly what she had feared, but she wasn't going to let on. "I'm secure there. The fact I didn't get fired is a positive sign."

"It is," he said.

"So how about you? I don't know many little boys who want to be venture capitalists when they grow up."

Adrian laughed. "No, probably not. You know the routine for us VC guys: undergrad at Wharton, MBA at Harvard, used family connections to talk my way into an analyst position at a first-tier firm in Boston. Where I would still probably be languishing had I not stumbled on a promising start-up and convinced the partners to invest."

"What deal was that?"

"Ever heard of a little company called ProjeScape?"

Ana's eyes widened. Everyone knew ProjeScape. It was a productivity app that had exploded practically overnight and was used by half the businesses in America. Including Massey-Coleman. "That was you?"

He nodded. "Got lucky. I went to school with the founder and he came to me first. I could tell it was going to go big, but trust me, it wasn't an easy sell."

"But once it did . . ."

"I could write my own ticket."

"So why come back to Denver?"

Adrian shrugged. "I grew up here. I like the city. Better quality of life, great outdoor activities. There really was no comparison for me between Boston and Denver."

Ana leaned forward, frowning. "So, if you went to school on the East Coast, how do you know Bryan? I assumed you went to college together."

"Ah. You know those family connections I mentioned? My dad and his dad did business together. We spent many evenings playing pool in Bryan's basement while the adults talked business."

"You should have spent a little more time practicing then."

Adrian grinned, but he didn't reply because the first course arrived.

The food was just as good as Ana expected it to be, and the conversation downright pleasant. Adrian definitely had the touch of arrogance she'd come to associate with finance guys, but he was also personable and easy to talk to. By the time they left the restaurant more than two hours later, she had to admit to herself that she'd had a nice time.

They chatted easily on the way back, and when they entered the lobby of Ana's building, he paused. "Can I walk you up?"

Ana considered. There was her one-month rule, but she was pretty sure that Adrian was neither an obsessive stalker nor a rapist. She hadn't yet decided whether she wanted to see him again. She hadn't decided whether she wanted to kiss him either.

He rode up the elevator with her, keeping a respectable distance, and followed her out onto her floor, where they stopped in front of her door.

"So," she said.

"So." He smiled down at her. "Can I see you again?"

She smiled back. "I'll think about it."

The moment stretched, their eyes locked, and she could feel the instant he decided to move in for the kiss. She waited, curiously unmoved, while his hand slid to her waist and his lips met hers.

It was nice. He was a good kisser. Not too aggressive, not too passive.

And she felt absolutely nothing.

He must have picked up on her lack of interest, because he pulled back and placed a solid foot between them. "Just be straight with me, Ana. I have no chance here, do I?"

She closed her eyes and sighed, and when she opened them, she knew the truth. "No. And it really has nothing to do with you."

"I figured as much when you hesitated on Tuesday." He shoved his hands back in his pockets and gave a resigned shrug. "Tell Bryan I authorized the wire transfer this afternoon. The money should be in his account first thing Monday morning."

Ana studied his face. "You're really going to invest that fast."

A faint trace of amusement colored his expression. "You think I shouldn't?"

"No, of course you should. I just . . . I was planning on weeks if not months."

He shrugged. "It's not a lot of money in the scheme of things, Ana. Nothing ventured, nothing gained and all that. Sometimes you've just got to take your shot and see what happens."

She had the feeling that he wasn't just talking about Solid Grounds now. She couldn't help but smile. "Thanks, Adrian. I'm sorry."

He smiled back. "Me too. Have a good night, Ana."

She waited until he disappeared around the corner, then let herself into her condo and released a long sigh.

There was nothing wrong with Adrian. He was handsome, successful, easy to talk to. Maybe slightly self-congratulatory, but she was used to that by now. All in all, it was the nicest date she'd had in a very long time.

And yet when his lips touched hers, she knew something she'd known all along but hadn't wanted to admit.

She pulled out her cell phone and tapped out a text message to Bryan. Okay, I'm in. What time do we leave?

Chapter Fifteen

ANA'S UBER DROPPED HER at Denver International Airport at the yawn-inducing time of four fifteen on Monday morning. Bryan had gotten a deal on tickets from Denver to St. Louis, but the hitch was that the flight left at a quarter to six. No wonder it hadn't been filled. The sun wasn't even thinking about peeping over the horizon yet.

She pulled her roller case through the glass doors, rummaging through her shoulder bag for her driver's license, which she would need immediately for going through security. Like she normally did when she traveled, she'd split the difference between polished and comfortable: dark jeans, a lightweight sweater, and ballet flats. Nothing with any metallic parts, nothing to hold her up in security. Even the sticks thrust through the bun on top of her head were wood.

"Ana!"

She turned at her name and saw Bryan jogging toward her, a large backpack on his back. "Hey. I was waiting for you near the check-in desk."

Ana held up her phone. "Checked in online."

"Of course you did." He smiled. "Ready for an adventure?"

She laughed as they fell into step together, bypassing the escalators that led down to the security lines in favor of bridge security—a local traveler hack that shaved dozens of minutes off the wait. "I'm not sure I would call this an adventure."

"We're flying eight hundred miles to look at a twenty-thousand-dollar piece of used equipment, which we may or may not be bringing home in a U-Haul. How is that not an adventure?"

"This coming from a man who routinely flies around the world and hitchhikes in foreign countries?"

He winked at her. "They're not foreign if you go enough."

Ana just shook her head and tightened her grip on her suitcase. He was awfully chipper for this early in the morning, even if he looked rumpled enough to have just rolled out of bed. Jeans, T-shirt, wrinkled canvas jacket, Converse. He clearly hadn't shaved in several days, because the beard was starting to make a comeback. It was such a far cry from the polished professional who had showed up to the meeting with Adrian, it was hard to believe he was the same person.

And she was hard-pressed to say which version she preferred.

She cleared her throat. "So, how is this going to work exactly?"

"The seller is expecting us late this morning, so we'll go straight to his warehouse and check out the roaster. If we like it, I get a cashier's check, and we go get a U-Haul to drive it home. It's a twelve-hour drive, so I figured we'd stay overnight in St. Louis and drive home tomorrow morning. We should be back in Denver by dark."

"Okay then." She threw him another glance. "How sure are you that this is what we need?"

"Absolutely sure, assuming it's in good condition. And he's

including the ventilation system, which saves us thousands. I'll just need local installation and we'll be good to go."

"Wow." This whole time, the business had been somewhat abstract in her mind, an exercise to keep her busy while she was on leave from her real job. Maybe that was because her job *was* abstract. After all, she routinely dealt with things like publicity and reputation, which were completely mental, not physical. But in two days, Bryan would have four thousand pounds of green coffee beans from a farm that he owned in Colombia . . . and hopefully something to roast them in.

That was about as substantial as one could get.

"What's wrong?" Bryan picked up on her musings as they approached the TSA officer at a little stand. Ana moved forward, handed her license to him, and set her phone facedown on the scanner. It beeped when it accepted her boarding pass QR code. He nodded and waved her through.

Ana waited for Bryan on the other side while he went through the same procedure with a paper boarding pass, then picked up the conversation again. "I just started to think about how much work is actually ahead of us. I mean, once you get the roaster and the beans, we have a physical product. We need to be able to sell it within a reasonable amount of time, right? Beans don't stay fresh for that long." She plopped her suitcase onto the belt for the X-ray machine and toed off her flats.

Bryan followed suit, revealing gray socks emblazoned with penguins. The funky design barely registered through her sudden anxiety. "I'll just be doing test batches for now—we'll foist them off on our family and friends until I'm done fine-tuning the roast. But yeah. We need distribution. Like, yesterday."

She blew out a breath. "Okay. Then that's what I'll focus on. That means as soon as we get back, we'll need at least some basic marketing collateral. And I'll need samples to take around to interested coffee shops and restaurants. Half-pound bags should do it. Or at least that's what all the internet forums tell me."

"You've been reading those too?" Bryan grinned at her. "There's some really bad advice in there."

"But some good advice too." Ana went through the scanner without a beep and then waited at the end of the line for her suitcase and handbag.

Bryan found a place next to her to wait and glanced down. Then he smiled. "You have flowers on your toes."

Ana looked down quickly, inexplicably embarrassed by the white glittered flowers on her pink toenail polish. "Yeah, I got a pedicure on Friday."

"It's nice." Then he seemed to realize why she'd gotten the pedicure and lifted an eyebrow. "I didn't ask. How was the date with Adrian?"

"It was fine." She stared at the tip of her suitcase peeping out of the X-ray machine as if she could will it to move faster. Then it got sucked back in for a second look. She sighed. "It was good, actually. The Cellar is a great restaurant."

"I see." He crossed his arms and rocked back on his heels. "You going to see him again?"

She didn't look at him. "Nope."

"Why not?"

There were a million ways she could answer that question. It wasn't a good idea to mix business and personal. She didn't have time for dating. The truth was, there just wasn't any spark. But she was reluctant to state it that flatly, because it would only draw attention to the fact that she was feeling sparks toward the one person she couldn't act on them with.

"He drives a Tesla," she finally said. "The expensive one."

A smile quirked up the corner of his lips. "You have something against electric cars?"

"No, the car is fine." She rolled her eyes while she tried to explain. "Everything about him was just so calculated, you know? I mean, he's gorgeous and he's actually a nice guy. He doesn't need to try that hard."

The suitcase finally got released from security purgatory and slid down the rack of rollers toward her. She was so focused on getting it and her purse off the rack and out of the way that she almost missed the expression that flitted across Bryan's face. Once more, it looked suspiciously like jealousy. Because she commented on Adrian's looks? Come on, anyone with eyes could make that determination. It wasn't a preference; it was just a dead-on fact.

"I asked him how he knew you, and he said he was one of the kids crowd at your parents' functions."

"Yeah," Bryan said. "He always stunk at pool."

"Still does," Ana said, and they both laughed, the tension broken.

Bryan's backpack finally came through the machine, almost the exact opposite of Ana's Vuitton luggage—it was battered green nylon, the seams held together by duct tape, the bungee laces starting to fray across the back. The irony of criticizing Adrian for being concerned with appearances struck her. No, not irony. Hypocrisy. How was she any different? She fixed images for a living. She crafted her own to display exactly what she wanted to show the world. The designer duds, the expensive car, even the French luggage. Bryan, on the other hand, had never pretended to be anything other than what he was. Even when she didn't necessarily agree with or like that person, he was a hundred percent honest about himself. And now that he'd changed, he was honest about that too.

"What's it like?" she asked as they moved away from security and down the sloping ramp to the A concourse, where they'd pick up the train to their gate.

"What's what like?"

"Coming back and starting over. Being a different person."

Bryan considered it seriously. "Hard. Everyone expects me to act like I did before, and when I don't, they figure I'm working an angle."

"That must be frustrating."

"It is. But it's no less than I deserve." At her sharp look, he said, "No, I'm not punishing myself for my past mistakes. I just mean that we have to accept the consequences of our decisions. At least until we manage to completely reinvent ourselves and convince everyone else."

"Yeah," Ana said softly. "It takes longer than you think."

"I'm finding that out," he said with a smile, and she was grateful he didn't push further.

Given how early it was, security had taken them almost no time at all, and they were at their gate a full hour before their flight left.

"I'm going to grab some coffee. You want anything?"

Ana plopped into one of the seats at the gate. "Just a drip. I'll watch our bags."

"Are you sure you want a drip? This is airport coffee. You might want to dilute the taste a bit."

"A latte, then." Ana laughed. "You've become a coffee snob, huh?"

"Of course; I'm a third-wave artisan roaster. Or at least I will be if this trip is successful." He dropped his backpack on the ground beside Ana's suitcase. "I'll be right back."

Ana watched him go, surprisingly pensive. He never ceased to surprise her. She'd known him for two years, so she'd thought she had his number. But she was beginning to feel that there was a lot more going on inside that he didn't let on. Yes, he might be honest. But he wasn't exactly transparent. For all the illusion of shallowness, she figured she hadn't even come close to seeing the bottom.

Bryan came back a few minutes later with two paper cups and a white paper bag. He handed over the coffee and then pulled out a paper-wrapped bundle.

"What's that?"

"Spinach and egg-white wrap. I couldn't remember whether you ate wheat or not, so I went with the gluten-free tortilla. Hope that's okay."

"Thanks," she said, surprised. "I eat almost everything, but that was thoughtful. What did you get?"

"Sausage and cheese. Though if you prefer this one, I'm willing to trade. I was making no comments on your figure."

Ana laughed. "I didn't think you were. And you're right. When I'm not with Rachel and Melody, I eat very clean."

"You'd have to with those two as friends," Bryan commented. "Speaking of . . . Do you think they'd do a trial run with our coffee at Bittersweet?"

"Of course. I've already asked. They say send them the beans when you're ready. They also asked about display signage, so we're going to want to get on that pretty quickly."

Bryan paused with the burrito halfway to his mouth. "I don't even know where to begin with that."

"Don't worry; I do. Or at least I know someone who does." She'd done enough marketing work on the side to have a pretty good handle on the graphic designers she could depend on. Before she moved over to the crisis management division, she'd worked a lot with smaller companies who really needed a full-service marketing firm, not just a publicist. But she'd kept them at Massey-Coleman by finding independent contractors who could do the work for a fraction of the cost.

That was another reason her leave rankled. She could guarantee not another associate in the business had gone to that sort of trouble. And now they were getting her clients. Never mind that she didn't particularly like them. She'd laid all the groundwork, so it wasn't fair for someone else to get all the credit.

If she were going to have to start over with her list anyway, what was to keep her from going back to the business publicity department? Even better, what was to stop her from pitching a marketing arm to Lionel? She'd already been doing a fair amount of strategic marketing with her publicity clients. The firm might as well get paid for it. It would expand the business, something that Lionel was always looking to do.

And Solid Grounds would be the perfect proof of concept. She would handle all the marketing and publicity, build as much buzz as possible, and use that as her case study. An example of what she could do when there was a consistent vision applied across a company's communications.

"Ana?" Bryan asked, looking into her face curiously.

She realized she was chewing the burrito mindlessly. "Sorry. You got the wheels turning. I need to get all of this written down while it's fresh in my mind."

"You know, there's still the issue of the value of your advisory shares," Bryan said quietly.

"I know. But I haven't done anything yet."

"You've done a lot. I'm thinking—"

Ana waved a hand. "Nope. Not yet. Once I actually do something worth paying me for, we'll discuss it. All I did was get you a meeting, and I would do that for any friend. You're the one who gave a great presentation, and you're the one who convinced Adrian to invest. As far as I'm considered, my stake in this is still zero."

Bryan didn't look convinced, but he didn't press, which was good because her mind was on other things—all the work they'd need to do in a short time to get this business off the ground.

Which was exactly where her mind belonged. On work. And off him.

Chapter Sixteen

BRYAN AND ANA ORDERED an Uber at the St. Louis Lambert International Airport and went directly to meet the seller, who was located on the edge of the city just off I-70. The car dropped them off in the center of an industrial park in front of a sign that said Fourth City Roasters. A Closed sign hung in the window.

"That doesn't look promising," Ana said under her breath.

"Why else would he be selling?" Bryan countered, though inwardly he'd been thinking the same thing. It was always depressing to buy equipment off a failed business, like picking over a carcass left to rot in the sun. He slipped his backpack straps over both shoulders and nodded to Ana before walking with purpose toward the front door.

It was unlocked, so he pulled the door open and they stepped into the cool, dim interior. The scent of char still hung in the air, though from the looks of things, they'd been out of business for a while. The front of the unit had been set up like a small coffee shop, but the bar had already been gutted of its espresso machines and refrigerators, just leaving the hull of a countertop and an empty bakery case.

"Hello?" Bryan called.

A moment later, an older, bearded man hustled out from the back of the office space. "Hallo. You must be Bryan. I'm Louis."

Bryan shook his hand. "Louis from St. Louis?"

"What can I say, my mom had a sense of humor." He turned and extended his hand to Ana. "Louis Lamont."

Bryan saw the corners of Ana's mouth twitch against a smile, but she wrestled it down. "Nice to meet you, Louis. Can we see the roaster?"

"Of course. Come with me." He jerked his head over his shoulder and then moved with the same bound-up urgency with which he'd appeared. They followed him into a big, open bay that resembled Bryan's space and stopped before a large barrel-chested machine.

"Here it is," he said. "Twelve-kilogram, double-walled drum roaster, electronic variable gas settings, USB data logging."

"How long was it used?" Bryan asked.

"Less than a year."

"Do you mind me asking why you're selling?"

Louis shrugged. "I used to roast as a hobby out of my garage, and when I retired, I needed something to do. But it's a pretty big leap from roasting a kilo for your own use to hundreds a week. Just never got off the ground. Problems with the roast, problems with the bean suppliers. Honestly, it all became too much work."

That statement was almost a relief. So many times, people jumped from the hobby to the business without understanding what it took to succeed. Granted, Bryan had yet to successfully roast his first batch of beans, but at least he had experience with the larger drum roasters and he had been smart enough to bring in someone like Ana to help. He had no illusions that this was going to bring him a quick influx of cash . . . he'd be happy to cover his expenses while he got it off the ground. The words *thirty-six and living at home* haunted him every time he walked through the door of his parents' mansion. By thirty-six, Mitchell Shaw had developed his first downtown block. To say Bryan was working against a deficit would be an understatement.

"Can we see it in action?" Ana asked.

"I don't have any beans, but yeah, we can turn it on."

He began twisting the knobs and flipping switches, which fired the gas jets that lay in a long line beneath the now slowly rotating drum. He stepped back for Bryan to look.

He got in there and squinted at the color of the flames, fiddled with the air intake valve. "You have a match or a lighter?"

Louis dug in his pocket and handed him a Zippo. "My wife's always on me to quit."

"Your wife is right." Bryan flicked the lighter and held the flame in front of the intake until it started to waver toward the open space.

"What are you doing?" Ana murmured at his shoulder.

"Adjusting the draw." He looked at the flames again. Blue with just a tip of yellow meant it was burning the right amount of oxygen.

"You have the probes for this?" he asked Louis.

"I do, but I don't have my laptop here. It does connect via USB, though."

"Good." As long as it had the capability to transmit the readings from the temperature probe to his profiling software, they were in business. Bryan turned on the fan and the cooling tray agitator, which were meant to stir the beans in a circular motion to stop the roasting and cool them.

"Can I flip on the afterburner?" Bryan asked.

Louis nodded.

He flicked another switch on the metal vent, and the afterburner flared to life midway up the exhaust. This was meant to burn off the chaff before it reached the outside air. Denver's air quality regulations meant that he'd have to do something to cut down on the amount of smoke and debris his operation put out, and the afterburner was the most efficient way to do so.

"Okay," Bryan said. He turned off the gas and shut down the roaster. Everything looked to be in perfect operating condition—another reason he'd chosen to go with a model he was familiar with. Had he not known exactly what a fully operational roaster of this model looked and sounded like, he wouldn't have known if he was getting a good deal or not. Part of wisdom was knowing what you didn't know. "You're asking twenty thousand?"

Louis nodded again.

A calculating look flashed across Ana's face for a moment, a sure sign she was thinking about how to work the situation. Then she sighed. "Listen, every dollar Bryan has is tied up in this business. You know we're serious if we came all the way out here, but I really hate to pay more than seventeen for this. Of all people, you should know how hard it is to get a roasting business off the ground. Three grand can make or break us at this stage."

Louis looked between them, considering, for a long moment. Then he nodded. "What if we split the difference? Say, eighteen-five?"

"Okay," Bryan said. "You have a deal."

Louis beamed and shook his hand. "Perfect. So, the next question is, how are you getting this out of here?"

They finally settled on an agreement to have Louis get it prepared and crated for transport, and Bryan would return the next day with the truck to pick it up. In less than an hour, he'd secured the centerpiece of his roasting business, for fifteen hundred dollars under budget. Ana and Bryan exchanged pleasantries with Louis for another minute and then walked back out the front door.

"Well, well," Bryan said. "Where did this 'honesty is the best policy' Ana come from? I thought for sure you were thinking of ways to spin the story for a better deal."

"I was, but it just didn't feel right." Ana grimaced. "Maybe you're rubbing off on me. Making me grow a conscience or something."

Bryan nudged her with his elbow. "Would that be so bad?"

"If it had cost you fifteen hundred bucks, it would be," Ana shot back, but she was smiling.

"I just hope we can actually get it on the truck. I have no idea how he's going to get it on a pallet. It must weigh a thousand pounds."

"Which is why you didn't pay for it now," she said. "Aren't you glad you brought me along? You would have paid his asking price without blinking."

She was right, and that was exactly why he'd brought her along.

Okay, not exactly.

"We have an entire day now. What do you want to do?"

"Eat," she said without hesitation. "What are our options around here?"

"I only know one thing, and you're probably not going to like it."

She arched an eyebrow.

"Barbecue."

Ana laughed. "I could go for some barbecue. When in St. Louis, right?"

"I'll believe it when I see it," he teased and saw the answering light of challenge in her eyes. She could make a competition out of anything.

"Okay, doubter, you're on. Get us an Uber, we'll drop our luggage at the hotel, and then we'll find the best barbecue place in the city."

*　　*　　*

The Uber driver dropped them in front of their hotel, an all-suites sort of place that catered to business travelers. Once the receptionist checked them into their rooms—on different floors, no less—they went their separate ways to drop their bags and freshen up.

Ana set her bag on the tiled bathroom floor and made a circuit of the hotel room to assure herself it was clean and bedbug free—one couldn't be too careful—and then paused in front of the full-length mirror on the closet. The woman in the reflection *looked* like Ana, but had it been her, she would have never appeared so uncertain.

"Where did this 'honesty is the best policy' Ana come from?" Bryan's words came back to her with uncomfortable clarity. Was that what he really thought of her? That she was a liar? Yes, she could spin with the best of them—it was a requirement in her line of work—but she'd never really thought of it as dishonest.

"Gah!" The syllable came out as a grunt of frustration, and she spun away to retrieve her hairbrush from her bag. She pulled the sticks from her bun, which had started to look more like the Leaning Tower of Pisa, and brushed out the tangles furiously. Why was she torturing herself? This was Bryan she was talking about. Part of the reason they got along so well was because they could accept the other person as they were. She never needled him about his past conquests, and he didn't voice whatever his opinion of her job might be.

Now she wasn't sure she really wanted to know.

A text from Bryan buzzed through her phone: Waiting in the lobby. Should I call an Uber?

She typed a quick reply: Sure. Be down in 3.

Time to get a grip, Ana. She shoved the sticks back into her bun, which was only marginally neater than before, grabbed her handbag, and marched out of her room before she could do any more ridiculous second-guessing.

The Uber was just pulling up in front of the hotel's glass doors when she reached the lobby. Bryan gestured at her from the curb and opened the back door for her, while she hurried across the tile floor.

"Ready to prove your barbecue devotion?" Bryan teased.

Ana flashed a smile, glad they were back to their usual playful banter. "You'll be sorry you ever doubted me."

But it was doubt that registered on his face when the driver dropped them outside a disreputable-looking brick building in an older part of St. Louis. Bryan looked at the restaurant with its peeling sign and whiteboard by the front door and threw a glance at Ana. "Are you sure you want to go here?"

"Both the Yelp reviews and our driver said this place has the best ribs in the city. Are you having second thoughts?"

"Not a chance," Bryan said. He yanked open the glass door and held it for Ana, then stopped short. The line from the counter stretched all the way to the door.

"See? It wouldn't be packed if it wasn't good. It's not even noon yet." The interior was just as she'd expect from a barbecue joint: picnic tables covered with red-checked plastic tablecloths, dark wood paneling, old metal signage from gas stations and markets. Ana fell into line without question, then looked at Bryan, who still had the doubtful expression on his face. "What? I thought you were the type who ate crickets and grubs in South America."

"I was climbing, Ana, not starring on an episode of *Survivorman*. It was more like camping and living off trail mix and beef jerky."

"Then this should be a step up." She flashed him a grin and hoisted her handbag more securely onto her shoulder.

Despite the length, the line moved quickly, and when they

got up to order, she could see why. It was a simple process: pick a meat and two sides. Everything came with corn bread. Ana ordered spare ribs, as did Bryan, and just in time; after the girl at the counter called back their order, she removed *ribs* from the whiteboard showing what was available.

"Now aren't you glad we didn't hesitate?" Ana said after Bryan paid and they took their red plastic glasses to the fountain drink machine. "When they're out, they're out. We've got good luck."

"Getting the roaster for fifteen hundred under asking and then getting the last batch of ribs? I think you are my luck." Bryan winked at her, a tiny bit of that trademark flirtation creeping back in, and Ana's heart gave a little leap. They grabbed a corner table that had just been vacated and plunked their table tag on the edge. Ana cleared her throat, looking for something to say to fill the suddenly awkward silence. Or maybe it only felt awkward to her. Bryan seemed completely comfortable.

She didn't have to wait long because a waitress brought their barbecue out on two rectangular metal trays, the plates piled with sauce-covered ribs, collard greens, and barbecue beans. "There's enough food here for three people," Ana said.

"I'll eat your leftovers if you want." Bryan made a move to steal one of her ribs, but she slapped his hand.

"Hands off. I didn't say I wasn't going to eat them."

"Now that I would like to see."

"Sounds like a challenge." Ana picked up a rib. "Watch and learn."

As it turned out, she couldn't make good on her boast— there was just too much food for her after an adulthood of dieting. But she made a good-enough dent that Bryan looked at her approvingly. "I'm impressed."

"Being able to eat almost an entire slab of ribs is all it takes to impress you? I wish I had known that earlier. I wouldn't have had to hustle Adrian for the meeting." She grinned so he knew she was just kidding.

"You've got some sauce right there." He pointed at her cheek, then gave up and swiped at it with one of the wet wipes on the table. "There."

"Thanks."

"You know, you surprise me."

"Because I eat real food?"

Bryan laughed. "No. I just didn't think this was really your speed."

She cocked her head. "Sounds like you're calling me a snob."

"Not a snob. Not exactly."

"Then what?"

A smile played at the corner of Bryan's lips. "High-maintenance maybe?"

"Oh, thanks. That's so much better."

He chuckled. "You already admitted that you drive the Benz because it's intimidating. I guess I don't understand why you work so hard to be unapproachable."

"Maybe I don't want to be approached." Ana cleaned her hands with another wet wipe and shoved her plate away. "I'll let you in on a secret. I don't particularly like most of my clients. So yeah, I cultivate an image. It keeps people at a respectful distance. They only see what I want them to see."

"What about people you don't want to keep at arm's length?"

Ana took a sip of her tea. "There are very few of those. Rachel and Melody know the real me. Isn't that enough?"

"I don't know." He gave her a searching look. "Is it?"

She shifted uncomfortably in her seat. Of all the people she would have expected to penetrate her facade, Bryan was the last. "That's funny, coming from you."

"What's that supposed to mean?"

She leveled a look on him now. "Life of the party. Total flirt.

Never met a woman he wanted to see twice? Maybe I'm unapproachable, but you rarely let anyone close enough to see the real you either."

He sat there for a long moment, like he was considering. "You're right."

"I'm . . . what?"

"You're right. You want to know why I quit climbing? Because the guy who did that is a guy I don't like very much. I don't want that life."

The way he was looking at her—open, serious, maybe even a little bit vulnerable—made her insides shudder in a peculiar way. The last thing she wanted was to feel something right now. Attraction she could brush off. But a true connection? Way harder to disregard. She knew she should change the subject, but instead she found herself asking, "Then who do you want to be?"

Another laugh, and the moment was broken. "Beats me. I've spent so long proving I'm not my father that I haven't given much thought to who I wanted to become myself."

"What's wrong with your father?"

"Absolutely nothing. And that's the problem."

Ana still didn't understand, but the way he was looking away told her that he wasn't going to say any more. And yet for some reason, Ana still found herself talking.

"Trust me, I get that."

Now he was focused back on her, and she didn't like how that light of curiosity in his eyes made her heart leap. "Oh yeah?"

"Yeah. Firstborn comes with a certain responsibility, and I haven't exactly lived up to that."

"You mean your parents didn't want you to be wildly successful?"

Ana rolled her eyes at the comment. "Not when it means cleaning up for people who probably deserve what's coming to them. They tell our overseas relatives that I work in marketing. Which I suppose is close enough."

He studied her for a long moment, and she toyed with her fork so she wouldn't analyze his expression. "Tell me about your siblings then. Surely there's a mime or an encyclopedia salesman in there to take the heat off you."

Ana laughed, grateful for Bryan's trademark humor. "Sadly, no. My next youngest sister is a nurse. Then pharmaceutical sales rep, web designer, and physical therapy student. My brother, the youngest, is still in high school, but he's leaning engineering."

"And just when you thought you could count on the lone brother to run away with his rock band and make crisis publicity look respectable."

The tone was teasing, but Ana flushed hot and then cold. He couldn't have known the joke would hit home. She piled her used napkins on her plate and stood abruptly. "Shall we go?"

Bryan had to have picked up on something amiss, but he didn't press. Instead, he took both of their trays to the trash, where he scraped the leftovers and piled them into the bus tub. "What do you want to do now?"

Ana thought for a moment. "Well, we're in St. Louis. We can't leave without seeing the Arch, right?"

"Let's do it. We're here; might as well take in all the sights."

Ana held up her phone. "Already called an Uber."

"Of course you did." But he nudged her with his shoulder. "Time to go play tourist."

*   *   *

Bryan was having a hard time not thinking about this trip like a date. A really long, odd date that involved buying industrial equipment, but a date nonetheless. Good food, sightseeing in an unfamiliar city, and the unmistakable urge to kiss his companion.

So maybe the last one had been a regular thought since he'd known Ana, but the more he got to know her, the more he began to think he'd had her all wrong. In his less . . . self-aware . . . days, she'd been a challenge. She returned his flirtation but brushed off his advances; any attempt he'd made to get closer to her had been neatly sidestepped. And after a while, he'd settled into the push-and-pull of their relationship, friends solely because of mutual friends.

Once he'd come back, he'd realized what it would actually do to their close-knit group if they were to date and break up and vowed that wasn't even on the radar, although he still wanted to kiss her. Then he'd seen her with Adrian and the thought of her with another man had made it pretty clear that he was failing badly at the friend-zone thing.

And now she pressed against him, peering through one of the windows in the cramped top of the Gateway Arch. Strong winds put a distinct sway into the building where they stood, over six hundred feet in the air, the city spread out beneath them. From here, it was surprisingly green, even this early in the year. Bryan tended to forget that spring existed everywhere else in the country, while the grass didn't even start growing in Denver until May.

"It's gorgeous," Ana breathed. "I didn't know Missouri was so pretty."

"Never been?"

She shook her head. "No. You?"

"Nope. No reason to until now. Would you ever move here?"

"Now that I know I could live on barbecue? It's a possibility."

"Seriously?"

She looked up at him and brushed a stray lock of black hair from her eyes. "Honestly? No. Denver is my home. Rachel and

Melody are as much my family as my actual family. I can't imagine leaving them behind."

"I can understand that."

She must have sensed something in his tone, because she shifted around so her back was against the window niche and she could look directly up into his face. "Why didn't you go into real estate? It sounds like your dad has always held a place open for you at one of his companies."

"He has." He looked out over the city as he chose his words. "If he'd had the choice, it would have been Alex he mentored. But Alex had his own family traditions to push back against."

Ana frowned. "I don't understand."

"You know Alex lived with us when we were seniors in high school, right? While his parents were in Russia?"

Ana nodded.

"Well, Alex and my dad got close. And have stayed close. They're much more alike than he and I are. Alex is . . . well, you know Alex. Principled. Steady. Not sure he's done a single wrong thing in his life."

"Hard to be compared to that, I bet."

He looked down at her. "When you're young, or not that young, it's better to not play the game than to lose at it."

"So that's why you became a climber? So you wouldn't fail at being your dad's successor?"

"Oh, nothing that intentional. I loved climbing. I was good at it. It got me attention for things that neither my dad nor Alex was any good at." He threw her a faint smile. "It got me the attention of girls."

"Pretty sure it's the muscles that did that, but okay."

Bryan threw back his head and laughed. "It was a good motivation to keep going. And then I realized I could make money out of it without having to sit in an office all day, without being responsible. Without being accountable. But the problem with lacking accountability is that it's all too easy to take advantage of it."

He shrugged. "Anyway. I'm not cut out for real estate development. As much as I know my dad is trying to preserve Denver's character, growth is out of control. It's nothing like the city I knew and loved as a child. So it would be hypocritical for me to work for a developer, even my dad, when I oppose development."

"But you're okay with living off them while you get your own business started?"

"What can I say? I'm hypocritical about hypocrisy."

They were getting called back onto the tram, so they moved with the group of people down the stairs and onto the pod-shaped car and took their seats again.

Ana nudged his shoulder with hers. "For the record, I don't think you're a hypocrite. And however hard you are on yourself, I also don't think you're a bad person."

He looked at her in surprise.

She shrugged. "I think you're like most people, just getting along the best you can. Trying to own up to your mistakes and make them right. Some are easier to fix than others, but that doesn't mean we shouldn't try. No matter how long it takes."

A touch of sadness had crept into her voice, but she was looking away from him, so he couldn't see her face. Gripped by something he couldn't exactly name, he turned his hand palm up on his knee. And was surprised when she placed her hand in it so he could interlace his fingers with hers.

She didn't look at him all the way down, the only connection the warmth of their palms pressed together. And then the tram arrived at the bottom and she jumped out of her seat, breaking the contact. "Let's walk a bit," she said, nothing of their moment showing in her voice. "I feel like exploring."

They walked across the wide expanse of grass at the bottom of the arch and then through the city. Just like Denver, downtown was compact. They started with the Old Courthouse and admired the Federal architecture that made it look like a mini Capitol building, White House, and Jefferson Memorial all in one. Then they meandered farther south into Ballpark Village, the shopping-mall-like complex just outside of Busch Stadium. By the time they'd finished exploring, the sun was dipping toward the horizon. They chatted about the business, the city, about Denver, but Ana stayed carefully away from serious topics as they walked. That was fine by him. He didn't particularly feel like mining his own neurosis and insecurity. But curiosity still nibbled at the edge of every interaction. Ana spoke like someone who knew something about regret. What could she possibly have to regret?

When their last Uber of the night dropped them at their hotel and they stepped onto the elevator, Ana turned to him. "That was fun. I'm glad I came."

"I'm glad you came too. Ana—"

Two men stepped onto the elevator just before the doors closed, their bulk and their roller bags separating Ana from him before he could get out whatever he'd been about to say. Which maybe wasn't a bad thing considering he had no idea what he was about to say.

The elevator slid up silently, but the businessmen were on a higher floor, so it arrived at Ana's before Bryan had a chance to say anything. He held the Door Open button while she slipped around the businessmen and stepped out.

"Meet you in the lobby at eight tomorrow to get the truck?"

Ana nodded. "Sounds good. Good night."

Bryan punched the Door Close button and leaned back against the side of the elevator with a sigh. One of the businessmen threw a surreptitious look his way, but he pretended not to notice. Just like he pretended not to think about Ana for the rest of the night, alone in his hotel room.

Chapter Seventeen

ANA DIDN'T SLEEP WELL, and she blamed the hotel mattress, even though it was perfectly comfortable. Whatever discomfort she felt stemmed from the way things had gone with Bryan yesterday.

She'd held his hand. Voluntarily.

Not that that meant anything to him, not in any real sense. He had obviously picked up on the things she didn't want to say and sought to comfort her. She wasn't surprised. Whatever he might think about himself, he was an essentially kind person. Even in his wilder days, he hadn't been predatory or untruthful; no doubt every single one of the women had known what she was getting into with him. Bryan never pretended he was something he wasn't.

But he might be pretending not to be something he was.

Enough, she told herself. She was spending a lot of time thinking about a guy who was unsuitable for her in every way, not the least of which being their web of interconnected friendships and the fact she was investing her time in his company.

A company that was going to need their full attention to avoid meeting the same fate as Fourth City Roasters.

Getting the cashier's check and picking up the truck went seamlessly, even though there was a brief question as to the weight capacity when they signed the paperwork and found out they'd been given a smaller truck than Bryan had rented. They'd assured him it was capable of hauling a thousand-pound machine with no problem, assuming it would fit in the back. So they'd busted out a tape measure and checked against the crate dimensions listed on the roaster manufacturer's website.

"Let's hope Louis managed to get it in the crate," Bryan said when they settled onto the ugly patterned-fabric bench seat. Yes, the truck seemed to be from 1990. But the diesel engine started with a reassuring rumble, so Ana hoped it would get them the eight hundred miles back home.

By some miracle, when they arrived at Fourth City Roasters, Louis was waiting for them, the machine disassembled and crated, all components shrink-wrapped so they wouldn't move during hauling. Just to make sure, Bryan looped tie-downs around the crate and secured them to the anchors in the floor of the truck bed. This thing wasn't going anywhere.

Bryan handed over the check, Louis handed over the bill of sale, and Ana and Bryan were on their way west with a nearly twenty-thousand-dollar piece of roasting equipment in the back of a rental truck. The truck, which had felt so light and powerful moments before, now felt sluggish and heavy.

"At least we don't have to go through mountains. Were we coming from the West Coast to Colorado, we might have a bit of trouble."

"That's not reassuring." Ana cast a look at the side mirror, as if the view of the moving truck would tell her anything useful about its mechanical competence.

"Oh, it'll make it. It just might be slow. And cost us a lot in fuel. Good thing you're a killer negotiator."

"Let's just hope he didn't damage anything while he was packing it up."

"These things are pretty tough," Bryan said. "They're essentially big metal barrels with nozzles to shoot fire."

"And now I know why you're so interested in roasting." Ana smiled so he knew she was kidding. "What next then?"

"Well, I already set up an appointment for assembly on Thursday, so assuming all goes well and it's operational, I should be able to roast my first batch on Friday."

Ana blinked. "That soon?"

"Just in time. Beans get here tomorrow. Which is another reason this truck has to make it. I have to be there to accept the freight tomorrow afternoon."

Ana studied Bryan in the seat next to her, once more startled by him. Right now, he looked more like his climber self—his hair was getting long enough again that it curled against the collar of his hooded sweatshirt; the growth on his face had passed five o'clock shadow days ago and was headed into full beard territory. She had the sudden impulse to run her fingers across his jaw and see what it felt like.

Which of course she wouldn't. Couldn't. No, wouldn't.

He glanced at her, evidently noticing her perusal, but not uncomfortable. "What are you thinking?"

"I'm thinking that you probably get underestimated a lot."

"Oh yeah?"

"You come off as kind of a hippie."

Bryan laughed. "Pretty accurate."

"But you *own* a coffee farm in Colombia. You've overseen the harvest and the beans are arriving and we have a roaster in the back of a rental truck."

"Yes, I'm well aware of the progression. Which is the reason why I'm going home to my parents' house after this. Because I'm broke."

"One of the people who underestimate you is yourself. You're doing this, Bryan. This is a huge deal."

He flicked her another look. "You're freaking me out a little."

"Sorry. I just mean . . . this is cool. This is a good thing. And we're going to make it successful."

"We?"

"Absolutely *we*. I'm invested now. I wouldn't be driving halfway across the country in a really uncomfortable moving van if I didn't believe you could do this."

"Diva."

It took her a second to realize he was referring to her crack about the van. "Okay, fine, don't be serious."

He didn't look at her, but for the second time in as many days, his hand found hers and squeezed. "That means a lot to me. Seriously. I'm not sure anyone's believed in me before."

"I'm sure that's not true," Ana said, but the bloom of warmth in her chest said it didn't matter.

Great. She actually cared about this guy.

In order to stave off that uncomfortable realization, she pulled her tablet and keyboard from her purse and set it up on her lap.

"What are you doing?" he asked.

"I'm getting to work. We have a roaster and we'll have beans tomorrow. That means I need to get going. There's packaging design, branding, distribution, advertising . . ." She pressed a hand to her forehead. "No, first things first. . . . I just . . . don't quite know what that is yet." It was as if this was suddenly becoming real. It had been so long since she'd actually run an entire marketing campaign that she almost forgot what it was like to be responsible for the success of a product. Not to mention everything else that a start-up entailed.

"If it's too much, Ana, let me know. I don't mean to throw this all in your lap. We can hire someone. Hire a firm, whatever."

"You don't have the money for a firm, at least not a good one. No, I can do this. I just need to wrap my head around it."

By the time they crossed the state line into Kansas, she had pages of nested timelines and lists in her project management software—ProjeScape, ironically—and the grip of panic was easing a little bit. It wasn't as extensive as it looked. She'd start with what seemed like the most immaterial issue but would affect the most areas: branding. She sent off an email to a graphic designer friend, asking her to come up with some logo possibilities for Solid Grounds. They'd work on the brand book from there—font styles and colors that would carry across their packaging and website. Which meant that she needed to get on the schedule for her preferred web designer, since he tended to book up quickly. Fortunately, he owed her a favor, so she got an almost immediate email back saying he'd fit her in whenever she needed him.

"Two down, nine million thirty-six to go," she quipped.

Bryan grinned at her.

Given their late start, they decided to drive straight through, stopping only for restroom breaks and fast food before hopping back into the truck. By the time the sun was down, Ana's neck and back were kinked, but she'd made some significant headway on her work. And as they crossed the Colorado state line, she put the finishing touches on the design brief for the website.

"I can't believe you," Bryan said. "You just seriously knocked out a month's worth of work in ten hours."

Ana rolled her head, easing the kinks in her neck from looking down the entire day. "Amazing what you can accomplish when you have no distractions. Makes me think I should lock myself in a concrete box at work with no phone." She reached up and kneaded a particularly stubborn knot from her neck, twisting her head one way and then another to try to loosen it.

"Come here." Bryan gestured for her to slide closer on the bench seat. It was a testament to her exhaustion that she did as he said without questioning, unbuckling her shoulder belt and rebuckling the center lap belt beside him.

Bryan didn't take his eyes off the road as he reached over and began to knead the knotted muscles in her shoulder and neck.

Ana sucked in a breath. "Ouch. Your hands are stronger than you think they are."

"Sorry. Climbing." He eased off the pressure but didn't stop, and she let herself relax into his touch.

Until she became aware that it was *Bryan* who was touching her, his calloused fingertips rough against her soft skin, something that should be unpleasant but was anything but. Desire shot straight through her, sharp and unmistakable, as far removed from the stirring of attraction she'd felt earlier as a direct strike of lightning from the crackle of static. She jerked away and he immediately dropped his hand.

"Did I hurt you again? I was trying to be careful."

"No, I'm okay. Thanks. That feels better." She unbuckled her belt and slid back to the far side of the cab, silently letting her breath out in a steady stream while she made sense of what had just happened.

She'd known she liked Bryan. She'd known she was attracted to him. But until now, she hadn't known she *wanted* him.

*   *   *

They pulled up in front of Ana's building just past midnight, bleary-eyed and cramped into a permanent sitting position.

212

Or at least Bryan was. He had no way of knowing what Ana was feeling because she'd spent the last two hours not talking to him.

He pushed the gear lever in the steering column to park and turned off the engine, then sat there in the dark for a long minute, trying to think of what he should say. "We made it."

"That we did." Ana started gathering up her things, shoving them into the depths of her huge tote.

"Thanks for coming with me. I wouldn't have wanted to make that trip on my own."

"Sure. I'm glad to help. It was fun." She didn't sound like she was mad, but there was a false note of perkiness in her voice. Before, he might not have picked up on it, but after spending two entire days in her presence, he felt like he knew every nuance of her voice. She thought she hid her emotions well, but if you knew how to listen, she was pretty transparent.

And right now, it was clear that he'd done something dramatically wrong.

"I'm going to be at the space early tomorrow to unload this and receive the delivery. If you need me, you can reach me on my cell or just drop by."

Ana nodded. "Okay. I'll let you know when I've got something to share. Maureen said she'd have some basic logo designs for us to look at in a couple of days."

"That's great. Thanks, Ana."

Ana nodded and levered open the truck door, then hopped out. Her knees buckled for a moment when she hit the pavement, but she righted herself quickly with a self-deprecating smile. "Maybe I need to give my legs a second."

Bryan chuckled. "You know we could have stopped and walked around if you wanted to."

"No, I wanted to get home. It was a long drive." She hauled her roller case out of the cab of the truck. "Thanks for inviting me. I'll be in touch." And then she slammed the door and headed into the lobby of her posh building.

Bryan watched until she disappeared around the corner to the elevator and sighed. He'd thought they were making progress. No, he'd thought they were becoming friends. And then he'd made the mistake of touching her. His intentions had been completely innocent, but obviously she didn't believe that because she'd jerked away like he'd stabbed her. Or betrayed her. Or something equally horrible.

She said she thought he underestimated himself, but now he knew that he had a good reason for doing so. He'd never escape his well-deserved reputation. Especially with a committed Christian woman like Ana Sanchez. He needed her, no question. She had the skills, ability, and experience to make this business a success; he didn't even know if he could roast his beans. Which meant that from here on out, he had to be on his best behavior. No touching. No compliments. Just business.

However difficult that was beginning to feel.

Chapter Eighteen

IT DIDN'T MATTER that she'd gotten home after midnight. Ana's daily routine still called. She dragged herself out of bed at 5 a.m., then several blocks to her gym, where she once more put herself through a grueling spin class and then went straight to yoga in the studio next door. She might have proven to Bryan that she wasn't afraid of eating, but she also knew it was time to pay the piper—there was no way she could down a plateful of ribs without consequence to her waistline . . . or more likely, her backside. By the time she staggered back to her vehicle, her legs were so shaky she could barely walk, but at least she'd burned two days' worth of calories in two hours . . . and all by 8 a.m.

At home, she showered, dressed in jeans and a pin-tucked floral blouse, and sat down at her dining room table with her laptop. She threw an uneasy glance at her Bible and devotional book, stacked just where she'd left them, unopened, but the gnawing feeling in her stomach pulled her attention back to her to-do list. Somehow, the victory she'd felt the night before paled in comparison to the list of things that still remained.

She tunneled her hands through her hair while she squinted at her laptop and waited for the files to sync between her devices.

There was no need to panic. Graphic design and the website, and consequently branding, were already under way. Bryan had said that he had the technical side of packaging under control. That meant she just needed to work on marketing messaging and distribution.

She spent two hours working on a few variations of the company's story, which would be used on the website, marketing collateral, letters, and social media ads—direct-to-consumer sales would be the most lucrative channel, even though wholesale was more stable. Once she had a rough idea of how to craft that messaging, she moved on to distribution—which looked a whole lot like copying and pasting contact information from Google into a spreadsheet. There were a shocking number of independent coffee shops and restaurants in the Denver area alone; she could spend the next couple of days expanding the list into Fort Collins to the north and Colorado Springs to the south. Those contacts would have to be mostly by mail, but she could hand-carry samples to the local restaurants and shops. She was always more persuasive in person anyway.

With those out of the way before lunch, she opened the electronic folder that contained the information for Rachel and Alex's wedding. The spreadsheet recorded every contract deadline and amount, from the location to the table-and-chair rentals. Or at least it was supposed to. The lines for the costs and details of the rental decor were still blank. She double-checked her email to see if Melody had sent her copies of the contract, but the only wedding-related thing in her inbox was a link to a Craigslist ad for a couple dozen hurricane lamps.

She picked up her phone, intent on calling Melody to ask, but a quick look at the time convinced her otherwise. It was only 2:45; the kitchen would close down for hot food orders in fifteen minutes, which meant that Melody would be putting out the last batch of fresh bread for the day and Rachel would be shutting down the hot line.

Well, she hadn't had lunch. If she hurried, she could grab something before the kitchen closed. She packed her laptop into her bag, slipped on her ballet flats, and headed straight down to her car.

Ten minutes later, she was parking in the alley behind Bittersweet Café and pushing through the back entrance.

"Ana!" Melody was the first one to see her, her arms full of a stack of plastic containers as she headed for the walk-in. "What are you doing here?"

"I had some wedding questions for you. And I wanted lunch. Am I too late?"

Rachel looked up from where she was wiping down her section of the countertop. "Depends on what you want. I've already shut down the range and the grill for the day."

"I've got some minestrone left on the warmer," Sam, Rachel's sous-chef, spoke up. Since the last time Ana had seen her, she'd gone from ringlets to rows of braids. "It's pretty good if I do say so myself."

"Your minestrone is fabulous. I'd love some."

"Coming right up." Sam grabbed a bowl and began to ladle the fragrant soup, while Melody rustled up a couple of slices of ciabatta and dropped them on a plate.

"You got a couple of minutes to go over wedding stuff?"

"Yeah. We can grab a seat in the break room." Melody cast a quick look at Talia, her pastry assistant. "Keep an eye on the oven?"

"You don't need to ask," Talia said, not even breaking her rhythm in rolling out her laminated dough.

"Rach, you joining us?" Melody called.

"Yeah, just a second." Rachel spoke quickly to Sam in hushed tones, then pulled off her apron and headed toward the tiny break room with Melody and Ana.

Once inside, Ana pulled up one of the molded plastic chairs to the scarred Formica table. "Sorry to pull you out of work, but we only have two months until the wedding and I wanted to make sure we haven't forgotten anything."

Melody and Rachel exchanged a look as she opened her laptop to a spreadsheet that was a graphical representation of her type A personality. "We've got the venue taken care of, along with the flowers, obviously. But there's still the matter of all the decor rental. Tables, chairs, lighting . . . plus whatever we need to run all the lighting and music. Does anyone know if we're going to need generators?"

"No, there's power run in the barn, which is our choice of setup for the reception. And we're going to do a late-afternoon ceremony in the garden, right?" Melody shot a quick look at Rachel to make sure they were all on the same page. Rachel nodded. "We've already gotten the lanterns off Craigslist—the ones I showed you—and I've got a lead on some really cool picnic benches that we can bring in for seating."

"You've got a lead or you've got them nailed down?"

"I should know in a week or so if my guy can get them."

Ana paused, her hands poised over her keyboard. "What guy? Should I follow up for you?"

"No, it's fine. I've got a reminder in my phone." Melody narrowed her eyes at Ana. "What's going on? You seem unusually tense over this, even for you."

"Gee, thanks." Ana smoothed a lock of hair behind her ear. "I've just got a lot going on. I'm working on the entire marketing and promotion plan for Solid Grounds at the same time I'm supposed to be helping with Rachel's wedding. I feel like I'm going to drop a ball if I don't have the full picture."

Rachel chuckled and put her hand on Ana's shoulder. "Okay,

first of all, calm down. You were only supposed to be helping with all the venue and contract stuff. Melody and I were taking care of all the details. You're off the hook there."

"That's when I still had a job," Ana said. "You guys work full-time. It's only fair I take up some of the slack."

"Sounds like you've got a full-time job now too," Melody said, "flying to St. Louis at a moment's notice and everything. How'd that go?"

Ana shrugged. "Fine. Flew there, looked at the roaster, drove home. I managed to get him down $1,500 on the price, which I figure pays for my plane ticket and my hotel room. Not sure I'd ever drive eight hundred miles in a twenty-year-old moving van again, though."

"No, that's not it." Melody stared at Ana closely. "Something happened."

Rachel gasped. "Between you and Bryan?"

Ana shook her head, but heat was already creeping into her cheeks.

"It did!" Melody said. "Tell us everything!"

She had to shut this down before they started going off on the wrong track entirely. "Nothing happened between Bryan and me."

"But you look like a tomato, so *something* happened." Rachel looked at her closely. "Or is it that you wish something had happened?"

Ana's traitorous face confirmed the suspicion by heating even further. Why was it that she could control her expression in every other situation but this one? "Guys, it's no big deal."

Melody rubbed her hands together almost gleefully. "There is something going on there! You, what? Have feelings for him?"

Ana buried her face in her hands, hoping that those feelings weren't written as plainly on her face as she suspected they were. "I don't know. You know I've . . . been attracted to him . . . since we met. But I haven't acted on it because frankly, he was a bit of a dog. And I didn't think he was serious about me anyway."

"But now . . . ," Rachel prompted. "He's come back, seems to be a changed man . . ."

"Ana and Bryan sitting in a tree . . . K-I-S-S-I-N-G," Melody singsonged.

Ana picked up an empty Styrofoam cup and launched it at Melody's head. The baker dodged it, laughing.

"There was no kissing at any point. There was maybe a little hand-holding."

"Ooh la la," Rachel said.

"No, not ooh la la. It wasn't even like that. We were talking, we had a moment . . . he took my hand. That's it."

"Even better. Sharing moments." Rachel waggled her eyebrows until Ana shot her the Look of Death. "Okay, seriously, though. I've always liked Bryan. Deep down he's a good guy with a kind heart. And from what Alex tells me, he really has gotten in touch with his faith again. You know, before Vivian, he was this committed, one-woman guy. I don't know what she did to him, but whatever it was, it messed with his head."

"I'm not sure if that's reassuring or a warning," Ana said. "It's supposed to make me feel better that he's been damaged by past relationships?"

"Haven't we all?" Melody said wryly.

"What are you going to do?" Rachel asked.

"What is there to do? Nothing. Regardless of what I may or may not have felt in a moment of weakness, this isn't a relationship that would make any sense. We're friends. You know what would happen if we got together and then broke up. It would be weird. Alex would side with Bryan, you guys would side with me, and then it would be really tense. Totally not worth it."

"Unless it is," Melody said with a smile.

Ana kneaded her temples with her fingertips, already regretting her openness. All this talk about Bryan made her head hurt, and now her friends were going to be rooting for something that should never happen. That she'd never let happen. She and Bryan would go on like they had been going on. She would just ignore the fact that every time she remembered the feel of his fingertips on her neck and shoulders, it sent a shiver through her entire body.

Because that was not helpful at all.

"I shouldn't have brought it up. Nothing's going to happen. I'm not going to let it happen. It's not—*he's* not—what I want."

Rachel held up her hands. "Okay then. We're sorry. We just happen to love you both, and we think it's an interesting idea, the two of you together. You know, you're not as dissimilar as you might think."

"Right."

Melody counted off on her fingers. "You're both fitness freaks. You're both super-smart even though he hides it sometimes. And you both really don't like people to crawl beneath that armor of yours to see the real person underneath. His just happens to be the life of the party and yours is . . ."

"Unapproachable. Yeah, I know. Bryan told me."

"And you let him live?" Rachel asked.

Ana shrugged. "He's not wrong, exactly. The only difference is that he seems to think it's a problem and I see it as an asset."

Rachel and Melody exchanged a glance, but Ana ignored it as she shut down her laptop and shoved it into her bag. "I feel better now that I know I haven't forgotten anything. Melody, you'll email me as soon as you get the final confirmation on the tables and benches?"

Melody nodded. "Sure will. But you didn't even touch your soup."

Ana paused, having completely forgotten about her lunch on the table next to her. "Any chance I can take it to go? I want to pop in and see if the coffee beans got delivered as planned."

Another glance exchanged, but Rachel rose. "Sure. I'll put it in a to-go container for you." She picked up Ana's dishes and headed back into the kitchen.

Ana sensed Melody looking at her, trying to broach a subject while she packed up. Finally, she just turned to her and asked, "What?"

"I'm sorry if we made you uncomfortable. Don't stop talking to us, okay? When you guys didn't approve of Justin, I stopped talking to you and I missed so much. I don't want that to happen again."

Ana softened. Melody looked truly worried. She gave her a quick hug. "Trust me, I'm not going to ditch you guys because you want to set me up. We've been through too much together. But, Mel, just let me handle this, okay? I don't need anyone getting more involved in my love life than I am."

Melody laughed and squeezed her tight. "Okay, just checking."

Rachel came back into the room and handed over a paper bag. "Your lunch to go. Let us know how things are going over there. I'm looking forward to trying the coffee."

"No more than we are." Ana gave Rachel a quick, one-armed hug. "Okay, I'm off. Check in with you later."

Ana strode decisively out of the bakery and to her car parked in the alley, her resolve strengthened. No matter how great they thought the idea of her and Bryan together was, their very investment proved that it was a bad idea. Not that she needed any reinforcement for that thought. Her own experience had proven as much already.

Chapter Nineteen

Even knowing objectively that four thousand pounds of green coffee beans were small potatoes—mixed metaphor intended—compared to the big coffee farms, it still came as a shock to Bryan when the truck arrived and delivered his tiny pallet to his warehouse.

Twenty-eight bags. Only twenty-eight.

He lugged them to the climate-controlled room he'd had built specifically for bean storage and piled them on the bottom shelf of one of the units, realizing just how unprepared he was for this venture. Yes, he'd known that he was going to have to source beans from other farms for the roastery just to break even this year. But somehow, he hadn't realized that his own would be such a paltry yield. When he'd worked with the roaster in Oregon, they'd had row after row of shelving units, all containing beans of different varieties and origins. They must have warehoused tens of thousands of pounds at a time or more. And they churned through them at a shocking rate.

He was still standing in the storage room, the sinking feeling in his stomach hardening into a knot, when he heard the front door chime and Ana's voice ring out into the warehouse.

"Bryan? Are you here?"

"In storage," he called.

She strode into the room, her hard-soled shoes tapping the concrete, and then stopped short. "Where are the rest?"

"This is it."

"That's four thousand pounds?"

Bryan nodded slowly. "Twenty-eight bags."

"Somehow I thought there would be more."

He grimaced. "So did I."

Ana took a deep breath and let it out slowly. "Well, it's still four thousand pounds that we need to sell, right? And they have a limited shelf life, so we don't want too many. It's okay."

"Are you trying to reassure me or yourself?"

Ana threw him a wry smile. "Both, I think. I just didn't . . ."

"Yeah, me neither. I think I'm going to have to move up that next shipment."

They exchanged a glance, and as their eyes met, he felt suddenly calm. It would be okay. They were in this together. Simply knowing that he wasn't stuck out here by himself trying to make this work eased some of the tension from his shoulders.

"What's next?"

"Well, I can do a very small batch in the sample roaster, but the drum roaster won't be fully operational until tomorrow night. Assuming nothing got damaged in the disassembly or the move."

"Let's do it then."

"Really?" He glanced at her. "You want to hang out?"

"Sure. You said it doesn't take very long in the sample roaster. How long before we can cup it?"

"It needs to rest between eight and twenty-four hours

before we grind it. So we should be able to taste it tomorrow morning."

"I've got to drink someone's coffee tomorrow, so why shouldn't it be yours?"

Bryan took a deep breath, the nerves coming back. He felt like he was about to on-sight a 5.14, not roast a few grams of beans. But this was the first test of whether he'd made a good decision in buying the farm, whether the beans were of decent quality. He hadn't been there throughout the growing season; for all he knew, something could have veered it off course from the quality he anticipated.

Ana was still looking at him expectantly, though, so he dragged one of the bags off the shelf and onto a nearby table, then carefully opened it. He scooped out a small cup of beans and then gestured with his head for her to follow him into the cupping room.

"Can I see those?" She reached for the cup without waiting for his answer and took a handful of beans, turning them over in her hand. "It's hard to believe that these turn into something drinkable, isn't it?"

"I'd venture to say that you've never tasted anything like this." He forced a grin. "I'm just hoping it's a good thing, not a bad thing."

She dropped the beans back into the cup and gave his arm a squeeze. "Don't start doubting yourself now."

Her touch sent a blaze of heat through his arm, which he tried to suppress. She was being supportive. She wasn't flirting. Now to talk himself into actually believing that . . .

The jitters continued as they proceeded into the cupping room, still sparsely decorated, but more appealing than the warehouse. A long countertop sat along one side of the room, holding a sink hooked up to a reverse osmosis filter. Beside it was the sample roaster, a small but heavy steel machine with two separate barrels. The difference between roasting on one of these and on the drum roaster was like the difference between a Zippo lighter and a flamethrower, so there wasn't much parity between the roasting times and temperatures he'd get on this machine versus the big one. This was solely to determine the quality of the beans and to find any faults in the coffee itself. This was the science, the tangible part of the process. The roasting was the art, the intangible, what would determine if his product was fantastic or just mediocre.

"Here we go," he said. Ana stood a few feet away, close enough to watch but far enough to stay out of his way. He fired up one barrel of the sample roaster first to heat the interior before he put in the beans. While it was heating, he carefully measured the volume of his beans on the gram scale and made a notation in his notebook. As a matter of course, he'd measure them when they came out roasted to determine the moisture loss.

When the readout on the display showed the barrel temperature was right, he poured the beans into the hopper with a clatter and flicked the lever to drop them into the barrel. Ana hovered in the periphery, even though there wasn't much to see. As the beans moved through the roast, the smell changing from grassy to bready to coffee-like, Bryan pulled out a little metal sample tube to observe the beans every couple of minutes, scrawling notes on his pad each time.

Then finally, the roast was done and he lifted a lever to drop the beans into the cooling tray.

Ana edged closer as he stirred the beans with a wooden spoon. "Those smell amazing. This is, what, a bit past a city roast? That was only a single crack, right?"

He glanced back at her, surprised. "You're right. I find that South American beans taste better at a medium roast. You get the delicate flavors of the beans without the char. African beans, for example, hold up better to darker roasting because it intensifies and complements the flavors."

"Twenty-four hours, huh?"

"Or eight. Depending on whether you want to come back at midnight."

"I don't have anything planned."

"You're kidding, right?" He studied her face, trying to determine if the usual straightforward Ana had chosen this moment to become a jokester. "You want to drink coffee that late?"

"Now that you put it that way, I'm second-guessing the idea. But yeah. I'm not going to sleep until I know how this turned out, if the beans are any good." Ana looked suddenly uncertain. "Unless of course you don't want to come back."

"Oh, no, I'm going to be here the rest of the day. I've still got things to set up in the office and warehouse before the installer gets here tomorrow to put in the roaster."

"I've got things I can work on at home then," Ana said, sending a flood of disappointment through him. What, was he expecting her to hang out with him for the next eight hours? "I'll be back here about eleven thirty."

"You really don't have to. As soon as they cool, I'm going to package them up. Eight hours or twenty doesn't make much difference in that case."

"I want to." She smiled. "I'll see you later tonight."

Bryan watched Ana turn and go without a backward look, then absentmindedly reached for one of the roasted coffee beans and popped it into his mouth. It tasted good, but chewing on beans wasn't the best indication of their quality. Still, the taste and maybe the caffeine gave him a little boost of confidence.

He knew how to do this. He'd spent two months doing nothing but roasting coffee, after all. His farmworkers were experienced, the soil was good, and the climate had been favorable.

There was no reason why this venture couldn't be successful. Whether it would be as successful as his climbing career was uncertain, but all the signs pointed to good outcomes.

Now it just remained to be seen if his confidence was proven out.

*　　*　　*

It was a stupid impulse that had made Ana agree to return to the roastery, but it was her word that actually had her climbing into her SUV and driving back for the grand reveal. She hadn't been able to help herself. Once again, Bryan's confident, jovial mask had dropped to show her just how uncertain he was about this whole venture. He needed the moral support. This was his redemption, his chance to show his family and friends that he could be more than the climber who got by on his muscles and his gregarious personality to do something stable, something of value.

She got that far more than she'd like to admit.

When she pulled up in front of the roastery, all lights were blazing, but the front door was locked. She rapped on the window with her car key, bringing Bryan running immediately from the back. He was dressed in different clothes, which told her at least he'd managed to get out of the shop for a little while, maybe to work out. Had she not killed herself with two sequential classes at the gym this morning, she might have done the same thing.

"Showtime," Bryan said brightly, flipping the lock again once she was inside. He worked a key off his key ring and handed it to her. "Here. I keep forgetting to give you a copy."

"Thanks." She clipped the key onto her ring and then took a deep breath. "Are we ready?"

"Ready as I'll ever be. Time to validate or crush all my hopes and dreams."

"No pressure, though."

He grinned. "None at all. Come on. I'm all set up."

And he was. He had the beans in a small vacuum-sealed bag, waiting on the countertop next to an expensive burr grinder like the high-end coffee shops used, along with the scale and an electric kettle. He flipped on the switch to get the water boiling and then immediately cut open the bag with a box knife.

"This makes it easy to boil water for coffee," he said, and Ana got the feeling he was just trying to fill the quiet. "I like to brew mine at 202, and water boils at 202 here, so there's no testing temperatures or waiting. Straight out of the kettle makes a good cup."

She nodded, because there wasn't much she could say once he turned on the grinder and its high-pitched buzz filled the room. He tapped the machine to get the rest of the grounds out and leveled them in the collection. Then he set one glass cup, followed by the other, on the scale to measure the precise amount of coffee in grams, then poured water from the kettle to the same weight. He clicked on a timer with a beep.

"We'll test at exactly nine minutes. And then we'll repeat the process at a different grind, possibly, depending on the extraction."

Ana threw him a sidelong glance. "So basically what you're telling me is that roasting and making coffee is best done in a lab."

"The perfect cup? Pretty much. But by fine-tuning our brewing process, we'll know exactly how good the beans can be and then offer suggestions to our customers on how to best use them." He looked momentarily abashed. "Obviously this has to be repeated on the big roaster. For now we're just looking for general bean characteristics and faults."

"Which are?"

"Harsh or off flavors mainly, faults from the growing or

fermentation process. You can save some lower-quality beans by roasting them dark, which also can give you more consistency across suppliers, but at that point, you're really tasting the roast itself and not the beans."

"So even if they're bad, we can still use them by roasting dark?"

He grimaced. "Worst-case scenario. Roasting a Colombian past full-city is tantamount to sacrilege."

"Noted. I don't want to be struck by lightning over coffee beans."

Bryan cracked a bare smile, but she could tell his mind was still on the coffee. At the four-minute mark, he used a spoon to break the crust on top of each cup and removed the grounds and foam. He gestured for Ana to bend close to inhale the aroma.

"Smells amazing," she said, breathing deeply. "How much longer until we can taste?"

He glanced at the timer, then clicked it off. "Five more minutes."

"That's forever."

"Patience is a virtue."

"Not at midnight, it isn't."

He grinned at her, but he didn't budge. When the timer finally beeped to indicate nine minutes was up, he handed her a spoon that had a deep, round bowl. "Time to taste now. Ladies first."

"No, I wouldn't dream of it. This is your farm, your beans, your company. I insist."

Bryan dipped his spoon into the coffee and slurped his first taste. Ana waited expectantly, watching his face for any clues to his thoughts. "Now you."

"You're not going to say what you think?"

"I don't want to influence you." He took her spoon, dipped

it into her cup, and held it out to her. She breathed in the scent of fresh coffee and then leaned forward to sip the coffee out of the spoon.

Flavor exploded on her tongue. "It's good!"

"Don't sound so surprised."

"No, I'm not, it's just that . . ." She took the spoon from him and dipped it in herself to take another taste. "I taste something vaguely nutty and kind of . . . sweet. Chocolate-like. That's the only way I can describe it."

"That's a characteristic of Colombian beans," Bryan said. "Personally, I think this could be roasted a little lighter. But the sample roaster roasts hotter, plus it's all done by eye. I'll have the probe data to work with on the drum roaster."

She went back for another taste, and then she had to cut herself off. Considering it was nearly midnight, any more than a few sips of coffee would have her up for the rest of the night. She caught Bryan watching her in quiet satisfaction and realized that he hadn't been quite as concerned as he'd suggested. "You're not surprised."

He shook his head slowly. "We had the coffee graded at the farm, so I knew the beans were good. There's just always the possibility of improper packaging or damage in transit . . ." He let out a breath and for the first time gave her a full smile. "It's a good harvest. We may not have much to work with, but it's top quality."

He looked so pleased and relieved that Ana couldn't help throwing her arms around his torso and giving him a hug. "Congratulations, Bryan. I'm so happy for you."

Slowly, his arms went around her, his fingers tightening against her back, and she caught her breath, realizing she was pressed up against him. As quickly as she could manage without looking conspicuous, she pulled back and straightened herself. "What now?"

"We get the roaster installed tomorrow, and then I fine-tune my roasting process."

"On these beans?"

He grimaced. "I chickened out as soon as they arrived and bought some inexpensive Colombian greens from a local supplier. The last thing I want to do is ruin all our good beans."

"That sounds sensible. How soon do you think we'll have samples for me to give out?"

"If all goes well? A week, maybe two."

"Then I need to get on top of the packaging. Logos will be in tomorrow. Are you okay with doing something simple, like a clear label that we can put on generic bags, until we get customized packaging?"

"Absolutely. Whatever we need to do."

Ana hoisted her bag and gave a decisive nod. "I'll be in touch, then. And . . . congratulations again, Bryan. I'm really happy that you're happy."

"Thanks. I appreciate you coming over here. It would have killed me to wait."

"Honestly? Me too."

Ana stood there for a long moment for a reason she couldn't name, then turned and left.

No, that wasn't correct. She fled.

Chapter Twenty

THE INSTALLER ARRIVED first thing on Thursday morning, a guy with a Southern drawl, a plaid shirt, and a beard that made him look like a member of ZZ Top. He was one of the recommended technicians for this brand of roaster, however, and the instant he walked into the room, he put Bryan at ease with his knowledge and his confidence.

It seemed like it would have been an easy enough thing to install a twelve-kilogram roaster in a small warehouse, but as Bryan watched from the outskirts as the construction team arrived, he realized it was far more complex than he thought. The roaster got precisely positioned so that the stack would clear the steel rafters, then bolted down to the concrete floor. Then each part was checked, tightened, and reassembled as needed, the gas supply hooked up, and the vent and afterburner parts assembled. Then it was all the construction work, cutting a hole in the ceiling for the exhaust vent and weather-sealing the opening. Considering how much was involved, it went fairly quickly and smoothly.

Then came the fun part: firing up the roaster and testing everything from the thermocouple that would tell him the drum temperature as he was roasting to the computer link that would upload and analyze all the data coming from the machine. A lot of the process was still done by eye, but establishing a profile for each bean and each shipment would help ensure consistency that was sometimes lacking from roasters who did everything completely by feel. Like climbing, roasting was equal parts touch and physics.

Bryan found himself holding his breath as the first information began to filter onto the screen, plotting a temperature curve on the x and y axes. The technician fiddled with the manual adjustments on the roaster, changing gas and air flow until the flames burned a precise orange-tipped blue.

"Nice machine," he said finally. "You got a good deal."

Bryan let out a breath. Up until now, some part of him had wondered if his eighteen-thousand-dollar gamble would pay off.

"I'm not going home until tomorrow," the technician said. "Roast a sample batch or two tonight to make sure everything's working properly and you understand all the adjustments. I'll drop by in the morning and make sure you're satisfied."

Bryan shook his hand and thanked him for his help, and then he was alone in his roastery with his new-to-him equipment and a bag of mid-quality beans. He pulled out his phone and texted Ana: Roaster installed and working properly. About to test-roast my first batch.

Several moments later, her reply came back: So glad to hear that. Tell me how it turns out.

He pushed down the feeling that bubbled up at her response. Surely it wasn't disappointment. She was helping him on the business side; the roasting was his responsibility. Still, he'd begun to think of them as something of a team, even if he'd been stupid to think she'd want to witness this event. It meant a lot more to him than it did to her. It symbolized the start of a new business. A new life. Maybe one in which someone like Ana might be interested in someone like him.

He turned on the roaster, brought up the software, and started the roaster heating. This was a double-walled design in which a smaller steel drum rotated inside a larger one, which was in turn heated by the burner. The air space between the two transferred heat to the inner drum by convection; in Bryan's opinion, it was preferable to a direct-heat method because it cut down on the possibility of scorching the beans early in the roast, something like heating chocolate in a double boiler rather than in a pot on the stove. He'd made that mistake young, when he'd attempted to make hot chocolate by melting Hershey bars over high heat on his mom's range.

He started by weighing his beans. The roaster had a twelve-kilogram capacity, but it worked best at three-quarters full, so he weighed out nine kilos. Then he checked the beans' humidity with a hygrometer and noted it in the space in the software that kept track of the profile for a particular bean. He was going to start at 450 degrees on this one, knowing that high-altitude Colombian beans liked a hotter temperature than Ethiopian or Kenyan.

Once the roaster hit temperature, he carefully poured the beans into the hopper, the sound as they hit the hot drum like marbles on a tile floor. Almost instantly the grassy smell of green coffee beans hit his nostrils. He glanced back at the computer and watched the drum temperature plummet as the cooler beans were inserted, waiting for "the turn," where the temperature would begin to rebound.

It climbed almost immediately. And kept climbing. The pop of the first beans at six minutes was his first indication that the roast wasn't going the way he wanted it to, but he decided to let it go and find out what would happen. The software told him he was leveling off at his desired roasting temperature, but it was progressing far too fast. When he hit second crack at only nine minutes, he shut the roaster down and emptied the beans into the tray where agitator blades churned them until they cooled to room temperature. He scowled at them, dark and oily. He had been going for a medium brown with barely a sheen. As soon as they were cool enough to handle, he pulled a couple from the tray and popped one in his mouth. And immediately spit it in the trash.

He'd still cup it, but it would be more for educational purposes than decision-making. This batch was a bust.

Bryan pulled out his cell phone, about to text Ana an update, but shoved it back in his pocket just as quickly. She didn't need to hear about his failures. He knew there would be some, but in order for her to do her job properly, she needed to have confidence in the product they were selling. What he had in front of him right now, he didn't want to drink, let alone sell.

He saved the profile so he could refer to it later, shut down his computer, and turned off the lights in the roasting room. It was just past eight o'clock, and he'd now been here for fourteen hours. This time he did send a text, but to Alex: Whatcha doing, bro?

A couple of minutes passed, and Bryan locked up all the doors and shut down all the lights but the one in the reception area. His back pocket beeped.

Dinner with Rachel. Why?

No reason. Going home then. He wasn't going to interrupt his friend's time with his fiancée, especially since Rachel was so busy. But it only served to highlight the fact that he had absolutely nothing waiting for him at home. It wasn't even a home. It was his parents' house, where he was a welcome but slightly frustrating houseguest. No doubt they looked at him and wondered where they'd gone wrong.

The gym then. He kept a bag in the back of his car so he could pop in when the impulse struck. He drove across town to the climbing gym, swiped his card at the front desk, and proceeded straight to the locker room. It brought him past one of the climbing walls, where two climbers, a woman and a man, were working their way up the multicolored holds set in the concrete wall. A wash of longing hit him with unexpected force. How long had it been now? Seven months? Eight? Already his calluses were beginning to soften. Were he to attempt an outdoor route, the rough rock would probably rub his fingers raw. Kiss of death for a professional climber. No, worse than that. A sign of shame. An indication that he'd given up, gone conventional.

He sped up again, dumped his stuff in his locker, and changed into a T-shirt and shorts before heading to the weight room, where he could punish his body with free weights until he forgot what it felt like to be hanging in space by his fingertips, managing his adrenaline to conserve his energy, knowing exactly how long he had before his muscles gave out on him.

That man—the thrill seeker who made bad decisions based on how they made him feel, who used women who didn't matter to him so he could forget the one who did—was long gone. He didn't want him back. Wouldn't risk encountering him again on the slab and not being able to leave him behind.

He was already back in the locker room, heading for the showers, before he realized the woman he was trying to push from his mind tonight wasn't Vivian, but Ana.

*   *   *

She was not avoiding Bryan.

No, the real reason Ana was staying away from the roastery this week had to do with her massive to-do list, not the fact that she'd had another . . . moment . . . with a man she was trying hard to keep at arm's length.

She started her day early as usual at the gym, pushing herself through a ninety-minute hot yoga class that left her feeling wrung out like a limp rag. A shower and a protein shake later, she turned to her list, which involved following up on some details on the wedding venue with Darcy. The farm's phone just rang, however, and Ana left a message to call her back as soon as possible.

That meant turning her attention to the page-long list of tasks for Solid Grounds. She hadn't been happy with the first batch of logos she got from her graphic designer, so she sent them back with a critique for a second round of designs. Until that got nailed down, she couldn't do anything about packaging, signage, or marketing materials.

She could, however, finish writing all the copy for the website. Her designer was already working on the shell of the site, ready to plug in the graphics and the content as soon as she could provide it, which basically meant she was behind on the whole process. Their selling point was the story: how a professional climber had come to be involved with a nonprofit co-op, then bought a coffee farm in Colombia. She just had to cast it in a way that was not only engaging and exciting, but also easily repeatable. It was one thing to sell people on the coffee and the concept; it was another to let them use it as a value-added offering for their own brand. Denver was a socially conscious city that already prioritized local businesses over chains; to be able to offer coffee with a wider vision but home-based roots was an opportunity that they wouldn't let pass by.

She was so absorbed in crafting the messaging for Solid Grounds that she didn't notice the sun going down through her wide apartment windows until she looked up into full night. No wonder her stomach was beginning to feel hollow.

She hadn't stopped for lunch and it was already edging past her usual dinnertime.

She quickly scanned what she had written and felt a glow of satisfaction at the accomplishment. It may have taken her all day, but she'd finally come up with something that was interesting and mildly inspirational without being hyperbolic. She already knew that Bryan would give her pushback on how she had portrayed him, but that was one battle she was not going to lose. He'd put her in charge of messaging, so he was going to have to defer to her judgment.

It wasn't so different from what she did for her other clients, she realized. She worked on their images by giving them humanitarian activities, things that would show they really weren't the heartless, immoral capitalists that everyone assumed they were. The only difference was, Bryan's activities were a legitimate outgrowth of change that had taken place long before she got a hold on him.

It was nice for once to tell a story that actually existed rather than having to craft one from scratch and then bully the client into climbing on board.

She saved the file, attached it to an email, and sent it to Bryan with the cover note, *Your new website copy. Let me know what you think. And no, I'm not taking you out of this, so don't ask.*

She smiled as she pressed Send, then sat in her quiet apartment, wondering what to do next. Dinner, she supposed.

A half hour later, sitting in front of a steamed sweet potato and a hastily sautéed chicken breast, she wondered if she should have gone out. Even when she didn't have company, sometimes it was enough to be in public, surrounded by people. It cut the lonely feeling that came from living in this city and working the long hours that most Denverites worked. The vaunted Colorado work-life balance basically just meant they spent their free time climbing, biking, or kayaking rather than binge-watching Netflix. It didn't necessarily translate to more connection or less work.

She clicked on her television for the noise and tuned it to a network channel before switching it off just as quickly. Music competitions held no interest for her, not anymore. She knew all too well everything that went on behind the scenes in that industry. Instead, she took out her phone and texted Melody and Rachel: I'm bored.

Melody texted back immediately: Ana?

Yes?

I was checking to make sure it's actually you. I've never heard you say you're bored.

So that means you're free?

A sad-face emoji came through from Melody followed by the message: Sorry. With Justin tonight.

Rachel's reply followed close behind. And I'm with Alex. Funny, Bryan texted something similar about an hour ago.

Ana paused. Somehow she hadn't thought about Bryan doing the same thing she was, working late and eating alone. Well, it was too late to do anything about the eating alone part, but . . . No, what was she thinking? She was trying to stay away from him.

But why? Because she was attracted to him? That was silly. She'd been attracted to other men over the years without acting on it. And she liked him, *legitimately* liked him, as a friend.

Melody: You should call him and see what he's doing. A long pause and then a second message came through. I promise, this isn't me trying to set you up.

Ana looked at her phone for a moment, trying to decide what to do. She could always text him and see if he was free for coffee. Or maybe not coffee considering their new line of work. At this hour, drinks would sound like she was looking for a hookup. Bowling was . . . not her thing. Which left absolutely no innocent reason to be texting him.

She almost said as much to Melody but found she didn't have the energy to go into the whys. Instead she went to her bedroom, climbed into her pajamas, and settled under her summer-weight comforter with the devotional she hadn't cracked in a week, if not longer. At least she could get some Jesus and fill in those blank squares in her planner that had been staring at her accusingly. And for an hour or so, at least, she could convince herself that she had no need of human contact.

Chapter Twenty-One

THE GOOD NEWS was that Bryan had the spare beans for his trial. The bad news was that he needed them.

There was something he wasn't getting about the process of roasting, and he wasn't sure what the variable was. He was familiar with the machine. He was using the same profile he'd used for similar Colombian beans in Oregon. He attempted to follow the curve exactly, messing with time and temperature and airflow. He slowed down the roast, which only resulted in overdeveloped beans. He sped up the roast, which resulted in beans that had a grassy flavor and underextracted because they hadn't lost an adequate amount of their mass in the roasting process. Before long, he had kilos of failed roasts, beans that could only be used to fertilize gardens. He certainly didn't dislike anyone enough to make them drink it.

And his optimism, which had been so high only days before, began to plummet.

It wasn't only that this was harder than he expected; it was that he couldn't figure out what he was doing so differently between his apprenticeship and his own shop. He pulled some of his coffee books off the shelf in the office and scanned the passages about roasting in the hopes that something would jog an idea loose.

"Pretty intense look you've got there."

Bryan jerked his head up and found Ana standing just inside the front door, holding a paper bag. She took his lack of greeting in stride and plunked the bag down on his desk. "I thought you might like some dinner."

"Dinner? What time is it?" He twisted around and checked the clock.

"Five thirty. I understand it's a little early, but I was hoping to make a class at my gym later tonight and I hate working out on a full stomach. You like Lebanese, I assume?"

Bryan straightened and put aside his books, unable to deny the sudden lift of his mood at Ana's appearance. "I can't say I've ever had Lebanese specifically, but I like most Mediterranean food."

"Well, this is the best, and it better be, because I had to drive all the way to Aurora to get it."

Bryan chuckled. Aurora was an eastern suburb of Denver, only about twenty minutes away without traffic, but it might as well have been a different planet as far as most downtown dwellers were concerned. "If it's imported, that makes it all the better."

Ana laughed and pulled up a chair on the other side of the desk. "Did you have a chance to look over the web content I sent you?"

Bryan made a face. "So that's what this is about? A bribe to make me let you use that?"

"Oh no, this is just dinner. You don't have a choice with the content." She began unpacking containers from the bag. "What's wrong with it anyway?"

"It makes me sound . . . heroic."

"I hate to break it to you, but I just told the bald-faced truth. If it sounds heroic, that's because it is."

He made a face and peered through the clear lid of his container. "Steak?"

"If you'd prefer the chicken, I'm happy to swap. I'll eat either."

"No, steak's good." He lifted the lid and inhaled the aroma of Middle Eastern spices. In addition to the sliced grilled steak, his plastic plate was heaped with creamy hummus, tabbouleh, and saffron rice. He took a plastic fork and stabbed a piece of meat, hoping that if he had his mouth full, Ana would cease with the direction of the discussion.

"It's a good message, Bryan. It's got 'think global, act local' all over it. And it's even better because it's completely authentic. It wasn't concocted by someone like me. I was thinking we should shoot a couple of short videos for the site and social media, have you talk about Colombia and what the drug trade has done to the farmers, why you wanted to help."

He kept chewing and didn't look her in the eye.

"You know I'm not going to go away just because you're not looking at me, right?"

Bryan choked on a laugh, his mouth still full. He chewed and swallowed before he could speak again. "I was hoping maybe you'd get the hint."

She stabbed her own piece of chicken and chewed placidly, purposely drawing out the time before she answered. "You want to make a living at this? You take my word for it. This is the way to do it."

"And if I don't?"

"Then you can find another marketing expert, but they're just going to tell you the same thing." Ana shrugged. "People pay me tens of thousands of dollars to craft this sort of opportunity for them. If you don't take it, you're an idiot, and I don't do business with idiots."

"Ouch. Just be honest with me, will you?"

Ana smiled sweetly. "I always am."

"Well, if we're being honest, then I guess you should know that we may not even have a product to sell."

Ana sobered immediately. "What? Why? Something wrong with the equipment? The beans?"

"Only the ones up here." Bryan tapped his temple and then told her about all his failed batches that day. "I just can't seem to grasp whatever intangible is interfering with the roast. I'm using similar beans, the same profile, and it's not cooperating."

"It's tough translating processes and recipes to a new place." Ana forked tabbouleh into her mouth and chewed, her expression thoughtful. "I remember when Melody and I moved to Denver and she got her first pastry job. I thought she was going to lose it. She was so confident in all her recipes from San Francisco and Paris, and then she had to adapt them all to Denver. The humidity and the altitude wreak havoc on baked goods."

Bryan stared at her. "What did you say?"

"I said Melody's recipes didn't work here." Ana frowned. "Why?"

Bryan tipped back in his chair, his jaw slack. "I'm a total idiot."

Ana blinked. "I don't understand."

"Roasting beans. We're baking them. The process of roasting requires a Maillard reaction to caramelize the sugars and brown the beans, just like baked goods." He leaned forward. "It's the altitude, Ana."

A smile started on her face. "That would make a difference, wouldn't it?"

"Without a doubt. I've lived here all my life, but I've never roasted here. I didn't even think about it." He started to laugh. "You've just saved me."

"Well, technically, I think it's Melody who saved you."

"Nope, definitely you and your well-timed Lebanese take-out." He went back to his meal, but his foot was tapping impatiently as he thought through the adjustments he would make to his next roast.

"You're dying to try something, I can tell." Ana smiled. "It's okay. Pretend I'm not here."

Bryan jumped up and rushed to the roasting room, where he turned on the flame to preheat the drum. His laptop woke up as soon as it started receiving input, already charting the minute rise in temperature. Then he went back to the office and pulled a yellow pad from his desk drawer, almost forgetting that Ana still sat there, watching him curiously.

If he compensated for the ten-degree difference in the boiling point, that meant he was getting to first crack much sooner than he should, leading to the underdeveloped flavors. Which meant turning down the temperature for the first phase of the roast . . . He scribbled figures on the page for each point of the roast and then drew a time-to-temperature curve so he could visualize how he was going to plot it in the software.

Ana was craning her neck to get a look. She glanced up at him with a sheepish smile, and only then did he realize that she was surprised.

"What, you didn't think I could do math?"

She shrugged, a bit of pink coloring her cheeks. "You're just so relaxed about everything all the time. I honestly don't know what you're capable of."

"Until recently, maybe I didn't either." He paused. "You want to hang around for a bit, see how this all shakes out?"

She hesitated, then nodded. "Sure. I want to see if this does the trick."

"Okay." He smiled at her and returned to his food, polishing it off in minutes and then tossing the container back into the bag. "Am I mistaken or is that baklava in there?"

Ana pulled the container from the bag and scooted it out of his reach. "It is, but it's dessert. Which you can earn by figuring out your roasting problem."

"You're mean."

"I'm good at motivation."

She was, but it was more her presence and the fact he didn't want to fail in front of her that was driving him to get this right. That and the need to prove this was not the risky, impossible venture his father seemed to think it was. He was betting his life savings on the four thousand pounds of beans in the storage room, and so far he was too afraid to break into them for anything more than a sample roast.

Ana finished her food and added her own container to the bag, then pushed herself to her feet. "Okay. Are we going to do this then?"

"Yep. It will take a few more minutes to preheat the drum, and then we can get going. Come on, I'll let you weigh the beans."

"Oh, goodie," Ana said, but the excited glint in her eye spoke of anticipation. She threw the paper bag in the trash can and followed him from the office.

"There's the scale," he said, pointing to the table that held the plastic tub of opened beans and a gram scale. "We're going for nine kilos."

"I feel like I'm involved in an illicit operation. You know, Americans don't use kilos for anything but drugs."

"Something you know a lot about, do you?"

"Only what I see in movies." She scooped beans from the tub into the container on the scale, watching the digital readout carefully until it showed 9,000 grams. "What now?"

"Showtime." He pointed to the computer, which showed the drum temperature, much lower than where he'd been starting his roast. Starting at a lower temperature would soften the rate of rise on the rebound, leading to a longer first phase and, hopefully, a better result. He just prayed that he had it right this time.

"Do the honors. Pour them in that hopper there."

Ana moved to the roaster and poured the beans in where he indicated, though she had to stretch on her tiptoes to do it. Without her high heels, he realized how tiny she really was; he towered over her and he was just a hair above average height. But that was not what he should be focusing on now. He turned his attention back to the computer and gestured for her to look at the software, which was now plotting the temperature curve in real time, sampling the drum every thirty seconds.

"Why does the bean temperature drop like that?"

"The drum temperature drops. Just like when you drop pasta into boiling water and it stops boiling and then it gradually comes back to a simmer? Same thing. The pasta—and the beans—are continually rising, but it takes a while for the drum to heat up again. We're just looking for a nice steady curve here." He pointed back at the line, which had immediately begun to climb.

He peeked at the flames, fiddled with the air mixture, and pulled a sample with the small cylindrical trier. The beans were starting to get a nice, even color. No black spots.

"Smell that? That bready phase indicates a Maillard reaction. That's basically when amino groups start getting rearranged into different flavor compounds. As the caramelization process begins, it's going to start breaking down sucrose, which contributes to the acidity of the final coffee."

Ana looked up at him, her expression hovering somewhere between curious and admiring. Her mouth opened, but she obviously thought better of it and shut it again.

He didn't pursue what he saw in her eyes, not now, going between visual inspection of the beans in the roaster and his software. Finally, he heard the first telltale pop, followed by a cacophony of cracks as the others split open. A quick check of the color, a sniff of the beans, and he decided he was done. He pulled the lever and spilled the beans from the drum into the cooling tray, which immediately began churning.

"That's it?"

"That's it." He checked the time. Much longer than it had taken him to get to first crack before, but he was optimistic that the beans were far better developed than the first short attempts. Just inhaling the aroma of the finished product gave him the sense that he'd gotten it right.

"And then we need to wait eight hours?"

"Don't worry, I'm not going to ask you to come back at 2 a.m. But I will make you a cup of coffee first thing tomorrow if you come by."

Her eyes shone with excitement, picking up on his optimism. "Deal. I'd venture to say you've earned your baklava." She pushed herself away from the table, disappeared into the office, and returned with the plastic container.

"Your prize." She flipped the container open and offered it to him. He selected one of two pieces of pastry, sticky with honey, a dusting of chopped pistachios falling off onto the floor.

He took a bite and chewed. He didn't particularly like baklava, even though this was a good one, crispy and flaky and sweet. Ana, on the other hand, sighed with pleasure at her first bite, rolling her eyes.

"It's been so long since I've had this," she said. "I don't usually do pastry. It's so bad for you."

"So is coffee."

"Bite your tongue. Coffee is life. I would inject it directly if I could."

"There's a product line we could think of expanding into. Do you think it would catch on?"

"If it were legal, absolutely." She licked the honey off her fingers, and he barely restrained himself from suggesting that he help with the process.

"I guess now would be the time to tell you I don't really like baklava?" He held up his half-eaten pastry, dancing it in front of her face. "I think you should eat it."

She lifted her eyebrows at him. "Because you hate me and want to see me pay?"

"You know, not everything enjoyable has to be bad for you."

Two little spots of color surfaced in her cheeks, and he realized she'd taken his comment as innuendo. A smile played at the corners of his lips and he moved the baklava closer. "Come on, you know you want it."

She narrowed her eyes at him, but when he put it to her lips, she took a bite. "Okay, so it's totally worth it."

"Totally," he agreed, stepping closer before he even realized what he was doing.

Her eyes widened a fraction as he got closer, only a few inches between them, the air suddenly charged with energy.

"You've got something right there," he murmured, swiping away a tiny piece of pastry from the edge of her mouth. Her lips parted, her eyes locking with his, but she didn't move away.

Part of his mind whispered that what he was about to do was stupid; the other half whispered that he'd be stupid not to. He put down the baklava and rested one hand on her waist, slowly drawing her closer to him. She came along, seemingly unable or unwilling to pull away as he dipped his head toward hers.

The first soft touch of his lips to hers brought a quiet exhale, a barely perceptible softening against him, which he took as assent. He kissed her slowly, carefully, tasting honey and pistachio and something that had to be her alone, holding her so lightly she could have drawn free with a breath. And then he broke the contact, lifted his head to look directly into her eyes.

Ana was staring at him with an expression halfway between shock and wonder, as if she couldn't believe it had actually happened. She took a deep, shuddering breath for the count of three. And then she slid her hand behind his neck to pull his lips down to hers again.

* * *

She was kissing Bryan.

The thought broke through for a bare second and then disappeared just as quickly, pushed out by all the other sensations she'd rather focus on: the soft brush of his lips against hers and the pressure of his fingertips on her back, holding their bodies so tightly together she wasn't sure where she ended and he began.

No, she was kissing him, and all she could think was that this felt *right*. That she was made to be kissing him. That they were puzzle pieces that first looked to be incompatible but fit together in both the strangest and most logical way. And then she wasn't thinking about anything, because she couldn't catch her breath, couldn't get enough of him, drinking him in like she hadn't known she was dying of thirst.

He lifted her onto the table to level their heights, his mouth never leaving hers for a moment. And then something penetrated her fog of desire. "Wait," she whispered against his mouth.

He lifted his head a bare inch. "What? Too fast?"

Ana shifted and pulled out the object she'd been sitting on. "No. Clipboard."

Bryan laughed, surprised, and grinned at her before bending down for another kiss. She let herself fall into it for a minute before she pushed him back a bit. "Wait, Bryan."

"I know there's not another clipboard under there."

She laughed and dropped her head against his chest. "That's not what I meant."

"Too fast? Too . . . me?"

Ana jerked her head up, hearing the thread of insecurity in his voice. "No. It's not that. It's just . . ."

"We're friends and we're working together?"

She smacked him in the chest, but only succeeded in stinging her hand. The guy was chiseled from rock. "Will you shut up a moment and let me think?"

"Sorry. Shutting up while you think." He shoved his hands in his pockets, grinning down at her like she'd done something amusing.

"Who said you could let me go?"

"Has anyone told you you're bossy?"

"Is that a problem for you?"

"No, not considering you want me to keep holding you." He slid his arms around her waist and pulled her to him again. "Is this helping you think?"

She laughed breathlessly. "Not really. It's just . . ."

He dipped his head and kissed the corner of her mouth. "It's not that complicated, Ana. I like you."

"I like you too; it's just that . . ."

He kissed the other corner of her mouth. "Our friends will find out about this and have us married by the end of the month?"

"That's one thing . . ."

He nuzzled her neck and whispered in her ear, "We're just kissing, Ana. It's not a proposal and it's not a proposition. And you can tell me to get lost at any time."

And put that way, she couldn't think of a logical objection to what was a much better way to spend an evening than going to the gym.

Chapter Twenty-Two

ANA SHOWED UP at the roastery at precisely nine o'clock the next morning, feeling giddy and ridiculous. She'd left late, never making it to the gym, instead waking up early and powering though two classes in an effort to deflate some of her buoyancy. It didn't work.

She and Bryan. Together.

Kissing.

A lot.

Which of course wasn't the main point of any relationship, but it definitely marked a change in what had been up until now a flirtatious friendship. She'd taken extra care dressing and doing her makeup after the gym, even as she told herself she didn't need to. This was Bryan, after all. He'd seen her sweaty and disheveled, running the steps at Red Rocks. Not to mention the fact that he didn't seem like the type of guy to expect his woman to be made-up at all times.

She would never admit to thinking about being any man's woman, let alone his.

She parked out front on the nearly empty street and unlocked the door with her key, then flipped the latch behind her. "Bryan? Are you here?"

She heard a rustle a moment later, and he poked his head out of the cupping room. "Good morning!"

She held up the brown sack she was carrying. "Look what I brought."

"A paper bag?"

"Cute. I dropped by Bittersweet for breakfast."

"Oh, you are the best." He caught her around the waist and then lowered his head for a languid good-morning kiss. She sighed happily, feeling every bit as sappy as she'd accused her friends of being.

"I really am, aren't I?" she said, earning a laugh from him. "I do remember you promising me some coffee. I can't wait to test out the new roast."

He grimaced.

"You didn't."

"I couldn't help myself. I was so confident I'd gotten it right, but I used the inferior beans. It wasn't a good example. So after you left I did another batch with the Flor de Oro."

"And?"

He smiled. "It's good, Ana. It's really good."

Excitement welled up inside her. "Can I have some?"

"Of course. Let's go into the cupping room and I'll make you a pour over."

She grabbed the bag and moved into the cupping room, where Bryan immediately started weighing beans from a glass jar and then putting them into the grinder. She unpacked the Styrofoam containers that held their breakfast along with plastic utensils and settled onto a stool at the tasting bar. He'd said he'd been studying roasting, but evidently he'd been working on his barista skills, because he did the pour over exactly as she would have . . . on the scale, with a timer, giving each incremental amount time to absorb and drip through the paper filter before he poured the next. The slow, steady supply of water extracted the beans to just the right degree, while the heavy paper filter removed the oils and sediment for a clean, crisp cup of coffee. When he finally set the brewed coffee in front of her in a warmed cup, he looked about as excited as she felt.

Ana inhaled the aroma first, clean and bright with only a little bit of the roast's char evident. Pretty much a perfect medium roast. Then she took her first sip.

"So?" Bryan said.

She set down her cup carefully, a smile spreading across her face. "You're right. It's really good. I think you could go a little further to bring out the caramel or stop sooner and get more floral, and either would be excellent."

"I was thinking the same thing." He poured the rest of the coffee from the glass carafe into his own cup and sipped it experimentally. "The question is . . . is it good enough?"

"I say we let the experts decide. Tonight is friends-and-family night at the supper club again."

Bryan looked suddenly uncertain, and for whatever reason, she found that insecurity incredibly endearing. It was a sign that he cared about what he was doing, the flippant, devil-may-care climber who had done whatever he wanted for as long as he wanted. It was a change in the man she'd known. And not an unwelcome one.

"Would you rather hear it from them or from the shop owners and chefs when I start sampling?" Ana asked reasonably.

"Good point. Will you text Rachel and get us on the list?"

"We're already on it. I asked her a couple days ago if we could take over the coffee responsibilities. You can talk about the beans and I can play barista. If I recall, last time you asked me to make you a cortado."

Bryan circled the bar and perched on the stool next to her. "Was that only a month ago?"

She blinked. She guessed it was. Only a month since she'd been put on leave. A month since Bryan had come back into her life. How had her life made such a drastic turn in only a few short weeks?

"Uh-oh, I can tell you're analyzing things. I shouldn't have said anything."

"No, it's just that . . . a month ago, I would have never thought that I would be working full-time on your coffee company. Not in a million years would I have dreamed we'd be . . . you know . . ."

"Thanks a lot."

She flipped open her food container, which contained Rachel's famous spring crepes. "I didn't mean it that way. You did disappear for eight months. I wasn't sure we were going to see you again."

"If it makes you feel any better, I've been interested in you since the moment I met you. Remember, at Alex's Fourth of July barbecue? He was trying to impress Rachel, but I couldn't keep my eyes off you." He opened his own container and gave her a nod of thanks when he saw she'd gotten him the same thing. "And before you say it, I wasn't trying to get you into bed. I could tell that wasn't your style."

She flicked him an amused look. "That's not the impression I got."

"Maybe I didn't know how to go about it. It's a lot easier to flirt than to come up to an obviously intelligent and intimidating woman and tell her you think she's amazing."

"You think I'm amazing?" She let the *intimidating* crack go, because he was right.

"I do." He leaned over and planted a light kiss on her lips. "And I'm glad you haven't freaked out yet."

Ana stabbed a piece of potato. "I'm still considering it."

"You didn't seem to have any issues last night. I think I'm just going to keep kissing you so you can't think about it."

Inwardly, she thought that sounded like a very good idea. "If you do that, I'm going to forget that I have another batch of logos for you to look at."

"Rain check on the kissing, then. For now."

Ana chuckled as she pulled her tablet from her shoulder bag. She'd known he was sarcastic and charming and edgy, but this silly side was something completely new. The idea that she brought it out of him made a little flutter start in her stomach. She booted up the tablet and then pulled up the email from the graphic designer.

Bryan took the tablet from her hand and scrolled through the six designs in the file. "These are pretty good. But this . . . this is the one." He pointed to her favorite of the batch, designed to look like a passport stamp with a line-drawn mountain range in the center and *Solid Grounds* printed in a circle around it.

"That was the one I picked too." Ana smiled. "I'm thinking we use black, red, and cream for the brand colors. I'll make up a brand book so we can make sure everything's consistent across website and packaging."

"How long will that take? The website?"

"The back end, with the secure ordering and the product database, will be done in another week. The front end, the design part, hasn't even been started. He needed a logo to build it around."

Bryan found her hand and laced his fingers with hers. "Thank you, Ana. I couldn't have done this without you. I wouldn't know where to start."

She smiled at him. "Then we can start talking about my advisory shares of what is going to be a very successful company."

*   *   *

When Bryan got to Bittersweet Café that night, none of the guests had yet arrived; only Alex, Rachel, and Melody were there, the two women already hard at work on the meal. Bryan brought in a canvas bag that held the roasted beans and plunked it on the coffee bar, his stomach already in knots.

"Hey, where were you this morning?" Alex asked. "I thought you were meeting me at the gym."

"Sorry. I got caught up at the roastery." That was one of the reasons, at least. After Ana left, he'd started fine-tuning the roast with the Flor de Oro beans, finding the exact right point for both the drip grind and a blonde espresso; he refused to destroy the unique, delicate character of his beans by charring them into an unrecognizable mass of carbon. Do that, and his offerings would be no different from the chain coffee shops that dominated every street corner and airport in America.

The bigger reason was that he'd promised Ana he wouldn't say anything to their friends about their new relationship, but he was loath to lie. And between over two decades of friendship and Alex's multiple degrees in psychology, it would take him exactly four seconds to determine Bryan was hiding something.

Even now, Alex was studying him with narrowed eyes. "What's going on?"

Bryan took a deep breath. "I have to admit, I'm really nervous. It's one thing to think I'm good at this; it's another thing for people to say they'll pay for it."

Alex clapped him on the shoulder. "Welcome to my world. Every time I put out a new essay or article, it feels like being put in the stocks while the sun rises, waiting for the townspeople to start throwing rotten vegetables."

Bryan threw him an arched-eyebrow glance, and Alex laughed. "Okay, so weird analogy. Just know that putting yourself out there for any reason is pretty terrifying. What did Ana say? She's the biggest coffee snob out of all of us."

"She thought it was good. Of course, she had her suggestions about what I could do differently next time . . ." He didn't say that he had taken those suggestions and experimented with some tiny batches in the sample roaster. Tomorrow when he cupped the beans, he'd know if she'd been right or not.

"Speaking of . . ." Alex nodded toward the front door, through which Bryan could see Ana crossing the street to the bakery. Even from a distance he would have recognized her; he'd been cued into her for some time—her movements, her walk, the way she flipped her hair over her shoulder when she was trying hard to be nonchalant. Which was exactly how he knew she was just as nervous as he was at this moment, though for potentially different reasons.

"Did you know she used to be a barista?" Bryan said. "She's going to show off her skills tonight."

Alex looked at him closely for a moment, and Bryan wondered if he'd said something that had given him away, but he didn't have any more time to wonder because Ana was coming through the front door.

"Hey, guys." She pushed her sunglasses up onto her head, sounding perfectly normal. "Are we the first ones here?"

Alex nodded. "Rachel and Melody are cooking, of course."

"Good. I wanted to talk to them about what drinks they want us to make for dessert. Bryan and I thought it made more sense to serve the same drink to everyone. Easier to judge the quality of the coffee if we remove variables." She plopped her bag on the counter, smiled vaguely between the two men, and then retreated to the kitchen, where her friends were working.

Bryan watched her leave before he realized he was being conspicuous and turned back to his bag of beans. Alex stood there thoughtfully for a long moment. "So how's that whole thing going?"

"What whole thing?"

"You and Ana."

Bryan didn't look up. "Good, I think. We've got the logo nailed down, and she's called in pretty much every favor she's owed to get our website and marketing up and running fast. She's smart."

"And that's it?"

Bryan glanced up at his friend. "What's it?"

"She's smart?"

"Well, she's smoking hot, but you've got eyes." Bryan tried for his usual flippant tone, but from the smile that was creeping onto Alex's face, he thought he might have missed it by a few degrees.

"I do. As do you." Alex rapped his knuckles on the counter and took a step back. "I'm going to go talk to Rachel."

Bryan sighed. "Don't."

"Don't do what?"

"Don't go speculate with Rachel, okay? It will make Ana uncomfortable." There. He hadn't exactly told him anything, but he'd implied enough for his friend to fill in the blanks.

"Okay," Alex said simply. "But I give it until the end of the night before everyone knows. You are a terrible liar. Ana, however, is frighteningly good."

"She is until you get to know her," Bryan said without thinking, and then shut his mouth firmly.

Alex laughed. "Okay then. I do need to talk to Rachel, though." He held up a hand. "About a completely different topic."

Alex slipped from the room, leaving Bryan alone at the bar. So much for keeping things under wraps. What had it been? Sixty seconds before Alex knew everything, just from the look on his face? There was a reason why he'd never been any good at poker. Same reason he'd never been very good at pleasing his father—he couldn't prevent everything he thought and felt from surfacing directly in his expression and words. And most of the time, they were thoughts that probably should be kept to himself.

He spent time going over the bar setup. He'd worked briefly in the coffee shop attached to the roastery in Oregon, learning coffee-making techniques and best practices, but he couldn't say he was anywhere near a professional. The best he could do was check to make sure the espresso machine and the milk frother were clean, that the milk and nondairy alternatives in the refrigerator were fully chilled. He'd grind his beans as close as possible to brew time, so there was very little to do but run a damp rag over the polished bar top and hope for the best.

Ana emerged from the kitchen not long after. "You ready?"

"Yep."

She studied him for a second. "There's no reason to be nervous. The coffee is good. And really, 90 percent of the people here aren't going to know what they're drinking anyway."

"I'm not sure whether that's encouraging or not."

Ana plowed on, unperturbed. "I thought we'd start the drip when they're finishing up the main course and bring the cortado out after dessert."

"Good plan." He rubbed his hands together, a nervous gesture he'd developed in his climbing days, even though his palms weren't covered in chalk. He'd be a lot more relaxed if he could pull her close and kiss her, but before he could even think about making good on that idea, the door dinged open to their first guests.

It was friends-and-family night again, so Bryan had at least met most of the guests, even if he didn't know any of them well. He and Ana greeted them and ushered them to the table, which was soon filled with people, their relaxed chatter filling the small café space. Definitely an easier audience for their first time out of the gate. Did Rachel and Melody feel this nervous when they debuted a new menu item? Probably not. They were professionals; he was hoping to be a professional someday.

"Relax," Ana whispered, bumping him with her hip as she passed behind the bar. "It'll be fine."

He grasped her hand under cover of the bar and rubbed his thumb across the back, felt her slight inhale in response. At least he wasn't the only one having a hard time keeping their budding relationship under wraps.

Finally, Alex called them to the table and they filed into their places, Ana on the opposite end from Bryan, thankfully. Then Rachel and Melody brought out the salad course, which they never ate themselves. It was good, but his mind was split between Ana four seats down and their coffee debut in less than an hour; food was a bare afterthought.

The first-course plates got cleared, and then the women came out with the second course. Rachel stood at the head of the table to address the group. "This one is special tonight. We're having coffee-and-ancho-rubbed tenderloin over roasted potatoes, the coffee for which was provided by Denver's newest micro-roaster, the Solid Grounds Coffee Company, owned by our very own Bryan Shaw."

Bryan's gaze shot to Ana, who just grinned at him. So that was why she'd asked if she could take the remnants of the sample beans. He took his first experimental bite of the beef, wondering if he could recognize his own beans in the rub. He couldn't, but it was delicious all the same.

When that course was finished, Ana excused herself from the table to start the drip behind the bar. Bryan paused for a minute and joined her.

"I should have told you," Ana said, "but I wanted to surprise you."

"It was good, wasn't it?"

"It was. And this is going to be good too, so relax." Ana took the glass jar of beans, weighed out the proper amount, and poured them into the newly cleaned grinder.

"Not too fine. I'm finding that they overextract if . . ."

Ana shot him a look. "Bryan, I'd venture to say I've done this a lot more than you have. *Relax.*"

He grinned and backed off. Whatever might be going on between them, it didn't make a dent in her assertiveness. He just leaned against the back counter and watched her grind the beans, put them in the coffee machine, and start the drip going into the huge insulated dispenser. The way she moved around the bar said she hadn't been exaggerating about her work experience; however long ago it had been, she definitely knew what she was doing. What a surprise to find that the polished, high-powered professional could do something as . . . normal . . . as make coffee on a commercial machine.

Or maybe it was just because everything she did was fascinating to him and always had been.

He had it bad.

"If you pour, I'll serve," he said in a low voice, leaning over to check that the cups were warm on top of the espresso machine.

"Deal." She didn't look at him, just checked the progress of the coffee and then started pulling cups from the stack to fill, neatly and precisely, all to the same level. He put them on saucers and took the first two out to the table before he thought to grab a tray from under the counter and take out the next six together.

And then he held his breath, waiting for their responses. He shouldn't have been surprised when Ana fished cards out of her purse and began passing them around. "I know this is unusual for a supper club, but this is also our very first focus group. If you wouldn't mind filling out the cards while you drink your coffee and eat your dessert, we would really appreciate it."

He shot her a grateful look down the table, and she winked at him in reply as if to say, *Don't worry. I've got this.*

Bryan picked up his own card. It was short and anonymous with questions to be rated on a scale of 1–5, *strongly disagree* to *strongly agree*: *I thoroughly enjoyed my coffee. I thought it was too strong. I thought it was too weak. This is the style of coffee I like to drink for pleasure.* (On that one, he wondered what other option there was . . . what you drank for pure caffeination?) *I would buy this coffee for use at home. I would order this coffee at a local shop or restaurant.* At the bottom, a final question: *What is your favorite coffee drink?*

Melody and Rachel brought out dessert then: flourless chocolate cake with a dusting of confectioner's sugar and fresh raspberries. He suspected that Ana had coordinated the offering with them to complement the drinks. There was no denying that chocolate and coffee were a magic marriage of flavors.

When the guests had gotten mostly through their desserts, he and Ana went back to the bar and started pulling two shots at a time for the cortados: a drink served in a double shot glass with equal parts milk and espresso. It was a nice way to show off the flavor of the beans while still appealing to those who couldn't handle the bitterness of an undiluted shot. Ana worked the Bezzera espresso machine like a pro, the years away obviously not dampening her memory or her touch for it. He took these out two at a time while she made them, so they'd be piping hot when they hit the table, then thought to collect the cards and pass out another round for the espresso.

He dipped his head to whisper as he passed, "You make coffee look sexy."

She flushed, but she didn't miss a beat in tamping the grounds and placing the portafilter into the group head. "Back atcha."

He couldn't help himself; he reached out and squeezed her waist, his thumb tracing a trail across her lower back . . . just as Rachel walked back through the door. Her eyes lit on their position and widened, followed by a sneaky grin.

"Uh-oh," he whispered. "I think the jig is up."

Ana twisted around, almost spilling the finished espresso shot, but Rachel had already moved on. "Are you sure?"

"Pretty sure."

Ana sighed. "Was it too much to ask for twenty-four hours to ourselves?"

"In this group, probably."

"Fine." Her voice took on a resigned tone that stung a bit, and she added the steamed milk to the last two cortados. "We'll deal with that later."

Bryan's euphoria of a moment ago dissipated as he walked back to the table and placed the last two shots in front of Rachel and Melody. He shouldn't let it bother him. Ana simply didn't want other people getting into their business. But maybe that wasn't the entire truth. She'd resisted him for the longest time because she thought he was a player . . . and honestly, he couldn't blame her. He hadn't given her any reason to think otherwise, with the long parade of pretty and sometimes vapid dates. He'd just thought she understood that he'd changed, that he wasn't that man anymore, that he didn't want to remember that man.

Or maybe it was far simpler than that. She dated men like Adrian—polished, rich, intelligent—not former climbers who lived at home with their parents while they tried to make a dubious business venture work.

She was fine with stolen kisses in the roasting room, but didn't necessarily want to be on his arm in public. And while he wished that were enough for him, watching her take her place with her friends at the opposite end of the table, for the first time he knew for certain . . . he wanted more.

Chapter Twenty-Three

THE SUPPER CLUB GUESTS cleared out, but Ana stayed behind the counter, cleaning the machine and returning the bar to the state in which she'd found it. In truth, she was avoiding the discussion that she knew was going to follow as soon as her friends got her alone.

But Rachel and Melody went back to the kitchen to clean up and wash dishes and get the bakery ready to open the next morning, so Ana came out to the table where Bryan was sorting the comment cards into six different piles.

"How are they?" Ana asked. "Judging from everyone's reactions, I'm guessing overall positive?"

"For the most part." Bryan looked up and smiled at her, and a little part of her annoyance melted. She slid into the seat across from him and pulled a stack of cards toward her. These were obviously the high-scoring ones of the drip batch, because almost all the circled numbers were fives.

"Six out of twelve said it was excellent. That has to make you feel good."

"Yeah, but six out of twelve didn't." He pushed the other two piles toward her.

She picked up the first card. This person's impression was lukewarm, but the last response clinched it: their favorite drink was an iced blended mocha. She flipped through the rest and saw a similar trend: Frappuccino, white chocolate mocha, dirty chai.

"This is totally fine," she said. "That's why I added the control question. The people who were iffy about it are the people who really don't drink coffee so much as they drink sweet caffeinated drinks. If you serve them a cup of black coffee instead of a mocha, they're not going to love it. Their taste buds are calibrated for the sugar."

"I noticed that too," Bryan said. "Similar trend with the cortado. It's not a drink that non–coffee drinkers are going to be familiar with."

"All this tells us is that you know your target market." She reached across the table and squeezed his wrist. "This is encouraging, Bryan. We're on the right track."

His mouth tipped up at the corner. "Thanks to your foresight."

Ana shrugged. "It's my job. Trust me, I threw this together at the last minute. I hate to miss an opportunity to gather data."

A clatter in the kitchen made them jerk their heads toward the swinging door, startled. Bryan folded his hands in front of him. "So, what do you want to do?"

"About what?"

"About them. Alex already knows. He saw me watching you and figured it out. He's a mind reader."

Ana sighed. "I know. I didn't really think we'd be able to keep it quiet, but I was hoping . . . Anyway, I'll tell them tonight. They're not going to let me out of here without an interrogation."

Bryan nodded thoughtfully. "Well, since we aren't sneaking

around anymore, how about having dinner with me next weekend?"

Ana blinked. "I can't."

He chewed his lip for a second, obviously turning something over in his mind. "Are you embarrassed to be seen with me, Ana?"

Ana's jaw slackened. "No! Why would you ask me that?"

"You don't want our friends to know and now you won't go out on a date in public . . ."

"That's not the reason!" The words spilled out of her in a rush. "I literally can't. I'm going to California for my dad's birthday next weekend. I'm leaving on Friday and I won't be back until Sunday night."

He laughed, relief threaded through the sound. "Oh. I thought . . ."

"No! Not it at all. I'd love to go to dinner. Wednesday maybe?"

"Good. Wednesday it is. I'll close down early." He rose from the table and gathered his cards. "I'm going to let you get to it and look over these at home. See you back at the roastery sometime this week?"

She nodded and got to her feet too. He gathered her to him and kissed her softly, tenderly. And despite the fact they were in public, that her friends could walk in at any moment, she wrapped her arms around his middle and kissed him back.

"See you soon, Ana."

"See you." She stood there, watching him walk out of the café, her heart feeling unexpectedly fluttery. Yes, they'd spent a few sweet hours kissing in secret, like forbidden first love, but this was the first time he'd kissed her in public. The first time he'd acted like her boyfriend.

"So . . ."

Ana spun and saw Rachel and Melody standing in the doorway, grins plastered on their faces. "Guys—"

"Is there something you'd like to tell us, Ana?"

Her face flamed with heat and she plopped back in her chair. "It's not that big of a deal."

Melody got there first, sliding into the seat across from her. "It is a huge deal. You and Bryan! Seriously, this has been so long in coming—"

"Mel," Rachel said quietly, and Melody probably realized that she wasn't helping matters. She shut her mouth and leaned back in her seat, but she was still grinning widely at Ana.

Rachel joined them, a tiny smile playing on her own lips. "When did all this happen?"

"Yesterday."

"Yesterday?" Melody burst out. "I can't believe . . ."

Rachel silenced her with another look. "Is it serious?"

Ana shook her head. "No. I mean, not yet. I don't know."

Rachel thought for a long moment. "I know Bryan seems to be pretty tough and flippant, but he's actually kind of a sensitive guy."

"Are you really telling me not to break *his* heart right now?" Ana asked. "The guy who has had a string of women and barely avoids getting slugged in bars by ex-girlfriends' brothers?"

"Oh, I haven't heard this story," Melody said. "Do tell."

Rachel ignored her. "He doesn't look at them like he looks at you. Like he always has. I'd venture to say he's been waiting for you to turn his way since he met you, but you haven't shown any interest. Just . . . be careful."

"I'm always careful," Ana said automatically.

"With *him*." Now Rachel let herself smile. "I care about both of you. He's like a brother to Alex, and you are practically my sister. I want both of you to be happy."

Ana shifted uncomfortably in her seat. Why did the weight

of this relationship—if you could even call it that—fall on her shoulders? "I expected you guys to have my back."

"We do," Melody said. "Always. It's just different when we're all friends."

"And that's exactly why I didn't want anyone to know." Ana shoved back her chair and began to collect her things. "We like each other. He kissed me. That's all this is, guys. Don't make it into something it's not." She hoisted her bag onto her shoulder. "I've got to go."

"Ana, we're sorry," Rachel called after her. "We didn't mean to upset you."

"Who's upset?" Ana threw back. "Just . . . let us figure this out on our own, okay? If there is a relationship, it's between me and him, not me and him and the rest of you."

She didn't wait to hear their response, just let herself out the café's front door and crossed the street to where her SUV was parked. The cool air hit her face, dissipating some of the angry heat gathered there. She hauled herself into the car and slammed the door, then just sat there in the dark, breathing in and out. She wasn't sure if she wanted to yell or cry, and she couldn't figure out why either of those were options in the first place. She knew her friends meant well, so she had no reason to be angry . . . and the crying part was so out of character for her that she'd almost forgotten what it felt like.

And then she knew why the tears felt like an option. The look on Bryan's face when he'd thought she was turning him down for dinner, coupled with Rachel's warning, made her feel like a terrible person. She hadn't meant to be abrupt, and she really didn't want him to feel bad. She just wasn't sure how to handle the situation.

She hadn't had a real, legitimate relationship since she was eighteen, and that had ended in a total disaster that she was still living down.

Ana pulled out her phone, then composed and deleted messages to Bryan until she settled on I don't really feel like being alone tonight. Want to watch a movie or something?

The bubbles started dancing, indicating his reply. Sure. Did you have something in mind?

She pulled up the movie app on her phone and flipped through the late-night options, but everything was either too violent or too steamy. You want to come to my place? Just for Netflix. No chill.

Almost immediately, his response: Understood. With you I have no chill anyway.

She laughed out loud at the reply. He was clever; she'd give him that. See you in 30 then? He might not know it, but she was making a statement—not to him, not to her friends, but to herself.

*   *   *

Ana's stomach jumbled with nerves while she waited for Bryan to show up at her place. Which was silly, because women had guys over to their place all the time without anything happening. But those women weren't her. As far as she knew, she'd never actually had a man in her apartment . . . well, ever.

Wow. That was kind of sad.

It was also understandable. She worked so much that she was rarely home, and when she dated a new guy, most of them never made it past the first date, much less the one-month, definitely-not-a-murderer threshold. But this was Bryan. She'd known him for two years. They were a part of each other's solar system, not planets but satellites that circled around other bodies and managed to intersect once in a while. Which was maybe the nerdiest reference she could have possibly come up with.

She had herself thoroughly worked up by the time the knock came at her door, and she opened it with a nervous jitter in her middle.

"Hey." He bent down to lightly kiss her hello, but that was it. He moved past her when she held the door open and lifted a paper bag. "I didn't know what you had in mind, but in my opinion, you can't do movie night without popcorn and candy."

The nervousness vanished. It was so sweet and normal and silly that she couldn't remember what seemed so daring about this invitation. "Of course you can't. Microwave?"

He pretended to look shocked. "Never microwave." He dug in the bag and pulled out a glass jar of popcorn. "This is fair trade, organic, grown on a fifth-generation family farm. And, I suspect, picked kernel by kernel by angels, considering what they charge for it. We can only make this the old-fashioned way."

"I've got pots in the kitchen." She gestured toward the space just to the left of the entryway. "You might be the first person besides me to ever use it."

Bryan sobered as he looked around. "Wow. This is amazing, Ana. I had no idea."

"Yeah, you really can't tell from the outside. But it has a great view too." She swept a hand toward the windows, to where downtown was spread out before them in a sparkling carpet of lights.

"Why didn't you host when Rachel needed a place for the supper club? This is every bit as nice as Alex's place."

A niggling bubble of guilt surfaced. She'd considered it, of course, but the idea of having a lot of people in her private space, strangers traipsing through her sanctuary, had been enough to give her a panic attack. "With my job, I don't like anyone knowing where I live. I'm repairing the reputations of people who sometimes don't deserve to have them repaired. And there are those who are pretty unhappy about it."

Bryan looked at her closely, real concern etching his face. "Have you ever been threatened?"

"Not with anything more than nasty letters and phone calls to my office, fortunately. Occupational hazard."

She went to one of the cabinets and pulled down a large stainless-steel pot, set it on the commercial-style range, then searched in another cabinet for a big jar of coconut oil. "I'm assuming we need butter too?"

"You assumed right. Got a measuring cup and spoon?"

She found one for him, and Bryan scooped coconut oil into the heating pan, then dropped a couple of kernels into it and shut the lid. "Test kernels. When they pop, we know the oil is hot enough."

"Interesting." She cocked a hip against the counter. "Do you know how to cook anything else?"

"Nope. Pretty much popcorn and coffee are the extent of my culinary skills. Though I do make a fantastic turkey sandwich, if that counts."

"Kind of." She smiled as she watched him measure the kernels. What was it that drew her to him? He was the exact opposite of anyone she'd thought she might want. He was good-looking, yes, in a boy-next-door-meets-surfer sort of way. He had a body carved from rock—she could have figured that much from having her arms around him, even without having surreptitiously checked out his magazine spreads and videos online. That would probably be enough for some women, but good-looking, well-built guys were a dime a dozen, whether in Los Angeles or Denver.

The first kernels popped and he lifted the lid to dump in the rest, then shook the pan, she assumed to coat them with oil. He looked completely at home in her expensive kitchen in his T-shirt, jeans, and flip-flops, his attention focused on what was going on inside the pot.

No artifice. No trying to impress. Just being exactly who he was and hoping that it was enough for her. He hadn't even tried to gloss over his past behavior to make himself look better, just explained how he was different now, how he wanted to leave that past behind. She worked in a business where everyone tried to be something that they weren't, paid hundreds of thousands of dollars to craft an image. By contrast, the public and the private Bryan were exactly the same.

She might be able to trust a man like that. She might even be able to love him.

"Do you have a big bowl?" Bryan asked, oblivious to the thoughts skittering around in her head.

"Yeah, right here." She absently opened yet another cabinet to reveal a big ceramic bowl. He took it down and set it aside while he tossed the hot popcorn with a few pats of soft butter, then poured it all into the bowl. "Here we are. Did you have any idea what you wanted to watch?"

He was taking her completely at her word, that he was there for movie-watching only. It was so sweet that she had a hard time repressing her smile.

He cocked his head at her. "What?"

Heat warmed her cheeks. "I really like you. You're a good guy."

Slowly, a smile spread across his lips, transforming his features. "I'm getting pretty fond of you myself." He took her hand and pulled her closer, then bent to kiss her. The only parts of them touching were hands and lips, but she felt the warmth through her entire body. Happiness.

How long had it been since she'd actually felt happy? Excited? Content? She took pride in her work, she thrived on the stress and the pressure, but it was a hard-edged satisfaction. Right now, she just wanted to wrap herself in this cozy feeling and never leave it.

Maybe she was wrong. Maybe it wasn't a matter of being able to fall in love with a guy like him. Maybe she was already there.

"Movie," he whispered, kissing the tip of her nose. "If you don't pick one, I'm going to choose some ridiculous foreign film just to show off."

"I forgot, you speak Spanish," Ana said. "Do you speak anything else?"

"A little French from school, a little more Portuguese, but Spanish more than anything. I was conversant before I spent all that time in Colombia, but I think I can call myself fluent now."

"I'm impressed."

"You're bilingual too. You speak Filipino, don't you?"

"Yeah. Taglish mostly." At his quizzical look, she said, "Tagalog plus English. I could speak it straight if I had to, but no one really does. It's all a mix of Tagalog and English and Spanish in my family."

"What are they like?" he asked curiously as they moved to her living room sofa and plopped together on the end of the sectional.

"They are . . . a lot."

"Meaning . . ."

"Loud, enthusiastic. They'll tell you exactly what they think, no holds barred."

"So basically exactly like you?"

Ana smacked him on the shoulder. "Thanks." She shook her hand. "I need to stop doing that. That hurt."

He laughed and pulled her to him, then took the remote from her hand. "Since you haven't picked anything, I'm going to choose."

"Nope, my house, my remote. I get to choose." She stole it back from him, then paused. "I know what I want to watch, but you're not going to like it."

"I'm not that picky."

"You promise you won't be mad?"

He frowned. "Why would I be mad because you picked a bad movie?"

Ana didn't say anything, just surfed through the documentary section until she found what she was looking for. She knew it was in here, because she'd seen the Netflix listing when she googled Bryan. She swallowed hard and clicked it, tensed for Bryan's reaction.

The main title came up: *On the Edge*, with a still image of a climber clinging to the edge of a granite slab.

Bryan stiffened beside her, the tension radiating through his body. "Ana . . ."

"Please?" she said quietly. "I know you said you've given it up, but it's a big part of you still. I want to understand. With you here to explain it to me."

He looked down at her, the conflict evident in his face. "That's really how you want to spend our evening?"

"Yes." She shot him a mischievous look. "Climbers are sexy."

He chuckled. "Okay, then. When you put it that way . . ."

She settled back against him and twined her fingers together between her knees, squeezing hard. The documentary followed five climbers, including Bryan, through various parts of their season. Ana found herself glued to the screen, fascinated by the technical details and interviews, cringing at the heights and the falls. Gradually, Bryan relaxed next to her, seemingly caught up in watching it until it came to his segment. The tension instantly radiated through him.

The female interviewer asked, "What would you do if you couldn't climb anymore?"

A younger Bryan laughed at the question, then looked into the distance as he considered. "I don't know. I really can't envision a life for myself that doesn't involve climbing."

Bryan reached for the remote and clicked the TV off, sitting there stiffly in silence.

"Bryan?"

He licked his lips but didn't respond, almost like he was listening to something beyond himself.

"Do you miss it?"

He twisted to look at her, whatever spell he'd been under broken. "Yeah. I miss it. Every day."

"Then why don't you still do it?" Ana asked softly. "I don't believe that setting hand or foot on a rock is going to turn you back into the person you were. You need to have more faith in what God has done with you, how you've changed, than that."

"It's not just that," he said, his voice hoarse. "It's . . . everything in that part of my life, from this documentary on . . ."

"Please. Just tell me."

He paused as if he were trying to think of where to start. "You should know the woman asking the questions in that video was Vivian, my ex-girlfriend."

That was the last thing she'd expected Bryan to say. "*The* ex-girlfriend?"

"You've heard about that, I see," he said wryly.

"No, not really. I just heard that the last time you disappeared, it was because of a woman. So I assumed."

"That was her. We met on this shoot and really hit it off. She's a climber too, by the way, or she was, before . . ." He gestured vaguely. "It doesn't matter. Suffice it to say that I fell for her hard, like I'd never fallen for anyone. We were together for a couple of years. And then I asked her to marry me."

"What happened?" Ana asked, even though she could already guess the answer.

"She said no." He shrugged. "Said that she never knew I was that serious about her and she wasn't ready to settle down. She was taking a job in California, and I was still based in Colorado. I would have moved for her, but she didn't want me to."

Ana took a moment for a slow inhale, considering her words. "I'm sorry. That must have been crushing."

He glanced at her, a wry look in his eyes. Maybe a little bitter. "It was. And I tried to get over her, but I think you know how I managed that. I was just thinking maybe I'd moved on when she showed up in Colombia, looking for me."

A stab of jealousy shot through her. His ex, his true love, had come back to him in Colombia? Was that why he'd stayed away?

He laughed harshly when she voiced those thoughts. "Not exactly. It turned out she just needed to get me out of her system. Before she got married. To my sponsor."

Ana's jaw dropped open. "You're kidding me."

"Nope. And when he found out that she'd come to see me, he figured that I'd been the one to lure her there or something. So he fired me. Canceled my sponsorship contract under some sort of buried exclusivity clause. He'd known I had a sponsorship from another gear manufacturer, but his approval wasn't in writing. I didn't have a legal leg to stand on." He laughed. "Ironic that he fired me over an *exclusivity* clause. He should have had one with his fiancée."

Ana stared at him, digesting that crusher. He'd barely gotten over the woman and she'd what, dangled herself in front of him? And then told him she was getting married?

"I'm . . . sorry. That's inadequate, I know. It's horrible. And just . . ." She shook her head. "I don't know what to say."

"Yeah, it was pretty awful. I got the job offer in Colombia, acted as a translator for a while, did some physical labor to keep my mind off it, and ended up buying a farm. Life's weird."

"Do you still love her?" She hated how insecure and needy her words came out.

He flicked his gaze to her, obviously surprised. "No. I would never have started this if I still had feelings for her."

"You had feelings for her the whole time you were dating a lot of other women before," she whispered.

"I wouldn't call those relationships." Regret tinged his soft tone. "What happened in Suesca . . . that pretty much killed any love I might have had left. She was using me, knowing how I felt about her, and that's just not something I could ever forget."

Ana must not have looked convinced, because he twisted on the sofa to face her fully. "Listen, I'm just going to lay it all on the table here, Ana. I'm crazy about you. I have been since I met you, but I could never get you to see I was more than a dumb climber."

She flushed. "I never thought—"

"Yes, you did. And that's okay. Because honestly, you wouldn't have wanted to be with the man I was back then."

She shifted around, the question she'd wanted to ask for a while rising to the surface. "What happened in Colombia, exactly? I mean, I understand about Vivian now, but . . . what changed?"

"My come-to-Jesus moment, you mean? Literally?"

She nodded.

He settled back against the cushion and let out a long breath. "It wasn't one big dramatic thing. It was the process of stepping out of my life, I guess. Getting some distance. When I didn't have all the distractions of the city—the clubs, the women, even my climbing—I realized that there wasn't very much to me. God took the opportunity to show me how empty I truly was, how the things I was holding on to really didn't matter in the grander scheme." He gave a self-conscious shrug. "I know that probably sounds foreign to someone like you."

Ana broke the eye contact, feeling suddenly horrible. "I wish you wouldn't say things like that."

"Why not? It's true."

She laughed helplessly and ran her fingers through her hair. "You seem to think I'm this paragon of Christian living, and I'm not. I can barely manage to crack my Bible, and I haven't been to Mass in like a month, even though I let my mom still think I'm going . . ."

Bryan smiled, but it had a sympathetic cast. "Faith isn't supposed to be a to-do list, Ana. Trust me, I had to come to grips with that myself." He reached for her hand and squeezed it. "Where's this all coming from?"

For a split second, she wanted to tell him, let all the things come pouring out that no one knew, not even her friends. But fear took the upper hand and she shoved the words back.

"Nothing. Sorry. I'm just dreading this trip back home. Every time I go back, all I hear from my parents is about how I've thrown away my youth on this horrible job when I should be getting married and having their grandkids. Don't get me wrong—I love my family; they just . . . don't understand."

Bryan stayed quiet for a long moment. "Then let me go with you."

She blinked. "What?"

"I'll come. I'm your boyfriend, after all. Or at least I want to be." He smiled again, and her heart stuttered at the way he was looking at her. "That should get the relatives off your back for a while."

"You don't want to do that. For one thing, you won't understand anything anyone is saying . . ."

"You already said they speak Taglish. I can figure it out from the English and Spanish."

"And for another, we're going to get asked about the wedding date at least two times before we leave, if not more. I don't bring guys home."

"Ever?"

"*Never* ever. Because like I said, they're a lot."

He lifted her hand to his lips and kissed the back of her fingers. "You're important to me, Ana. I would face any number of nosy relatives for you, and far more than that. What do you say?"

It was a terrible idea. Either he'd decide he'd made the worst decision taking up with her once he got put through the third degree from her aunties, or they'd break up and her family would perpetually ask her about the nice Colorado boy. Because despite what he seemed to think about himself, he could charm just about anyone.

"I think maybe you're a glutton for punishment."

He brushed his fingers against her cheek. "No, Ana. I'm just in love with you."

She only had time to gasp before his lips were on hers. And at that point, there was really no decision to make.

Chapter Twenty-Four

"WE SHOULD NOT BE GOING," Ana muttered as they walked down the Jetway, a stop-and-go process as the plane loaded.

"I thought we'd been through this," Bryan said. "We go. I meet your family and convince them that you're not going to be an old shriveled spinster, and then we come home. Easy."

Ana rolled her eyes at him. "Thanks for that image. I was talking about the business. I just dropped off all those samples and sent out the brochures. We need to be home in case we get prospective customers wanting to come by."

"I'm the owner of the business and I'm not worried. So why are you stressing over it? Are you having second thoughts about me coming along?"

"No, I'm having second thoughts about *me* going. You're the only reason I'm actually going through with it." She twisted around and lifted her face for a kiss, and he willingly obliged.

A man in a suit cleared his throat behind them, and Ana broke away to see that the line was moving again. She pulled her roller case along, aware of Bryan following, and couldn't resist a glance behind her. Partly because she really was grateful and partly because she just liked looking at him.

He'd made an effort for her family, she noted. In place of the usual jeans and T-shirt, he was wearing a nice pair of slacks and a button-down shirt, though the sleeves had gotten rolled back the second they got into the Uber. He'd offered to shave and get a haircut, which she'd talked him out of. She'd come to like the way his long hair felt when she ran her fingers through it, the tickle of whiskers against her face and neck. And maybe she also didn't want Bryan to feel like he needed to change for her or her family. All in all, he looked like the perfect millennial businessman, which had made Bryan laugh until he choked when she said so.

"Just shoot me now," he'd said.

"If the coffee roasting business fits . . ." she'd fired back, but he'd just kissed her and told her she could call him whatever she wanted.

That's when she'd realized she was in love with him too.

She blew out her breath now at the recollection, trying to settle the jitter in her stomach. This was moving fast, at least the part that had to do with feelings. They'd spent almost all day every day together the past week, packaging samples and applying labels to bags, Bryan roasting while Ana worked on her laptop in the office. And he'd insisted on driving her to drop off the samples, partly because it was easier than finding parking at every one of the locations, and partly because neither of them particularly wanted to be out of the other's sight.

"This is us." He stopped at row twelve and tugged her back when she almost walked right by, lost in her own daydreams. He took her suitcase and hoisted it into the overhead bin, then followed with his own—he'd temporarily retired the green backpack for this trip, going with a respectable black Samsonite instead. "You want the aisle or the middle?"

She sent him a chiding look. "Really? You think I'm going to stick you in the middle? Your legs are twice as long as mine."

"Which look very nice in those jeans, might I add."

Suit Guy now sighed loudly. Bryan threw him a look. "Come on, man, give me a break. I'm dating the most fantastic woman in the world. Can you blame me?"

For a second, he looked like he might crack, but he just said, "Pick your seat and sit down already, will you?"

"After you," Bryan said to Ana, waiting for her to slide into the row. Bryan smiled placidly at the impatient businessman and took his time settling into his seat.

Ana covered her mouth and laughed into Bryan's shoulder. "You're terrible."

"The guy clearly has no sense of humor, and it's not like the plane can leave without him." He reached for the seat belt and buckled himself in.

"What if someone calls about the coffee?" she asked, picking up where they'd left off.

"I've got the office phone forwarded to my cell, and I have the ordering software installed on my laptop. I can do anything from California that I could do from here. Probably more, since I won't be in the roasting room." He reached for her hand and squeezed it with an amused glance. "You'd think you were the one who was hanging her entire existence on this venture."

Ana sobered now. "I don't want you to think I don't have full confidence in you, because I do . . . but what would you do if this didn't work?"

Bryan looked at her silently for a long moment. "I don't know. I still have the farm to deal with, so I would work on the export part, but I don't think that would actually make me a living, at least not considering Denver rent prices. Go back to Colombia and live on the farm?"

"You're that opposed to an office job?"

"No, just too old with too few skills to get one. And before you say it, no, I wouldn't go work for my father."

The man seated in the window spot arrived, and they shuffled around to let him in, then reseated themselves.

"I don't understand your relationship with your dad. It seems to be pretty friendly, if you're living with them, and Alex gets along so well with him."

"That's because Alex is the son that he always wanted," Bryan said flatly. "I never had a chance."

Ana blinked. It wasn't the first time he'd referred to how close Alex and Mitchell Shaw were, but it was the first time he'd let on that it bothered him. "You blame Alex?"

He whipped his head toward her. "No! Not at all. If Alex weren't there, my dad and I still wouldn't be close. It just makes it easier on him, thinking that his friendship with Alex is somehow benefiting me."

Ana still stared, uncomprehending.

"Just imagine what it's like when a self-made man with a driving need to leave a legacy for his son finds out that son has no interest in what he does and is, in fact, somewhat opposed to the whole concept of urban development?

"On one hand, I know he's not doing anything wrong. He's doing business ethically, at least as far as he's concerned. He's paying fair market value for the properties he buys. On the other hand, I've seen gentrification force out people who have lived in their homes for generations to make way for rich white software engineers. It's a conflict I can't get past in my own head. And before you remind me, I realize I'm benefiting from his success, which also makes me a hypocrite."

Ana sighed and leaned her head back against her seat. "I'm beginning to think there's no way around being a hypocrite unless you live in a cave."

"You don't have a hypocritical bone in your body."

"Then I effectively have you fooled." She threw him a smile so he'd think it was just banter, but inwardly, the words stung with barbs of truth.

The flight attendants shut the door and began their safety spiel, which Ana pretended to pay attention to, even though she was still thinking over what he'd said. Bryan could be extremely successful and wealthy if he would just get over his squeamishness and go into the family business. Instead, he'd followed his own path, first as a climber, then as a coffee farmer and roaster—two things he'd only gotten into because of his desire to help people.

Meanwhile Ana was making massive amounts of money helping people she neither liked nor believed in, simply because they paid her to do it. No wonder her parents thought there was something unsavory about her job.

And soon, she'd be back to work. Back to long hours spinning stories around people who probably did deserve their downfalls, back to living in her office and only coming home to work out or sleep. Back to a life that had no time for Bryan.

She glanced at him, but he was looking over the safety card, apparently taking the flight attendants' instructions seriously. No, just because they wouldn't be working together every day didn't mean they couldn't still have a relationship. They'd carve out whatever time they could manage together, even if it was just at the gym. If she could convince him to teach her to climb, that would even be something they could do together.

She lifted her thumbnail to her teeth, then dropped her hand before she could mess up her manicure.

Bryan didn't miss the aborted gesture, capturing her hand again. "Relax," he whispered. "It's all going to be okay."

And for a short period of time, she actually believed it.

*   *   *

It was dark when Bryan and Ana's plane touched down at Ontario International Airport. The "Inland Empire" spread out beneath them in a gleaming patchwork, neighborhoods and streets marked out in grids by the streetlights, the freeways like parallel ropes of white and red. He'd spent a fair amount of time in Southern California, given that Pakka Mountaineering was headquartered there, but from the air, it became clear that it was as far removed from Denver as from his small Colombian town.

They hadn't checked any baggage, so they deplaned and went straight to the ground transportation area of the aging airport. "Are we renting a car or taking an Uber to your parents'?" he asked as they breached the airport's air-conditioning for the still-warm, slightly moist night.

"Uber, but we're not going to my parents' house tonight." Ana pulled out her phone and pulled up her ride-share app, requesting a ride from the airport to some location she apparently knew by heart. "I got us a hotel." At his raised eyebrows, she amended, "I got us two rooms at the same hotel."

"Is there a reason why we're not staying with them? Not enough room?"

"Oh, there's room. Everyone except my brother and youngest sister have moved out. But trust me, you'll be much more comfortable at a hotel for the weekend."

A niggling feeling of disquiet began. "Are you worried that they're not going to like me?"

She laughed. "They're going to *love* you. Don't worry about that. They're just a bit . . . much . . . even for me." She flushed. "That sounds terrible."

"It's not terrible. You just don't want two full days of their opinions on your life choices." Bryan got it. He'd been afraid of the same thing when moving home, but in practice he barely saw his parents. They had their own lives; his dad had long work hours, his mom had her charity work, and both of them had their friends and acquaintances. It wasn't an exaggeration to say that his parents had a better social life than he did. Well, than he'd *had*. The time spent with Ana upped the quality of his own considerably.

"It's your weekend, so we can do whatever you want. I just didn't want you going to a lot of trouble for me. I'm used to camping for months straight with the clothes I have on my back. I don't mind couch surfing at your parents' house should the situation call for it."

Ana's expression lightened and she moved closer to him, slipping an arm around his waist. "Thank you. I'm just happy you're here with me. This could be a long weekend otherwise."

There it went, that degree of concern that seemed to go deeper than uncomfortable questions from her parents. What was she so worried about?

The Uber arrived, a lowered white late-model Civic with tinted windows and a ground effects kit that sprayed blue light beneath the chassis. Bryan exchanged a glance with Ana that clearly said, *You're kidding me, right?* and then opened the back door for her.

Ana climbed in and introduced herself, but Bryan bent down to talk to the driver, who couldn't be more than the minimum driver age of twenty-one. "Hey, man, can I put the luggage in your trunk?"

Wordlessly, the driver released the latch. *I guess that's a yes.* He hoisted first Ana's case then his own into the trunk and slid into the space that Ana had made for him in the back of the car.

Still without a word, the driver pulled away from the curb. Bryan studied him from the side, thinking maybe he didn't speak English, but he seemed thoroughly American. Just not talkative apparently. Or maybe he was too busy listening to the throbbing techno music that poured from the speakers. Ana was watching their progress against the map on her app, however, and it seemed like the driver knew where he was going, so Bryan just sat back and watched the Southern California cityscape slide by outside his window.

Hard to see much of anything in the dark, but pockets of streetlights illuminated newer-looking strip malls and clusters of palm trees, not so unlike Denver's suburbs. Well, minus the palm trees. Even knowing they were significantly inland, it made him think they were going to get a glimpse of the ocean at any minute.

The driver, still bobbing his head to the beat, silently merged onto a freeway, which was somehow still congested at this time of night. As time stretched, it became clear they were still a fair distance from the city in which Ana had grown up, freeway exit after exit passing without any sign that they'd ever get off. And then finally the driver exited and navigated streets that looked strikingly similar to Ontario's to finally stop in front of a multistory business hotel.

"Thank you," Ana said, immediately climbing out. This time the guy pulled their luggage out of the trunk, still without a word, climbed in, and drove off.

"So that was interesting," Bryan said.

"Stuck in the nineties." Ana smirked as she watched the blue glow of the Civic disappear down the street. "I know this place is kind of generic, but it's close to my parents' house. Close enough to walk if it's not too hot, even."

"It's just fine." He followed her into the hotel, where she went straight to the counter to check them in.

"I've got this, Ana," he said, but she shook her head, that familiar stubborn look coming over her face.

"You're doing me a favor; therefore, I pay. And you're not

going to convince me otherwise, so you might as well save us both some time."

He held up his hands. "Yes, ma'am."

The desk clerk looked between them with amusement, though she was trying hard to keep a straight face. "Ms. Sanchez, you are in room 302, and Mr. Shaw, you are in room 205." She pushed their room keys across the desk. "Is there anything else I can help you with?"

"No, thank you." Ana took her suitcase and strode toward the elevators without having to look where they were.

"I take it you've been here before," he said.

"I always stay here when I visit. I don't like to be a bother to my parents. My mom feels like she has to cook for me and pick up after me anytime I'm staying in their house."

"Isn't that what moms do when their grown kids come home?"

Ana shot him an unreadable look and said nothing.

There was definitely something weird going on.

The elevator took no time to go up one floor to Bryan's room, but he stuck his foot out to keep the doors open. "What time do you want me ready in the morning?"

"We don't have to be there until eleven, so feel free to sleep in if you want."

He was beginning to learn Ana's cues; this clearly meant she had other plans in mind. "What are you going to do?"

"I'm going to a yoga class in the morning. There's a 7 a.m. at the studio down the street."

"Let me guess: that's the other reason you stay here."

Now amusement lit her eyes. "I can't get out of the house early enough and without a full breakfast if I'm at home. And if I tell my mom I can't work out on a full stomach, she'll have *tocino* going on the stove at five."

That didn't sound so bad to him, but there was obviously a lot he didn't understand about her family.

The door started to make a dinging noise, indicating its irritation that they were still blocking it from closing. "Okay. What time do you want to leave?"

Her eyebrows went up. "You're going with me?"

"Sure. Why not?"

"Well, for one thing, I didn't think you did yoga. And this is hot vinyasa, too . . . it's pretty demanding."

He shrugged. "I'm game if you are. What time should I be ready?"

He could tell she still didn't know what to do about his willingness. "I want to leave here by 6:25. It'll take a few minutes to walk there and then we'll have to fill out waivers and things."

"Sounds good. I'll meet you in the lobby at 6:25." He leaned forward to give her a quick, chaste good-night kiss, then let the door slide closed. Just before she disappeared from view, he gave her a little wink and saw her answering smile.

Good. Let her think he didn't know what he was in for.

She didn't know everything about him. In fact, he'd venture to say she knew very little.

Chapter Twenty-Five

ANA WOKE BEFORE her alarm went off, thanks to a body clock that was set an hour ahead of local time, with a feeling in her stomach that could either be dread or anticipation. Maybe both. Dread over the forthcoming family reunion, anticipation for the yoga class that would also serve as her entertainment for the morning. She dressed quickly in her yoga clothes, then pulled on a sweatshirt and flowy pants over top, knowing the overnight temperatures had cooled just enough to be nippy when they ventured out on foot. Her hair went back into a tight ponytail, face splashed with water, teeth quickly brushed. She never wore makeup to the gym; in this case, she'd sweat it off before she even got a quarter of the way through the class.

She'd half-expected Bryan to change his mind, but he was waiting for her in the lobby when she arrived, dressed in athletic shorts, a T-shirt, and a sweatshirt of his own. "Ready?" he asked, even more awake and raring to go than she was.

She chuckled. "There's still time to back out, you know."

"Why would I want to back out?"

"I don't know. Just saying you don't have to impress me."

He put up his hands. "I'm just trying to get a workout. That's all."

Well, if that's what he was after, he'd definitely get one.

They pocketed their room keys and left the hotel, Ana leading the way down the street. Fog covered the city, shrouding it in dim blue light even though the sun should already be up. She readjusted the strap that held her yoga mat on her shoulder, drawing Bryan's attention to it for the first time.

"You travel with a yoga mat?"

"Yep. You have no idea how many mats I had to go through before I found one that would fold up compactly enough for a carry-on. I hate studio mats."

"What about me, then?"

"Studio mat."

"Oh, okay, I see how this is going to be." He bumped her with his shoulder and then took her hand. She barely repressed a sigh at the warmth of his hand wrapped around hers. Who would have thought holding hands with a man would become one of her greatest, simplest pleasures? And why had it taken her so long to realize it?

Because she hadn't been friends with any of the men she'd dated, she realized. Most of them hadn't reached that stage for obvious reasons, but even the ones who lasted more than a handful of dates seemed to want to bypass the sweet courtship stage of holding hands in public and go straight to bed. She would never in a million years have pegged Bryan as the hand-holding type.

Despite the early hour on a Saturday, the studio was already packed, the parking lot filled with cars. Ana led the way into the small reception area, where people in various states of dress milled around. For a hot class, most people wore as little clothing as possible. As she passed a beautiful twentysomething in an outfit with barely more coverage than a bikini, she questioned the wisdom of bringing Bryan here in the first place. She wasn't normally self-conscious about her body, but next to Yoga Barbie, she looked like Soccer Skipper.

"Drop-ins for the seven o'clock," she told the girl behind the desk. She had blonde dreadlocks and tattoos down both arms; her own skimpy outfit made Ana think she was probably the instructor and not the receptionist.

She gave Ana a bright smile. "Drop-ins are twenty dollars. If you'll fill out these releases, I'll check you in." She pushed two clipboards, each with a sheet of paper and a pen clipped to it, toward them.

Bryan took his and glanced at it, his eyebrows lifting. "Death or *dismemberment*? What, are we going to be juggling chain saws?"

Ana shot him a look to hush him up as curious glances came their way. "It's just boilerplate." She scribbled her signature at the bottom with the date, dug in her pocket for cash, and headed back to the desk. Bryan beat her to the punch and handed over two twenties before she could.

"Thanks," the girl said. "Studio A. You can go in and warm up if you like."

They dropped their stuff in the cubbies in the hallway, and then Ana began to strip off her outerwear. Bryan was looking at her with something of a stunned expression.

"What? They heat the room to 95 degrees. Trust me, you're going to want to wear as little as possible." She adjusted her top to make sure it covered everything it needed to cover and tugged down the hem of her boy shorts, suddenly feeling exposed and uncomfortable.

"Okay, then." He pulled off his shoes and socks and then whipped off his shirt, giving her her own moment to blink in appreciation. With the hair and beard and lean body that most yogis worked years for, he'd fit right in. Until, of course, it came time to twist himself into a pretzel. Didn't matter how strong or fit you were; yoga tended to make you feel like a hopelessly uncoordinated oaf until you got the hang of it.

"Oh, I forgot to ask for a mat. Be right back." Bryan wove his way among the bodies back to the desk, and this time Ana didn't miss the passing glances of appreciation from the women and more than one of the men. She looked away.

He came back with a mat—pink floral—which he held up with a rueful glance. "Am I going to have to turn over my man card if I use this?"

"I don't think you've got anything to worry about," she said without thinking and then flushed.

A slow smile spread over his face. "You ready?"

"I could ask you the same thing."

He shrugged. Poor sap didn't know what was going to happen to him. She grabbed her mat and followed him to studio A, the whole time repeating to herself that this was an athletic endeavor and she really shouldn't want to reach out and touch the muscles that rippled across his back with every movement.

Heat hit them the second they walked into the studio, the wooden floor of which was already littered with the yoga mats of people saving their spaces. A few students stretched or contorted into various positions, evidently taking advantage of the heat's effect on their muscles. Ana and Bryan picked a spot in the corner with enough room for two mats, unrolled them, and settled onto the floor to stretch out.

Bryan looked completely unperturbed, but Ana was now feeling a little shaky and insecure. About what, she couldn't say. Letting him watch her contort into difficult positions while scantily clothed? That was part of it. But more than anything, she was letting him into her private world. She'd counted on doing this alone, as she always did, and now he was here beside her.

The dreadlocked girl—she'd been right—glided into the room and attached her cell phone to the speaker in the corner. "Welcome to hot vinyasa," she said smoothly, smiling at all of them with that glowing sort of friendliness all yoga teachers seemed to have. "I'm your instructor, Miranda. Welcome to our members and guests this morning. I'll be giving modifications for the more difficult asanas, so please feel free to work to your level."

Ana glanced at Bryan, but he was just sitting cross-legged, placidly watching Miranda talk.

"Now we're going to begin with a little meditation . . ."

Normally Ana used this time to breathe and pray, but she was too aware of Bryan sitting next to her to focus her attention on anything but him. She'd thought that maybe he was just going along with this to be with her, but he seemed to be taking it seriously, breathing in and out with calm concentration. And then Miranda started them into the flow, the first simple sequence moving through forward bends and plank position, then back to downward-facing dog.

Now we'll see, Ana thought, watching Bryan from the corner of her eye.

He flowed through the sequence as naturally as if he'd done it hundreds of times, perfectly in control.

Well, he was a climber, so he had strength and flexibility. And this was just the first vinyasa. She knew from experience that newcomers dropped like flies at the quarter mark of the class.

And yet Bryan hung in there with the best of them, tackling each pose with seemingly no effort. Even the moves most men struggled with, like dancer, where they had to clasp their ankle behind them and then raise it to shoulder height, he managed as if he knew exactly what he was doing.

Because he did.

"Liar," Ana hissed at him as they transitioned into the next pose and back to the vinyasa: lowering to plank, through to cobra, and then back to down dog.

He turned his head and grinned at her. "Shh. I'm concentrating. This yoga stuff is hard."

She stuck her tongue out. "I hate you."

Miranda frowned at them from the front of the class.

Not only did Bryan not have any difficulty with a class that Ana was panting and sweating through, but when they moved to arm balances, the teacher actually called him out for demonstration of eight-angle pose, a particularly difficult asana that Ana had been struggling with for at least a year.

"Watch how he—what's your name?"

"Bryan."

"Watch how Bryan transitions into this pose. See how he positions his knee behind his right shoulder?"

Ana watched all right as he managed the pose with ease, balancing forward on his palms, legs twined to the side around his right arm as if he defied gravity, strong, fluid, graceful. He was gorgeous, in a sense of the word she usually reserved for ballet dancers and gymnasts. Why did this surprise her? After all, wasn't climbing basically vertical yoga? She wiped her forehead, feeling silly that she'd thought she was going to show off for him, then bent forward to make her own attempt at it again.

And promptly collapsed on her shoulder.

Bryan immediately unwound himself and crouched beside her. "You okay?"

"Yeah, nothing bruised but my ego," she muttered. And then they were moving on in the class, inversions that of course he handled with aplomb.

When they said their final namaste and bowed to their teacher, Ana just sat there, exhausted and sweating. She cracked an eye open at Bryan. "I think you've been holding out on me."

He had the grace to look abashed. "In my defense, you never actually asked if I'd done yoga before."

"You could have volunteered!"

He shrugged, but a little smile played on his lips. "I wanted to see the shocked look on your face when you found out I wasn't a total klutz."

"I should have known." Ana wiped down her mat and began rolling it up into a little cylinder. Bryan stood up to retrieve the spray cleaner and a rag and wiped down his own borrowed mat.

"When did you start?"

"A couple of years ago, when I was getting injured a lot. Another climber recommended that I take up yoga to balance out my strengths and weaknesses and I kind of liked it."

She looked at him and shook her head. "You are full of surprises."

"So are you. Geez. Standing splits?"

Now Ana smiled. "You're trying to make me feel better."

"Is it working?"

She laughed. "Yeah."

Ana excused herself to the bathroom, where she saw she looked just as sweaty, flushed, and disheveled as she feared. When she returned, Bryan was talking to the instructor and a petite blonde girl who, were it physically possible, would have had little cartoon hearts in her eyes as she gazed up at him.

"That's so fascinating. So you don't climb anymore?"

Bryan caught Ana's eye. "No, not anymore. If you'll excuse me, I need to go. Thank you for the class, Miranda."

"Any time. Visit us again."

Ana didn't miss the way their gazes followed him until the very moment he pulled his shirt back on.

And then he placed a hand on her bare, sweaty waist, bent down, and kissed her lightly. "Ready to go, sweetheart?"

Warmth bloomed in her chest. He didn't need to make the point that he was taken, but he had. "Yeah, I am." She thanked Miranda on the way out, feeling daggers from Heart-Eyed Girl, and took a deep breath the minute they hit the cool outside air. "So that was fun."

"It was. Or are you being sarcastic?"

"A little of both." She paused for a second. "Are you hungry? I was thinking about getting a smoothie. We passed a juice bar on the way."

"Of course we did."

She frowned. "What's that supposed to mean?"

"Just that it's a very California thing to do. Especially after hot yoga."

"Oh yeah, because Denver is so lacking in yoga and smoothies. Says the hipster."

"Take it back."

"If the *astavakrasana* fits . . ."

"I think yoga is mainstream enough that it proves I am, in fact, not a hipster."

"Yeah, except you did it before it was cool."

He pretended to think. "You may be right. Should I keep growing my hair? How would I look with a man bun?"

"You'll never know because I'm going to sneak in and cut your hair while you sleep."

"Okay, no man bun, then?"

Ana laughed. "Please don't."

He let go of her hand and put an arm around her shoulder so she had to walk closer to him. "Have I ever told you that I think you're amazing?"

"Um, where is this coming from exactly? Because I won't let you wear a bad hairstyle?"

"No, because there's pretty much nothing you can't do. You're beautiful, smart, athletic, beautiful . . ."

"You said *beautiful* twice."

"I know. I would have said *smart* twice if you hadn't interrupted me."

Ana giggled, and the giggle kept going until it turned into a full-fledged laugh. Maybe it was tiredness or maybe it was just him, but nothing ever seemed so bad with Bryan around. When was the last time she'd just laughed for no reason?

"You're punchy."

"And you're really good at this yoga thing."

"Thank you."

"I can only imagine what you're like climbing. I mean, I saw the video, but I bet you're amazing."

Apparently, the workout and the admiration had left him in a good mood, because rather than immediately shutting her down, he shrugged. "Just because you're good at something and you used to do it doesn't mean you have to keep doing it." He paused, his expression mock-thoughtful. "Maybe I'll become a yoga instructor."

"Teach shirtless and you'll pack out every class." Ana flushed furiously as soon as the words left her mouth. She'd obviously sweated out her filter.

"Is that a fact?"

"It is a fact and you know it. But back to the climbing . . . if you have no intention of going back, why do you keep this up?"

"So I can impress girls, of course." She narrowed her eyes at him, and he chuckled. "Maybe I like it for its own sake. And maybe I just like having something for myself that I don't tell anyone about."

"Not even Alex?"

"Not even Alex, though he probably suspects because he's seen my yoga mat in the car."

"What else don't we know about you?"

"Hmm. I don't eat seafood unless Rachel cooks it."

She blinked up at him. "What?"

"Got sick in Mexico once, won't eat it at restaurants any-more. I trust Rachel, though, so I'll eat it when she makes it."

Ana thought. "That just seems like plain good sense to me. I don't eat a lot of things unless Rachel cooks them."

"You're saying I have to do better? Then . . . I like foreign films."

Now she pulled away and stared up at him. "No."

"Yes, seriously. An old date was trying to make me more 'cultured' and introduced me to all these great Italian and French films. They're weird, but I like them. The Spanish stuff is the best because I don't have to read the subtitles."

"So let me get this straight. You own a coffee farm and roast your own beans. You do yoga. And you watch foreign films."

"When you put it that way . . ."

"Sorry. Gotta say it. Hipster."

Bryan swiped at her, but she dodged out of his way and darted down the empty sidewalk, running as fast as she could toward the strip mall ahead. It didn't take long for him to out-pace her, given the difference in their strides, and he caught her around the waist. She didn't put up a struggle, just let him turn her around toward him. He didn't kiss her, though, just looked seriously into her eyes. "I love you, Ana."

She blinked. "Why?" The word spilled out before she could think of a better response.

"Because you're exactly who you want to be. You say what you want, do what you want, regardless of what anyone else thinks. I admire that sort of honesty. I kind of thought I was the only person who went through life that way. It's not easy, but it's freeing."

He couldn't have said anything that would have made her

feel worse. She swallowed hard and disentangled herself from his embrace. "I think you probably have the wrong impression of me, Bryan. I am the last person you should be calling honest. Look what I do for a living."

He shrugged. "You think half of what's been written about me in interviews is true? I mean, it's kind of true, but people tend to draw their own conclusions. But there's a big difference between public life and private life. This . . ." He waved a hand up and down to indicate, she imagined, her disheveled, out-of-breath, sweaty appearance. "This is the real you. Who falls out of eight-angle pose and tries again. Who almost sprains her eyeballs trying not to ogle the hot specimen of manhood right next to her in class."

Ana's mouth dropped open and she smacked him in the arm. "I did not!"

"You were totally checking out my *chaturanga*."

She threw her head back and laughed. "Okay, I was. Come on. I'm hungry." She pulled him into the smoothie shop, which turned out to be more of a healthy café, though the buzz of high-speed blenders spoke to the accuracy of its name.

Fifteen minutes later, they both walked out with small Styrofoam cups of smoothies—orange-mango for her and coffee-cacao for him—and egg-white wraps. The foot traffic had begun to pick up along the street now, and they had to dodge people walking dogs as they ate silently side by side. Deep down, though, his words had left a niggling sense of disquiet. He thought she was so honest and transparent, even after discounting what she did for a living.

He had no idea she'd been lying to them all.

Chapter Twenty-Six

BRYAN COULDN'T HELP BUT be nervous as he showered and changed to get ready to go to Ana's family's home. This morning had been fun, if for no other reason than to show off a little and get in a workout, but he could tell that Ana was seeing him in a new light. Just not a different-enough light to say that she loved him.

Maybe she didn't. He'd said it twice now, once in her apartment when he'd volunteered to come with her and once this morning, and she'd gotten uncomfortable both times. She should know him well enough by now to know he wasn't saying it to ramp up the physical intimacy of their relationship, and she should know equally well that he wasn't a sappy guy by nature. Which left only one possibility—she didn't feel the same way.

And yet sometimes, he'd catch her looking at him with an expression that made him sure she was in love with him too.

He shook his head and tried to push out the thoughts. It was so much easier when there weren't any real feelings involved. Vivian had taught him that. But the three years between bookended heartbreaks had also taught him that avoiding feelings just made him . . . less. Shallow. Maybe even untrustworthy. He never wanted to be that guy again. Every day he got up trying to prove he was that person no longer.

Ana, on the other hand . . . there had been something in her eyes when he told her how much he admired her honesty that reminded of him of an animal, frightened and trapped. Was that him projecting based on her instant demurral, or was she really hiding something?

He dismissed the thought. This was Ana he was talking about. She was the most together and up-front of any person he'd ever met, not to mention straitlaced. Anything she was hiding had to be the equivalent of stealing a candy bar from a convenience store when she was nine.

Best that he focus on proving himself to her parents so they approved of their relationship. He combed his hair neatly and trimmed his facial hair, which was somewhere between "forgot to shave" and full beard, but Ana had specifically told him not to change it, so he wouldn't. He slipped on slim-cut dark jeans and a crisp blue button-down shirt, just formal enough to say he took the occasion seriously, casual enough for what he understood to be the Southern California dress code. He considered showing up downstairs in his flip-flops as a joke, but instead, he pulled out the suede Oxfords and a pair of funky socks, this time cats on surfboards.

Oh man. He really was turning into a hipster.

He pushed off that unfortunate realization, snapped on his single nice watch, and shoved his wallet in his pocket. Ready. For anything. He hoped.

Ana was already waiting in the lobby, tapping away on the keyboard of her cell phone. She looked up when she saw him, her mouth rounding into an O. "You look great."

"So do you." The white floral sundress displayed her tanned shoulders and arms, the deep V and tight waist accentuating her beautiful figure. A pair of low-heeled strappy sandals showed off a robin's-egg-blue pedicure that he'd missed during the yoga class. Her hair was caught back in a long fishtail braid, making her look casual and relaxed and much younger than her age. He wanted desperately to kiss her, but she'd already applied some glossy pink lipstick, so instead he took her hand. "Are we walking or Ubering it?"

"Neither." She held up her phone. "My sister Marisol is coming to pick us up."

"Marisol." Bryan racked his brain, but he couldn't remember if she'd actually told him all her siblings' names. "Which one is she?"

"The nurse. The next oldest. She's also the least likely to give you the third degree. She's married to a white guy, so she's been through the whole routine herself."

Bryan paused. That was an aspect of the trip he hadn't even considered. "Is that likely to be a problem?"

"Oh no. I just mean that you'll have another 'outsider' to talk to at the party. Her husband has picked up a few words of Tagalog but not enough to figure out what's going on when the older folks get going." She nudged his arm. "Wait, are you getting nervous?"

"Since you just called me an outsider? A little."

"Don't worry, it's not a bad thing." Before he could ask her how being an outsider could not be a bad thing, she perked up, pointing through the hotel's glass doors at a white Toyota Camry that had stopped out front. "There she is. Come on."

They were approaching the car when the driver stepped out. Bryan blinked for a moment. She wouldn't have had to tell him they were sisters: Marisol had the same long, thick black hair, the same nose, the same high cheekbones as Ana. But she was several inches taller and clothed in green scrubs.

"Ana!" she squealed, rushing to the curb and throwing her arms around her sister. "You're here!"

They did the little hoppy-happy thing that long-separated girls tended to do upon reunions, looking each other over and commenting on new hairstyles, weight loss, and manicures. Then finally Ana turned his direction. "Mari, this is my boyfriend, Bryan."

The word *boyfriend* gave his insides a jolt like an electric charge. They'd danced around the whole relationship-definition thing, but this was the first time she'd ever introduced him as such. He liked it. A lot.

"Hi, Marisol." Bryan held out his hand, but she went in straight for the hug.

"It's so good to meet you, Bryan." She stepped back and looked him up and down, then shot a grin at Ana that clearly conveyed approval.

"It's nice to meet you, too. Here, I'll sit in the back so you can talk." He ignored their objections and climbed into the backseat of the sedan.

"I can't believe you actually came," Marisol said when she pulled out of the hotel parking lot onto the street. "We were taking bets on whether or not you'd be able to get away from work."

"Miss Daddy's sixty-fifth? Never."

"Well, you missed Mom's sixtieth, because of . . . what? Some tire emergency."

"It wasn't a tire emergency; it was a product liability issue . . ." Ana broke off. "Yeah, it was a tire emergency."

"Well, you should know that Mom has been praying loudly for you to rethink your career choices. She wants me to tell you it's not too late to go into nursing."

Ana rolled her eyes. "Last time it was web design like Helena. Her company still doing well? Last time I talked to her, she had just gotten that big studio contract."

"Oh yeah. We barely see her. She's almost as busy as you."

Bryan kept waiting for Ana to say something about her leave of absence, but when she fell silent, he took it as an opportunity to insert a question. "Marisol, where do you work?"

"Providence St. Joseph. Oncology." She flipped a look over her shoulder at him. "I switched shifts today so I could come pick you guys up. And please, call me Mari. Everyone else does."

"Okay, Mari. Are all the siblings going to be here?"

"Oh, you bet. I just picked Bettina up at the airport. She's a senior at UVA, but we flew her in for the weekend. Helena and Jacqueline live in the area, so they're driving up this afternoon."

"Married?" Bryan asked. Now that he was here, he realized how little Ana actually talked about her family.

"Jackie and I are. Helena and Ana are still the holdouts, which of course you're going to hear *all* about. Brace yourself." But the way she said it was playful and not ominous.

"Don't worry, I don't scare easily. I'm an only child, so my mom has been hinting hard for grandchildren for about ten years."

"But you resisted?"

"Took me a while to find the right woman, I guess."

Mari caught his eye in the rearview mirror, looking pleased by the statement, but he saw how Ana just turned to look out the window. Flattered, embarrassed, or something else? Well, he certainly wasn't going to pretend that his feelings were casual, especially not around her family. They should know that she was important to him.

"Anyway," Mari said, "this is going to be small by our standards. The kids and their significant others, a few of Mom and Dad's siblings, and some family friends. Which still means fifty or sixty people, but you should see the family's wedding receptions. Jackie had ten bridesmaids."

"That's because she's a Kappa Alpha Theta." Ana turned to speak to Bryan over her shoulder. "Both Jackie and I went to USC, but I was never the sorority type."

"Really? I'm surprised. I'd think you would have joined and ended up president of your chapter."

"He's not wrong," Mari said.

"I was just focused on getting through school," she said. "Jackie and Helena have always been the social ones. Well, and Edward. Did he really take two girls to prom this year?"

"Yep. Little Casanova. Smack him upside the head while you're here, will you? He's insufferable."

Bryan smiled as he listened to the banter between the sisters. This was something he'd never experienced himself, given the fact he was an only child, even though he often thought of Alex as a brother. Ana might think her big family was going to scare him off, but if they were anything like Mari, he had a feeling he was going to enjoy today.

He watched the city slide by his window—wide streets, newer strip malls in desert colors of creams and browns and pale oranges, palm trees pretty much everywhere. Mari turned into a nice neighborhood filled with modest midcentury houses, tucked among lush greenery. She pulled into the driveway of a low-slung one-story set back behind a white iron fence, the street on both sides of the driveway filled with cars.

"Here we are. Casa Sanchez." She put the car into park and threw Bryan a grin. "Sure you're ready for this?"

"Couldn't be readier." He levered open the back door and climbed out, smoothing down his shirt, then opened Ana's door for her. She sat there for a second, breathing in and out, and then took his hand to step out.

He took the chance to pull her close and whisper in her ear, "Why do you look so nervous? Afraid I'll embarrass you?"

"What? No!" She dropped her head and muttered, "I'm afraid *they'll* embarrass me."

"I'll remember to ask your mom to pull out the baby pictures and get it out of the way then." He squeezed her hand. "Relax. How bad could it be?"

She laughed and stretched up for a kiss. "I'm going to remember you said that."

It wouldn't make the right impression to arrive wearing Ana's lipstick, so he bypassed her mouth and instead kissed her jaw just under her ear.

She shot him a wry smile. "Come on. It's now or never."

He followed the sisters up the cement driveway to a perfectly ordinary entryway, flanked by painted brick and featuring a polished oak door with a stained-glass insert. Mari walked in without knocking and announced, "They're here!"

Immediately, he could hear voices, and he trailed Ana inside. The smell of soy sauce and vinegar and cooking meat wafted from the kitchen, or maybe it was brought by the rush of people into the front room. He wasn't sure where to look first, at the family members who were greeting Ana in a mix of English and Tagalog or at the house, which was simultaneously pristine and a time capsule of 1980s decor, complete with ivory sofas and rose-colored swag draperies.

A petite woman, even shorter than Ana, pushed her way through the group and regarded him through her glasses with a frown. And then her face broke into a smile. "You must be Bryan. Welcome. I'm Ana's mom, Flora." She gestured for him to bend down and kissed him soundly on the cheek, enveloping him in rose-scented perfume.

"I am. It's nice to meet you, Mrs. Sanchez."

She linked arms with him and began to drag him toward the kitchen. "Are you hungry? Have you had Filipino food before?

You're going to love it. You're not one of those trendy boys who doesn't eat rice or soy or any of those things, are you?"

"No, I eat everything."

"Oh, good." She patted his arm. "Ana, your dad is in the back with Tito Orly and Carding. Ask him when he wants to turn on the barbecue."

Bryan threw her a helpless look, but Ana just grinned at him and headed for a side door, which he guessed was the exit to the backyard.

The kitchen was as dated as the rest of the house, though it was just as impeccably clean and smelled even more strongly of soy sauce. An elegant-looking woman with her dark hair in a knot carefully fried chicken in a pan with a pair of steel tongs, a frilly apron tied over her slacks and blouse.

"This is Ana's boyfriend, Bryan," Mrs. Sanchez said. "These are Ana's aunts: Macaria, Marguerite, Marisol—yes, Mari is named after her—and Dolores."

Bryan smiled and nodded to each of the aunts in turn, though he was already wondering how he would remember them all. Then a tall, dark-haired Caucasian man came in through the sliding-glass door, holding a plastic tumbler. He went straight to Mrs. Sanchez. "Do we have any more Pepsi? Dad said there might be some in the garage."

"I'll check," she said. "John, meet Ana's boyfriend, Bryan."

His expression turned briefly appraising and he shook Bryan's hand firmly. "Nice to meet you, Bryan. I'm Mari's husband."

He could have guessed that much, but he just nodded. "A pleasure."

"Come on, you can help me with the drinks." He looked at the assembled ladies. "Mind if I borrow him for a bit?"

"No, no, you go," Macaria—at least he thought it was Macaria—said, not looking up from her chicken. Bryan followed John out of the room, down the hall, and then made a sharp left through a door into an empty garage where a large refrigerator was plugged in at the back.

"A bit overwhelming, isn't it?" John said, opening the refrigerator and pulling two-liter bottles of pop from the door.

"They all seem nice." Not that he would know in the thirty seconds he'd been there.

"They are. They're determined to be welcoming." John chuckled. "This is the first English I've heard out of them all day."

"I appreciate that. Ana said you don't speak much Tagalog?"

"I've picked up bits and pieces, but you'll notice Ana and her sisters rarely speak it unless they don't want anyone to know what they're saying."

"So if I hear my name and a bunch of Tagalog, I should worry?"

"That just depends. You don't have to understand the words to get the context. Here, take these." He handed several bottles to Bryan and went back for more. "How long have you and Ana been together? Sounded like you were a bit of a surprise to everyone."

"Not that long, even though we've known each other for a couple of years. Her best friend is marrying my best friend."

"Ah." John shut the door and adjusted his hold on the pop. "Don't worry, the family is great. I don't have any relatives here in California so they pretty much adopted me."

"How long have you and Mari been married?" Bryan asked.

"Eight years. We met in school."

"You're a nurse too?"

"Physician's assistant. Here, we can go out this side door to the backyard and bypass the auntie gauntlet."

Bryan followed John out the door, around the stuccoed side of the house, to the backyard. And stopped. He would never have guessed from the front, but it was something of a tropical paradise—large swaths of grass and a huge sparkling-blue kidney-shaped swimming pool. Mature foliage hid it from the neighbors, a cluster of palm trees in one corner, a pergola in the other. It was beneath the pergola that the men were hanging out, one of whom he could only guess was Ana's dad. Ana was nowhere to be seen.

John took it upon himself to make the introduction. "This is Ana's boyfriend, Bryan. Bryan, this is Ana's cousin Carding—um, Ricardo—and her father, Mr. Sanchez. Her uncle Orlando was just here a second ago . . ."

Ana's dad rose from his chair, not challenging but not exactly warm either. He was considerably taller than Ana or her mother, just a shade shorter than Bryan, with a full head of black hair and a trim physique. He held out his hand. "It's nice to meet you, Bryan." Ana's dad had only a trace of an accent, his English bearing a clear American stamp. Bryan shouldn't be surprised; Ana had said they'd moved to the US decades ago.

"It's my pleasure, sir. Thank you for letting me come along for your big day."

Mr. Sanchez smiled then, but it was an assessing sort of smile. He nodded toward an empty chair, which one of the other men had pulled up. "Have a seat."

Bryan did as he was invited. "It's a beautiful day to sit by the pool. Believe it or not, there's snow in the forecast in Denver next week."

"Are you from Denver?" Mr. Sanchez asked.

"Born and raised. But I've traveled a fair amount."

"Have you ever been to the Philippines?"

"I have, actually. In my former life, I was a rock climber." He was loath to pull out his climbing career so soon, but there was no way to answer the question without doing so. "I climbed in Iloilo and Cebu for about two weeks, and then we went on to Thailand. I've been wanting to get back for years now."

"Well, maybe you will. Talk Ana into going back and seeing

her extended family. Then again, we barely see her and she only lives a two-hour plane ride away."

Bryan wasn't going to make the mistake of taking sides on this one. "She is pretty busy. She's quite successful."

"Yes, she is. If you're no longer a climber, what is it that you do?"

So Bryan found himself telling Ana's dad about the coffee farm and the roastery and what he wanted to do with the business long-term.

"You know, Carding's wife's family owns a coffee plantation in Mindanao."

"Yes," Carding broke in, "but they grow robusta, which isn't in great demand for export. Mostly used locally."

"That's interesting," Bryan said. "As I understand it, farmers went away from the traditional variety and planted robusta because it was rust-resistant. But there's a resurgence of interest in *kapeng barako*. . . . Any thoughts about maybe switching back?"

Carding blinked at him, clearly surprised that he knew the Tagalog name. Thank goodness he'd been flipping through one of his coffee references a few days ago. "I'll have to ask her if they have. I don't know."

"There's also the problem of direct export," Mr. Sanchez said.

"If you're interested, I might be able to connect you with the exporter I work with in Colombia. They came out of a missionary organization, and there may be some interest in Mindanao."

That's where Ana found him what could have been minutes or hours later, talking about coffee and farms and managing workers and the difficulty of import-export. Far from being unfriendly, Ana's father and cousin were knowledgeable and eager to share their experience with him. But when Ana appeared, all the conversation broke off.

"Happy birthday, Daddy," she said, hugging him.

He beamed. "I'm so glad you came. Sit down. Bryan was just telling us about his farm. He says you're working with him."

"Just part-time to help him out," she said. "Can I borrow him? Mom wanted help with the decorations. We still need to put the lights up on the patio."

Her dad waved a hand. "Leave them. I don't need lights."

"Yes, but Mom wants lights."

Mr. Sanchez gestured with his head to Bryan. "You better go then. What my girls want, they get."

"And don't forget it," Ana said with a smile. She slid her hands into the crook of Bryan's elbow and pulled him away. As soon as they were out of earshot, she said, "So that looked like it was going well."

"Why do you sound so surprised?"

She shrugged. "It's been so long since I brought anyone home, I didn't know what he'd do."

"They were both really helpful. I came away with some new ideas and a possible new coffee supplier."

"Wow, you work fast. I'm sure you impressed him. My dad was a bank president. He knows more about commodities than I could possibly learn in a lifetime. He could probably quote you prices on coffee futures from memory." She stopped before several large plastic bins, one of which contained a mess of twinkle lights. "My mom wants these strung up on the patio cover."

Bryan squinted at the lattice overhead. "Okay. I can do that. Do we have a ladder or a step stool?"

"Nope."

"That might be slightly more difficult, then." He looked around and found a patio chair that didn't look like it would break under his weight. "What are you going to do?"

"Tiki torches to keep away the bugs." She picked up one from a bundle on the ground along with a small mallet. "It was either that or cooking, and trust me, you don't want me to cook."

"Surely you can't be that bad."

She fixed him with a look. "If you're dating me thinking I'm ever going to feed you anything that didn't start out frozen or pre-marinated, you're after the wrong woman. You should have taken your chance with Rachel while you could."

Bryan laughed. "I never had a chance with Rachel." There went that look again, this time with more heat, and he held up his hands. "Don't worry, I'm dating you for your brains."

"Sure you are."

Bryan took a quick look around to make sure no one was watching, then pulled her against him and gave her a brief kiss. "And your family coffee connections."

"Oh, is that right?" One more kiss, this time lingering a bit longer.

The sliding-glass door rattled open and Mrs. Sanchez's voice rang out. "Ana, can you come in here for a second, please?" The door slid closed again.

Ana sighed and tipped her head against his chest. "This is her version of flicking the porch lights."

"It's all starting to make sense now."

She chuckled and pulled away. "I better go. If I don't look suitably abashed for smooching on the patio, she might not let us sit together."

Bryan laughed, but when Ana didn't so much as crack a smile, he sobered. "Really?"

"Don't want to find out. Chop-chop with the lights."

"Yes, ma'am." He bent over the box and pulled out a jumbled string, which was going to take longer to untangle than it would to hang. When he straightened up, Ana's dad was watching him with an unreadable expression.

Back to best behavior. Definitely.

Chapter Twenty-Seven

HER MOTHER'S EMERGENCY turned out to be picking candles for her dad's cake, or so she claimed. As soon as Ana dug out a pack of sparklers from the pantry, Flora started with a casual, "So, Ana . . . Bryan seems nice. Why haven't we heard about him before?"

Ana glanced around, looking for some distraction, but her aunts had everything well in hand. She wasn't getting out of this. "We haven't been dating for very long, Mom."

"But you brought him here, so you must like him."

She knew better than to volunteer anything that had not already been entered into evidence. "Yes, I do like him."

A little smile surfaced on her mother's lips. "Does your father need to have the talk with him?"

Tita Marguerite stopped wrapping a Pyrex dish with tinfoil and looked between them, suddenly interested. "*Ano* 'talk'?"

Ana jumped on the distraction. "You mean she never told you about the talk? Any time one of the girls gets serious with someone, Daddy sits the guy down and gives him a lecture on how he expects his daughters to be treated. And then gives him the third degree on every aspect of his life. I heard he practically wanted John fingerprinted and background-checked."

"Absolutely true," Mari called from across the room.

Flora looked over her glasses. "Well, you know, Ana, that was because of you. After . . . you know . . ."

"Yeah, Mom, I know." She sighed. It had only been a matter of time before her past came up, though in this case, she couldn't help but think it might be warranted. "In answer to your question, though, no. I don't think we're at talk status yet. Sorry to disappoint you."

Her mom shrugged, but it was clear she had hoped for something more. Some sign her eldest daughter was settling down. She'd just have to settle for the fact that Ana had brought someone home. By anyone's standards, that was progress.

Ana wandered back to the sliding-glass door, where she could watch Bryan untangle twinkle lights with a surprising amount of patience. She had no idea what she'd been so nervous about. Bryan charmed everyone, from her mother to her aunts to her dad, even if they weren't about to allow them to be alone together.

"What's the deal with him?" Mari asked quietly at her shoulder, watching him too. "You haven't mentioned anything about a boyfriend."

"You think I hired an escort for the weekend or something?"

Mari shrugged. "The thought did cross my mind."

"Thanks a lot."

"No, but really . . . where did you meet him?"

"Mutual friends. We've known each other for almost two years, and we've been dancing around it for a while, but things just finally . . . happened."

"Well, I like him. And I like the way you look at him."

"How's that exactly?"

Mari smiled. "I don't know. You've always been so busy. But

you get this kind of soft look and just stop and watch him. I have to believe he's good for you."

Ana blushed, actually blushed. "I like him. He's . . . himself. No pretension. What you see is what you get."

Mari looked doubtful. "No guy wants to be called simple, Ana."

"I didn't say he was simple." Anything but, actually. Every day she spent with him, she learned some new and surprising fact. "I just deal with image and perception all day, so it's nice when someone is exactly who he seems to be."

"Mmm," Mari said.

"Mmm, meaning you don't agree?"

"Don't start reading into my *mmm*s. Maybe I was just admiring those arms of his."

Ana's mouth dropped open. "Mari!"

"What? You mean you haven't noticed?"

She looked back out onto the patio, where Bryan was stretching overhead to hang the lights. Oh no, she'd definitely noticed. She'd noticed enough to almost break her nose in yoga today.

Mari grinned. "I'll just leave you here speechless. You might want to go out and get a closer look . . . I mean help him out."

"Mom wants me to help with the food. And by help, I mean put it in dishes and then stay away from it. Hey, when are the others going to be here?" She didn't need to elaborate for Mari to understand she meant their four other siblings.

"In a bit. When the party starts. You don't think they'd want to hang around with any of the old people, do you?" Mari's grin said she included herself in that description, especially since their next oldest sister was still in her twenties, if not for long.

"Heaven forbid." Ana turned away from the window and the too-tempting view of Bryan, back to her aunties. "Okay, who needs help?"

By the time the first guest arrived at a quarter after six, all the food was finished, the cold dishes set out on the kitchen table, the warm dishes covered in foil in the oven. There was the usual hugging and kissing from older relatives; barely veiled criticism couched in surprise at her presence; a lot of inquiries about her marital status and suggestions that she date people's sons or brothers. Pretty much status quo for one of her parents' parties. Bryan helped in the last regard, ready to place a possessive hand on the small of her back or to bend and whisper something in her ear when she wanted to get away. He knew what he was doing, and she was immensely grateful for it.

After they made their rounds of the party, Ana and Bryan heaped their plates high and took them out to a cluster of chairs on the opposite side of the pool, away from the noise and heat and laughter of the house. The twinkle lights made the backyard look festive, a cool breeze rustling through the bushes and sending the palm trees swaying overhead. Bryan sat quietly, working his way through the mounds of food on his plate.

"What are you thinking?" Ana asked.

"I'm wondering how I can get your mom or your aunts to adopt me. This is amazing."

"They can cook for sure. But now you see why I don't eat Filipino food very often. I'd be as big as a house."

Bryan didn't laugh like she intended him to, instead studying her quietly in the deepening shadows. "Is that why you kill yourself every day at the gym?"

Ana blinked. She opened her mouth to answer but found that every reply she could give was inadequate or shallow. "Would you have even given me a second look if I didn't?"

"Yes."

Ana looked away. "I don't believe that."

"Trust me, you'd be gorgeous no matter what. Besides, the very first thing I told Alex about you was that you don't take any garbage from anybody. *That's* what I remember from when we met. Not your dress size."

"Easy to say when it can't be tested."

Bryan stared at her. "You know, you think that says something about you, but really all you're saying is that I'm too shallow to love you if you don't meet some arbitrary standard of perfection."

The words struck with more force than he probably intended, and Ana opened and closed her mouth, trying to think of a reply. Before she could form even a single word, however, a slender woman approached and plopped herself in the chair next to them. "Hey. You must be Bryan. I'm Ana's sister Bettina. But you can call me Betsy."

Bryan threw a glance at Ana and then stuck out his hand. "Hi, Betsy. Nice to meet you."

"Same here. It's about time Ana brought someone home. Maybe Mom can stop lighting candles for her."

Ana covered her eyes with one hand. "Betsy, stop. You make me seem even more pathetic than I feel."

Betsy leaned over to Bryan, voice lowered to a commiserating tone. "Our mom is amazing, but she's a trip. Do you know she used to be a pearl importer? Then she quit work when Ana was in high school and all that focused attention was on us. By the way, thanks a lot for that."

Ana laughed. "You complain, but she's the only reason you stayed eligible to play tennis, so you should be thanking me. If not for that focused attention, you wouldn't have passed economics."

Betsy made a face, then straightened suddenly. "Ana? Please tell me that's not who I think it is?"

Ana followed Betsy's gaze to where a good-looking man had

just exited the patio door and was scanning the corners of the backyard. The blood drained immediately from her face, leaving her light-headed and weak. She had the sudden impulse to cringe down in her seat, make herself small, as if that would keep him from seeing her.

"Ana, what's going on? Who is that?"

"That is Robert Lumala." Ana took a deep breath and let it out as slowly as she could manage. "My ex-husband."

*   *   *

Bryan stared at Ana, stunned. "Your ex-husband?" He looked back at the man who was steadily advancing on them, sizing him up. Tall, handsome in a foreign-movie-star way, nicely dressed.

But *ex-husband*?

Ana seemed transfixed by his approach, so she would obviously be no help. He cast a quick look at Betsy. "Give me the short version. Love, hate, or tolerate?"

"I believe the last time she saw him, she told him that he broke her heart and if he ever approached her again, she'd return the favor by breaking his nose."

"Okay, so we're going with hate." At least he knew there was no competition with the guy. The question now was how to make him go away as quickly as possible so Ana didn't need to deal with him.

He knew just as swiftly that it wasn't his place. When the ex got within a few feet and Ana rose, Bryan did the same, sticking right by her side.

"Ana," Robert said, offering a cautious smile. "It's nice to see you. I didn't expect you to be here."

"It's only my father's sixty-fifth birthday. Why would I be?" She seemed to get a handle on herself and said calmly, "Robert, I'd like you to meet my boyfriend, Bryan."

"Hello," Bryan said, offering his hand. Robert looked him over, up and down, then gave a dismissive smile as he shook his hand. Bryan hated him already. And Ana had been married to this guy? What on earth had she seen in him?

Then Robert made the cardinal mistake of guys everywhere, the aggressively hard handshake that was meant to establish dominance. Bryan didn't play those stupid games, but he couldn't resist giving Robert's hand a squeeze hard enough to make him flinch. *Yep. I cling to rocks for a living.*

Except, of course, he no longer did.

Robert pulled his hand back and shoved both in his pockets, looking back to Ana. "Could I have a word with you? Alone?"

Ana gave him a chilly smile. "Anything you want to say to me, you can say in front of Bryan and Bettina."

"Actually—" Bettina gave a helpless shrug—"I'm going to get some food." And then she hightailed it out of there.

Robert glanced at Bryan, and he stared blandly back. Ana was the only one who could ask him to leave, and she didn't seem inclined to do so. Robert obviously figured that out, because he moved aside and tried to pitch his voice low. "I've actually wanted to talk to you for a long time. I'm sorry that things are so bad between us . . ."

"You're sorry that things are *bad* between us?" Ana replied incredulously.

"That's what I said—"

"You're not sorry about anything else."

"Obviously, I wish things could have turned out differently, but Ana, it's been almost sixteen years. Don't you think it's time to get over this?"

Bryan looked between them. He'd never seen Ana in anything less than full control of her emotions, but he could practically feel the fury vibrating from her body.

"Right. I should just get over it. You are unbelievable. Even now, you can't admit responsibility for what you did to our marriage."

"We were young. I made a mistake."

"Right, a mistake. You were walking down the street, and oops . . . you slipped and accidentally got another woman pregnant?" She shook her head. "You're not sorry for anything. You're just mad that I won't forget everything and make it easy for you and your parents to be friends with my family. And as far as I'm concerned, that's your problem. *You're* just going to have to get over it."

Ana glanced back at Bryan. "I'm going inside. They're about to put the candles on Dad's cake." Robert started to say something, and she fixed her fiercest gaze on him. "No. We're done here. And if you come within six feet of me again, I'll make a scene you'll never forget. Got me?"

Robert's eyes widened and he nodded. Ana looked like she was going to say something else, but she stuffed it down and strode back to the house like a woman possessed. Bryan grabbed her plate from where she'd left it on the chair and followed her, not caring that it looked like he was trailing her like a puppy.

All he cared about was making sure she was okay. And finding out why she'd felt the need to hide her past from him.

*　　*　　*

Ana blew through the kitchen, where her mom was putting candles on a chocolate-frosted sheet cake, ignoring her when she called Ana's name. Instead, she navigated swiftly through the crowd and straight out the front door.

"Ana?"

Bryan's voice came softly behind her. He'd followed her out. Great. It was bad enough that he had to be surprised by her ex-husband, worse that he'd seen her lose it in front of her family and their friends.

But he was still waiting, so she drew a deep breath and turned toward him, helpless humor lacing her voice. "Surprise. I was married once."

"I kind of gathered that," he said levelly. "How old were you?"

Ana shrugged and moved out to the brick planter in front of the house, plopping herself down on the edge. She hissed in annoyance when her skirt snagged on the rough brick. "Eighteen. Our families have been friends for ages. His dad is actually my godfather. We were always together, but no one really thought we'd ever be interested in each other. And then, senior year of high school . . . we fell in love. Or at least that's what we called it." She rolled her eyes. "When you're eighteen, can you really be in love?"

"Maybe," Bryan said.

"Well, my parents didn't think so. They forbade the engagement, for good reasons. He'd turned down a college scholarship in order to tour with his band after we graduated. He was talented, no question, but I don't need to tell you what the parents of a teenage girl would say about marrying a musician with no other means of support, family friend or not."

"No, you don't."

"Anyway, we didn't listen. We eloped. Ran away to Vegas and got a quickie marriage. And consummated it as quickly as possible, so we couldn't be forced into an annulment." She threw him a wry look. "Let's face it, we were eighteen, sheltered, and Catholic. That's probably a good part of the reason we got married in the first place."

He chuckled softly, but he didn't try to touch her, even though he was close enough to.

"Anyway, I deferred my USC admission for a year, spent my days as a barista and my nights acting the supportive wife while his band played seedy bars. Meanwhile, he lived off my paltry paycheck and slept with other women. He got to live his dream and all I got were my mad pool skills." She forced a smile, as if that could erase the pangs of hurt and shame that came with the retelling.

He blinked. "Wow. So much for sheltered and Catholic."

"Yeah. He had his parents fooled too, so I guess I shouldn't feel too bad I didn't see him for what he was. In any case, he promised to clean up his act."

"How long was this after you were married?"

"Four months."

"Ouch."

"Yeah." She went in for the kill. "And then his ex-girlfriend showed up . . . nine months pregnant."

"What?" The shock on his face was thoroughly gratifying. "So he was dating you, sleeping with her, and then he married you?"

"Yep, pretty much. That was the last straw. I put my tail between my legs, moved home, and filed for divorce. I went to USC in the spring and never looked back."

Bryan stayed quiet for a long moment, digesting the information. "Why do I have a terrible feeling there's more?"

"Do you mean the part where Robert got a job working for my dad at the bank? Or the part where my mom makes oblique comments about my having divorced the only man willing to marry me?"

Bryan's mouth dropped open. "Surely you're joking."

"I wish I were. I mean, they were horrified, of course. But Robert spun it into some sort of story about youthful indiscretions and how I was the only woman he ever really loved, how I was the one he wanted to settle down with. And the families being as close as they were, they pushed hard for us to get back together."

"But you never did."

"Are you crazy? He showed up at the house one time and I tried to back over him with my car."

Bryan cracked a smile. "And just when I thought I couldn't possibly love you any more."

A reluctant smile came to her lips in return, a bit of the tension draining from her body. "Our families didn't appreciate my murderous inclinations. The thing is, I might have been able to forgive him, but it's unfair to expect me to act like it never happened, like we're best friends. My family should have my back. Not spend the next fifteen years telling me I'm going to stay single forever.

"Anyway. Now you know why I dread coming home. There's either the risk of running into him—though I really didn't think he'd have the guts to come here tonight—or having to hear about how great Robert is doing, how many women would just love to be with him, but he's still broken up over losing his one great love." She rolled her eyes again, wondering how she'd ever believed the lies that tripped off his lips so easily. "Trust me. He's not exactly lacking for female companionship."

"Wow. I'm really sorry, Ana. Why didn't you tell me? It's not like anyone could fault you for the divorce considering the situation."

He was right, but shame still burned inside her at the word *divorce*. She stared at her hands. "I'm literally the only person in my family who is divorced. I'm not a successful businesswoman; I'm just the divorced daughter who helps bad people keep their jobs. Do you have any idea what it's like to have your life dragged out as party chatter? One bad decision, and their view of me is damaged forever."

Bryan settled himself beside her on the planter and threw her a rueful smile. "You do remember who you're talking to, right?"

She flushed. Of course. Except while he had been completely

honest about his past, she was still hiding hers from everyone close to her. She didn't intend to confess, but words slipped out anyway. "You're the first person from my life in Denver who knows. I haven't even told Melody and Rachel."

"Why not? They're your best friends."

She shook her head, her braid sliding back over her shoulder. "I couldn't. They depend on me for advice. I'm supposed to be the sensible one. And now it's been so long, I don't know if they'd forgive me for keeping it a secret."

He reached for her hand and twined their fingers together. "Melody and Rachel love you. They'll understand if you explain it to them. But, Ana, you're carrying a burden that you were never meant to."

She glanced at him, her brow furrowing in confusion.

Bryan smiled faintly. "The only one who expects you to be perfect is you."

She held his gaze in the dark, taking in the compassion in his eyes. He meant what he said. If anyone knew what it was like to come back from bad decisions, it would be him. But he hadn't made a career out of fixing other people's problems. Her clients expected her to have it all together. Her *friends* expected her to have it all together. If she wasn't that person, then who was she?

She let go of his hand and pushed to her feet, brushing down her skirt. He meant well, but he couldn't possibly understand. She shoved down the emotion that had welled to the surface and put on a determined tone. "Sometimes it's easier just to put things in the past. I'm not that person anymore."

He didn't look convinced, but he rose and put his arms around her. "Well, I for one am glad that you came to your senses and didn't stay married to that schmuck."

"Oh yeah?" She lifted her face to his, relieved at his playful tone. "Why is that?"

In response, he dipped his head and kissed her, carefully and almost chastely, but Ana still half-expected the porch light to flicker on and off. When she stepped back, her heart swelled with emotion. There could be no question she loved him. But when she opened her mouth, the words still wouldn't come.

Bryan must have sensed her turmoil, because he cleared his throat. "Should we go inside for cake?"

"Let's. I'm kind of hoping that Robert will be having trouble holding a fork."

Bryan chuckled, though he put on an abashed expression. "You noticed that, did you?"

"He deserved it. Always has to be top dog in any situation."

Ana twined her fingers with his again, the contact tugging once more at her heart. She could no longer deny that what she felt for him was more than fleeting infatuation.

And yet she couldn't help feeling that once more, she'd let an opportunity slip away.

Chapter Twenty-Eight

"SO THAT WAS FUN."

Ana cast a look over her shoulder as they crept forward in the boarding line onto the 737 that would take them back to their real lives. She listened for any sign of sarcasm, but no, Bryan sounded completely serious.

"You're kidding, right?" She moved forward another foot and murmured an apology to the first-class passenger who took the brunt of her roller bag in the knee.

"No, I mean, I got to impress you with my *natarajasana*, met an ex-husband I didn't know about, and got propositioned by your seventy-year-old great-aunt. How is that not fun?"

Her victim jerked his head their direction at Bryan's words, and Ana had to stifle a snicker. After this weekend, what some random passenger thought about her was pretty far down on her list of things to worry about.

"To be fair, I really don't think Lola Ildefonsa meant it that way. Call it a translation error."

The line moved forward enough to get them to their seats, and Bryan hoisted their carry-ons into the overhead compartment. She settled into her window seat and shoved her purse under the seat in front of her.

"So, would now be the time to tell you that my parents invited us over to dinner tonight?"

Ana whipped her head around. "What? Tonight?"

"They actually invited you last week, but I figured we should see how this went before I sprang it on you."

Ana just blinked. She hadn't exactly been worried about bringing Bryan to meet her family because in the grand scheme of things, their approval or disapproval meant very little to her daily life. But the Shaws were different. Bryan lived with them for one thing; for another, Mitchell was close to her best friend's fiancé. This was far more make-or-break for them.

"You look kind of green," Bryan said. "I can cancel if you don't want to go."

As if she could do that. Not after the family and the ex-husband revelation. Fair was fair. "No, I'll go. Dress code?"

"Casual. They're not fancy."

No, they just lived in a multimillion-dollar historic mansion. She'd definitely dress up for the event.

"So, I was thinking . . ."

Her heart started beating harder at the significant tone of voice. "Yes?"

"Rachel has been so supportive . . . what if we buy out a supper club event for potential customers and distributors, maybe media? Would she be willing to devise a coffee-forward menu for the event showcasing our beans?"

"Oh." Ana laughed a little breathily when she realized he was transitioning to work. "I'm sure she would. I can ask her and see."

"It's an interesting story, so I think if we get the word out about what I'm trying to do with the farm and what Café Libertad is doing in the region, it might drive some interest to Solid Grounds."

"It's a good idea. I'll pitch it to Rachel. She'll enjoy concocting an interesting menu on Adrian's dime."

He gave her a half laugh. "Adrian." Then he cast her a sideways look. "You really have a type, don't you?"

"What? Rich, dark, and handsome?"

"Robert's rich too?"

"Investment banker. I'm surprised he didn't tell you when you met, considering all the territory-marking."

"I don't get involved in battles I can't win."

She shot him a look. "You don't actually think I care about those things, do you?"

"Maybe not consciously. But you forget I've been to your condo."

"Just because I live in a nice place and drive a nice car doesn't mean I'm shallow."

"I didn't say you were shallow, and I never mentioned anything about your car. I'm just wondering . . ." He broke off.

"What? What are you wondering?"

He leaned over the armrest and pitched his voice low. "Ana, those things are never going to be important to me. I spent my life savings on a coffee farm that may never earn me a dime. I'm wondering if that's the kind of person you could see yourself with. Long-term."

She lifted her gaze to look him in the eye, surprised. "Are we thinking about the future now? Already?"

"Ana, honey, I've always been thinking about the future when it comes to you."

She sucked in a breath. He was sincere; she had no doubt of that. He didn't play games. And right now, on a plane, he was asking if he was enough for her.

"I guess that all depends. Can you see yourself with a woman who earns more . . . a lot more . . . than you?"

"Honestly?"

"Yes, honestly."

He flashed an impish smile. "It's pretty much the ideal arrangement."

A smile spread across her own face. "You don't have to be so enthusiastic about the prospect of being a kept man."

"I prefer the term *trophy husband* myself."

"Slow down there, cowboy. No one is proposing yet."

"You'll give me fair warning when you do, though, right? I want to make sure my hair looks good on the proposal video."

Ana threw her head back and laughed, suddenly light-hearted. "If I propose, I'll make sure you're camera-ready."

"Good. I appreciate that." He flipped up the armrest so he could take her hand and remained that way as the flight attendants started their routine.

Ana listened with half a mind, but really she was watching Bryan out of the corner of her eye. He didn't joke around because he lacked depth; quite the opposite, actually. He was shockingly perceptive, and he knew just how to defuse tense situations in a way that didn't make her feel handled or managed. He told her he was in this for the long haul but put the control squarely in her hands.

For the first time, she looked at a man and had no reservations. In some miraculous way, he was perfect.

Somehow, Ana fell asleep on the flight and woke to the bounce of the plane as it touched down at DIA. She lifted her head in confusion to see Bryan beside her, reading a book on the phone held in his left hand, his right still clasping hers. "We're home?"

"Safe and sound," he said. "I figured we'd drop you off at your house first so you can nap and get ready and then I'll just pick you up later?"

"I can drive myself—"

"Let me. That way I have an excuse to escape the house afterward." He smiled and she returned it. She'd met Mitchell before and found him to be perfectly pleasant, but she was sure that Bryan thought her family was absolutely wonderful as well. It was one thing to be a guest, another to actually live with your parents as an adult. She shuddered just thinking about it.

They were walking down the long hallway from their gate, dragging their bags behind them, when Bryan said, "I checked my email on the plane. We got a nibble."

Ana looked at him blankly, still groggy from her nap.

"The beans?" he prompted. "Your samples? From a restaurateur . . . um . . ." He checked the phone quickly. "Caleb Sutter?"

Ana started laughing. "That was kind of a last-minute Hail Mary because he's a friend of Rachel's. But I didn't mention that in the letter. He's big into local and sustainable, so I suspected the story behind the company would appeal to him. What did he say?"

"He wants to try it in both his restaurants. Sample order of thirty pounds. If it goes well and the customers like it, he'll give us and our logo a featured spot on his menus and his websites."

Ana stopped abruptly, causing some grumbling behind her from passengers who were following too close behind. "Are you kidding me?"

"No, I'm not kidding. Look for yourself."

Ana squealed and threw her arms around Bryan's neck, hugging him tight. "This is amazing!"

"It's only one order for two restaurants, Ana."

"No, Caleb is a trendsetter. Everyone watches what he does, especially at Equity. If he picks it up, others are sure to follow. This is a good thing, Bryan."

He smiled down at her, eyes gleaming, she thought with

happiness. He took her hand and waited for her to grab her suitcase, and then they climbed onto the moving walkway down the center of the terminal. "This is all because of you, you know."

Ana made a dismissive sound. "No, it's not. It's because your farm produced some great beans and you did a great roast. I just got them to the right people."

"And without that, it would just be a bunch of beans in sacks in my warehouse." He nudged her. "We make a good team."

"That we do. We have to capitalize on this, of course. If I can get an in-person meeting with other high-end chefs, I can subtly drop that we're in Equity and it gives us instant credibility."

"Why don't we wait until we're sure that the customers actually like it?" Bryan suggested.

"They're going to love it, trust me. We need to take this little bit of momentum and run with it. Don't start getting all humble on me now."

The whole way home in the Uber, Ana was making both mental and electronic lists of what they'd need to do next. She wouldn't say it aloud, but she'd been waiting for the first feedback before she started working on her marketing push. If they didn't get any interest, it would be a sign that they had to rework either the roast or the marketing message. But Caleb had impeccable taste, so she was sure more emails would be coming in before long. Most chefs and managers got tons of samples every day, and while they usually tried them when they were fresh, it could take weeks for them to actually get back to the suppliers.

The Uber pulled up in front of Ana's place and the driver hopped out to get her suitcase. Bryan poked his head out of the back door. "I'll pick you up about six thirty or so?"

"I'll be ready. Looking forward to it." She was nervous too, but riding the high from their good news, she had nothing but confidence it would be a successful and pleasant night.

*   *   *

Ana never managed to take the nap that she claimed she was going to grab. Instead, she sat down with her laptop and worked her way through the hundreds of messages that had come in over the weekend. Most of them were junk until she got to one from Lionel Massey, marked with the little red exclamation point that meant *urgent*.

Hope you're enjoying your vacation. I know we said we were going to keep you out on leave for a little while longer, but we have another prospective client, and she says she will only work with you. Think I can convince you to cut your vacation short? Or at least come in to close the deal?

He'd included a link at the bottom to a *Washington Post* article headlined: *Louisa Holliday steps out on Academy Award–winning husband.* A photo of the starlet emerging from a hotel wearing dark sunglasses and shielding her face from the paparazzi made her look embarrassed and ashamed, when she probably was just annoyed at the attention.

Ana stared at it as she processed. Everyone knew who Louisa Holliday was, and it was a sign of Ana's preoccupation with personal matters that she hadn't even heard of this latest scandal. How had a Hollywood star even gotten Ana's name, let alone determined that she was only going to work with her?

She considered her words carefully before she clicked Reply. *I'm working on a consulting project, so it all depends on what she has in mind. Do I need to fly to New York or is she coming to us?*

She clicked Send and then tried to put the thought aside, even though it was rattling around in her head while she emptied the rest of her inboxes of varying spam messages. She was about to shut down when the envelope icon appeared on the tray again, and she clicked it to open it.

Lionel had already responded. *She'll do whatever she needs to do. Are you in?*

She sat back in her chair and considered, shocked that it even took consideration. The fact was, after the first couple of restless days, she hadn't missed her job. She had found an outlet in Bryan's roastery, a way to use skills that usually took a backseat to the more important strategic planning and image casting that she was paid very well for. She'd always expected to go back, but now that she was faced with the reality of it . . .

She must have sat there for ten minutes, staring at the message. Finally she closed the lid of her laptop without responding and went into her bedroom to change for dinner. But the presence of the email, what it could mean, nagged at her.

Lord, is this Your doing? Are You handing me a way back into a job I thought was gone? What about Bryan? What about the roastery?

What am I supposed to do here?

She hadn't truly expected a voice from heaven in reply, but she'd hoped for . . . something. An insight. A feeling. A nudge in one direction or another. Maybe she should talk it over with Bryan. He would walk through all the pros and cons with her, regardless of whether it worked out in his favor. Which was exactly why she loved him. He wasn't trying to make her into his own image of what he wanted in a girlfriend; he took her exactly as she was.

That thought put a smile on her face as she chose her clothes for dinner. He might have said it would be casual, but in this case, she didn't quite trust his judgment. Instead she picked a slim purple skirt, one of her floral chiffon blouses—so she'd succumbed to a sale as soon as the spring fashions came out—and a pair of neutral pointy-toed flats. She looked cute but put together, casual but still elegant. Ready for whatever might get thrown her way.

She was just fashioning her hair into a loose fishtail braid when a knock came at her front door. She grabbed her earrings and her watch from the bathroom counter and made her way to the door, putting on the jewelry as she walked. Sure enough, Bryan was standing there waiting for her, already changed— she suspected more for her benefit than his parents'.

"Ready?"

"Let me grab my purse. You can come in and have a seat if you want." She turned and went back to her bedroom, where she quickly shifted her wallet and makeup case from her travel shoulder bag into a fold-over clutch. When she came back, Bryan was standing near the windows, looking out onto the twilit city.

"Another purse?"

Once she got over the surprise that he actually paid attention to her handbags, she shrugged. "I have a substantial collection. Silly not to use all of them."

"No offense," he said, accompanying her to the door, "but do clients actually care about those things?"

"Clients come to me wanting me to fix the mess they've made of their lives. They might not consciously notice whether or not my purse and shoes complement my outfit, but subconsciously, they'll register that all the parts work together. There's nothing in the image that makes them doubt my ability to put everything to rights. And when we're talking about people who are facing at least the loss of their careers, if not jail time, that's reassuring. If they think anything at all is off, they'll go somewhere else."

"That's a lot of pressure." Bryan stepped outside and waited as she closed the door behind her, the electronic lock automatically latching. "Doesn't that ever get to you?"

"Sometimes. But it's part of the job."

"It doesn't have to be."

Ana let the comment pass. She'd been about to tell him about the offer she'd gotten from Lionel, certain that he would push the decision back to her, but now she wasn't so sure. Given the way he felt about authenticity, it wasn't so far-fetched that he would urge her to get out of a profession that put such a premium on image and into something in which she could be herself.

And she might not have the ability to resist that logic.

Bryan escorted her to his battered hatchback parked a couple of blocks down the street and held the door open for her like the gentleman he was. When he climbed in, he looked over at her. "Ready for this?"

He was just pulling away from the curb when his cell phone rang. He glanced at the screen, but then sent it to voice mail. "My mom. We'll be there in a few minutes and she can tell me whatever she's calling about in person."

A text message beeped in next, and he glanced at the phone quickly. "Mom again."

"Don't you think you should call back? It could be important."

"I just saw her ten minutes ago. How important could it be?"

Ana didn't say anything, but as the messages and calls piled up, her usually accurate instincts started poking at her. She'd spent a lot of time with Bryan in the last few weeks, and never once had his mom been so insistent on getting ahold of him. The occasional phone call or text, yes. Five in as many minutes? Never.

But they were pulling up the driveway of the Shaws' house now, so there wasn't much point in calling back. Bryan pulled into his usual spot and frowned. Ana followed his gaze to a sporty gray sedan parked at the opposite end of the driveway. It had California plates.

"Did your parents invite other guests?" Ana wondered aloud.

Bryan seemed just as baffled as she felt. "Not that I know of. Could be an employee dropping something off for Dad."

He turned off the ignition and moved to open her door, but she climbed out before he could. Then they walked to the front door together, Bryan pushing the door open and gesturing for Ana to go ahead.

She tried to keep the awe off her face, but it was difficult when she stepped into an ornate art deco entryway, complete with extensive wood carvings and stunning crystal chandeliers. The Shaws might use the space casually, but it was easy to imagine the balls that would have been held here in the Prohibition era, probably serving bootlegged liquor to elegantly dressed flappers and their dashing escorts.

"This is all original?" Ana asked.

"Most of it. And what isn't was reproduced using original methods. My dad was very exacting in his preservation efforts."

"Bryan?" Kathy Shaw's voice came from the adjacent parlor and they moved toward an equally beautifully decorated room. Kathy broke off when she saw Ana, a stricken look on her face.

A queasy feeling hit Ana's stomach. Had they gotten it wrong somehow? Was she not expected? Had something terrible happened, a family emergency?

While she was trying to work out the situation, she noticed that Mitchell and Kathy were not alone. A dark-haired woman sat in one of the armchairs near the fireplace. Her head swiveled toward Bryan and she slowly rose from her chair.

"Vivian?" Bryan breathed.

Ana's mind shifted gears abruptly, first registering that *Vivian* meant Bryan's first love, the one who had broken his heart and ended his career.

And second, taking in the woman's round, pregnant belly.

Chapter Twenty-Nine

BRYAN STARED AT VIVIAN, too stunned to form words. After she'd left him in Colombia, he'd expected never to see her again. But she was here.

And she was pregnant.

His mind didn't want to comprehend that second fact, any more than it wanted to comprehend that Ana was standing next to him, taking in the scene with a look of shocked horror on her face. Vivian seemed to pick up on that as well, because she shifted uncomfortably.

"Is there somewhere we could talk in private?" she asked.

"Uh, yeah, I guess we can . . ." He broke off and looked to Ana, unsure, in his shock, how to handle the situation.

"I'm just going to go. There are obviously things you need to work out." She kept her tone perfectly level, but there was something beneath it that told him inwardly she was seething. And then she seemed to remember how they'd gotten here. "But I don't have a car."

"Take mine. I'll come by to get it. We'll talk later." He willed her to look him in the eye, hear what he wasn't saying aloud. *I'll explain. This can't be as bad as it looks.*

But deep down, he knew this was exactly as bad as it looked.

"Okay," she said finally, holding out her hand. It took him another moment to remember that he'd offered his car. He dug his keys from his pocket and dropped them into her hand, then moved to kiss her goodbye. She turned her head so he only caught her cheek. His heart sank.

As soon as Ana let herself out the front door, Vivian looked at him, her expression sorrowful. "I'm so sorry. I never meant to . . . That was not my intention. I just didn't know how else to get ahold of you."

Mitchell and Kathy were watching the whole thing with carefully neutral expressions, but who knew what she'd already told them?

"Let's go talk out on the patio," Bryan said quietly, holding out a hand for her to precede him. Vivian hesitated and he realized she'd never actually been inside his parents' house. Funny that in all the years they'd been together, he'd never introduced her to his parents. Was that from some sort of unconscious understanding that they wouldn't make it in the long term?

He led her through the house to the French doors that opened onto the immaculately landscaped backyard, his heart hammering in his chest, his stomach churning. The last time he'd felt this panicked had been on the way to the hospital with Vivian, sure she wasn't going to live. Now it was *his* life as he knew it that was on the line.

She went straight to the patio table, as graceful and athletic as ever, even with the huge belly, and lowered herself into one of the chairs. Bryan took a seat directly opposite her and waited.

"So, I don't think I need to tell you that I'm pregnant." A twinge of humor laced Vivian's words.

Bryan saw nothing amusing in the situation. "I think I figured that one out for myself."

She reached across the table and laid her hand on top of his, even though he had the strongest urge to pull it away. "Bryan, the baby is yours."

He'd known that's what she was going to say; why else would she be here? But the air seemed to swirl around him, his balance compromised, making him light-headed and dizzy. "How do you know?"

"Well, we had sex."

"And you said you were on the pill."

"It must have been the antibiotics they put me on in the hospital," she said quietly. "Bryan, you have to understand, it's not like I planned this. It's not like I wanted this."

Bryan took a deep breath and wiped a hand over his face. As much as he wanted to believe that it was impossible, he knew it was all too possible. A quick count back put the . . . incident . . . in Suesca at nearly nine months. And from the looks of her, she didn't have much longer to go before she popped. Which raised the question, why did she wait so long to tell him?

Vivian hung her head and studied her chipped manicure when he asked. "I didn't want to believe it. I was engaged to Luke. At first, I just assumed it was his baby. But all the tests and ultrasounds . . . they don't add up to when he and I . . . you know."

Bryan was having a hard time drawing in full breaths. Vivian was pregnant. With his baby. Vivian. Had it been a few months earlier, he would have taken it as a sign he was getting a second chance. However nontraditional Viv seemed, she'd want her child to have both parents. And he would have married her without question.

But that was all in the past. Looking at her now, he felt only regret over his poor choices and panic over what this meant for him now.

Because he no longer loved Vivian, if he ever really had. He loved Ana.

Someone who had already been betrayed by a man she loved, who had already had a pregnant "other woman" show up on the scene, an event that had been so traumatic that she hadn't had a serious relationship in over fifteen years. And now, just as she was finally beginning to trust him, she had proof that no matter how much Bryan wanted to be different, he would never escape his past.

"Bryan?" Vivian pleaded. "Say something, please."

He jerked his head back to Vivian, thrust back into the here and now. He tried to order his jumbled thoughts as he took deep breaths. "What does Luke say about all this?"

She swallowed hard. "As you may know, Luke is not the most forgiving man."

Bryan laughed harshly in reply.

"I'm not sure when he figured it out, but he worked backward to the conception date and asked me point-blank if it was your baby. And when I said, 'Yes, I think so,' he threw me out."

Bryan wiped a hand over his mouth. "You two are done."

She nodded.

"Well." Another deep breath. "I'm not going to abandon my child, if that's what you're afraid of."

The tension seemed to melt out of her body. "Bryan, I'm so sorry. I've been so horrible to you. I should never have come to see you in Colombia. I should have told you about Luke. But I think deep down, I wanted you to fight for me. I don't think I've ever completely gotten over you—"

Bryan held up a hand. "Viv, stop. I'm going to take care of my baby, because what's happened isn't its fault. It didn't have anything to do with our bad choices. But that doesn't mean

I want to get back together. We're over. We were over when you slept with me, knowing you were engaged to another man. We were over when Luke fired me but took you back."

A tear trickled down her cheek. "I don't blame you. You have every right to hate me."

He sighed. "I don't hate you, Viv. But I've moved on."

"The woman you came in with?"

Bryan nodded.

"I'm so sorry. I didn't mean to interfere in your relationship."

"Well, after this, there probably isn't a relationship." He rose to his feet. "Do you have someplace to stay?"

She shook her head. "No. I came straight here."

"Then we'll get you set up in a hotel. And we'll talk more in the morning."

Vivian nodded, pushing herself up from her chair with difficulty. "Okay. Thank you."

He opened his mouth to reply, but it turned out he had nothing to say, so he just nodded. "Ana has my car, so we'll have to take yours."

They went back into the house, where his parents were still sitting in the parlor, conversing quietly in a pair of wingback chairs.

"I'm going to get Vivian checked into a hotel and then I'll be back. After I check on Ana."

Mitchell Shaw just nodded, but there was something in his eyes that Bryan could only read as disappointment. Kathy wouldn't even look at him. When she'd begged for grandchildren, she probably hadn't expected this to be the way she got them. Would his parents ever forgive him?

Even as he walked Viv to her car, he knew that the bigger question was, would *Ana* ever forgive him?

He had a sinking suspicion that the answer was no.

*   *   *

Ana drove back to her condo in a fog, parked Bryan's hatch-back, tried and failed three times to lock the doors with the key fob. It was as if the minute she'd laid eyes on that woman's pregnant stomach, she'd been taken back to the moment when Robert's baby mama had shown up at their apartment, angry and defiant and eager to burn down everything Ana knew about her life.

But no, this situation was different. Bryan hadn't cheated on her. He hadn't pretended to be something that he wasn't. He had changed.

And yet that didn't stop history from replaying itself.

She barely registered the doorman's greeting, rode the elevator up in a daze. Found herself a little surprised that she could still punch in her code from muscle memory, because right now her mind was a blank of horror and fear and dis-appointment. She tossed Bryan's keys on the countertop and made her way to the wall of windows in her gorgeous apart-ment where the city still hummed by, unaware and uninter-ested in the fact that twenty floors up, her life was crumbling around her.

"Don't be dramatic," she told herself aloud. "Let him explain before you jump to conclusions."

But what explanation could there be when his ex-girlfriend, the woman he'd admittedly pined after for years and once wanted to marry, came back pregnant? If it were someone else's baby, she wouldn't have been sitting in his parents' liv-ing room. Bryan might not pick up on it, but Ana knew how women in damage-control mode thought. Vivian's arrival had been calculated to make sure that she couldn't be ignored, that he couldn't make her go away quietly. She knew that his parents would want to know their grandchild, whether or not its mother was married to their son.

It. The baby wasn't an *it* but a *him* or *her*, a human being, one who had the right to have two involved parents, regardless of how unideal the circumstances were.

It felt like she stood at that window, thinking, forever. Maybe she had. When the knock she'd been waiting for finally came at the door, her muscles seized from standing motionless in one position for too long. She lurched toward the door, opened it, turned around before Bryan could even greet her.

He shut the door behind him. "Can we talk?"

She gestured to the sofa and plopped down on the far end, hugging a pillow to her as a physical barrier. Bryan sank down on the opposite end, about as far from her as he could manage and still be on the same piece of furniture. He opened and closed his mouth so many times, Ana couldn't stand it any longer.

"Is the baby yours?"

Bryan swallowed. "She says it is."

"And you believe her?"

He let out a long breath and slumped against the sofa. "It would be really easy to dismiss her, given the way it happened. But what if it is my baby? I'm not going to let a child grow up without its father because its mom is unreliable."

"But it's possible?"

A long pause, and then he nodded. "If her due date is what she says it is, yeah, it's possible."

"So what are you going to do?"

"Well, it's really easy for me to say I'm going to support the child, but we both know I have very little income right now, so I don't know how that would work. I'm going to have to figure something out." He scooted closer to Ana, and involuntarily, she squished herself back into the sofa. He looked hurt, but he froze in place. "What reason would she have for lying?"

"I can think of several." Ana jumped to her feet and paced the room fitfully. "Did you even ask her what happened to her supposed fiancé?"

"She said he figured out the baby wasn't his and kicked her out. And I hate to say it, but Luke can be cold. I wouldn't be surprised."

Ana stopped. "Ask for a paternity test."

He blinked. "I can't . . ."

"You can't what? Ask for proof that the baby is yours before you commit to supporting a child for eighteen years? You can't demand proof from a woman who slept with you while she was engaged to another man?"

"Ana, you don't understand. Vivian and I . . . we have a lot of history."

"Unless you don't want to know for sure. Unless you're looking for an excuse." The idea almost knocked her off her feet. "This is what you've been waiting for."

Bryan jumped up. "No, that's not true. I don't feel anything for Vivian, not like that. I love you. I know it's probably not what you want to hear right now—"

"I'm going back to Massey-Coleman." It was unrelated, but it spilled from her mouth before she could stop it.

He seemed jolted by the change of subject. "What?"

"Lionel asked me to come back. There's a big new client that they can't land without me. I've decided to take it."

He frowned, now switching gears along with her. "Okay. What does that mean for Solid Grounds?"

"I'll finish sending out the samples, and then I'm going to find you a good marketing consultant. I have a feeling that I'm not going to have any time for side projects once I get going with this new client."

"So . . . this is punishment?"

Ana blinked. "No. I got the message today, and I've been debating whether to take it. But it's a huge break, Bryan, my biggest client yet. If this goes well, Lionel might make me a partner. And that's all I've ever wanted."

Bryan nodded slowly. "I trust your judgment, and we have the money for a consultant thanks to Adrian. Send me your picks and I'll consider them."

She faltered. She'd expected him to say that he needed her, that he couldn't do this without her. But that was silly, because nothing she was doing for him couldn't be done by any other marketer. She hadn't founded the company or come up with the idea. All she'd done was write some copy and arrange for a website. Nothing more than she would have done for any of her friends.

"Then I guess that's it."

"What about us?"

She looked at him. "What about us?"

"You and me. This hasn't changed anything. I still love you, Ana. Vivian might be the mother of my child, but I don't want a relationship with her. Not in that way."

Ana couldn't help it. When the words *mother of my child* left his mouth, she flinched.

Understanding registered on his face. "I see."

"Bryan, I'm not saying that I can't . . . get over it. I just need some time. And you need some time. You've got to sort this whole thing out for yourself first."

"That's a cop-out, and you know it. First it's that I need to figure out this whole thing, and then it'll be that the baby is born, and then that I have to figure out how to co-parent with a woman I can barely stand." He rose and took her by the shoulders, forced her to look him in the eye. "Tell me right now, Ana: Do you love me or not?"

Ana swallowed, her heart clenching in her chest. "Yes."

He relaxed, letting his breath out in a long stream.

"But sometimes that's not enough." She stepped back out of his grasp. "I don't know if I can handle all this, Bryan. It's a lot to ask of any woman—"

"—let alone someone who's already been through it once." He took a big step back and dropped his chin to his chest, defeated. "I get it. I wish to God your answer was different. I wish to God that I hadn't thought I could do a better job of ordering my life than He could. But I did, and I guess now I'm having to deal with the consequences."

He looked like he wanted to say something more, but he just picked up his keys on the way out and left without another word.

Ana waited until the door closed behind him and then let out all the feelings she'd been pushing down in a long, keening wail that didn't even sound human to her own ears. Big, gulping sobs poured out of her, and she sank to the Persian rug, her entire body shaking with the force of her tears.

She let herself fall apart there on the rug for a handful of minutes, until her throat was raw and her head ached. Somehow, through her blurred vision, she managed to find her phone and type out a message on her group text with Melody and Rachel: I need you guys now. And just as quickly, she deleted the text before she could send it.

Then she did what women like her always did.

She picked herself up, washed her face, and began repairing the mask that protected her from the rest of the world.

Chapter Thirty

BRYAN SAT IN THE DRIVEWAY of his parents' house for he didn't know how long. His head felt dull, his stomach knotted, his chest tight. Too much had happened. So much that he didn't even know what had happened. For example, had he and Ana broken up? She'd asked for time, and he'd pushed the issue, feeling like she was giving him the polite brush-off. In the end, he'd just walked out, and he had no idea if he'd thrown away the person who was most important to him.

He pulled his keys from the ignition and trudged up the front steps, letting himself into his childhood home. Most of the lights were dimmed except for the kitchen, so he made his way through to the back of the house, where his dad was sitting at the island, doing something on his cell phone. Mitchell looked up when Bryan entered.

"Hey," Bryan said.

"Hey." Mitchell looked him up and down. "You look like you could use a drink."

Bryan raked his hands through his hair. "Yeah, I guess you could say that."

His dad got up and pulled two lowballs from the cabinet, dropped a couple of ice cubes in each, and then poured amber liquid from a decanter. Bourbon, Bryan thought. His dad had never been much of a Scotch man, thought it would make him seem pretentious. Mitchell shoved one glass over to him.

Bryan took a sip. He had been right about the bourbon at least. He waited for the beginning of the lecture that he knew was coming, knew he deserved.

"So, what now?" Mitchell lowered himself onto the barstool and looked at his son.

"That's it?"

Mitchell shrugged. "You're a grown man. I'm not going to treat you like a teenager who knocked up his girlfriend. What now?"

"I've got her settled in a hotel for now. Said I'd come by tomorrow and we'd discuss everything further. I need to think."

"She willing to take a paternity test?"

Bryan took a gulp of the bourbon. "I didn't ask her."

"Why not?"

"Because I don't want to be the guy who tries to weasel out of his responsibilities."

Mitchell nodded and thought for a second. "Here's the thing, though. This *is* a responsibility. Not just financial, but emotional and spiritual. I know you, Bryan. You aren't the type to just send a check. You'll want to be part of your child's future."

"And that's a bad thing?"

"No, that's not a bad thing at all. Obviously, it would be better for you to be married to his or her mom, but there are plenty of couples who successfully co-parent. But, Bryan, what if the baby isn't yours? She was engaged to someone else at the time."

"She says—"

"Right, she says." Mitchell paused thoughtfully. "What if she's wrong and it really is Luke's baby? Don't you think he has a right to know his own child? Trust me, Son, you want to know all the facts in this situation."

"That's pretty much what Ana said."

"Ana's a smart woman."

"Yeah. Smart enough to see this mess and run as far from me as possible."

Mitchell took a long, deep breath and then placed his hand on Bryan's shoulder. "I know I've been hard on you. I know I haven't been shy about showing my disapproval. But I believe you're a good man who has made some bad decisions and now you're trying to remedy them the best you can. Don't let whatever image you have of yourself cloud your judgment now."

"You mean just because I've done nothing but screw up until this point, don't assume I screwed up this particular time?"

"I'm saying don't be so quick to fix a situation that might not be yours to fix."

His dad was making sense, but at the same time, questioning the baby's paternity felt sordid and seedy. Like they were going to show up on the *Maury Show* to learn the results of the test and people were going to boo him for trying to get out of his child support.

And yet the way Vivian had come to him in Suesca, knowing full well that she was marrying another man, knowing full well that he would think they were getting back together, hadn't exactly been honest. She'd been living for the past eight months with her fiancé, who had taken care of her while she recovered from her injuries. Bryan wanted to believe that the Vivian he'd loved couldn't be capable of playing some complicated game, but that wasn't true.

"You're right," Bryan said finally. "I'll ask her tomorrow."

Mitchell nodded and finished his drink, then slipped off the barstool. "Whatever happens, Bryan, your mom and I are here for you. I hope you know that."

"Thanks." He smiled at his dad, genuinely warmed by the gesture, but deep down he knew the truth. He had gotten himself into this mess, and he would have to get himself out.

*　　*　　*

The next morning, Bryan showed up at Vivian's hotel room at nine thirty and rapped sharply on the door. After a bit of rustling inside, she opened the door, her expression surprised. "Bryan. Hi! I didn't expect you so early."

"Can we talk? I'm not interrupting anything, am I?"

"No, not really." She held open the door for him and stepped back. "I was actually just looking for an obstetrician to transfer care. Understandably, a lot of doctors don't want to take on a patient in her ninth month, even though I have all my records."

He slipped past her and settled himself in the desk chair across from one of the double beds. The room smelled familiar to him, a combination of Vivian's hand lotion and her herbal shampoo, unchanged after all these years. It struck an almost-indescribable yearning in him. Not for her, but for those days when he didn't know any better than to be blindly in love with her. Had she told him she was pregnant back then, he would have been thrilled because it meant that he could hold on to her, pin her down long enough to marry him. Even now, as she lowered herself carefully to the bed, a part of him wondered why this couldn't work. They could be a family, just the three of them. It wasn't as if she were the only one who had made mistakes; he was more than culpable.

And yet the thought of being with her, sleeping next to her, spending the rest of his life with her, made him feel ill because he knew that once the sense of responsibility wore off, there would only be unhappiness. He and Vivian hadn't been a match; he could see that now. Their relationship had been passionate, but it had also been volatile, a string of breakups and makeups. He'd never been sure if they'd be on or off. And while at times it had been exciting, it had been exhausting as well.

He felt no such reticence toward Ana.

Vivian was watching him, her hands clasped in her lap. "What did you want to talk about?"

"Well, just how this is going to work. Are you sure you don't want to go back to California until the baby is born? You said you're having problems finding a doctor. Wouldn't you rather have your OB from home do the delivery?"

Vivian shrugged. "I don't really like him all that much. But he was on my insurance."

"Okay. In that case, do you still have insurance and does it cover treatment here?"

"I think so. It should." She blinked. "I don't really know. Regardless, I want to stay here with you."

This was not the way he'd expected this conversation to go, and this was not the Vivian he remembered, forceful and decisive. "Viv, you need to know, if you stay here, I can't pay your expenses. You'll need to get an apartment of your own."

She blinked again. "I thought . . ."

"I'm living with my parents right now. I'm starting a business. Pretty much every dime I have is sunk into it."

"But your parents . . ."

"Are not responsible for either of us. I want you to know that I'm not going to try to shirk my duties to my child, but I'll be making so little until the company gets on its feet, there's not much to give you." Now was the time to drop the real bomb on her. "And before we make any child support agreements, I want a paternity test."

Now her entire demeanor changed. "You're calling me a liar?"

"No. But you can't blame me for questioning. You were engaged to another man at the time you say you got pregnant, and you went back to California and lived with him."

"The doctors were pretty clear. They—"

"Get due dates wrong all the time. Genetics don't lie. Viv, if it really is Luke's baby, don't you think he'd want to know? Would you really want him to miss out on his kid's life?"

Vivian rose from the bed stiffly. "I'd like you to leave."

Bryan nodded slowly. "If that's what you want. You have the hotel room until Friday. Let me know what you're going to do."

He quietly left the room, feeling her furious gaze on his back, but his initial niggling disquiet had grown to a full-out cacophony. He waited until he got to his car, then pulled out his cell phone and found Luke's number.

To his shock, Luke picked up on the first ring. "Bryan. I had a feeling I'd been hearing from you. Is Vivian with you? She's not taking my calls."

"Yeah, she's in Denver." Bryan took a deep breath. "I think there are a few things we need to discuss."

Chapter Thirty-One

AT MIDDAY, the restaurant was jumping with activity, the noise level hovering somewhere between loud and deafening. For the third time today, Ana wondered why her potential client had picked this venue for their first meeting. The details of her situation were delicate; they weren't the type of thing you wanted to shout over the conversations of your fellow diners.

Ana gave her name to the receptionist and immediately the manager appeared at her side to lead her into a small back room. Now she understood. Louisa Holliday commanded enough recognition that she could choose any restaurant in town and they would accommodate her need for discretion. The manager opened the door to the private room and let Ana in, then just as quickly excused herself.

Louisa sat at one of the handful of tables, looking as delicate and exquisite in person as she did on screen. The translucent ivory skin and vibrant copper hair made her look like an illustration from an art nouveau advertisement. But when she turned to greet Ana, her voice was unexpectedly deep and sultry. It wasn't hard to see why she'd taken Hollywood by storm.

"I'm so glad to meet you, Ana." She didn't rise, just extended a hand and gripped Ana's with a surprising amount of strength. "Please, have a seat. I hope you don't mind. I ordered wine for us."

"I don't mind at all. Thank you for meeting me." Ana took her seat and placed her clutch on the edge of the table.

Louisa's eye went directly to it. "That's a great bag. Is it the new Prada?"

"It is." She'd bought it as a way to bolster herself before diving back into her job. She wasn't even officially back to work; her triumphant return all depended on her ability to snag this account today. Lionel hadn't even been apologetic, and he hadn't meant to be. That was the way things worked.

"I like your style," Louisa said.

"Thank you." Ana took a sip of her wine, a Riesling that tasted way too sweet for this early in the meal, but she wasn't going to say that aloud. "Lionel told me you asked for me by name. I'm curious to know why. There's no shortage of publicists in New York and Los Angeles who could have taken you on. In fact, they've probably been tripping over themselves to bring you on board."

Louisa chuckled. "Oh, they have been."

"So why me?"

She put down her glass and looked directly at Ana. "For one thing, everyone expects me to hire a publicist from New York or LA, some power player who will minimize the damage and allow life to go on as usual."

Ana smiled slightly. "That's generally what publicists do."

"And how much of that do you actually think the public buys? Come now, they're sensitive to all the spin. They know when they're being played. But if an actress were to go back to her hometown, where everyone knew her, where she could get support after the terrible ordeal she'd undergone . . ."

"I'm sorry. I think I'm missing something. I was under the impression that the scandal was about you being caught in a hotel room with another man. While still married to someone who, by all estimations, is the most powerful director in Hollywood." Ana spoke bluntly, watching Louisa's expression as she did.

"Who terrorized me and tried to control my life," she said. "He's really not the person everyone thinks he is."

Who is? Ana thought, but the obvious answer immediately sprang to mind. She shoved the thought of Bryan away and folded her hands on top of the table. "Let's not play games here. Tell me exactly what you expect me to do for you."

"I expect you to do exactly what you did for Beth Cordero. You know, even I was surprised when she went on the talk show circuit talking about the pressures of competitive sports on children and how she escaped from under her father's thumb. Everyone has completely forgotten the blood-doping issue. Did you hear that based on her speaking, there's been an inquiry into harassment and abuse in winter Olympic sports? It's brilliant." She smiled. "When I saw that, I knew I wanted you."

Ana was beginning to feel sick at the implications. "To my knowledge, everything that Beth is saying is true. That wasn't concocted."

"Oh, please. Her father was a nightmare, no joke, but to say that she was afraid for her life should she not perform?" Louisa chuckled, this time a little nastily. "That was a stroke of genius."

"How . . . how do you know all this?"

"Oh." Louisa's eyebrows lifted. "You really don't know. Beth and I go way back. We grew up together, kind of. Enough to say hello and catch up on old times if we run into each other at charity functions. Breckenridge is a small town. There's no one who doesn't know everyone else's business. You think that no one would have intervened if there was real abuse going on? She was the darling of the entire town. Well, next to me, of course."

Ana couldn't wrap her head around what Louisa was telling her. Beth Cordero had lied, had smeared her own father in order to repair her career and preserve her endorsements? Had all the corroboration been set up? Had the "witnesses" been paid off? And by whom? Beth? Or someone else entirely?

Louisa was rattling on. "Basically, I wanted to make sure I got started as soon as we could, laying the groundwork. It will only be a couple of months before I'm showing, and I need to make sure the public is firmly on my side before that happens. It will still be nasty—have you been on social media lately?— but 'driven into the arms of another man' is a far better headline than 'ungrateful upstart cheats on industry powerhouse.'"

Lionel. It had been Lionel who had taken the responsibility for fact-checking Beth's story. Now she remembered. It would be better for Ana not to be involved in that part, he'd said; she should focus on finding appropriate charities and speaking engagements for Beth while he made sure everything was on the up-and-up. Too sensitive, too high-profile to get wrong, he'd said.

And now Louisa wanted Ana to do the same thing for her. Before anyone knew she was pregnant with her lover's baby.

It was so ridiculous, so close to her own messed-up life, that Ana started to laugh.

Louisa's eyes narrowed. "What's so funny?"

"Sorry. I . . ." She wiped her eyes, careful not to smudge her makeup. "I'm afraid I can't help you, Ms. Holliday. And I'm afraid that Lionel was being too modest when he said that I was completely responsible for Beth Cordero. He played a big, really an essential part in the whole narrative, so I have absolutely no doubt that he will be able to do the same thing for you."

"But you're a woman. It looks better if my publicist in this case is a woman who understands."

"I wish I didn't understand quite so well." Ana rose and took her purse. "Thank you for the wine. I'm sorry I can't help you."

And without another word, she turned and left the restaurant.

Once outside on the curb, Ana pressed a hand to her flushed forehead. Had she really done that? By walking away from Louisa Holliday, she'd ensured that she was never going back to Massey-Coleman. She'd probably ensured that she'd never get another crisis publicity job in Denver or anywhere else Lionel had connections. And for the first time, she realized she didn't want one.

She'd spent years trying to clean up other people's messes, thinking they deserved a fighting chance in the court of public opinion. And maybe they did. Maybe her clients were just people who had made mistakes. But they had compounded their mistakes by trying to paper over them, by trying to pretend they weren't human, by trying to make them go away. Instead of owning up to them and taking the consequences of their actions.

Like Bryan had.

She gave her valet ticket to the man at the stand and waited as he ran for her SUV, still parked down the street. She'd gotten it washed and waxed this morning to remove any errant water spot or swirl. They'd offered to detail the inside, but she'd said no thanks. She'd known she wouldn't have to drive anyone today, so there were still cracker crumbs in the seat and a slight smear of almond milk down the inside panel where she'd spilled her latte on the way to the car wash. It didn't matter. All anyone would care about was the exterior.

The car came to a stop in front of her, and the valet opened the door so she could climb in. There was the faint leftover taint of old coffee inside. She threw her ridiculously expensive Prada purse on the passenger seat and slid off equally expensive shoes so she didn't ruin them on the floor mats. And she sat there.

She was every bit as shallow and mercenary as the Hollywood starlet inside the restaurant.

Bryan had never claimed to be perfect. He'd been a hundred percent up-front about who he was, the mistakes he'd made. Now that one of those mistakes had caught up with him, he was attempting to deal with it with integrity. And she'd rejected him for it because it made their relationship messy. Because it reminded her of how Robert had betrayed her.

How she hadn't been enough for him, and her flaws had made him go sleep with other women even while he was married to her.

How for all her money and her success and her beautiful wardrobe, she was just as lost and confused and hurt as any of the people she worked for.

She didn't have anything together. And Bryan made her realize that for all their differences, they were exactly the same. Imperfect people trying to climb out of bad decisions.

Ana realized that tears were sliding down her face, probably taking her eyeliner with them. The valet was peering into the car with concern now, unsure whether to tell her to move on or ask her if she was okay. She made the choice for him: she put on the signal and pulled away from the curb.

At the stoplight, the guy in the car next to her stared at her and then quickly looked away. Funny how uncomfortable people got at a real show of emotion. It was okay if you could cry pretty; their discomfort came more from the disruption of the proper order of things than the feelings themselves.

Then she glanced in the rearview mirror and started. Okay, she didn't blame him for looking away quickly. She was frightening, like some creepy corporate zombie-clown from a not-quite-funny horror movie. As soon as she pulled into the garage of her building, she grabbed a wet wipe from her glove compartment and began to scrub the smeared makeup from her face.

Then she stopped. Why was she so worried about what anyone thought about her? Why was she determined to keep everyone from knowing that she actually had emotions?

She tossed the soiled wipe in her cup holder, grabbed her purse, and climbed out of the car. When the doorman did a double take, his face concerned, she just gave him a nod and climbed onto the elevator, where she rode up to her perfect apartment and walked into her perfect kitchen to place her cell phone on the charger.

Only then did she notice that the light on the phone was blinking, indicating a message.

She pressed the button for her voice mail and listened. One message.

"Hi, Ana. It's Bryan. I don't like the way we left things . . . actually, I don't even really know how we left things. We should talk. Call me."

Ana deleted the message and placed the phone on the charger. Then she went to her room, changed out of her work clothes, and washed her face clean of the makeup she'd worn for her meeting. The girl who stared back at her looked young—young and crushed and uncertain.

For the first time in a long time, she was actually looking at herself.

She walked out of the bathroom and took a circuit of her home like she was seeing it for the first time. It was beautiful, tasteful, *perfect*. It could have come straight out of the pages of *Architectural Digest* or *Domino*, titled something sufficiently aspirational like "Elegant Oasis in the City." And yet no one would walk into the space and know anything about her other than she had money. And liked clothes and shoes and hand-bags, based on the overstuffed state of her closet.

What had seemed to be the trappings of success, her just deserts, now seemed like a shallow attempt to cover up the truth.

She didn't feel good enough and she never had.

Wasn't that why she worked so hard to keep up her own image? Wasn't that why she went to two churches of different denominations, so she didn't have to make a choice and risk disappointing her family? Wasn't that the real reason she'd immediately backed away from Bryan? Not because his life had suddenly become complicated, which it had—she had no doubt that being in love with a man who was co-parenting a child would be difficult and frustrating and at times unfair. But that hadn't been the first thought that went through her mind. She'd jumped straight to how the situation would reflect on her. What people would think about her. What her parents would say.

Whether or not God would still love her.

Put that bleakly, it seemed ridiculous, and yet the question still resonated deep inside her. Hadn't she secretly thought that her divorce was her fault? Hadn't she believed it was caused by some deep deficiency as a wife and a person? She'd been work-ing all these years to be perfect, to make up for those perceived faults, in the hopes that maybe God would deem her worthy again. That maybe He would bring her another chance for love.

He had. And she'd thrown it away because that man was no more perfect than she was.

She sat on her four-thousand-dollar custom sofa, selected because it had been handmade in North Carolina using only well-paid American labor and was guaranteed not to exploit workers in the developing world. In short, it was just as perfect as the rest of her image.

And it meant absolutely nothing to her.

Which was good, because this was all going away. Louisa Holliday wouldn't have wasted any time calling Lionel to tell him what happened. By the end of the day, he would be phoning Ana to say they no longer needed her services at Massey-Coleman, something that she'd known in her heart long before this moment.

It turned out she didn't care about that any more than she cared about the stupid sofa.

But there was someone she did care about, and he was halfway across town, probably roasting beans and wondering how to go forward since she'd so abruptly left him in the lurch with their business, not to mention their relationship. He deserved more than that. He deserved the truth, even if it was too late for them.

And there were two women who loved her unconditionally, who would have stood by her through all her doubts and feelings of inadequacy, if only she'd had the courage to let them in.

She retrieved her cell phone and tapped in the message to Rachel and Melody that she should have sent a week ago. I need you guys now. And then, a second one.

I have some things to tell you.

*   *   *

When Ana texted, she hadn't considered that it was the middle of the workday, and Rachel and Melody would just be finishing up the lunch rush. Which was why she was instantly flooded with guilt when they showed up, still in their chefs' whites and without the usual food offerings that accompanied an emergency visit.

She let them in with a horrified gasp. "I'm so sorry! I didn't even think. I didn't mean to pull you away from work. I just—"

"It's okay," Rachel said. "We're through the rush and Sam and Talia are holding down the fort. What's going on? Are you okay?"

She ushered them in and gestured for them to sit down—on that blasted sofa—beside her. Melody and Rachel exchanged one of their now-trademark worried glances, clearly unsettled by her out-of-character behavior.

"What's going on, Ana?" Melody asked, her brow furrowing with concern.

Now that it came to it, her big emergency seemed silly. She'd dragged them away from work to tell them about something she'd been keeping a secret for sixteen years. Surely it would have kept for another few hours. But they were here, watching her expectantly, so there was no turning back.

And yet, she chickened out and reached for the less shameful of her announcements, only confirmed moments before. "I got fired."

Rachel blinked, like she wasn't sure she'd heard right. "I'm sorry, you got *what*?"

"Technically, my temporary leave was made permanent, but it's the same end result. I am no longer a publicist with Massey-Coleman. Effective immediately."

Rachel gasped and reached to give her a hug. "I'm so sorry. Are you okay?"

Ana nodded. "I am. I know it sounds weird, but it's freeing. I sat down with a new client and realized that I can't do it anymore. I can't plaster over other people's mistakes." She drew in another long breath. "And I can't stop hiding from my own."

Now she had their full attention. Rachel backed off and folded her hands into her lap patiently.

"I was married once."

"*What?*" Melody's mouth dropped open. "When? How?"

"When I was eighteen. It ended badly." She poured out the story in even greater detail than she'd given Bryan, forcing herself to unburden every last sordid element. "So now you know why I'm so weird about dating. I figured if I kept my standards high—unreasonably high—there was no way I could make a mistake like that again. I'd rather be alone than wrong. And that's a lonely way to live."

"Ana, honey . . ." Rachel reached for her hand and squeezed it hard. "Why wouldn't you tell us? Why did you keep it from us? You know we'd understand. It wasn't even your fault."

Ana hung her head for a second, not sure if the sudden burst of shame was over her past or the fact she'd been hiding things for so long. "I guess I didn't want to be that person anymore. And I was afraid if you knew . . ."

"We'd figure out you were exactly like us? Human?" Melody sent her a wry smile. "I hate to break it to you, but we kind of already knew that."

"Everyone—including you two—expects me to have the answers. How can I give advice to anyone else when I really have no idea what to do about my own life?"

"Well, look who's bought into her own PR?" Melody bumped Ana with her shoulder. "You know, we're friends because we like you. Not because we like having our own personal publicist."

"Though," Rachel interjected with a smile, "it is kind of a plus."

"Well, that's the only kind of publicity I'll be doing. Lionel made it clear that there would be no crisis work for me in Denver anymore. Which is fine. I'm tired of spinning the truth. For other people, for myself. I've been hiding behind all this— this *image*—for too long. It's time to face my life."

Melody smiled. "I knew Bryan would be a good influence on you."

"He was. But . . . that might be over."

"What?" Now they both looked shocked. "What do you mean?"

Ana stopped. If Bryan hadn't told anyone about Vivian's pregnancy, it wasn't really her place to break the news. And without that, there was no way of explaining why they were no longer together.

Though they really hadn't made that determination. They'd just . . . stopped talking.

She remembered the message he'd left today. She'd assumed from his level tone that he was talking about the business and not their relationship. But if he hadn't told Alex they'd broken up, did that mean he was still holding out hope? Did that mean she still had a chance?

She popped to her feet. "I'm sorry, guys. I have to go. I have to see him."

Rachel and Melody rose as well. "You won't make it to the roastery before he leaves. He and Alex had plans today."

"Do you know where?" Ana asked, a tinge of desperation creeping into her voice.

Rachel smiled. "Seems like you're not the only one reevaluating your life choices this week."

Chapter Thirty-Two

BRYAN WAS BEGINNING to believe that he actually had a future in this roasting business. He'd gotten back to work as soon as he returned from California, roasting full batches of beans to fulfill their first order, watching both the beans in the roaster and the profiling software like a hawk to make sure he was doing things as close as possible to his sample roast. He'd quickly discovered that the first batch of the day came out quite different from the later ones, a function of the residual heat in the drum from successive batches, which led to a change in his process. Even though it wasted fuel, a long, slow heating process seemed to give him more consistent roasts throughout the morning. Fortunately, he'd already dialed in the city roast that would be used for drip and a lighter, Scandinavian-style coffee that would appeal to third-wave coffee connoisseurs. The blonde espresso was proving to be slightly more elusive, but he was close enough to be confident that he'd have it figured out by the end of the week. That would make three different products from the same beans, something almost unheard of in this business.

What to do with that information was another story. Since Ana had made her big exit—from the company, but also possibly from their relationship—he was a bit lacking on the strategic side. He knew he needed to sample, he knew he needed to fulfill orders, but besides that, he had no idea what to do next to build this from an interesting idea to a viable business. He'd become dependent on Ana and he hadn't even realized it.

No, that wasn't quite the truth. He'd recognized it the minute she told him she needed some time to think. During the week he'd found himself reaching for his cell phone to text her news of his roasting victories and the trickle of orders that had come in from her prospects, before he remembered that she wasn't a part of it anymore. He had to restrain himself from picking up the phone and asking if she wanted to grab a bite to eat and watch a movie. His life since coming back from Colombia had involved Ana in every aspect, and her absence left a gaping, obvious hole.

He packaged the day's roast in the vacuum-sealed bags with one-way valves, their foil exteriors emblazoned with the logo that Ana's designer had created. Those went into cardboard boxes, to be hand-delivered later—he wasn't willing to cut into his meager profits by shipping. Besides, he was hoping that when he delivered them, he'd have a chance to pump the front-of-house manager for customer feedback. So far the only consumer input they'd had were the little cards from the supper club, once again a brilliant idea of Ana's.

No matter where he turned in this building, he was faced with reminders of her presence and, as a result, her absence.

It was killing him.

Which was why he'd broken down and left her that phone message. He realized that voice mail wasn't exactly honoring the spirit of "space," but he couldn't stand not knowing what was going through her mind. Was she trying to wrap her head around that fact that he could be a father? Had she decided she was disgusted by his past behavior and written him off? Was she delaying the inevitable in order not to hurt him? Alex had been no help; Ana evidently hadn't told Rachel anything, and at Bryan's request, Alex had kept the situation to himself.

He wasn't sure if that made him feel better or worse. Maybe she was fine. Or maybe she was happy that he was out of her life.

"Hey, you ready to go?" Alex popped his head into the room, obviously having let himself in with the key Bryan had given him in case of emergency.

"Yeah, let me finish packing this batch." He counted out twenty bags and carefully fit them into a cardboard box stamped with their company logo and labeled with the roast type. He set it aside on top of several others like it and then pulled off his gloves. "Guess it's time to face the music."

Alex waited patiently as Bryan gathered his keys and wallet from the office and then locked up the roastery. Only when they headed to Alex's car did his friend finally speak. "You know, you surprised me when you said you wanted to go climbing. I really thought you'd given it up for good."

Bryan gave a little shake of his head in answer. He'd thought by abandoning his climbing, he'd be able to leave that inglorious phase of his life behind him, but it still hadn't kept his mistakes from coming for him. If Vivian had proven one thing to him, it was that he might be paying for his actions for a good long while. But his father had been right: he needed to stop fixing things that didn't need fixed, punishing himself for sins that had been forgiven.

He kept up that thinking until they arrived at their climbing destination, Castlewood Canyon State Park. They unpacked their gear from the back of Alex's wagon and began the hike down to the start of their climbing route. A hawk soared overhead, searching for small animals for its supper, and Bryan remembered how he'd pointed out the eagle to Ana while they'd been hiking at Red Rocks. How hard he'd struggled against his attraction toward her.

He should have stuck with that vow. Had he been smarter, they'd still be friends. He could deal with the idea of not being with her romantically if it meant she was still in his life.

"You want to lead?" Bryan asked as they started to set up for their climb, racking their equipment on their harnesses, checking and double-checking knots.

"No way," Alex shot back. "This is your comeback. That honor goes all to you."

Bryan just nodded and took his position. He'd climbed this route dozens of times, so it shouldn't be a challenge, but nervousness still swirled in the pit of his stomach. He'd loaded the act of climbing with so much significance that he felt like he was about to break a spell. As if the first brush of a fingertip against rock would transform him back into the person he feared to be.

"Did we come to climb, or sit here and admire the rock formations?" Alex asked, his smirk evident in his voice.

Bryan shot his friend a dirty look, even though he was stalling. He worked out his first holds and dug the toe of his climbing shoe into the rock face. The rough surface of the stone abraded his fingers, his calluses already softened from almost nine months of disuse, but it was a good kind of pain, the kind that reminded him of the pleasure he'd always taken in the challenge. Gym workouts and yoga had managed to keep most of his muscles in good shape, but by the time he reached the first anchor point and clipped in, he was already feeling the unaccustomed strain in the tendons of his fingers.

"You building a summer home up there?" Alex called.

Bryan grinned at the sound of his own favorite gibe coming

back to him and reached for the next hold. By the second anchor, he was finding his rhythm, climbing almost as fluidly as he had before, even if the little tremors throughout his body told him just how far out of condition he really was.

And yet with every crimp and pinch, something settled inside him. His breathing evened into a deep, easy pattern, each movement becoming like a prayer, less conscious than words. *I'm sorry that I strayed so far. I'm sorry that I thought I could do a better job on my own. I'm sorry that I misused the gifts I was given for my own glory.*

Because wasn't that what he'd done? Made himself his own god, enjoying attention, accolades, the sensation of not having to play by the rules?

And now that he'd been brought low, lost something —someone—that truly had meaning, he realized just how much in need of help he really was.

The top of the slab loomed and hope bloomed in his heart for the first time in days, something he couldn't fully explain. Maybe the joy he felt in doing something he had always loved told him all was not lost, that his life wasn't stretched so far out of shape that it couldn't be righted. Or maybe it was just the knowledge that he didn't have to be imprisoned by his past. But when he finally hauled himself over the ledge, he felt reborn.

He clipped in to the final anchor. And immediately felt a surge of pain when he realized his first instinct was to text Ana and tell her he was climbing again.

"You did it."

He lifted his head, sure that his imagination had conjured her voice. But no, there she was, standing all of five feet away from him in jeans and a simple T-shirt. Smiling.

"What are you doing here?" He scrambled to release himself from the rope, then realized he hadn't yet called off belay. Alex's response was a little bewildered, but Bryan was too focused on the woman in front of him to think about his friend below.

"I came to see you," she said simply, her arms wrapped around herself protectively. "I was going to go to the roastery, but Rachel told me you and Alex would be here. What changed your mind?"

Bryan searched for a way to explain himself, but just as quickly gave it up. He didn't want to stand here and have a pleasant, meaningless conversation without having any idea where they stood. "Ana, why are you here?"

She uncrossed her arms and stepped closer, meeting his gaze for the first time. "I came to apologize."

"Apologize? For what?"

"For being pretty much everything you hate. Pretentious, image-conscious, shallow. Vivian showing up threw me for a loop. I didn't know what to say or do because in no way did you having a baby fit into the future I envisioned for us."

"Trust me, it wasn't exactly in the plan for me, either. But Ana—"

"No, wait. Let me finish. Bryan, I love you. I've been in love with you for a long time. But I don't need to tell you that this is not how I saw my life going. It was supposed to be perfect, you know . . . I was supposed to meet a successful man with a high-powered career, who didn't mind that I made my own money, even encouraged me in my ambitions. We'd get married, move into a tasteful house in the city that was just expensive enough to make all our friends jealous. And then we'd have two-point-five kids in the space of four years. Pretty sure prep school was on the list too."

Bryan's heart sank as she listed off all the criteria for her perfect life. He'd always had the suspicion that he didn't measure up to her expectations, and now he had proof. It didn't even matter that Vivian had come along. It had only been a matter of time before she figured out that he wasn't what she wanted.

But she was still speaking. "I realized it wasn't so much that I wanted those things; it was that I knew I would never find them. I was holding out for the perfect so I didn't have to deal with the real."

He stared at her. This was not where he'd thought she was going with this speech.

"Listen, you know that the whole thing with Robert messed me up. Anyone who knows me knows that I have control issues." She flipped him a helpless smile. "All this time, I've been trying to prove that I'm not the person who makes mistakes and bad decisions. And I'm ashamed to say that with Vivian in the picture, it made you seem like another one of my bad decisions."

"Ana—"

She waved him off and stepped closer, reaching for his chalk-smeared hand. "Bryan, you're not a bad decision. You're my best decision. Because you're real. You liked me when I was a coldhearted corporate shill. You liked me when you found out I was lying to my best friends because I was embarrassed to tell the truth about my past . . . which was stupid, because it didn't matter to them at all, just like you said it wouldn't. And I figure you'll like me even now that I'm unemployed and have no idea what to do with my life."

He couldn't hold himself back. "What? You quit?"

"I found out that I was just lying to myself and everyone else." She held up her hand. "Not to say that I have anything against my publicity colleagues. I'm not ashamed of my work. But I realized that it was easier to be a publicist for my own life instead of living it. When you deal with image all day, you start to forget that there needs to be some substance beneath it."

Tears glistened on her bottom lashes. "And I don't know that there is."

The flash of emotion destroyed any barrier he might have had against her. He pulled her into his arms. "No, Ana, I don't believe that for a second. You are intelligent and funny and caring. You love your friends and your family . . . even when your family has spent more than a decade throwing passive-aggressive jabs your way. You helped me even though you didn't have to. Those aren't the actions of someone who lacks substance."

"But I love you and I walked away from you when things got too messy."

"Life is messy, Ana. But I don't blame you. It would have been a lot for anyone to take."

"It's not." She shook her head resolutely. "I love you, Bryan. So you made a mistake. So you have a baby. I respect the fact that you're a man of character who owns up to his responsibilities. And if this . . . us . . . goes all the way, I'm prepared to be the best stepmother I can be. No matter how a child comes into the world, he deserves to have people who love him."

Bryan sucked in a breath, stunned by her words. The prick behind his eyes warned tears, but Ana wasn't exactly the type to approve of a crying man, so he blinked quickly until the sensation passed. "You have no idea how much that means to me, Ana."

She gave him a watery smile. "You have no idea how much you mean to me."

"But I have to tell you something. The baby isn't mine."

She stared at him. "What? You did a paternity test?"

He nodded. "Got the results back today. I'm not the father. I'll leave the question of whether it's Luke's for him and Viv to sort out."

He didn't tell her how Vivian had broken down when they'd

found out, how she'd admitted she'd been afraid to do the test because she didn't want the baby to be Luke's, not after their relationship had become so volatile and combative. She'd come to Denver with the hope that Bryan would take her back and accept the baby as his own without question; she'd really thought there was still a chance for them.

Now, it all just made Bryan's head hurt, and if he were honest, his heart too. Vivian was messed up and light-years beyond misguided, but he didn't want to see her in pain. He had a feeling she was dealing with her own past issues in as self-destructive a way as Bryan had.

"I'm so stunned I don't even know what to say."

"I know. I'm sorry to put you through that. But, Ana . . . even though the baby's not mine, I feel like I still need to check up on Viv once in a while. Make sure she's all right. I owe her that much. Is that something you can be okay with?"

Ana nodded. "I can. Even if it is like one big soap opera."

He took her face in his hands. "I love you, Ana. It means so much to me that you were willing to sacrifice your vision of the future to be with me."

"I love you, too," she whispered.

He leaned down to kiss her and she wrapped her arms around his neck, holding on to him like she wouldn't let go.

And even if she did, he wouldn't.

Epilogue

JUNE 19 DAWNED bright and sunny, with fluffy clouds chasing each other across the blue Colorado sky. The forecast predicted rain for later, but they were all praying that the ceremony would go off without a hitch before they moved to the barn for the reception.

"Are you ready?" Ana fluffed Rachel's skirt, checking for errant wrinkles in her wedding dress. She'd been a little militant with the steamer today, but that was only because she needed to stay busy. She was just as nervous as the bride and groom, maybe more. Because there was one thing that still needed to be settled, and she was far less confident of the outcome.

"Ana, relax." Rachel turned to regard herself in the mirror, perfectly calm and at peace. She looked stunning, the simple halter accentuating her figure and leaving her shoulders bare but for a cascade of dark curls. She'd decided to forgo a veil, instead wearing a spray of flowers on one side of her hair. She looked confident, beautiful, modern. The perfect bride.

"Oh, I'm so happy for you!" Melody threw her arms around

Rachel, nearly crushing her dress again, and Ana had to restrain herself from pulling her away before she did some serious damage.

"Watch it, Mel," Rachel said. "That ring is going to blind me if you're not careful."

Melody pulled away from Rachel with a laugh and held her left hand out before her. "I almost can't believe it. It's been three weeks and I still stare at it wondering if it's real."

"It's real," Rachel shot back. "Though I still can't believe we're losing you to Florida. Colorado—and Bittersweet Café—won't be the same without you."

They hugged again, murmuring watery endearments, and Ana blinked back tears of her own. She was thrilled for her friends, but today was the day everything changed. Rachel would be married, Melody would be moving . . . and in a few minutes they would no longer be the tight-knit little trio who had taken on the world as single women with ambitions for the future. She moved toward them and put her arms around their shoulders. "I'm going to miss this. This is the last time we'll all be single girls together. As happy as I am for you, Rachel—and you too, Melody—I can't help but feel a little sad."

"No." Rachel pulled them close again. "We're sisters, remember? That makes us all family. You're not losing a sister; you're just gaining a brother. And pretty soon, another one."

Ana brushed away the tears that had finally broken free as she hugged her two favorite women in the world, her heart full. She wasn't normally so sappy, but it was like casting off the remnants of her old life had cast off the chains that held back her emotions too. She was crying all the time these days, and unashamedly. Just not enough to let her happy tears ruin the hour of makeup their artist had gone through this morning.

"Okay, let's do this." She squeezed both of them and then reached for their bouquets, lined up on the table. She handed the bigger one to Rachel, a gorgeous cluster of Colorado wildflowers that spoke of summer and sunshine and new beginnings. The smaller ones, all white to contrast with their pale-green dresses, went to Melody and Ana.

"See you when you're married!" Melody called gaily, making a beeline for the tent flap.

Ana exchanged a long look with Rachel. "I love you, Rachel. I'm really happy for you."

"And I'm happy for you, too." Her knowing look made Ana blush, even though she and Bryan had been very open about their relationship. The fact that they were joined at the hip probably had something to do with it, too.

Ana took a deep breath, stepped out of the tent into the sunshine, and proceeded down the gravel walk to the small enclosed garden where the wedding was going to be held. They'd laid out the chairs in concentric squares around the little garden, a 360-degree view of the proceedings broken only by the red carpet leading through the gate to where the officiant and the groom already stood under the arbor.

She heard the soft murmur of Russian in the nearest chairs, Alex's family come from near and far to witness his wedding. And then she glimpsed Bryan and Justin up front next to Alex, all of them looking dapper and clean-shaven and excited for the proceedings.

The cellist began the first strains of the wedding processional, the prelude to Bach's Cello Suite no. 1. They had no flower girl or ring bearer, but Alex's sister, Dina, as the youngest, started down the aisle first. Then came Ana, and then Melody, taking their places opposite the men.

Finally, all heads swiveled to see the bride poised at the edge of the aisle, glowing with happiness, her eyes already fixed on her groom. Alex's face lit up, his gaze following Rachel all the way down the aisle until she came to rest opposite him in front of the reverend. He took her hand and bent to whisper something to her, which made her smile even wider.

Ana wouldn't remember the words of the ceremony later; she was too busy watching Bryan across the aisle, her heart pounding with nerves. He gave her a quick, questioning frown. Even from eight feet away he could tell when something was bothering her. She flashed him a smile in return so he knew that everything was okay and valiantly attempted to keep her mind on the ceremony.

And then it was over. The bride and groom turned and walked down the aisle, beaming at their guests as they went, resonating with happiness over their union. Ana was next, and Bryan met her again in the center to escort her back down the aisle.

"You're never this distracted," he whispered. "Is something wrong?"

"No, not wrong." At his curious look, she said, "I'll tell you later; I promise."

But later seemed like it would never come. There were the photos of the wedding party together, and then the reception, which was probably the most spectacular feast ever served in a barn, course after course of delicious food and drinks, courtesy of Rachel's chef friend Caleb and, of course, the Solid Grounds Coffee Company. When the evening finally turned toward dancing, and the day faded into a sparkle of lights overhead, Ana took Bryan by the hand and pulled him outside.

She took a deep breath, inhaling the cool quiet away from the noisy, warm interior of the barn. "It's a beautiful night. The rain was threatening, but I think we're finally in the clear."

"We are in the clear." Bryan glanced around and then tugged her around the corner of the barn and into his arms. "You know I've been waiting to do this all day."

"Me too," she whispered and let him prove exactly how much he'd missed her. When she finally regained the presence of mind to pull away, she was feeling even more shaky and breathless. "You know, someone's going to catch us."

"We're just kissing, Ana." His playful smile said he remembered the last time he'd told her the same thing, the night they'd finally succumbed to the pull of attraction and taken their relationship from friends to something more.

"And this isn't a proposition," she added.

He grinned. "Or a proposal."

"Well . . ." Ana gave him a sly smile, hoping it didn't look as shaky as it felt. "You told me that when it came time to propose to you, you wanted to make sure your hair looked good. Your hair looks pretty fantastic today."

He stared at her. "Ana?"

"I know it hasn't been long, but you also know when I figure out what I want, I don't waste time going after it."

"Um, yeah. You waited, what, one day before opening up your own business?"

"Shh." She placed a finger on his lips. "Don't interrupt. I had this all figured out."

He pulled her against him. "Of course you did."

"And what I've realized from the last two months is that you're exactly what I never knew I wanted. What I never knew I needed. I'm not sure exactly who I am yet, but I know I'm more of me when I'm with you than anywhere else." She took a deep breath. "So, with that said, Bryan Shaw, will you marry me?"

A delighted smile spread across his face. "Analyn Sanchez, I can think of nothing I want more." And then he crushed his lips to hers in a kiss that washed away any fears she might have had about his feelings for her.

When she pulled away, however, it wasn't because she'd had her fill of him—she was beginning to think that could take a lifetime. Rather, it was the distinct, cold plop of a raindrop on her forehead. Followed by half a dozen of its friends.

Ana squinted at the sky and blinked as one fell directly into her eye. "Really?" she demanded of no one in particular.

Bryan laughed, but still held her close. "I'm sorry the weather didn't cooperate with what was admittedly a pretty perfect proposal."

Ana sighed happily and looked into Bryan's face, his expression holding amusement and tenderness and so much love that it made her catch her breath again. She finally knew the truth.

"I don't need perfect. I just need you."

Author's Note

WHEN I WAS CONSIDERING writing the third book in the Supper Club series about coffee, I was inspired by the example of several faith-based organizations working in Colombia to help farmers convert coca to coffee crops. Farmers often find themselves with no other choice but to grow coca for the cartels, and government incentives to convert to coffee often don't materialize, leaving them unable to feed their families and pay basic expenses. Third-party organizations, on the other hand, are able to take some of the uncertainty out of the equation by guaranteeing higher prices for fair-trade and organic coffee to be sold to artisanal roasters in the US and other countries.

However, coffee is a price-sensitive commodity. In 2014, panic over coffee shortages led to widespread planting, particularly in Brazil. As of this writing in 2019, the market has been flooded with beans, driving the price below half of what it was only five years earlier. Unfortunately, due to falling prices, many of the farmers who converted to coffee years before have had no choice but to convert back to coca. Coffee prices are predicted to rebound, and it's possible that the pendulum will swing back the other way as it once again becomes lucrative.

I encourage anyone who is concerned about the impact of their coffee habit on the farmers who grow the beans or the connection to the drug trade to seek out fair-trade, single-origin coffee from micro- and macro-roasters. By buying high-quality beans sourced directly from the farmers or through a reputable co-op, we can help ensure a living wage for farmers and shift the demand, however slightly, toward a more sustainable coffee economy.

About the Author

CARLA LAUREANO is the two-time RITA Award–winning author of contemporary inspirational romance and Celtic fantasy (as C. E. Laureano). A graduate of Pepperdine University, she worked as a sales and marketing executive for nearly a decade before leaving corporate life behind to write fiction full-time. She currently lives in Denver with her husband and two sons, where she writes during the day and cooks things at night.

Discussion Questions

1. Ana is the definition of *driven*, always striving toward perfection. In what ways is this a good quality? How is it harmful? How important is it to you to "check the boxes" in your own life, literally or figuratively?

2. Bryan compares himself to the Prodigal Son of the Bible story (see Luke 15:11-32), wondering what happened when the Prodigal had to prove he was a changed man. How do you imagine the rest of the Prodigal's life played out? Have you encountered people who cling to an old perception of you? Were you able to persuade them that you'd changed?

3. Through the outward symbols of her success—her wardrobe, her car, her apartment—Ana carefully crafts the image she presents to the world. Bryan is also accused of hiding his true self behind his reputation as a shallow playboy. What "armor" do you wear when you want to protect yourself or project a certain image? Do you struggle, as Ana does, to let others see your vulnerabilities?

4. For a long time, Ana and Bryan resisted their attraction to each other, in part because of their interconnected friend group. Were they wise to do so?

5. Though she's mostly satisfied with her life, at times Ana feels left out and lonely once her two best friends begin working together and find romantic relationships. Have you ever felt like the odd one out in a group of friends? What happened?

6. Bryan and Ana both experience major disruptions to the careers they've built over many years. Have you ever had a sudden change to your life's direction? If you found yourself with the chance to start over and do something new, what would you choose?

7. Ana is great at her job, but sometimes bothered by the work she does to protect or spin clients' images. Do you think she's right to feel that way? How would you advise her if she came to you with her concerns?

8. Bryan never feels like the son his father wanted, so he gives up on the idea of pleasing him. Ana also fears she can't meet her family's expectations, but she tries by doing things like continuing to attend Mass. Do any parts of your life look different from what your parents might have wanted or expected? Which character's response do you most relate to?

9. Ana keeps a huge secret from everyone, including Bryan and her best friends. Did you understand her reasons?

10. As Bryan faces a crisis, Mitchell tells him, "Don't be so quick to fix a situation that might not be yours to fix." What do you think of this advice? When have you

tried to fix something that might not have been your responsibility? What was the result?

11. Ana, Melody, and Rachel all face big changes as the story ends. What do you think the future holds for their friendship? Who are the longest-running friends in your life, and what kind of changes have you endured together?

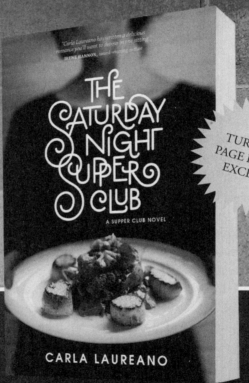

Chapter One

THREE HOURS INTO Saturday night dinner service and she was already running on fumes.

Rachel Bishop rubbed her forehead with the back of her sleeve and grabbed the newest round of tickets clattering through on the printer. Normally orders came in waves, enough time in between to take a deep breath, work the kinks out of her neck, and move on to the next pick. Tonight they had come fast and furious, one after another, tables filling as quickly as they were cleared. They were expecting two and a half turns of the dining room tonight, 205 covers.

It would be Paisley's biggest night in the six months since opening in January, and one they desperately needed. As part-owner of the restaurant, Rachel knew all too well how far away they still were from profitability. There were as many casual fine dining places in Denver as there were foodies, with new ones opening and closing every day, and she was determined that Paisley would be one of the ones that made it.

But that meant turning out every plate as perfectly as the last, no matter how slammed they were. She placed the new tickets on the board on the dining room side of the pass-through. "Ordering. Four-top. Two lobster, one spring roll, one dumpling. Followed by one roulade, two sea bass, one steak m.r."

"Yes, Chef," the staff answered in unison, setting timers, firing dishes. Over at *entremet*, Johnny had not stopped moving all night, preparing sides as fast as they came through on the duplicate printer. It was a station best suited to a young and ambitious cook, and tonight he was proving his worth.

"Johnny, how are we coming on the chard for table four?"

"Two minutes, Chef." Normally that could mean anything from one minute to five—it was an automatic response that meant *I'm working on it, so leave me alone*—but at exactly two minutes on the dot, he slid the pan of wilted and seasoned greens onto the pass in front of Rachel and got back to work in the same motion. She plated the last of table four's entrées as quickly as she could, called for service, surveyed the board.

A muffled oath from her left drew her attention. She looked up as her sauté cook, Gabrielle, dumped burnt bass straight into the trash can.

"Doing okay, Gabs?"

"Yes, Chef. Four minutes out on the bass for nineteen."

Rachel rubbed her forehead with the back of her sleeve again, rearranged some tickets, called for the grill to hold the steak. On slow nights, she liked to work the line while her sous-chef, Andrew, practiced his plating, but tonight it was all she could do to expedite the orders and keep things running smoothly.

"Rachel."

She jerked her head up at the familiar male voice and found herself looking at Daniel Kearn, one of her two business partners. She wasn't a short woman, but he towered above even her. Her gut twisted, a niggling warning of trouble that had never steered her wrong.

"Hey, Dan," she said cautiously, her attention going straight back to her work. "What's up?"

"Can I talk to you for a minute?"

"Now's not a great time." Dan might be the rarest of breeds these days—a restaurateur who wasn't a chef—but considering he owned four other restaurants, he should be able to recognize when they were in the weeds. The energy level in the kitchen right now hovered somewhere between high tension and barely restrained panic.

"Carlton Espy is here."

Rachel dropped her spoon and bit her lip to prevent any unflattering words from slipping out. "Here? Now? Where is he?" She turned and squinted into the dim expanse of the dining room, looking for the familiar comb-over and self-satisfied smirk of the city's most hated food critic.

"No, he left. Stopped by my table before he went and told me to tell you, 'You're welcome.' Does that make any sense to you?"

"Not unless he considers questioning both my cooking and my professional ethics a favor." She looked back at the tickets and then called, "Picking up nine, fourteen!"

"You really need to issue a statement to the press."

She'd already forgotten Dan was there. One by one, pans made their way to the pass beneath the heat lamps and she began swiftly plating the orders for the pair of four-tops. "I'm not going to dignify that troll with a response."

"Rachel—"

"Can we talk about this later? I'm busy."

She barely noticed when he slipped out of the kitchen, concentrating on getting table nine to one of the back waiters, then table fourteen. For a few blissful moments, the printer was quiet and all the current tickets were several minutes out. She took a deep breath, the only sounds around her the clatter of pans, the hiss of cooking food, the ever-present hum of the vent hoods. After five hours in the heart of the house, they vibrated in her bones, through her blood, the bass notes to the kitchen's symphony.

Her peace was short-lived. Carlton Espy had been here, the troll. Of all the legitimate restaurant reviewers in Denver, a scale on which he could barely register, he was both the most controversial and the least likable. Most people called him the Howard Stern of food writing with his crass, but apparently entertaining, take on the food, the staff, and the diners. Rachel supposed she should be happy that he'd only questioned her James Beard Award rather than criticizing the looks and the sexual orientation of every member of her staff, as he'd done with another local restaurant last week.

The thing Dan didn't seem to understand was that slights and backhanded compliments from critics came with the territory. Some seemed surprised that a pretty woman could actually cook; others criticized her for being unfriendly because she didn't want to capitalize on her looks and her gender to promote her restaurant. She had never met a woman in this business who wanted to be identified as "the best female chef in the city." Either your food was worthy of note or it wasn't. The chromosomal makeup of the person putting it on the plate was irrelevant. End of story. Tell that to channel seven.

As the clock ticked past nine, the orders started to slow down and they finally dug themselves out of the hole they'd been in since seven o'clock. The post-theater crowds were coming in now, packing the bar on the far side of the room, a few groups on the main floor who ordered wine, appetizers, desserts. The last pick left the kitchen at a quarter past eleven, and Rachel let her head fall forward for a second before she looked out at her staff with a grin. "Good job, everyone. Shut it down."

Ovens, grills, and burners were switched off. Leftover

mise en place was transferred to the walk-ins for tomorrow morning. Each station got scrubbed and disinfected with the careless precision of people who had done this every night of their adult lives, the last chore standing between them and freedom. She had no illusions about where they were headed next, exactly where she would have been headed as a young cook—out to the bars to drain the adrenaline from their systems, then home to catch precious little sleep before they showed up early for brunch service tomorrow. By contrast, Rachel's only plans were her soft bed, a cup of hot tea, and a rerun on Netflix until she fell into an exhausted stupor. At work, she might feel as energetic as she had as a nineteen-year-old line cook, but the minute she stumbled out of the restaurant, her years on the planet seemed to double.

Rachel changed out of her whites into jeans and a sweatshirt in her office, only to run into Gabrielle in the back corridor.

"Can I talk to you for a minute, Chef?"

Rachel's radar immediately picked up the nervousness beneath the woman's usual brusque demeanor. Changed out of her work clothes and into a soft blue T-shirt that made her red hair look even fierier, Gabby suddenly seemed very young and insecure, even though she was several years older than Rachel.

"Of course. Do you want to come in?" Rachel gestured to the open door of her office.

"No, um, that's okay. I wanted to let you know . . . before someone figures it out and tells you." Gabby took a deep breath and squared her shoulders. "I'm pregnant."

Rachel stared at the woman, sure her heart froze for a split second. "Pregnant?"

"Four months." Gabby hurried on, "I won't let it interfere with my work, I swear. But at some point . . ."

"You're going to need to take maternity leave." In an office setting, that was hard enough, but in a restaurant kitchen, where there were a limited number of cooks to fill in and new additions disrupted the flow they'd established, it was far more complicated.

Gabby nodded.

"We'll figure it out," Rachel said finally. "And congratulations. You're going to make a wonderful mother. I bet Luke is thrilled."

Gabby's words rushed out in relief. "He is."

"Now go get some sleep." Rachel's instincts said to give her a hug, congratulate her again, but that damaged the level of authority she needed to maintain, made it harder to demand the best from Gabby when she should probably be focusing more on her baby than her job. Instead, Rachel settled for a squeeze of her shoulder.

Andrew was the last to head for the back hallway, leaving Rachel alone in the kitchen to survey her domain. Once again, it gleamed with stainless-steel sterility, silent without the drone of vents and whoosh of burners. It should probably bother her more that she had no one to go home to, no one waiting on the other side of the door. But Rachel had known what she was giving up when she set off down this career path, knew the choice was even starker for female chefs who had to decide between running their own kitchens and having a family. Most days, it was more than a fair trade. She'd promised herself long ago she wouldn't let any man stand between her and her dreams.

Camille, Paisley's front-of-house manager, slipped into the kitchen quietly, somehow looking as fresh and put together as she had at the beginning of the night. "Ana's waiting for you at the bar. I'm going to go now unless you need me."

"No, go ahead. Good work as always."

"Thanks, Chef. See you tomorrow."

Rachel pretended not to notice Camille slip out with Andrew, their arms going around each other the minute they hit the back door. The food service industry was incestuous, as it must be—civilians didn't tend to put up with the long hours, late nights, and always-on mentality. There had been plenty of hookups in her kitchen among waitstaff and cooks in various and constantly changing combinations, but they never involved Rachel. On some points at least, she was still a traditionalist—one-night stands and casual affairs held no appeal. Besides, she was an owner and the chef, the big boss. Getting involved with anyone on her staff would be the quickest way to compromise her authority.

Rachel pushed around the post to the dining room and crossed the empty space to the bar. A pretty Filipina sat there, nursing a drink and chatting with the bartender, Luis.

"Ana! What are you doing here? Did Dan call you?"

Ana greeted Rachel with a one-armed hug. "I worked late and thought I'd drop by to say hi. Luis said it was a good night."

"Very good night: 215."

Ana's eyebrows lifted. "That's great, Rachel. Way to go. I'm not going to say I told you so, but . . ."

"Yeah, yeah, you told me so." Rachel grinned at her longtime friend. Analyn Sanchez had been one of her staunchest supporters when she'd decided to open a restaurant with two Denver industry veterans, even though it meant leaving the lucrative, high-profile executive chef job that had won her a coveted James Beard Award. And she had to give part of the credit to the woman next to her, who had agreed to take on Paisley as a client of the publicity firm for which she worked, even though the restaurant was small potatoes compared to her usual clients.

Luis wiped down an already-clean bar top for the third time. "You want anything, Chef?"

"No, thank you. You can go. I'll see you on Tuesday."

"Thank you, Chef." Luis put away his rag, grabbed his cell

phone from beneath the bar, and quickly slipped out from behind his station. Not before one last surreptitious look at Ana, Rachel noticed.

"Do I need to tell him to stop hitting on you?"

"Nah, he's harmless. So, Rachel . . ."

Once more that gut instinct fired away, flooding her with dread. "You're not here for a social visit."

Ana shook her head. "Have you seen the article yet?"

"The Carlton Espy review? Who hasn't? Can you believe the guy had the nerve to come in here tonight and say, 'You're welcome'? As if he'd done me some huge favor?"

Ana's expression flickered a degree before settling back into an unreadable mask.

Uh-oh.

"What is it? You're not talking about the review, are you?"

Ana reached into her leather tote and pulled out a tablet, then switched it on before passing it to Rachel.

Rachel blinked, confused by the header on the web page. "The *New Yorker*? What does this have to do with me?" The title of the piece, an essay by a man named Alexander Kanin, was "The Uncivil War."

"Just read it."

She began to skim the article, the growing knot in her stomach preventing her from enjoying what was actually a very well-written piece. The writer talked about how social media had destroyed civility and social graces, not only online but in person; how marketing and publicity had given an always-available impression of public figures, as if their mere existence gave consumers the right to full access to their lives. Essentially, nothing was sacred or private or off-limits. He started by citing the cruel remarks made on CNN about the mentally disabled child of an actress-activist, and then the story of a novelist who had committed suicide after being bullied relentlessly on Twitter. And then she got to the part that nearly made her heart stop.

> Nowhere is this inherent cruelty more apparent than with women succeeding in male-dominated worlds like auto racing and cooking. The recent review of an award-winning Denver chef suggesting that she had traded sexual favors in return for industry acclaim reveals that there no longer needs to be any truth in the speculations, only a cutting sense of humor and an eager tribe of consumers waiting for their next target. When the mere act of cooking good food or giving birth to an "imperfect" child or daring to create controversial art becomes an invitation to character assassination, we have to accept that we have become a deeply flawed and morally bankrupt society. The new fascism does not come from the government, but from the self-policing nature of the mob—a mob that demands all conform or suffer the consequences.

Rachel set the tablet down carefully, her pounding pulse leaving a watery ocean sound in her ears and blurring her vision. "This is bad."

"He didn't mention you by name," Ana said. "And he *was* defending you. You have to appreciate a guy who would call Espy out on his disgusting sexism."

Rachel pressed a hand to her forehead, which now felt feverish. "Anyone with a couple of free minutes and a basic understanding of Google could figure out who he's talking about." A sick sense of certainty washed over her. "Espy knows it, too. Without this article, his review would have died a natural death. He should have been thanking *me*."

Cautiously, Ana took back her tablet. "I'm hoping people

will overlook the details based on the message, but just in case, you should inform your staff to direct media requests to me."

"Media." Rachel covered her face with her hands, as if that could do something to stave off the flood that was to come.

"Take a deep breath," Ana said, her no-nonsense tone firmly in place. "This could be a good thing. You've told me about the difficulty women have in this business, the kind of harassment you've put up with to get here. Maybe this is your chance to speak out against it. You'd certainly get wider attention for the restaurant, not that it looks like you're having any trouble filling seats."

Rachel dropped her head into her folded arms. What Ana said was right. It would be publicity. But despite the old saying, it wasn't the right kind of publicity. She wanted attention for her food, not for her personal beliefs. To give this any kind of attention would be a distraction. And worst of all, it would make her a hypocrite. Playing the gender card for any reason—even a well-meaning one—went against everything she stood for.

"No," she said finally, lifting her head. "I won't. I'll turn down all the interviews with 'no comment' and get back to doing what I do best. Cooking."

"I thought you'd say that. I'll issue a statement to that effect. Just be prepared. Reporters can be relentless when they smell an interesting story." Ana hopped off the stool. "I'm beat. Call me if you need me."

"I will." She hugged Ana and watched her friend stride out the door, five-inch heels clicking smartly on the dining room's polished concrete floors. Rachel didn't move from her perch at the bar, though she was glad that Luis was already gone for the night. He would take one look at her and pronounce her in desperate need of a drink. The last thing she needed to do was send herself down that unwitting spiral again.

Instead, she would head to her office in the back as she always did, look over the pars that Andrew had calculated for her that morning, and pay the stack of invoices waiting in her in-box. Work was always the medicine for what ailed her, even if she was hoping that for once, her gut feeling was wrong.

Because right now, her gut told her everything was about to go sideways.

CHAPTER ONE

AT LEAST THEY COULDN'T FIRE HER.

Andrea Sullivan propped her elbows on the bar and buried her head in her hands. How had things gone wrong so quickly? One minute she'd been on the verge of closing a half-million-dollar deal. The next, she'd nearly broken her hand on the jaw of a client who thought her company's offerings extended to favors she had no intention of delivering. Three years of working her way up the ranks toward VP of Sales all down the tubes because one man couldn't keep his hands to himself.

No, her company certainly wouldn't risk an ugly public legal battle. They didn't have to. Her boss had other, more subtle means of showing his displeasure.

As punishments went, Scotland was a big one.

"What's so terrible about Scotland?"

Andrea jerked her head up and met the bartender's gaze. Had she said that aloud?

The man's eyes crinkled at the corners as he ran a towel along the polished mahogany surface of the bar, evidently amused by her slip. Round faced and topped with a thinning mop of dishwater-blond hair, he looked as stereotypically English as the London pub in which he tended bar.

She let out a long breath, her shoulders slumping. "Scotland's cold, it's miserable, and the food is horrible."

"Oh, it's not so bad as all that, is it?" His expression turned from amused to sympathetic. "Take in some countryside, tour a castle or two, maybe some high street shopping . . ."

"This is a business trip. Trust me. My dream vacation involves sunshine and umbrella drinks on the beach, not rain and fog in some backwater village."

If she'd only managed to keep her temper in check, she'd have been spending the next week in the tropics with the promise of a fat commission and a guaranteed promotion, not serving time in Scotland babysitting a celebrity client who suddenly wanted to dabble in the hotel business.

James MacDonald.

She'd never heard of the man. Then again, she didn't own a television. She spent so much time on the road, she wasn't even sure why she owned an apartment. She seemed to be the only one on the planet, however, who hadn't heard of the Scottish celebrity chef. Half a dozen restaurants, four cookbooks, his own television show. Even her taxi driver had been able to name MacDonald's three London restaurants without hesitation.

Andrea toyed with her half-filled wineglass, watching the golden liquid slosh around the bowl. "I should be on my way to Tahiti right now, not sitting in a pub drinking a rather mediocre glass of wine."

"That's because you go to Paris to drink wine," a deep male voice said over her shoulder. "You come to London to drink ale."

Andrea straightened as a man leaned against the bar beside her. He was tall and broad-shouldered, dressed in a pair of dark slacks and a business shirt, the collar unbuttoned and sleeves rolled up to show off muscular forearms. Dark hair worn a little too long, brilliant blue eyes, handsome face. Handsome enough she took a second look and immediately wished she hadn't been so obvious about it. His grin made her heart do things it was certainly not intended to do.

She couldn't prevent the corners of her mouth from twitching up in a smile. "Now you tell me."

He glanced at the bartender. "Get me a 90 Shilling, and whatever light's on draft for the lady." He looked back at her. "We can't have you leaving London thinking that pathetic chardonnay is the best we have to offer."

"That's very thoughtful." She offered her hand. "I'm Andrea."

"Mac." He held her hand just a moment too long while he studied her face. Her stomach made a peculiar little leap. She quelled it ruthlessly and drew her fingers from his grasp while he slid onto the barstool beside her.

"Now tell me why you're sitting here instead of on what sounds like a brilliant holiday in the South Pacific."

Because my temper finally got me into more trouble than I could talk my way out of. Aloud she said, "I'm doing research on the owner of this pub."

"Ah, the illustrious Mr. MacDonald. Brilliant chef, but not the full quid from what I hear." The sparkle returned to those devastating blue eyes, and she had the feeling she was the butt of a private joke.

Andrea couldn't pass up the opportunity to gather some local gossip. She plowed onward. "You know him?"

"That depends on why you're asking. Is it business, or is your enquiry of a personal nature?"

"Business. I'm supposed to meet him in Inverness tomorrow, and I'm looking for a little background."

"Are you always so unprepared for meetings?"

Andrea bristled. "Of course not. I only got the call from my office a few hours ago. I'm now fortifying myself for a long night of web browsing back at the hotel."

"I can see that. Well, I'd say this pub is a pretty good reflection of him. Comfortable, slightly sophisticated. Best selection of locally brewed beers in England and some truly inspired food."

Andrea looked around. Typical decor, lots of wood and brass, dim lighting. Stained glass and leather accents. Upscale but not uptight. Welcoming but not sloppy.

"Middle of the road," she murmured. "But that still doesn't tell me much about the man."

"And why do you need to know so much about him?"

The bartender returned with Andrea's drink and poured Mac's from the bottle into a glass, watching them as if they were his evening's entertainment.

"My job requires rapport," she said. "I can't convince someone we're right for the project if I don't know what he's looking for. I can't win him over if I don't know which buttons to push."

"Hmm." He sipped his ale, his eyes dancing over the rim of the glass.

Was he laughing at her? "What?"

"I've just never heard a woman worry about which buttons to push when she's wearing a skirt that short and heels that high."

Heat crept up Andrea's neck and into her cheeks as she tugged down her suit skirt. It wasn't as if she were wearing a miniskirt. The length was perfectly modest when she wasn't sitting on a barstool. The heels were admittedly less conserva-tive, but she wore them for height, not for looks. Then she realized he was watching her with a satisfied smile. She had taken the bait. Who exactly did he think he was?

She stilled her fidgeting and fixed him with a direct stare. "I could close a deal in jeans and tennis shoes. I just don't like being unprepared. Besides, I'm used to dealing with hotel groups with hundreds of properties, not celebrities with noth-ing better to do than play innkeeper."

"So MacDonald's a dilettante?" He swiveled on the stool and leaned back against the bar, arms crossed over his chest. Repressed laughter flashed in his expression.

"Frankly, I don't know the first thing about him. I've never seen his show, I certainly don't cook, and I can't fathom why anyone with a successful career in London would want to open a hotel on the Isle of Skye."

"Now that just sounds like bigotry. We Scots have an over-abundance of national pride."

Andrea's cheeks heated again. How could she not have noticed? His accent, while refined, had a distinct Scottish burr. She was really off her game if she had failed to pick up some-thing that obvious. Still, he had needled her about both her clothing and her professionalism, and she had to pry the apol-ogy from her lips. "I didn't mean to be rude."

He waved a hand in dismissal. "You've got bigger problems if you know so little about your client. Though you'll do fine if you avoid the pejoratives about his native land. I do think you have one thing in common."

"What's that?"

"You both think work is a terrible reason to cancel a trip to Tahiti."

A reluctant smile crept onto her face. "I can drink to that."

"*Slàinte*, Andrea." He clinked his glass to hers, took a long pull of the ale, and hopped off the stool. "I should get going now. I would suggest you do the same, Ms. Sullivan. You've got a long day ahead of you tomorrow."

She blinked at him. "How did you—"

"Night, Ben. Her drinks are on the house."

"Night, James."

Mac—or the man pretending to be Mac—winked at her and sauntered out of the pub.

"That was . . . He was . . ."

Ben seemed to be fighting a smile. "Mr. MacDonald, yes. I daresay that's the first time not only has a woman *not* fallen all over him, she's actually insulted him to his face."

Andrea's heart sank to the soles of her Jimmy Choos. "I think I'm going to be sick."

"I wouldn't worry too much. I rather think he liked you."

Right. She glanced back at the door, but James MacDonald had already gone. Why, oh why, did this happen now? She had to hook this account if she had any hope of getting back into her boss's good graces, and now she'd be spending the next few days trying to placate a celebrity ego.

She'd never been particularly proficient at groveling.

Andrea hopped off the stool and reached for her purse before she remembered Mr. MacDonald had taken care of her bill. She found a couple of one-pound coins in her change purse and set them on the bar as a tip, even though Ben had done nothing to signal her impending disaster. Would it really have been so difficult to give her a shake of the head, a raised eyebrow? But of course he'd stay out of the matter when his boss was involved.

"Thank you, Ben." *For nothing.*

"Good night, Andrea." He slipped the coins beneath the bar and added, "Don't think too badly of Mr. MacDonald. He's a good man, beneath it all."

Andrea forced a smile and hiked her handbag onto her shoulder, then escaped onto the dark London street. At nine o'clock on a Sunday evening, traffic had tapered off, and the usual haze of diesel fumes faded into the musty scent of damp concrete. She made a left and strode toward the Ladbroke Grove tube station, irritation speeding her steps.

How many times had she lectured her junior account managers on the importance of maintaining professionalism at all times? Every contact was a prospective client or referral. She'd just proved her own point in a particularly embarrassing manner.

Not that she excused James MacDonald for his role in this debacle. She knew his type. Wealthy, good-looking, famous. He expected women to fall at his feet, and God forbid one had a mind of her own. She'd probably be dodging his advances for the next three days while she tried to convince him she was more than a pretty face. He was lucky she hadn't smacked him for commenting on her clothing in the bar.

Truthfully, she hadn't been in much shape to do anything but put her foot firmly in her mouth. It had been years since she'd let a man rattle her, and it had taken only a smile and a lingering handshake to do it. Heaven help her.

She only made it a few blocks from the pub before the stiletto pumps began to rub blisters on her heels. She gave up on her plans of an indignant walk to the tube station and raised a hand to the first black cab she saw. She climbed into the rear and gave the driver her destination.

She could salvage this. She'd spend the rest of her evening with her laptop, finding out everything she could about the man. From here on, she would act with the utmost professionalism. She hadn't gotten this close to VP through years of seven-day weeks and grueling round-the-clock hours to blow it now. Her boss may have given her this assignment as some backhanded punishment—after all, it had been years since he'd wasted her on a barely five-figure deal—but there had to be some sort of cachet to landing a celebrity client like James MacDonald. Surely she could turn it into bigger accounts. But first she had to repair the damage she'd done with her big mouth.

The cab pulled up beside the imposing Victorian brick edifice of the Kensington Court Hotel. Andrea paid the driver and climbed out with a wince, once again regretting her choice in footwear. She limped into the richly decorated lobby and rode the lift to her fourth-floor room.

The lush carpeting muffled her footsteps to a whisper when she let herself in. She certainly couldn't complain about her accommodations. She had stayed in the hotel dozens of times over the years, and each room was impeccably decorated in its own style. Her current space featured an enormous tester bed, framed by blue silk brocade draperies that spilled from a gilded corona above the headboard. She gingerly eased off her shoes, sank onto the luxurious mattress, and heaved a sigh.

She was tired, and not the kind of tired a good night's sleep in a fluffy bed could solve.

She lay there for a long moment, then threw a glance at the clock and calculated back five hours. Her sister should just be getting supper ready in Ohio. She pulled her cell phone from her pocket and dialed.

Becky answered on the fifth ring. "Andy! Why are you calling me? Aren't you supposed to be on a plane right now?" Something sizzled in the background, punctuated by a child's scream.

"Did I call at a bad time?"

"No more than usual. I'm frying up some chicken for dinner—Hannah! Leave the cat alone!"

Andrea smiled. Becky was almost eight years older than

Andrea, and she had three children: a nine-year-old son and three-year-old twins, a boy and a girl. "I can call back later—"

"David! Don't hit your sister! I'm sorry, what were you saying? Aren't you supposed to be on your way to Tahiti?"

"Change of plans. Michael booked me a consultation with some celebrity client while I'm here. I'm flying to Scotland tomorrow."

"And you're okay with that?"

"I'd rather be in Tahiti, for sure."

"No, I meant—"

"I know what you meant. I'm okay. What's one more, right?"

"Oh, I don't know, the difference between a luxury vacation and a padded room, maybe?"

Andrea chuckled despite herself. Even from Ohio, Becky couldn't resist the urge to mother her. "It's my job. What am I going to do, say no?"

"That's exactly what you say. 'Michael, I've planned this vacation for over a year. Find someone else to do it.'"

"I know." The smile faded from Andrea's face. Had it not been for the disastrous outcome of her last appointment in London, she would have said exactly that. She'd gotten away with plenty of attitude in the past based on her unmatched sales record, but in this business, she was only as good as her last deal. "I'll be fine. Really. I'm meeting the client in Inverness tomorrow, and then we're driving to Skye. I should be back in New York on Wednesday."

"Maybe you should take a few days off while you're in Scotland. Your vacation is blown anyway."

"I don't think that's such a good idea. I'm staying at the client's hotel."

"Who's the client?"

Andrea paused. "James MacDonald."

The squeal that emanated from the speaker belonged to a teenage girl, not a thirty-eight-year-old mother of three. Andrea held the phone several inches from her ear until she was sure her eardrums were safe.

"And here I thought your job was completely boring!"

"Strictly business, Becks. I've got less than two days to put together a proposal, and he doesn't seem like the easiest client to deal with. It's going to be a long trip."

"I bet you don't even know who he is," Becky said reprovingly.

"Oh, I know who he is." *A self-absorbed celebrity with the sexiest smile I've ever seen.* She yanked her mind back from that precipice before she could slip over. "I need to do some research for my meeting now. I'll call you from Skye."

"All right, have fun," Becky said in a singsong voice. Andrea could practically hear her grin from four thousand miles away. "I expect an autograph, by the way."

Not likely. "Love you, Becks. Give the kids a kiss for me."

Andrea clicked off the line and pressed her fingertips to her eyes, trying to calm the urgent thrumming of her heart. The last thing she needed was to think of her client in anything but a professional fashion. Men like MacDonald were predators—any sign of weakness and she'd never be able to shake him. She knew all too well what could happen if she succumbed to an ill-advised attraction. She'd been there once, and she wasn't going back there again.

"Strictly business." The steadiness of her voice in the quiet room reassured her. She took a deep breath and levered herself up off the bed. Enough procrastinating. She still had work to do.

Andrea slipped out of her suit jacket and skirt, hung them carefully in the closet, and ensconced herself in a luxurious hotel robe. Then she chose an obscure Dussek piano concerto from her phone as mood music and dragged her laptop onto her legs.

James MacDonald chef, she typed into the search box, and waited. Page after page of results appeared: restaurant reviews, interviews, television listings. Andrea clicked through to his official website first and quickly read through his bio. Born in Portree, Isle of Skye, schooled in Scotland. Completed a degree in business at the University of Edinburgh, followed by culinary training at Leiths School of Food and Wine in London. A long list of assistant and sous-chef positions at some of London's most prestigious eateries culminated in his first restaurant, a gastropub in Notting Hill. That first location was quickly followed by smaller, more focused restaurants in Knightsbridge and Covent Garden, then Cardiff, Edinburgh, and Glasgow.

Last year he had been invited to prepare his take on traditional English food for the prime minister. A few months ago he had been named a member of the Order of the British Empire for his philanthropic work with at-risk youth.

She blinked at the screen. Wonderful. She'd just insulted a member of a British chivalric order. That was a distinction not many women could claim.

Andrea moved on to the newspaper articles, all of which called him the standard-bearer for nouveau-British cuisine, then scanned a Wiki page listing each of his six restaurants. All of them had received starred reviews in the Michelin Red Guide. The Hart and the Hound, the flagship pub she'd just visited, received one of only a dozen two-star ratings in Britain.

She should have bypassed the wine and ordered dinner instead.

MacDonald couldn't have accomplished all that by age thirty-five without a sharp mind and plenty of talent. Somehow that just stirred up her irritation. She'd half-expected to find evidence he had simply ridden his looks and charm to success, but every detail pointed to hard work and sacrifice. For heaven's sake, the man had even established a vocational cooking program for secondary-school dropouts.

"The perfect man," she muttered. "Just ask him."

She scrolled through the search results until gossip sites began to appear. Photos of MacDonald with a string of beautiful women—models, actresses, dancers—at exclusive parties and club openings. So he was that sort. Never with the same woman twice.

Great. Her hand still hurt after the encounter with the last wannabe Don Juan. Now she had to spend the next three days trying to get James MacDonald's signature on a contract while keeping things strictly professional. The fact he'd already turned her into a blithering idiot once didn't bode well for her quick thinking.

But she'd manage. She had to. She hadn't come this close to achieving her goals just to let a man get in her way.